A DEAD GAME

By

Mira West

authorHOUSE®

AuthorHouse™
1663 Liberty Drive
Bloomington, IN 47403
www.authorhouse.com
Phone: 833-262-8899

Published by AuthorHouse 02/13/2025

ISBN: 979-8-8230-4169-0 (sc)
ISBN: 979-8-8230-4168-3 (e)

Library of Congress Control Number: 2025901129

Print information available on the last page.

This book is printed on acid-free paper.

This book is a work of fiction. Places, events, and situations in this book are purely
fictional and any resemblance to actual persons, living or dead, is coincidental.

Dedication

To my family. I never feel cold.
Your endless love wraps me in
continuous warmth.

ONE

I t began during a midsummer month in the late 80's.

The sign on the door should have read: CAUTION! ENTER AT OWN RISK, not Women's Lounge. Jasmine staggered in dodging blasts of hairspray and perfume, cringing with every high-pitched whine and clanging locker door, then collapsed on the wooden bench in front of her locker and dropped her head in her hands. The thought of making it through the first hour seemed just as impossible as the long day ahead.

"Hey, you!"

Cracking an eye, Jaz rotated toward the disturbing yet fondly familiar voice. "Hi Yarah."

"Girl, what's wrong with you? It better not be contagious." She shut her locker and came over for a closer examination.

Jaz opened her burning eyes a tad wider and focused on the dial of her locker. "Long story and too tired to go into it." Twisting right to left then back again, the door opened to what should have been a stiff clump of gold polyester, but her vest was hanging rested and wrinkle free as if nothing even happened yesterday. Jerking it from the hook, she slipped her arms through the holes, buttoned it up and posed with a wide pretentious smile. "How do I look?" Yarah was just about to shoot off one of her smart-ass remarks when the door flew open, and Connie Russo burst in panicked.

"You don't want to go up there!" she ranted between gasps of air. She was just twenty-one and hadn't been seasoned to the steady stream of harassment. So any confrontation sent her into an immediate panic attack.

"What do you think *that's* all about?" Yarah said.

"I don't know, but she's right. I don't want to go up there."

"Well, I'm gonna go find out." Yarah marched over and returned with Connie. Her tall lanky body was trembling. Her pale blue eyes were bugged, and her short blonde hair was nearly standing on end.

"Are you all right, what happened?" Jasmine said, patting the bench next to her. She could relate to Connie's fear. There was a lot to learn in the art of surviving in the casino, especially for a female who thought working at the Palace would be a glamorous job. Connie sat down next to her clutching her thighs with tense, trembling hands. "Calm down . . . take a deep breath," Jasmine said, inhaling and exhaling.

"Okay." Connie took a shaky breath. "There's a man on my game winning big—real big. I saw all the pit bosses, even the casino manager!"

"Yeah, so what?" Yarah huffed.

"So! Have you seen him? He's disgusting! He has long, greasy hair. He farts, burps, drools, and smells like blue cheese." She shuddered. "I'm telling you, if Anthony hadn't pushed me out, I think I would've puked."

Jasmine was listening quietly while Connie gave her graphic depiction until her distress signal blared like a foghorn. She bolted off the bench and threw her hands in the air. "Not him! No way. I'm not dealing to him again. Look at me." She pointed at herself. "I didn't sleep a wink last night because of that, that beast. I dreamed he chased me around the neighborhood like some vicious rabid dog. As you can clearly see, no one came to my rescue."

Yarah cut in. "Going back to your question: 'how do I look?' I was going to say like shit, but I thought I'd be nice today. Girl, start talkin'. Who is this guy and what's goin' on?"

Jaz shook her head. "You have no idea. It was horrible."

"All right, so spit it out." The women in the lounge gathered curiously as Jasmine began her story.

"Yesterday I was at my blackjack game just standing there . . ."

Yarah glared. "The short version."

"I wish there *was* a short version." Jaz glared back. "This man," she huffed, "came to my game with a couple hundred dollars, supposedly from his social security check, and not only did I give him every chip in my rack, but I turned it into forty thousand!"

"You're kidding!" the women said in unison.

"It would have been more, but when David Sly punted the trash can the length of the casino, they yanked me from the game."

"I heard about him. He only plays with women dealers, right?" one lady asked.

"Yeah, he's a pervert. He gets off calling you the *"C"* word. I'm sure his sole mission is to make you so uptight and angry, you dump your rack."

"He called you a cunt?" Connie asked timidly.

"No, he called her *cutie!*" Yarah snapped.

"Oh!" Jaz rippled with a shiver. "I forgot to mention his black woolly socks."

"Black woolly socks?"

"Actually, you think they're socks but they're really not. It's his big, hairy feet covered in an inch of crusty, black muck. He rests them right up on the chair next to him for everyone to see and smell."

"Oh my God!" Yarah screeched.

Jasmine folded her arms. "Need I say more?"

"No, not one more word or I'm gonna be sick," Yarah mumbled, holding her hand over her mouth.

Gladys pointed at the clock. "I hate to say this, but we gotta go." The lounge quickly cleared with heads shaking and muffled chatter, fearing they'd have to deal to the beast.

"Are you comin'?" Yarah waved.

"Just a minute." Jaz peered in the mirror, fluffed her hair, then bent over and raked her hair. She came up and looked again, waving at herself. "It's no use. I'm a two today."

Yarah grinned. "But you make me look like a ten—so come on." She grabbed Jaz by the arm and led her upstairs to the casino floor.

Rounding the corner of the promenade, Jasmine Woods entered the casino pit, the place where it all happened. From corner-to-corner the ceiling was covered with mirrors, the walls with red velvet florets, and the carpet was splashed with a rainbow of colors, so if you drop your coins they're not easily found. Every square inch was dimly lit by teardrop bulbs on spindly chandeliers.

Night fell twenty-four hours in the Paradise Palace, and for a good reason. But there was a reason for everything when it came to making money. Daily, the casino performed more tricks under their rooftop than Barnum and Bailey's big-top. All it took was minimal lighting and absence of clocks, and the customer was lulled into a money-making machine. Without a clue, they roamed from slot-to- slot and game-to-game giving away their hard-earned money. It was amazing how something so simple had such big results.

In the distance, Jaz could hear a chorus of cheers resonating from a crowd of people. This was a red flag alert someone was winning, and the closer she got to the pit the louder it became. Now a hint of blood was in the air as the pit bosses circled like a school of sharks.

Glancing at the game, Jaz swallowed back what was coming up, thanking God she wasn't the dealer. But Tony Baxter, the pit boss, made a point of changing that fast.

He motioned her over with his greasy head and stood with a scowl on his face. Jaz knew the second he opened his mouth her freshly starched shirt would be soggy enough to wring. She was right. "What the *hell* took you so long!?" he snarled with a voice as sharp as his eyes.

"Why? I'm not late," she said in defense.

"No, but I want him out of here!" He pointed at Anthony.

Jaz looked at the dealer responsible for Tony's kill mode, when someone else caught her eye. Stepping closer for a better look, yesterday came flashing back with a sequel to her nightmare. "Oh my God, I knew it! He's still here!" Sitting like a duck amongst doves in his shabby weathered trappings was the beast.

"Yeah, that's fuckin' Joe Horn."

Jaz grinned. "The name sure fits. Looks like he's been blowing it all night long by the size of the crowd." As usual, her attempt to lighten the air only ignited Tony's temper.

He grabbed his crotch and glared at the man. "Blow this ya no good . . ."

His crude comment didn't ruffle Jaz in the least. She'd been conditioned and learned, to survive in the casino you must never forget it's a man's world. "What's his story, anyway?" she asked, curious of the man's peculiarity.

Tony took the toothpick from his mouth and pointed it at her. "His story! I'll tell ya his story. He's a goddamn vagrant from downtown. Lives in a cardboard box. Wanders in here yesterday with his measly social security check, and now he can buy a fuckin' mansion!"

Jaz swallowed, taking a step back from his gnashing teeth. "Sorry, that was me. I dealt to him. He was really, really lucky."

Tony's head sprang from his shoulders. "That was your fancy work that started this shit-storm?!" She nodded. "Well, you got a hell of a job cut out for you today. He's up to three hundred thousand."

Her eyes bugged. "That's my game?!"

"No, it's your fuckin' birthday party! Now go blow out the candles and say goodnight."

Most suspected the casino was connected to the mob—not because the bosses wore pinstriped suits, white ties and wing-tip shoes, or because they had distinct Italian accents. It was their strong-armed strategy to winning. They were a gang of *"good old boys"* that believed rough stuff and chauvinism were acceptable in the casino. Tony Baxter led the pack. He was a five-foot, beady-eyed, gangster throwback with an acute case of Napoleon syndrome.

Jasmine approached the game and drew in a deep calming breath. Her uncanny ability to win was a nerve-racking detriment. Regularly, she was given the job to eliminate a contender, which normally took place on the frontline. This was a string of high limit tables, where rules were dictated by the deepest pockets and each hand was just shy of a wrestling match. After three years of steady conditioning, she was able to deflect the shards and became a permanent fixture.

Looking back at Tony, pondering the thought of pleading insanity, she knew it was useless. He was already anticipating the thrill of the kill with his hands clasped and sporting a wide smile. Like a whipped mule, Jaz inched in and tapped Anthony on the shoulder.

"It's about time," he said from the corner of his mouth.

"I was hoping this wasn't my game," she whispered.

"So was I." Slapping the sweaty deck in her hand, he snatched the single chip off the table and dropped it in the toke box.

Here she was again, the casino's secret weapon. Jasmine stood five-eight, slender, and with attention-grabbing curves. She had wavy, copper-red hair that swirled down her back and over her shoulders. Her face was naturally appealing with defined cheekbones, full, pink lips, and a light spray of freckles across the bridge of her nose. Not until you were lured in by her warm country welcome and hypno-tized by her sapphire eyes would you know she was taking every last cent you had.

Tony crept up behind her as she began to shuffle the cards. Jaz could feel his hot breath on the back of her neck as he quietly gave his order. "Do whatever you gotta do, just get the fuckin' money back."

She nodded an okay as if blindfolded and standing in front of a fir-ing squad, while the players looked at each other like sacrificial lambs. They knew it was just a matter of time before the casino sent in the ringer. What they didn't expect was a young, pretty woman to tackle the job. Jaz smiled and quickly scanned the table to assess what each player was winning. Joe's checks zigzagged from one betting circle to the next like the Great Wall of China, teetering on the edge of three hundred thousand. At that point, it was insignificant what the other men were winning. The game was upside down and sinking like the Titanic.

As Jaz shuffled the cards, she wondered how these presumably sane men sat tolerant of the rotten egg next to them. The stench was over-whelming. But as the crowd kept growing it started to make perfect sense. The game was in the spotlight, and like any thrill there's an indescribable high that comes with it. In the casino, it's when an audi-ence has formed and you're on center stage. No way were these men bowing out before the show was over. They were there for the dura-tion or at least until the curtain dropped.

The men puffed on their musty cigars and glared over their cock-tails, not to miss one twist or tuck Jasmine's hands skillfully made. Joe Horn couldn't have cared less. He gazed up at her with one lazy eye, drooling pools of slime over his chips. *The same chips she would be touching!* She gagged with that thought.

"So Jasmine, you gonna be as nice as Anthony was to us?" one of the players said, shattering the icy silence. It was a question she'd heard ad-nauseam, and the truth of the matter as well as annoying fact, most players equated your disposition to how much money they won with you.

Jasmine smiled, playing a sweet southern tune. "Now, does this look like the face of someone mean?" she cooed and batted her lashes. That was her first mistake, leaving the door wide open for the beast.

"I know what I'd like to do with that face," the crusty, lizard-skinned man spewed with curdled breath.

Stifling a heave, Jasmine abruptly stopped him. "If you wouldn't mind, please keep that thought to yourself."

"Why?!" He lunged. "What are ya gonna do?" His eyes dared her to make a move, but her body stood stiff.

Clenching the deck, she stammered, "I'll-I'll call my boss over." Little did he know, Tony would just wave with a grunt.

The bum sneered and licked his brown stained lips. "We got us a wild one, boys." He raised his glass and gulped down a shot of tequila, ending with a sonorous belch. All the men laughed except one. He knew Jasmine wasn't there for amusement, and if looks could kill he would have been handcuffed and read his rights.

"Darlin', it's gonna take more than that pretty little face of yours to convince me you're not here to take my money." Her eyes locked with his, yet no words were exchanged. That was exactly why she was there. Without wasting another minute, she flicked the cards and a yelp of excitement resounded.

"She's easy money, men. Look at this!" One of the cigar-smoking yahoos slapped a snapper on the table, followed by a roar of hoots and high-fives. Jasmine smiled and paid the man while the hawking bosses mouthed swear words and shook their heads. It was known throughout the tiny town of Tahoe, the Palace sweated the money. In other words, they hated to lose.

Jaz had a six showing, the worst card. Pressure was on to make a winning hand, and in a flash the six turned into an eleven and she hit it with a ten. All the excitement softened to a muffled groan, giving the bosses a moment to exhale and wipe their shiny foreheads.

Not Joe Horn. "Bet you can't beat this!" he shouted. With a crash, he threw his chair to the floor and waved his skinny arms at the inquisitive crowd. Tony stood at attention but didn't move. The word from upstairs was to keep Joe at the Palace, and get the money back.

Standing with his eyes closed, Joe held his arms out and began humming a tune. Globs of slobber sprayed with each rancid breath as his wiry body tipped back and forth like a pendulum. The audience cheered and chanted for an encore. Joe let out a howl and began unzipping his tattered trousers. He was going to give them a show they'd never forget.

Finally, Tony took charge and rushed over before Joe's pants hit the floor. "Okay, okay, you've had your moment of fame. Let's finish the game." Grabbing the chair off the floor, he sternly positioned him in his seat.

Joe jerked from his grip, angered by the interruption and began stomping his feet on the brass foot rail.

Tony looked down at the black embedded dirt that covered every inch of skin from toenail to ankle bone. "Hey Joe, where's your shoes?"

"Ain't got none."

"What do ya say we get you a pair? You're about an eleven or twelve, right?"

"How the fuck do I know. Are we gonna play cards or not?" he said, running his fingers through his wild twisted sprouts of hair.

"All right, just forget about it." Tony backed off. Having settled a brawl earlier, he was fully aware of his explosive temper.

Jasmine proceeded to deal, avoiding eye contact with the sniveling swine, and noticed one of the players transfixed on her breasts. He was a chubby, middle-aged, balding man with glasses so thick she was sure he could see right through her vest.

"So, where you from little lady?" the peeping-tom asked.

"Montana. Missoula, Montana. Have you ever been there?"

"No, but I'm sure it's a good place to be from." He chuckled.

Jaz gave him her usual undisturbed smile. She'd heard that remark as many times as the question was asked.

Joe hit his fist on the table and shouted at the man. "Hey, cut the bullshit! Can't you see I'm trying to play cards?"

The chubby man flinched and sat back. "We're just having a friendly little chit chat."

"Have it somewhere else," Joe snapped.

"Maybe I'll just sit this one out," the man said. The other men decided to do the same, leaving the *Beauty and the Beast* to duel it out.

Joe bet two thousand. His top card was a ten. Jaz had a five. She pointed at his circle. "If you want a hit, scrape your cards in front of your bet."

"I know! Just hold your fuckin' horses, *cunt*."

What!? Her eyes narrowed, and her hand clenched into a tight fist. Every muscle in her body twitched, visualizing laying him out cold. The other men sat like statues, stunned and staring at her. It was uncommon for a customer to defend the dealer. The fear of confrontation with the possibility of getting kicked out sucked the life out of them. Closing her mouth and holding her tongue, she slowly unclenched her fist. Without hesitation, Joe pushed another stack of chips next to his initial bet and flipped over his cards. His strategy of playing blackjack defied all books and odds. It was like magic. Anything he did turned into a winner.

Jaz looked at him confused. "You want to split your tens?"

"Goddamn right."

"But I have a five showing. Are you sure?"

He nodded. "Yeah, split 'em."

Jaz placed his chips behind each card. With the combined hands, he had four thousand dollars riding on this bet. She could hear Tony nervously tapping on the podium, which sounded like Morse code for: *he wins, you die!* The first hit was a face-card, making a twenty. Joe waved and pointed at the next bet. Jaz hit it with an ace for a twenty-one. A loud roar echoed from the gathering crowd, yet a mere whisper to the noise Tony made. She wasn't sure what he hit; just thankful it wasn't the back of her head.

The Palace ran the casino like a back-alley cock fight. Every dealer was programmed to go right for the jugular, or it could mean their job. Management made that perfectly clear by firing Darrell Butler, a veteran craps dealer and one of the casino's best. No one could believe it. All he did was call a hand for forty-five minutes, and after the customers scurried off with their winnings, he was ushered out to his car.

Jasmine was thirty-three, and a single mother of two. She couldn't afford to lose her job. With a quick flip, she turned over her cards. The hole card was a four. She had a nine and vigorously slapped down another card, praying it was a two. No such luck. It was a ten. She had a nineteen—not enough to beat Joe Horn.

He was an anomaly that broke the code. The one that couldn't be beat. Joe had won so much money the social security check he'd started with was now pocket change. And by his appearance, his life didn't require a dime. There was no value to his stacks of checks. His profanity and obnoxious antics were a cheap sideshow for something money couldn't buy: attention.

After forty minutes, Jasmine had done more damage than the casino normally allowed. Thankfully, Anthony was back to push her out instead of the bosses kicking her out. He gave her the *why me* look, and she reciprocated the same, although refrained from saying: *"It's about time!"* Handing him the worthless deck of cards, she politely excused herself. "Thank you, gentlemen. I'll see you in twenty minutes." Turning with a sigh, she left for the help's hall to get a strong cup of coffee and say an extra-long prayer.

Finding a quiet table in the corner and close to the coffee pot, she flopped down and locked eyes on a potted mum. Sipping the coffee in deep reverie, she felt a hand clutch her shoulder.

"Looks like you've had a rough start."

Jasmine looked up. "Hi Vonda, yeah, to say the least."

"Mind if I sit down?"

"No, but I'm not much company."

"Are you all right? You look a little . . . pale."

"Is that a nice way of saying sick?"

"Well, in a roundabout way, yes." Vonda Simmons was an attractive, middle-aged German woman. She kept her hair dyed blonde, short and spiked, cutting ten years off her age. Although, her sympathetic ear and kind heart were her best attributes.

"I would've called in sick if I thought it was going to be a repeat of yesterday."

"What happened yesterday?"

"You didn't hear about the sewer rat who won all the money?!"

Vonda chuckled. "Oh yes, I did hear about him."

"That was me. I gave it to him, and now he's back!" She took a sip of coffee. "I think I just bought him a yacht to go with his mansion. Why do the drunk and rude always win with me? I don't get it."

Vonda cocked her head. "I am a little short on cash. Maybe I'll just tie one on and come see you later."

"Nice try, but it won't work. You have to be mean, too."

"Ha—I'm German! It's in our blood." Her lips slanted, and her eyes turned into slits. "How's that for mean?"

"Whoa, that's frightening, Vonda." Jaz set her coffee down and folded her arms. "I'm serious. He's won four hundred thousand and hasn't tipped a dime, not a dime! Not only that, the madder I get the more he wins."

"You're not alone. I'm the same way. Very rarely are the A-holes a George, but isn't that the way it always goes?" She took a sip of coffee.

"Unfortunately, yes," Jaz groaned.

Vonda glanced up at the clock. "Sorry dear, but we'd better drink up; break's over."

Walking and mumbling, feeling as if her nerves were tied in knots, Jaz turned the corner and almost dropped to her knees. Anthony was standing alone and beaming with a winning glow. All the men were gone, including the beast. Rushing up to him, she tapped his shoulder but felt like giving him a hug. "Thank you! Thank you! Thank you!"

He rubbed his knuckles on his vest. "Believe me, it was all my pleasure." Handing her the deck of cards, she was about to wrap her fingers around it when Tony rushed toward her like a sizzling fuse. The only thing missing was the dynamite.

He pointed at Anthony. "You stay here. This will be *your* game." Then he pointed at Jasmine. "You are *never* allowed to deal to Joe Horn *ever* again! Ya got it? Right now he's a gnat's ass from a million—a fuckin' million! As a matter of fact, he's signing autographs. Would you like me to get you one?"

The only thing Jaz wanted was her crocheted throw and a dark corner. As incongruous as the job was to her inherent benevolence, it provided a decent living for her and her children. She also believed that one path led to another and someday, whatever it was, would eventually come along.

After the two-day, non-stop gambling fest, Joe's money vanished along with his magic fairy dust. The once-in-a-million million dwindled to five thousand. His fans were reduced to a few disappointed stragglers. The spotlight dimmed, and the curtain dropped. To the Palace, it wasn't worth the risk keeping Joe there any longer. He was given the money from a mound of checks in his pockets and eighty-sixed from all the casinos on Tahoe's strip.

Joe Horn appeared nightly but never again on center stage. He stood outside peering through the glass pane window at what once was his moment of fame.

TWO

April was the slowest month of the year for tourists and gamblers. Taxes were paid and pockets were emptied, but that didn't stop the Palace from finding ways to draw in people—one was their annual blackjack tournament. A cash prize of two thousand dollars was awarded to the first-place winner, along with their photo on the Wall of Fame. There was no entry fee, which literally attracted hundreds of people from coast-to-coast. The other was their headliner entertainment. This week it was geared to bring down the house with a group of male strippers from Australia called the Macho Men. They were débuting in the United States, and the Paradise Palace was their first stop.

Jasmine looked across the pit and saw Yarah Da Silva, her senility savior. Though they were bonded and sealed as best buds, they were opposites in more ways than not. Yarah was an exotic Brazilian beauty who could've easily been crowned Miss Universe, if all it took was looks. She was tall, slim and muscular and moved in a hip-shaking strut. Her smile was flawless and her eyes like black diamonds. She wore her hair piled on top of her head and bleached it, creating a brilliant honey-orange hue. The only exception to her glorified attraction was her vernacular. It was as blunt as a butter knife with words that could cut like a machete. "Hey, Yarah." Jasmine waved across the pit.

With hips rolling, Yarah sashayed over to her. "What's up, girl?"

"Did you hear? The hotel is giving away free tickets to the Macho Men show. You want to go tonight?"

Yarah threw her hands on her hips. "You have to ask!?"

"I'll take that as a yes."

"No, that's a *hell* yes."

Jaz leaped to her toes. "Great. It starts at eight, but I want to be there early for a bird's eye view."

"Can we bring our binoculars?"

"Good idea." Jaz chuckled. "I'll call you after work."

As Yarah turned to leave, Jasmine spied a man in the distance meticulously tidying the area. Normally it wouldn't have caught her attention, but there was something very unusual about him. His attire was extravagantly over the top: black, double-breasted suit, gray silk tie and a white handkerchief in his breast pocket. She watched totally captivated as he straightened slot chairs, emptied ashtrays and picked up coin buckets like a custodian. Inching his way closer, she was stunned by his movie-star face. Then their eyes collided. Quickly averting her attention to the ongoing blackjack tournament, she fought to look away, but curiosity had her wandering back just as he approached her game.

"Hi, I'm Frank Pazzarelli, the hotel manager." He held out his hand.

Her pulse raced like a jittery schoolgirl and face heated to a shimmery pink. Jaz smiled, shoving out a sweaty palm. "Hi, I'm Jasmine Woods. I thought you were the best dressed porter I'd ever seen."

His lips parted with a Hollywood smile. "I thought I'd help out with the aftermath of the tournament." He smiled again, this time cocky. "But I have to admit, I've had my eye on you, and I do have an ulterior motive." Frank made it his mission to know the woman who stopped him in mid-motion with her eye-catching beauty.

She tilted her head. "A motive?"

"Yes . . . you."

"Me?" Her excitement rushed to her face again.

"You sound surprised."

"I guess a little . . . why me?"

"You're a beautiful woman, isn't that reason enough." He leaned closer. "Actually, there's a charity event coming up this Friday, and I was hoping you'd accompany me." His raven eyes danced. "You'd make me a very happy man if you said yes."

She wanted to give him Yarah's response: *"You have to ask?!"* "Is it black tie?"

"Yes, but you have carte blanche at any shop in town. Just have the store manager call me here at the hotel, and I'll do the rest." He baited the hook and jiggled it.

She smiled. "That's very generous, but I have my own gown."

"So, it's a date?"

"Yes, I believe it is."

"Great. What time is your shift over?"

"At six o'clock . . . why?"

He pointed at her. "You ask a lot of questions."

"Well, you're a very mysterious man."

"Fair enough. Just come by the front desk before you leave. You can give me your phone number then."

"Okay."

"See you around six." He winked and left.

Watching him swagger off to his hiding place, a zillion butterflies emerged from their cocoons and fluttered inside her stomach. It was an excitement long overdue and long forgotten, at least three years since her marriage with Carl, and he thought romance was a type of lettuce. Turning her gaze out the window, she felt the tingling fervor dissipate as the senior citizen tour bus pulled up. Today she was dealing roulette, since Tony was still fuming over Joe's good luck and her bad. It was located just as you entered the hotel and conveniently posed like an information booth. There was no escaping the multitude of questions as everyone came through the door.

Marching in two-by-two, twisting their heads back and forth, the seniors searched for a destination of relief. Jaz pointed to the sign.

They waved a *thank you* and she waved back, catching something from the corner of her eye. It was like nothing she had ever seen and equal to the mystery man. Muscles taut and rippling under tight white t-shirts, hair flowing like a horse's mane and skin bronzed to an exotic golden tan. There was no mistaking who the beautiful bodies belonged to. It was the Macho Men, and in a minute they were swarming her game.

"Ello, Matey," the leader of the pack greeted her. "I'm Giant John, but you can call me John."

I'd rather call you Giant! "I'm Jasmine," she said and swallowed back a stifled scream.

"Jazzy baby, think you could scrape up a bottle of brew for me and the boys, aye?"

"Sure." She spotted Julie across the pit and tried calling her, but only a few unrecognizable words sputtered from her mouth.

"Let me try." The muscle man waved wildly to the busy cocktail waitress. Julie saw him and immediately left a trail of thirsty customers in her dust.

"Here she comes," Jaz said.

"Literally," John joked, and the other men laughed.

"Hello there, boys," Julie chimed seductively as she gave each a mini lap dance while taking their order. That was exactly what Jaz needed—a minute to regain composure and seem somewhat in control. She spun the wheel and waited as Julie finished with their requests.

"Okay, you guys ready to play?" Jaz asked, but there was no response, not even a look. Their attention was far from playing roulette. She tried again. "Guys, what's your favorite number?" It was obvious the only numbers they were interested in were 36-24-36. Word got out and every waitress in the hotel came prancing by in their bikini bottoms and bosom-baring tuxedo vests. It didn't take a genius to realize, the Macho Men were only there for show and tell not gambling.

The day crawled by longer than usual, or the anticipation of seeing Frank Pazzarelli had stopped the clock. Jaz looked at her watch. Each second seemed like five minutes and each five minutes an hour. It was by far the longest day in history.

Just then a bell rang, and an announcement was made over the intercom. "Ladies and gentlemen, we have our winner of the blackjack tournament." The pit went still, and the racket softened to a rustling. Jaz bobbed back and forth, trying to see through the crowd, then raised on her tiptoes. She saw the casino host waving a giant check and holding onto a microphone. "The Paradise Palace would like to congratulate . . . Thelma Bradshaw! Come up here, Thelma."

A squeaky shrill cut the suspended silence, and a petite elderly woman garbed in a pink chiffon dress waved her hands in the air. She weaseled her way through the crowd and onto the center platform. "This is just amazing. I needed two thousand dollars to buy new teeth." She grinned wide as the camera flashed, and her toothless smile was displayed on the Wall of Fame with all the other smiling winners.

As the crowd scattered, Jaz felt a tap on her shoulder and heard a groan in her ear. "I'm here. Time to go home."

"Finally!" She cleared her hands for surveillance, and then hurried to the dealer's lounge to take off her uniform. Yarah was just walking out when she turned the corner. They came an inch from bumping heads.

"Well, excuuuse me!"

"Sorry," Jasmine said out of breath.

"What's the big hurry, girl?"

"I don't have time to talk but it's good. I'll tell you tonight."

"Remember, seven o'clock," Yarah said.

"I remember." Scurrying to her locker, Jaz took off her vest, ran a brush through her hair and dabbed her lips with gloss. Then, like a gazelle, she sprang up the stairs two at a time. Her copper locks bounced against her shoulders as if sensing her thrill. There was no way she was going to keep this man waiting—not one minute. Reaching the casino, she zigzagged between people in a hurried stride then slowed, took a deep breath, and confidently walked up to the front desk.

A young man greeted her. "Hello, may I help you?"

"Yes, I'm here to see Mr. Pazzarelli."

"Just one moment and I'll call him."

A nervous knot formed in her throat and slid down to her gut. She felt like slipping away just when he appeared. Awestruck, her mouth unhinged as wide as her eyes. The dreary casino didn't do him a bit of justice. He was heart-stopping handsome. The James Bond type, polished and debonair. Groomed black brows emphasized his deep-set, liquid brown eyes. His blue-black hair curled around his white starched collar, and a five o'clock shadow enhanced his perfectly chiseled, square jaw. She was speechless.

"Hello again," he said, reaching for her hand.

She lifted her arm and held out limp fingers. "Hello," gurgled out. "Uh . . . you said to come by the front desk when I got off. Well . . . here I am."

"Yes, I was waiting for you. I'm almost ready to leave, but I need to grab a few things from my office. Would you mind coming up with me?"

She couldn't see any harm in that. Yet as they entered the elevator an uncomfortable urgency enveloped her. "I don't have much time. My kids are expecting me home soon."

He smiled. "This won't take long. So you have children?"

"Yes, two, Shauna and Justin."

"That was lucky, a boy and a girl."

"Yeah, I feel pretty fortunate. Do you have children?"

"No. Never been married."

Never married! That's strange. He could have his pick.

The elevator arrived on the sixth floor, and they walked down the hallway to the last office. Frank unlocked the door and stepped aside for Jasmine to enter. She crept in and looked around. It was like a plush apartment; nothing at all what she'd imagined. His desk was of ornately carved ebony wood with two ox-blood leather chairs angled at each corner. Ten steps away was a fully stocked wet bar, and to the left was a sliding glass door to a terrace which overlooked Lake Tahoe.

Frank shut the door and sauntered to the bar. "Want a drink?"

"No thanks." She stepped lightly over an intricately woven rug, stroking the butter-soft, leather chair then casually wandered out to the terrace. Frank followed her, sipping a scotch, mesmerized by her wonder and irresistible beauty. "It's a beautiful view," she said, leaning over the railing and gazing down at the lake.

His eyes indulged on her swaying hips, long legs and the way the breeze played with her hair. "Yes it is." He wanted desperately to come up behind her and wrap his arms around her waist. To feel her supple body next to his had been a fantasized desire for some time. "But not as beautiful as you," he uttered.

She turned and smiled, resting her elbows on the top rail. "Thank you."

"You're welcome." Starting with her full, pink lips, his eyes slowly moved down her body. The crisp mountain air revealed her rigid nipples through the white tuxedo shirt. He envisioned kissing and caressing her breasts and felt the excitement surge like electricity to his groin. Jaz could see by the loose wave of his silk trousers he was quite aroused. Though the sight was a little startling, it made her feel alive and attractive. That, too, had been dormant and forgotten.

Standing in awe of each other, Frank stepped closer and traced her brow with a finger, then he swept a strand of hair from her face. An unspoken longing drew their bodies together.

His lips reached for hers, and she unexpectedly stepped back. "I, I better go." Frank didn't respond, ignoring her hesitation. He lived true to his reputation as being armed and dangerous, packing his heat-seeking missile holstered in white cotton. "Frank," she said, holding back his shoulders.

"I'm sorry, but you have me speechless." He drew in a breath and led her back inside his office. "Let me get a few things; then we'll go." While he thumbed through files and paperwork, Jasmine took another look around. She was now more intrigued than before with mystery man. Frank grabbed his briefcase, and they left his office. "Where are you parked?" he asked.

She waved. "Oh, it's all right. You don't have to walk me. I'm parked way in the back."

"I insist, and we'll take my car." When they arrived on the second level of the garage, Frank walked her to a sleek black 450 SEL Mercedes sedan.

"Wow, this is nice." Jaz started to touch it then pictured her fingerprints smudging the pristine gloss.

"Thanks." He opened the passenger door and helped her inside. The car was fully loaded, almost space age with all the gadgets and gizmos. It was dripping with extravagance like his office and like him.

There was more about this man than she knew what to think. *"Then don't, just have fun!"* The little voice in her head screamed.

Shifting into gear, Frank squealed out of the garage and down the ramp toward the back of the hotel. "Lead the way."

She looked around as they trolled the employee parking lot. "There's my truck." She pointed.

He pulled up behind a brown, short-bed. "This is you—a truck?"

"Yeah."

"I don't see you in a truck."

"What do you see me in?"

His eyebrows arched. "I'll tell you when we have more time."

A curious smile curled. "Another time then." She latched onto the door handle and started to get out as he clutched her arm.

"Wait a minute." She sat back down, hoping for the kiss she had stubbornly resisted on the terrace. "You forgot to give me your phone number."

"Oh, that's right . . ." Fumbling through her purse, she found a piece of paper and jotted down her telephone number. "Here you go."

Frank glanced at it and tucked it inside his suit pocket. "Do you stay up late?"

"Usually . . . why?"

"There you go again." He wagged his finger.

"I think that's a valid question," she replied.

Staring at her, something came over him he had never experienced. It was a sense of vulnerability. "Well," he smiled briefly, "just in case I get lonely and feel like talking. Sometimes that happens."

Jaz chuckled. "I end up talking to myself." She got out of the car and leaned in the window. "Thanks for the ride."

He nodded. "I'll talk to you later." Then he sped out of the parking lot and out of sight.

Jasmine had half an hour to find something to wear and be out the door to meet Yarah for the Macho Men show. Although, everything she put on didn't meet her daughter's opinionated standards. Shauna was just thirteen going on thirty. She was tall, slender and had already bloomed into a little lady. Her hair was long, like her mother's, but curly and the color of wheat. Despite her cute freckled face, she had one defining difference from other girls her age. It was her mature and highly precocious mind, which she spoke freely and most times too often. "Mom, you can't wear that," Shauna said, posing with her hands on her hips.

"Don't you have homework to do?" Jaz swished her hand.

"Yes, but I *still* think that dress is too short."

Jasmine tugged at the bottom edge of the dress. "Why don't you go see what your brother is up to?"

"I don't want her to see what I'm up to!" Justin blasted back a rapid response. He was the epitome of the Woods, not just physically but all the true characteristics. Freckled from head to toe, dark-brown curly hair, average in height for nine years old and meaty not skinny. Flexing his masculinity was the one Woods' trait that stuck out like a thorn; instilled by their patriarchal belief and taught as if required to become a man. As a result, Justin didn't like being bossed by his sister.

After Shauna left the room, Jaz took off the little black dress, neatly rolled it in a ball and tucked it in her purse. At the far end of the closet, she found a conservative, knee-length, loose fitting dress. She put it on and waved to the kids at the door. "Okay, I'm off."

Shauna gave her mom a nod of approval. "Bye Mom. Have fun. You look pretty."

"Thank you, I will. And don't worry, I'll be home early. Bye Justin, don't fight with your sister . . . I love you both." As soon as Jasmine turned the first corner on Kingsburg Grade, she pulled the truck over, opened her purse and slipped into the slinky black dress. Tonight was meant for fun, and she was long overdue.

Standing in the doorway of the showroom, it appeared every female in Tahoe had the same plan: to be there early. The first twelve rows were crammed into three, but Yarah's plume of orange hair was easy to spot. Jasmine cupped her mouth and screamed to her over the swelling excitement.

Yarah turned around and waved. "Climb over the chairs!"

"How? I'm in a tiny dress!"

"Who isn't!?"

After a hundred knee collisions and apologies, Jaz finally reached her. "So much for our bird's eye view. I had no idea it would be this packed."

"No kidding. It's stuffed tighter than my feet in these shoes."

"And me in this dress." They both laughed.

Suddenly, pulsating music began to rumble as smoke clouded the stage, and every woman felt the urge to bellow like a raving maniac. That was until the haze settled and eight scantily-clad men, standing with arms folded and legs wide apart, caught their breath.

Yarah grinned and elbowed Jaz. "This is like something out of a dream. Wouldn't ya just love to touch one of those gorgeous bodies .

. . or visa-versa?" Jaz didn't hear one word she said. She was mesmerized, hypnotized, and paralyzed by all that tan exposed flesh.

As the screams simmered to whines, the strippers announced they were looking for someone to participate in the next act. Then they separated and began scouring the crazed women.

Yarah hollered with arms flailing. "Over here! Choose me! Choose me!" As one came within arm's length, she ended the decision. Jaws of Life couldn't have pried her from his side. "See how easy that was?" she said to Jaz as he led her away by the hand.

"He had no choice!" she yelped.

The eight bronzed bodacious gods had Yarah lie down on the stage, and they straddled her body. Then bright lights flashed, and the music cranked to a hip-thrusting beat. Yarah lifted and gave Jasmine a thumbs-up while stroking their muscular legs. Not only did her dream come true, but she had the best view in the house.

When the show was over, Jasmine remembered to change into the other dress, just in case Shauna was still awake. There was no need to start something that would take all night to explain. She'd have to wait to fully understand, sometimes only a *little black dress* would do.

Quietly opening each bedroom door, Jaz snuck a peek at their sleeping face, then she went to her room to change into something comfortable. An evening was not fulfilled without her quiet time.

Wrapped in her throw, curled on the couch, she sipped on a glass of wine thinking of one sexy man not eight. It was odd, she thought, to have never seen Frank before today. A man of his distinguished stature and good looks would be hard to miss. Visualizing his face, it occurred to her, she'd forgotten to tell Yarah about him. She jumped off the couch and hurried to the kitchen to call before it was too late.

The first words out of Yarah's mouth instigated a debate. "Girl, you're all wrong. Hotel managers make a lot of money. They run the whole freakin' joint!"

"Not this much."

"Maybe he inherited it. Or maybe he hit it rich in the casino?"

"But why the fancy office? There's nothing fancy about the Palace, and this place was unbelievable. It just doesn't make any sense."

"Who cares? I don't and you shouldn't either. Men like him are trouble just waitin' to happen."

"Well, if I find out he's living in a lake view mansion, I'm going undercover."

Yarah glared at the phone. "Are you crazy, girl? That's too dangerous!"

"Don't worry. Just a little snooping, that's all. Hey, you wanna be my partner?"

"Hell no! I have enough craziness in my life. I don't need anymore. Besides, he's been watchin' you not me. So leave me out of it!"

"All right, but you might regret it . . . it could be fun."

"My fun and your fun are completely different. Not to mention, look completely different."

Jaz grinned, picturing his sexy smile. "Okay, but if you change your mind—"

"Forget it! Girl, I'm tired. I'll talk to you tomorrow. And do me a favor, stay out of trouble."

"Oh, good night." Jasmine had just returned to the couch to savor an hour of quiet time when the phone rang. She suspected it was one of Yarah's last-minute thoughts and answered with a brash attitude. "I see you changed your mind, didn't you?"

"About what?" a low, seductive voice asked.

"Ahh . . . who is this?"

"You've already forgotten me? That's not a good sign."

"Frank?"

"What, you didn't think I'd call?"

"Not tonight, I guess," she uttered.

"I can hang up and call you later."

She laughed. "No, I'm glad you did." She envisioned his dreamy, dark eyes and mouth-watering smile.

"So what are you doing?" he asked then sipped his scotch and rested his head on the ledge of the hot tub.

"Drinking a glass of wine and enjoying my quiet time."

"Mmm . . . sounds nice. What do you have on?" His eyes closed.

Her face turned hot. "Isn't that a little personal and more than you need to know?"

"Believe me, what a person wears says a lot about them."

"And how's that?" She leaned against the fridge as the conversation began to smolder.

He jiggled the ice cubes and took a sip. "If you're wearing a t-shirt and sweatpants, then you're the laid back, down-to-earth type. If you're wearing a night gown, you're up-tight and conservative . . . unless it's a short, sexy one. And if you're wearing nothing at all—"

"I got-I got it," she blurted.

"I thought you would." He grinned devilishly.

"All right, Mr. know-it-all, tell me this. What does it mean if I wear a t-shirt and sweatpants one night and a nightgown the next?"

"A sexy one?"

"Maybe," she whispered.

"I'd say you're way too confusing for me." He chuckled.

Her hips rocked. "Sooo . . . what do *you* have on?"

"Nothing at all. I'm sitting in my hot tub."

She slapped her hand over her mouth then remembered to start collecting clues. "And I bet you have a great view of the lake, don't you?"

"As a matter of fact I do. I just watched the sun sink into the icy blue water. Maybe you could join me sometime." He took another sip of his drink.

She saw herself snuggled against his chest, hair dripping wet, mist all around them, sinking deeper into the swirling water, embraced in an endless kiss. "It's a possibility."

"Mmm . . . we'll have to work on that."

His smooth, seductive voice aroused the cobwebbed corners of her womanhood and reminded her how good it felt to be turned on. Also, that it had been forever since she'd experienced eroticism of any kind. Closing her eyes, she kept the conversation going as his words stroked every inch of her body. "Tell me, Frank, have you ever met a girl from Montana?"

He swirled an ice cube in his mouth. "No, I don't believe I have. Are you from Montana?"

"Uh-huh," she whispered and took a sip of wine. The warm liquid trickled down her throat, leading her to another place—somewhere she hadn't visited in a long time. Her hand brushed over starved areas of her body, imagining it was his.

He detected something different in her voice as her breathing became more clear and audible. Curious of the change, he was provoked to embellish on the moment. "Oh, that feels good. There's nothing better than standing naked in the cool breeze. You don't mind if I dry off while we talk, do you?" There was no reply, then he heard a glass break.

Her eyes sprang open. "Frank, hold on a minute." Grabbing a dishtowel and broom, reality reclaimed its place back in the kitchen. Jaz mopped up the glass and wine then got back on the phone. "Sorry about that, I accidentally spilled my wine."

"I'm sorry I wasn't there to help." Snagging an ice cube from his glass, he rubbed it across his face. "Getting back to why I called; I'll be picking you up at six-thirty for our dinner date. Will that give you enough time to get home from work and get ready?"

"I think so. I'll try to get an early out."

"If you have a problem with that, let me know and I'll see what I can do."

"That would be great. By the way, where are we going?"

"The yacht club. Have you been there?"

She playfully answered, "The Yacht Club. Oh yes, I was just there yesterday. It was absolutely superb." She chuckled. "I'm just kidding, but I do like yachts. Does that count?"

"That's close enough." He was amused by her spunk. "Listen, I'll let you get back to your *quiet time.* And next time call me. I'll bring over the wine."

"All right, I'd like that," she said, innocent of his revelation. "Although I have to warn you, it's been awhile since I've had the company of a man. I'm not sure how to act anymore."

He grinned. "It's just like riding a bike: straddle it, sit down and start peddling. Now don't forget, Friday at six-thirty."

"I won't. Have a good night."

"Oh, I already have." He exhaled.

THREE

Tonight was the charity event with Frank, and the day was closing in on the final hour. The casino was thinning, and the action was down to a few five-dollar players as everyone left for dinner. Jasmine was thankful for that. Her mind had taken a detour from dealing cards to trying on dresses with the perfect hairstyle.

"Jasmine . . . oooh Jasmine," Frank said, standing right next to her. She turned, startled. "Oh, sorry, I didn't see you there."

"Where were you? I said your name twice."

"I suppose lost in thought." She didn't want to sound overly excited about their date tonight.

"Well, I just came by to tell you you'll be out in fifteen minutes." Her face lit up. "Did you make that happen?"

"I know a thing or two about women, and you need lots of primping time. Don't get me wrong, if I had a say in the matter I prefer au' naturel. The reason I like you."

She gulped, feeling a mist of steam rise from her shirt.

He patted the table. "Anyway, the limo will be at your house six-thirty sharp. See you then." As he turned and sauntered off, she fought back the impulse to scream *limo!*

Sitting at the end of the bed in a two-handed struggle with pure vanity, Jaz blared, "Who in their right mind would ever create something so stupid like pantyhose? And if that's not enough, throw in the life-threatening, tourniquet top."

"Mom, they make your legs look pretty," Shauna said.

"There's my answer—a man! Us women should invent a one size fits-all, waist high tube sock and see how they like it!" Shauna laughed. She loved her mom's rebellious humor. "How much time do I have?" Jasmine said with one last tug.

"It's almost six-thirty; you better hurry up."

Jaz looked in the mirror. She'd selected a black satin gown that draped in the back and plunged teasingly in front. It had a sexy yet classy flair. "It's a little tighter than I remember," she said, turning sideways. "I think just an olive or two is all this dress can handle."

"Just tell him you're not hungry," Shauna said, giggling.

"I don't think that'll go over very well if he's paying beaucoup bucks a plate." She glanced at her buttocks in the mirror. "But . . . I'm worth it."

Just then the door flew open. "Mom, there's a big white car outside, and a man is coming to the door," Justin yelped.

"Let Frank in, and tell him I'll be right there."

"Mom, you look sexy."

"Justin! You're too young to be saying something like that. Where in the world did you hear that?"

"In school." Then he and Shauna darted off to greet Frank at the door.

When Jaz heard the doorbell ring, her stomach did a triple somersault. She glanced in the mirror one more time, grabbed her wrap, and then teetered out on five inch heels.

Frank was standing in the entryway cradling a bouquet of pastel-pink roses. His mouth parted when she came into view. The uniform she wore at work may as well been a brown burlap sack. There was more woman in that dress than he'd seen in a lifetime. "You look stunning," he uttered, plucking a rose from the bouquet and giving it to her.

Jasmine took it, glowing with a wide radiant smile. "Thank you very much."

He looked at Shauna. "The rest are for you."

"These are for me?" She beamed with delight.

"I had a sneaky feeling you liked roses." Then he patted her on the head.

Jaz could hear her little voice. *"Danger-danger. He's good—reeeal good."*

Frank helped Jaz into the limo then scooted in close to her, leaving most of the seat empty. His lustful eyes sparkled devilishly as he envisioned the woman sipping wine during quiet time, doing whatever it was she was doing. "I have a surprise." He pulled out a chilled bottle of Dom Perignon from a bucket of ice. "Care for some champagne?"

"I love champagne. Wow, you really went all out. Or is this normal for you?"

Frank poured a glass for each of them, then he turned and rested a hand on her leg. "Let's just say, I favor the good life." He held up his glass. "To the beauty of perfection."

Jaz smiled and took a sip, gazing at him with an unsuspecting eye. The tux was as form fitting as a wetsuit, boasting his broad shoulders and trim waist. *I can't believe this man needed a date. He probably has hundreds of women sitting by their phone right now.* She fought back that pesky thought and took another sip of champagne.

Frank noticed her nervously nibbling at her lip. "Are you all right?"

"Yeah, just a little anxious I guess."

"The champagne should help." He added more to her glass, hoping for a two-bottle night.

As they entered the gates of the Yacht Club, limousines were looped around the circular driveway like a black pearl necklace. Frank had his driver park in front for everyone to see their grand entrance. Jaz stepped out and slipped her arm through Frank's as they parted the dignified crowd like celebrities at a Hollywood party.

It was a parade of jewels and furs with every woman wearing her finest. Frank escorted Jasmine around as if she were wearing the Hope Diamond, introducing her to several people. "You didn't tell me everyone calls you Frankie," she said curiously.

"They call me Frankie. You call me Frank." He gently tapped the end of her nose. She nodded in agreement. Frankie sounded juvenile, anyway.

As they strolled, Jasmine noticed most of the people had grouped with their own gender. The men were huddled smoking cigars, and the women were gathered in their own social circle. And for some reason they wouldn't stop staring at her. She tried to brush it off, but their pinched faces, darting glares and hands to their mouths, activated a defensive reaction. She began fiddling with her hair and crossing her arms over her chest, which brought on more attention, including Frank's. They were the jealous eyes of the women in his past.

Feeling responsible, he put his arm around Jasmine's shoulder and whispered, "Let's go outside and look at the boats."

"I was just going to suggest that," she whispered back.

Outside, the night air was dense and illuminated by a string of yellow bulbs draped along the pier. As they walked, hugged close together, Jaz glanced at a yacht secured along the dock. It prompted her to delve into her covert investigation. "That's a beautiful boat. Do you own one?"

"Actually, I do. It's quite fun. You'll have to take a ride with me some warm, sunny day." Then he gently backed her against a lamp post and uttered, "But it's not half as fun as this." His sultry brown eyes waltzed into her crystal blue eyes as his lips reached. "I've wanted to do this the day I saw you," he whispered in her ear.

"Do what?" She teased as her heart raced with his rigidness.

"Devour those lovely lips of yours." He began nuzzling her neck with delicate kisses, moving closer to her mouth. "I want you . . . Jasmine," he moaned, feeling her body cave to his touch.

"Hey, Frankie!" a loud voice echoed. They both froze and looked toward the doorway. A man with his hands to his mouth called out again. "Sorry, but the boss needs to see you."

"Tell him I'll be right there." Frank knew he couldn't keep Marco waiting. He looked at Jasmine. "This could take a minute." Leading her back inside, he went to find Marco while she attempted to mingle with the women.

After politely introducing herself, she eagerly jumped into a subject she knew well: children and horses. However, that instigated more eye-rolling smirks than when she had first arrived. It was obvious the women wanted nothing to do with her, and that was that.

Jaz backed out of the clutch and casually strolled in search of a glass of wine. Not knowing where Frank went or how long he would be, she felt less intimidated facing the bartender to pacify the time. Finding the bar, she took an open seat.

The bartender shuffled over to her. "What will it be, Miss?" he said with a hurried nod.

"A glass of cabernet, please." He turned to get her wine, and she looked in the mirror behind him, seeing a group of men in a heated argument. One had his back to her and looked like Frank. Then the man turned around. It was Frank, and he looked very upset. She wasn't sure if she should stay or walk away, but she definitely didn't want to be caught spying.

Taking her wine, she weaved through the people and stood before a big picture window. Looking out at the stars, the urge to go home surpassed the desire to stay. She didn't belong with all these stuffy people. She'd left that pretentious life of money and luxury three years ago, and it wasn't worth the painful price, and it definitely couldn't buy the one thing she wanted.

Feeling her past begin to surface, she turned to look for Frank and spotted him with a woman. More disturbing, the woman had her arms wrapped around his neck while fondling his hair. What really got her, he wasn't trying to walk away or even resisting. It looked like he was enjoying their conversation, talking with their lips almost touching.

Whirling around to face the window again, Jaz felt like a tea kettle ready to spew. *I knew it! Just one of many, I'm sure!* The humiliation and distrust she'd gone through with Carl had resurfaced as if yesterday. She fought back the tearful memories, but her patience with men and *other women* had run its course. She wanted to go home before she made a bigger spectacle of herself.

Frank caught a glimpse of Jasmine staring out the window. He immediately held Mimma back and slipped from her arms.

"Wait a minute, darling," she reached for him, "a kiss before you leave." Her red lips pursed.

Frank was already gone and walking up to Jasmine. He squeezed her waist. "Sorry about that. I didn't mean to be gone so long, but I ran into an old friend."

Without reservation, Jaz blurted out the words that were hanging from her tongue. "Frank, I'd like to go home."

He angled his head. "Are you sure, dinner hasn't even been served yet?"

She shot him a daring glare. "Yes, I'm very sure. I'm . . . not feeling well."

"All right, let me get your wrap." He left and then escorted her out.

The limousine swooped around and parked in front of them. Jasmine got in and slid to the end of the seat. Frank followed her and closed the gap. They looked at each other, stifling their questions, and then rested back and looked forward. The ride home was intensely quiet, but Jaz felt it was best to refrain from accusations than have a blowout on their first date. Besides, he was single and handsome. Why wouldn't any woman want him? The problem was her past had reared its ugly head, and no matter how far she moved the repercussions always found her.

Frank was confused. Something obviously made her upset. He wasn't sure if she'd heard the argument with Marco or witnessed Mimma groping him. To be safe, he decided to go with her excuse. "I'm sorry you don't feel well. Is there anything I can do?" He touched her leg. "You know, I give a great back rub." His lips curled into a sympathetic smile.

Her eyes narrowed. *I'm sure you do!* "Thanks, but I'll be fine." She smiled briefly and looked out the window as her mind dragged her through the mire of doubt.

Gently taking her hand in his, he squeezed it in an attempt to regain what he'd lost. "If I knew what to do I'd do it—anything, just name it."

Jaz listened to his sincere consoling and started to think she'd been a tad unfair. Her insecurity with men wasn't his fault. There was probably a justifiable reason he was so intrigued by that woman. Maybe it was an old friend like he said. She did look much older than him, and he seemed genuinely concerned about her feelings.

31

The driver pulled up in front of her house and turned off the engine. Frank brushed her face with a finger. "We're here, are you sure the night is over?"

She looked at him and could see his disappointment, but she *was* feeling sick—sick of getting hurt. "Yes, I'm sure. I really don't feel very well." She started to open the car door.

He stopped her with his hand and bewitching charisma. "Wait a minute. We have a little unfinished business first."

She raised an eyebrow. "What kind of business?" The words were barely uttered when Frank lowered his mouth over hers, and his spell had her submissively closing her eyes and parting her lips. They kissed as if starved, hungrily and eagerly. Her torment liquefied to a puddle and trickled between the crevices of her brick wall. But as his hand moved down her dress and over her breasts, the spell broke. She bolted forward, and her eyes snapped open. "I see! That kind of business."

Frank sat up, catching his breath. "Yeah, that kind of business."

Jasmine straightened her dress and brushed her fingers through her hair. "Well, just so you know, you're good at it." Frank tried kissing her back into his arms, but she defiantly resisted. "Please stop. I need to go in now."

"All right, all right, you win. I'll be a good boy." After helping her out of the limo, he walked her to the door. They stood silently staring at each other, seeing the same thing: two completely different people. He was spiraling with heated frustration while she was rebuilding her brick wall. And neither one knew where to go from there. "I wish this would have ended differently," Frank murmured, envisioning them sharing a pillow in bed.

"I know, but I still want to thank you." Jaz felt a twinge of guilt, ending the night because of her embedded distrust.

He shrugged and smiled. "Can I give you my phone number just in case you'd like to . . . whatever?"

"Sure." She gave a quick smile.

He pulled out a business card from his wallet and wrote down his home phone number. Handing it to her, he clutched her hand. "I hope you decide to call." His eyes conveyed his want.

"You never know." She gave him an answer that left room to ponder.

CHAPTER

FOUR

F rank fired up the engines of his 410 Cessna and was ready for takeoff, destination Guatemala. After nine years of service in the United States Navy, he was more comfortable in a plane than he was his own car. He had been a pilot and aircraft commander of the U.S. Navy P-3 Orion patrol squadron and didn't just fly your standard military plane. It was a four engine, turboprop, long distance, magnetic submarine locating aircraft.

Frank's assignment was to seek Soviet submarines by flying over the wave tops of the Pacific and Atlantic coastlines in twenty-hour hops. This not only required precise skill but the ability to fly under the radar at an altitude three to five hundred feet above sea level.

With the knowledge of the gaps in the American SOSA radar nets, he was invaluable to the U.S. submarine defense. Although, after his separation from naval duty neither airlines nor air charter services were interested in his aviation intellect. The only conceivable reason was too much knowledge did more harm than good.

After several interviews with no success, Frank contacted Paul Cusimano at the Paradise Palace in Lake Tahoe. He was a friend of a friend who owed a big favor—big enough that the position of hotel manager was soon available. Frank started the following week. The duties of the job were menial, compared to what Frank was used to, but that didn't last long. Airtel, a pilot recruiting service run by Marco Gamboli, tracked him down. He offered Frank a job flying to Honduras. It sounded simple yet had one requirement. One that if Frank hadn't found the depth of destitution and depression he would have said no. The instructions were to make the run and then make the exchange. The only requirement was to ask no questions. An advance of twenty grand made his decision a lot easier.

The course zigzagged through the radar nets of Central America to a remote uncontrolled airstrip in Southern California. After one flight, Frank knew exactly what was going on. The pilot recruiting service was a front for a drug run, and he was the mule. The way Frank saw it, it was an opportunity that couldn't have worked more perfectly. All his stored knowledge finally paid off, and the Palace kept him respectable.

He stayed with the hotel, having the ideal front, and flew three days a month. Paul's questions regarding his trips and plush office furnishing were quickly quashed with hush-money—enough that he never asked again.

When Frank gained trust with the impoverished country and a relationship was established, he made his own connections. It trickled through to Guatemala, where drugs were second in demand. They wanted guns. For Frank that was not a problem and wasted no time in finding an underground connection.

Mac served as an 82nd Airborne Division Ranger and named for his astute knowledge of machine guns. He became Frank's artillery supplier of the most sought after weapons. They ranged from war surplus 30-caliber U.S. light machine guns, U.S. surplus M-16, and AR-15 assault rifles, to a fabricated machine pistol Mac-10. With the supplier and buyer eagerly at hand, why include Marco in his multi-million-dollar operation? Frank was not only Kingpin, he was Warlord.

FIVE

Tony Baxter was in one of his belligerent, tyrannical moods again, pacing back and forth with nothing more to say than his favorite four-letter word. "What the *fuck* is she doin'? Has she gone completely fuckin' crazy?"

Jaz glanced over to see what his verbal fist fight was about this time and saw Connie hunched over her game in a nonstop shuffling frenzy. Her eyes were glued to her perpetual mission as beads of sweat dripped from her glistening red forehead. One by one, her customers were getting up, shaking their heads, and walking away from the game.

Tony waited like a tiger stalking its prey, and when all her players were gone he pounced in one giant leap. "Now that everyone has left, can you tell me what the *fuck* you are doing!?"

Connie cowed to his jutting jaw. "What do you mean?"

"What the *fuck* do you think I mean? You never stopped shuffling!"

"You told me to shuffle forty-five times."

"Are you fuckin' nuts? I told you to shuffle four to five times!"

She gulped. "Oh, you did, sorry." She lowered her eyes, knowing his were capable of burning holes.

Jasmine empathized with her embarrassment which Tony skillfully inflicted on his victims. She had been there more times than not and had one nubby fingernail to prove it. When she got tapped out for a break, she walked over to console Connie. "Hey." She gently touched her back. "I would have done the same thing. You never know about Tony."

Connie gazed up at her with glassy eyes. "I swear he said forty-five times."

Jaz nodded. "I believe you."

It started out to be a typical day for Jasmine. As usual, she was dealing the frontline. To her, this was where a player's opulence exceeded their mentality. To a bystander, they were show-offs with more money than they knew what to do with.

As Jasmine tossed the cards and scraped away the losers, a snippy, tight-faced, redhead said to her, "Honey, if you'd let us win, we'd tip you. That's how it works, you know." Her thick black lashes batted repetitively as though something was caught in them.

Sitting next to her was Ms. Barbie doll, her evil twin. Her platinum hair was teased so high it looked like cotton candy. She chimed in with her own request while sweeping her cards for a hit. "I'll take a nine, please."

Jaz tossed her a card, biting back a cynical reply: *"And which suit would you prefer?"*

Barbie's bewildered eyes darted up in total shock at Jaz. "Is that a nine? I asked for a nine—not a ten! I think you have a hearing problem." Both women cackled.

"I'm sorry, it's a little loud in here," Jaz said, keeping her head down and mouth under restraint. Dealers were not allowed to make derogatory comments or defend their innocence—casino rules.

"That's all you have to say? It's a little loud in here? Look at this crap she's giving me." Barbie shoved her cards in her husband's face.

He shook his head. "Just leave the dealer alone. She has nothing to do with what you get."

"It really helps if you know how to play," Jasmine said, feeling that was harmless and staying within the boundaries of policy rules. But she was wrong, and the battle began.

Fire shot from the woman's tapered nostrils. "I know how to play! You obviously need more lessons!"

Lessons! I'll show you lessons. Smiling with a stiff jaw, Jasmine began to shuffle-up, changing the system of the cards. She had reached her limit of stuffy stupidity and was ready to cash them in. A few twists, a couple tucks, add a quick strip, and then she eagerly dealt them out.

Both women looked at their cards. The redhead tucked hers, but the platinum blonde began tearing hers into confetti. "You know what you are—a bitch!? And you know what you can do with this fourteen?" She threw the freshly torn bits of cards at Jasmine, and they stuck to her hair like glitter.

Glancing around for help, Jaz saw the pit bosses laughing so hard they were holding their stomachs and slapping their legs. Finally, Tony moseyed up to the table. "You need a fresh deck?" He chuckled.

"Yes, thanks. Can't have a fourteen missing," Jaz said directly at the indignant woman.

Barbie stood up and flipped her hair over her shoulder. "Let's go, she's no fun."

As Jasmine watched them strut away, her eyes inadvertently relaxed in the direction of the front desk. Oddly, an empty feeling enveloped her. She hadn't spoken to Frank since the charity event, and that was two days ago. In a weird way she kind of missed him and started to regret how it ended. Then two poignant statements came to mind, given to her by Mariano Capeeza. He was a casino host at the Palace and well respected by his peers. He told her: "If you remember anything, remember these two things. Never burn bridges in this business, and connections are more valuable than knowledge." Taking his words to heart, she decided to go see Frank after work and see what he was up to.

While staring off, thinking of their last date, a giant man walked up to her game. He stood for a moment eyeing her and not saying a word. She noticed dribbles down the front of his white shirt and assumed he was completely intoxicated. Then he began sniffing which made him start coughing. Jasmine watched as his eyes bulged, and then he grabbed at his throat. "Sir, are you all right?" she asked, panicked. He tried to say something but continued in a strangulating cough. She scanned the area for a pit boss and saw Tony watching with his arms folded, teething a toothpick.

"Tony! Come help!" she cried out.

"Why? What does he want?" he hollered back nonchalantly.

Before she could answer, the man collapsed to the floor and began jerking and squirming like a human earthquake. "He's having a seizure!"

Tony leaped from the podium. "Throw a lid on your game!" Jasmine frantically grabbed the glass lid from under her table as Tony struggled with four hundred pounds of thrashing flesh. "Help me roll him over, he's choking!" he blared. Together, their adrenaline became bionic, and they flipped the enormous man over like a rag doll. "Call the paramedics!" Jaz jumped up and ran to the podium. She called the operator then came back to Tony's side as he restrained the man from choking. She had never seen Tony react so quickly and with so much concern. His face was strained, teeth gritted, and veins popped with the sheer will of saving this stranger's life.

"Watch out!" a voice called.

"The paramedics!" Jaz yelped.

Tony looked up. "It's about fuckin' time." He grabbed a chair breathlessly and inched his way up to the seat. "Now I need the para-fuckin'-medics," he uttered, wiping his brow with a sigh.

Today, Jaz saw something extraordinary and most likely never see again. It wasn't the horrific, life-threatening incident with the humongous man, or Tony's super-human strength. It was his exposed emotions and compassion. He was actually human after all.

As she reached out to touch his shoulder, he motioned her off with a quick wave. "Let's just call it a day. Leave your game locked and go home."

"Are you sure?"

"Yeah, I'm sure."

"All right. Thank you, Tony."

"Yeah–yeah–yeah. Just keep that between us." He took a winded breath. "I'm goin' home and make the biggest fuckin' martini ever known to man." He pointed. "My advice to you. Do the same."

She smiled and turned then looked back. "I want you to know you really impressed me—"

He held up a hand. "Keep that between us too."

Before going downstairs to change, Jaz headed to the front desk to tell Frank of the grisly experience. Despite the tragedy, it was the perfect opportunity to show her face and to see his.

"Hello, can I help you?" A clerk greeted her with a wide, practiced smile.

"Yes, I'm here to see Frank Pazzarelli."

"I'm sorry. He isn't here. He's out of town."

"Oh, for how long?"

"He'll be back on Wednesday. Would you like me to leave him a message?"

"No, that's all right. I'll see him Wednesday." She strode off deep in thought. *Out of town . . . I wonder if it's business or pleasure.*

Jasmine drove home consumed in the events of the day, which included Frank's trip, that cooking dinner seemed beyond her capability and far too energetic. Making a quick turn into the Burger Hut, she knew the kids would love the surprise and she the break.

Strolling through the door, Shauna was startled by her early arrival. "Mom, what are you doing home so early?" Jasmine handed her the two sacks of cheeseburgers and fries, which quickly changed her question. "This is dinner?!" She hollered to Justin. "Mom's home and she brought hamburgers!"

Justin came barreling out of his room. "No way!"

"Yep, I thought I'd surprise you," Jaz said and sat down at the kitchen table.

Shauna passed out the burgers and fries then went back to what was pestering her. "Really Mom, why are you home? You never come home early."

"Yeah Mom, did you get fired?" Justin asked.

Jaz set her burger down and took a sip of pop. "Actually, I helped save a man's life today. He had a seizure right in front of my game, but Tony and I was able to help him until the paramedics came. Then Tony told me to go home." She left out all the gruesome details.

"Did you get a raise?" Justin spouted.

Jaz chuckled. "No, I didn't get a raise, but it was rewarding to know we saved his life."

"Not the same!" He huffed.

Shauna glared at her mother. "So, is that *all* that happened, or are you leaving something out?" The kids loved listening to the bizarre stories that took place in the casino. They sounded so farfetched, like something out of a movie.

"That's pretty much it." Jaz continued eating her burger.

"Wow Mom, you're a hero! Can I tell my friends what you did?" Justin asked.

"Finish your dinner and homework first and then you can."

"Geez, you're no fun."

"I know. I've heard that all day."

The evening's agenda was nothing but total relaxation. Jasmine slipped on her favorite nightgown, folded the quilt to the bottom of the bed, fluffed the pillows, grabbed a book, and then slithered into bed with a cup of tea. Although, her mind was still racing with questions—Frank being the main subject. *Maybe he's decided not to see me at all . . . maybe I pushed him away too quickly . . . maybe it's a pleasure trip with another woman . . . I'll find out Wednesday.*

Frank glided his Cessna to a stop on a remote runway in California. He gathered two large duffel bags, one containing twenty kilos of cocaine, the other had two-hundred grand for the guns. With the leather straps over his shoulders, he stepped off the plane and strode to a black limousine waiting for him.

Clive Morgan jumped out to greet him. He was Frank's chauffeur, butler and cook. He was of English descent, tall and lean in stature, and wore his salt-and-pepper hair neatly combed back. Though he was nearing seventy years old, his vigorous demeanor masked it well. He and Frank had become close through the years but was never given details of his trips. As far as Clive knew, Frank had business associates all over the world. "Good to see you, sir. How was your trip?"

"Same as usual; too many meetings and not enough sleep. One more trip, and then I'm calling it quits." Frank heaved a duffle bag inside the trunk and then into a hidden locker.

"I believe you said that last time you came home," Clive said, closing the trunk.

"Yeah, but this time I mean it." Frank walked around the car and waited as Clive opened his door.

"As I remember, you said that as well."

Frank looked at him and grinned. "There's a reason now, before there wasn't." He slid into the cushioned leather seat, reached under and retrieved a metal briefcase. Unlocking it, he stashed the cash from the other bag and slipped it back under the seat. With a winded sigh, his head rested back and eyes closed.

Clive glanced in the mirror. "You'll see I stocked a fresh bottle of Chivas. That should help you relax."

Frank reached for the scotch and poured a long drink for the ride home. He took a hearty sip, stretched his legs and closed his eyes again. "Wake me when we get there."

"Very well." Clive shut the center window and tuned into his favorite mystery channel.

Four hundred miles had passed when Frank woke to the familiar curves, leading to his estate. He lowered the center window. "That was fast."

"Actually, it was just right. The last segment of who-done-it just ended.

"So, who done it?"

"Sheila, the waitress." He chuckled. "It's always the person you least suspect."

"Isn't that the truth?"

When they entered the gates of his five-acre estate, twin Dobermans ran out to meet them. They howled and barked, excited for Frank's return, and then happily jogged along the car until Clive parked. Reaching under the seat, Frank grabbed the silver case while the dogs panted at his window. He stepped out and slapped his chest, letting the dogs leap up on him. "How ya doin', Tank? Did ya miss me? I know Tasha did, didn't ya, girl?" After their celebratory licks, he tapped the side of his leg, and the dogs obediently heeled. Together, they marched through the large arched doorway and into his home.

Clive followed with the bag from the trunk. "I'll take this to the office and then prepare dinner."

"Thanks, but something light."

Clive nodded and set the bag outside the office door, then he left for the kitchen.

Frank unlocked the office door and placed the duffel and silver briefcase on top of his desk. Grasping the arm of his wing-back chair, he collapsed in the seat. This time he really did mean it. The trips had reached the point of completely draining him mentally and physically. It was time to settle down. That thought seemed incongruous, almost foreign, with only one explanation. It had to be the woman altering his mind, and that in itself seemed preposterous to consider.

Clive knocked at the door.

"Come in."

He stepped inside. "I just wanted to let you know there's a club sandwich in the refrigerator."

"Perfect."

"Then, if you no longer need me, I'll see you in the morning."

"Thanks, no, goodnight."

"Goodnight." Clive quietly closed the door.

Opening the duffle of cocaine, Frank eyed the white powder like a rat in a freshly filled dumpster. Then he retrieved a hollow book from his bookshelf that held a key to the top drawer of his desk. Opening the drawer, he located a list of phone numbers of buyers, suppliers and various people he'd met through the veins of the underworld. After dialing Chung Lee Chen, his broker and streamline to Los Angeles, he sat back and massaged the throb in his head.

"Hello?"

"Merry Christmas."

"I thought it might snow today."

"Meet me tomorrow at three o'clock."

"Same place?"

"Yeah."

"I'll be there."

Frank locked the drawer and returned the key to the hollow book, then he set the book back on the shelf. He walked over to a small oriental table with a Ming Dynasty vase sitting on top. Under the vase was a button that disengaged a sliding wall. It opened to a cubical made of cement with a Fort Knox vault door. After keying in the code, he spun the brass wheel to his private bank. Rows of wine crates were stacked to the ceiling. Inside each crate were bundles of cash. His last count was over fifty million. Stashing the money and cocaine, he gave the vault wheel a hefty spin then pushed the button on the table, and the wall slid back into place. His routine was as systematic as getting dressed. Everything was in sequence and everything in its right place. His stomach reminded him of the club sandwich. Now with everything securely tucked away, he headed for the kitchen to eat.

Tank and Tasha were sitting outside the door like sphinx statues. Brushing their heads, they followed him down the marble hallway to their favorite room. "You guys hungry?" They sat and licked their chops while he rummaged through the fridge. Finding a hunk of left-over roast beef, he held it up. "Let's hear it. Come on." Like a duet, they began bellowing a harmonious serenade. "Oh, that's beautiful. Here you go." He tossed each a slab of meat, and in one swift swallow it disappeared. "It's my turn now." He motioned with his hand, and they lowered their black, sleek bodies to the floor.

Sitting at the counter with his masterfully crafted club sandwich, something was missing . . . something cool, wet and soothing. *Yes, a glass chardonnay would be perfect.* Pouring the wine in his glass, a memory came to mind—one he would never forget. Jasmine and her *quiet time.* Lingering with his sandwich and wine, his mind wandered to her enticing curves, the fresh smell of her hair, and the sweet taste of her lips. *I wonder if she's home.*

After finishing his sandwich, he grabbed his glass and bottle of wine then headed up the spiral staircase to his magnificently decorated master suite. Priceless furnishings from around the world were throughout his private quarters. Dark polished hardwood covered the floor, and original oil paintings hung on the walls. He strategically positioned his king-size bed in the center of the room for a panoramic view of the sun rising and setting.

Sprawling out on the bed, Frank placed the bottle of wine on a French provincial night stand, grabbed the phone and hoped to hear Jasmine's voice.

"I'll get it," Shauna said and politely engaged in pleasantries with Frank.

"So, is your mom there?" he asked and took a sip of wine.

"Yes, just a minute." She held her hand over the phone and called, "Mom, it's for you!"

Jaz wrapped in her robe and came out to the kitchen. "Hello?"

"Jasmine?"

Her heart pounded against her chest. "Yes! Is this Frank?"

He grinned. "So you haven't forgotten me? I wasn't sure if you'd ever talk to me again."

"You! You have no idea what I've put myself through. I've replayed that night over and over in my head. I know I ruined the night and I'm really sorry."

"Don't worry about it. What do ya say we start over?"

"I'd like that . . . but I know a first impression says a lot."

Frank took another sip of wine. "I say we skip first impression and go right to third."

She giggled, "And what's a third impression?"

He adjusted his trousers. "Why don't you come over and I'll show you."

His statement wasn't shocking. The Palace had conditioned her to the fast-paced playboy type. But the one thing it didn't do, and couldn't do, was take the country out of her. Jasmine needed the slow meandering pace of a country mountain brook. "That sounds tempting but I'm already in bed." She didn't want to sound like a prude, as Yarah would call her.

A devilish grin curled. "Even better . . . maybe I'll come over there."

"Well, to tell you the truth, it's been a hot tea, flannel-nightgown kind of night. I had a pretty traumatic day at work. Actually, I came by the front desk to tell you about it, but they said you were out of town."

Frank gave her the same excuse he gives everyone. "Yeah, my mother lives in L.A. I help her out once a month. Stock up on food, do her bills, that kind of stuff."

"Hmm, I like that, a mama's boy." She pulled out a kitchen chair and sat down.

Frank swirled his wine and sipped. "A boy's gotta do–what a boy's gotta do." Then he quickly changed the subject. "Hey, did I hear you right? A flannel nightgown."

"I was wondering if you caught that."

"Now I am curious. How bad was it?"

"Bad enough that I debated on the long sleeve, down to the floor, button to the neck one."

He chuckled, "Sounds pretty scary."

"Truthfully, it was. A man collapsed at my game today. I thought he was going to die right in front of my eyes."

Frank set his wine down. "What happened?"

"This huge man came up to my game. I thought he was drunk at first, but he started coughing and choking and then fell to the floor convulsing. I have no idea what caused it, but it was terrifying." She shuddered, picturing the ghastly scene.

"Did the paramedics come?"

"Yes, thank goodness, and just in the nick of time. My boss and I helped him as much as we could, but he was enormous. He looked like one of those Sumo wrestlers. I bet he was at least four hundred pounds."

Frank stiffened. *Sumo said he was coming to Tahoe.* "Did you get his name?"

"No, he never spoke."

Something unsettling twisted in his gut. "Do you remember anything else about the man?"

Jasmine closed her eyes, picturing his features. "He was middle-aged, forty-fiveish—"

Frank interrupted. "Was he bald?"

"Yes."

"How was he dressed, suit or casual?"

She thought it was odd he was more curious about his appearance than his wellbeing. "Hmm . . . well he wasn't wearing a jacket, but he had on dark slacks and a white dress shirt. Oh! He had a big mole on his chin that looked like a heart." She shook her head. "Don't ask me why I remember that."

There was no doubt in Frank's mind who the man was. "Listen, I know you've had a stressful day. Get some rest, and I'll talk to you tomorrow."

"Sure, okay. Good night." She went back to bed now wrestling with more questions than before Frank called.

Frank picked up his wine and stared out the window. Tommy "Sumo" Tanaka was a man he hired when dirty work needed to be done. His size alone was intimidating enough, but his marksmanship was dead on. It wasn't like Sumo to arrive without calling, and why would he be at Jasmine's game? Something had to be going down. In the morning he would call the hospital and have a chat with Dr. Carmen Lucio. He was one of Frank's best clients and a physician there.

Jasmine fluffed her pillow and settled back in bed with her book, but each word and paragraph vanished the second she read it. Frank had possessed her mind and body, arousing her mundane life like spring in the winter. Just thinking about him was mind-boggling, not to mention erotic.

Now restless with his mysterious stir, she got up to pour another cup of tea when the phone rang again. She looked at the clock. It was now after ten. *Maybe he's in the mood for a little pillow talk.* She let it ring again then slowly lifted the phone. "Can't sleep, huh?"

"I'm not tired!" Yarah snapped.

"Yarah! I thought you were Frank."

"Uh huh, sounds juicy, tell me more." She had stretched the phone cord to the tub and was soaking in a cloud of suds.

"It's not what you think, if that's what you're thinking." Jaz angled her head. "When was the last time we talked?"

"Girl, the last thing I remember you were goin' to some highfalutin' shindig at the yacht club."

Jaz poured her tea. "Oh, we definitely need to catch up. That night didn't last long. I had him take me home early."

"You're kidding, right?"

"I wish I was."

"So what happened . . . and all the details."

"Well first I saw him in an argument, which was a little upsetting. He sounded so angry and so did the other man. Then some lady wrapped her arms around him like they were lovers. And that didn't go over well after what I went through with Carl. I guess everything kind of fell apart from there. Then I had him take me home."

"Probably did the right thing. Does Frank know you saw him in an argument and lovin' on the skank?"

"No. But he was confused with why I wanted to leave."

"You didn't tell him?"

"No. I thought it sounded immature and probably crazy."

"What are you gonna do now? Are you still suspicious of him?"

"I know he has a lake view home, and remember what I said?"

"Don't tell me you're goin' undercover?"

"Yes, doesn't that sound exciting? He's sooo tall, dark and mysterious."

"Girl, dark and mysterious says it all. If you ask me, he sounds more dangerous than a loaded gun."

Jaz sat back and took a sip of her tea as her mind shuffled through the pros and cons. "Dangerous, I don't think so. But there are a few things I haven't put together yet. Other than that, he seems like a pretty nice guy."

"Hey, talkin' about puttin' things together. Have you guys . . . ah, you know?"

Jaz laughed, "No, but—"

"But what!"

"I'm thinking I'd like to." She closed her eyes and bit her lip.

"I don't know, Jaz. He looks right, talks right, but somethin' ain't right. You know what I mean?"

"Oh stop worrying. I won't get into trouble. I'm just having a little fun."

Yarah looked at her wrinkled fingers. "Girl, I gotta get out of the tub before I turn into a freakin' raisin. I'll talk to you in the morning."

"Okay, see you tomorrow."

"You better."

"I will. Good night."

"Wait a minute! I almost forgot why I called."

Jaz pulled the phone back to her ear. "What?"

"Vonda is having a lingerie party at her house and wants us to model for her."

"Model . . . like what?"

"Nightgowns, teddies—that kind of stuff." Yarah was now out of the tub and posing naked in front of the mirror.

"Did you tell her we'd do it?"

"Not yet, but it sounds fun, and we get a free outfit for doing it."

"Really? So when is it?" Jaz asked.

"Next Friday night. You don't have plans with Frankie, do you?"

"No, and he doesn't want to be called Frankie. He made that very clear."

"Why?"

"I don't know. Just what he said. But anyway, tell Vonda I'll do it."

"Great! Talk to you tomorrow."

CHAPTER

SIX

I t was hump day at the Palace which was actually a Monday.

The mass of tourists had left the casino, taking with them the loud annoying rings followed by their hair-straightening screams. Only a muffled hum wafted through the air, giving those with things to ruminate the time to do so.

Jasmine thought about her conversation with Frank last night and was relieved he wanted to start fresh again. However his unusual questions and immediate hang up was still a little baffling. But rather than dwell on it all day, she shrugged it off as one of the things that made him so intriguing.

Yarah saw Jasmine gazing around the casino, too peacefully in her mind. She snuck up and clapped in her face then burst out laughing as she shot up in the air. "Thought that'd get your attention. When's your break?"

Jasmine caught her breath. "I'm not sure. My relief isn't back yet."

"I was hopin' we could . . ." Yarah stopped talking and sniffed. "What's that smell?"

Jaz sniffed. "Oh, that's Tony. He must be in the vicinity."

Yarah waved her hand past her face. "I knew I smelled somethin' rotten."

Jasmine's face softened. "He's really not that bad."

"Girl, if it looks like an asshole—smells like an asshole—it's an asshole!" They both erupted in laughter. "I better go. I'm back in the corner on the Big-Six today." Yarah rolled her eyes.

"Okay, I'll come by on my break. Maybe we can take it together."

"Sounds good." Yarah walked away pinching her nose and chuckling to herself.

Jasmine looked around for the tiny tyrant and saw Tony leaned against the podium, propped by an elbow, in his usual stance. She wondered if their bonding experience would have a lasting effect. But knowing Tony, it was probably a fleeting occurrence never to be seen again.

Suddenly his cologne became almost suffocating as he swaggered up to her game. "How ya doin' doll, you okay?" he said in an unfamiliar, caring tone. Jasmine looked into his eyes. They were different too, kind of misty.

"I'm doing okay. How are you?"

He massaged his forehead. "I'd be better if I didn't have this fuckin' hangover."

"Too many martinis?"

"That and. . . ." He hesitated and took a heavy breath.

She cranked her head, giving him a thorough examination. "Are you okay? You seem . . . I don't know . . . really different."

"Yeah, well, I don't know about you, but that really did a number on me yesterday."

"What do you mean? I thought you did great."

"It ain't that." He shook his head. "My old man died of a heart attack, God rest his soul, and I was there and did nothing. Between you and me, I ain't good at that life-savin' bullshit, and yesterday felt just like that day." He looked away and took another heavy breath. "I seriously thought I was gonna see it all over again."

Jaz wanted to reach out and hug him but wasn't sure how he'd react. "I'm sorry." She leaned toward him. "If it helps, I know how you feel. My dad died of a heart attack, too. I wasn't there like you, but—"

"I don't want to hear it. I say we forget about it." He turned and walked off, leaving Jaz with her mouth open and emotions dribbling out. *Nope, it's the same old Tony.*

Just then she felt a tap on her shoulder. "Break time," Earl said with bloodshot eyes and a pasty face.

"Are you all right?" she asked, staring into his eyes.

He mechanically shook his head back and forth. "No, I got a hangover."

"Well, you're in good company. Tony has one too."

"Oh, great, this should be fun," he grunted.

"Yep, he's all yours." She clapped, clearing her hands for the eye, then strolled through the casino to look for Yarah.

Turning onto the promenade, she passed a bellman carrying a vase of pink roses. He was heading toward her pit, and they looked identical to the roses Frank brought the night of their first date. *Hmm, I wonder if they're for me. It wouldn't hurt to ask.* "Excuse me, are those . . ." The bellman stopped and turned. "For me," she said and smiled.

He looked at the envelope, "Ahh . . . Jasmine Woods?"

"Oh, that's me!"

"You're Jasmine?"

"Yeah, see my name tag?" She held it out from her vest.

"Well, Mr. Pazzarelli told me to take them to pit two."

"Wonderful. Just set them on any podium in the pit."

He shrugged. "That's what I was going to do."

Jaz gleefully took off then remembered the card. "Oh, just a minute!"

He stopped and impatiently turned. "Yes?"

"I'd like the card please." Before he had a chance to give it to her, she plucked it from the bouquet. "Thanks."

"Sure. Anything else?"

"Nope." She eagerly opened the envelope and read the card. *Romance is nothing less than the finest form of art. And nothing but the finest for the woman of my heart. I'll call you tonight. Frank*

She smiled and slipped the card in her pocket then hurried through the casino in search of Yarah.

Frank was sitting with his feet crossed on top of his desk while gazing at the azure lake. It reminded him of the day Jasmine came to his office when the sun had cast a silvery sheen over the bouncing caps.

Closing his eyes, a smile stretched across his face visualizing her sensually tempting body draped over the terrace railing. He clutched his groin, remembering how he wanted to press his body against her. *Mmm . . . just one night in bed and she'd be mine.*

Just then the phone rang with a startling interruption. He sat up irritated and answered, "Yes!"

"Umm, Mr. Pazzarelli, I delivered the roses as you requested."

Frank forgot that he insisted the bellman call him. "Thank you. Did she see them?"

"Well, she actually stopped me in the aisle before I got there."

"Really?"

"Yeah, to see if they were for her." Frank chuckled. *A little presumptuous.* "Anyway, she took the card. But I did take the roses to pit two like you asked."

"Very good, Steven." He hung up and folded his arms, gloating with his ploy. A rap at his door interrupted him again. "Come in."

Linda, his secretary, peeked inside. "Excuse me, if you have the budget report done I'll take it to admin."

"Yes, I just finished it." He handed it to her then glanced at the clock. It was almost time to meet Chung Lee. "Ah, Linda, would you call the front desk and let them know I'll be out for a while."

"Will do." She took the report. "Do you know when you'll be back?"

"No, so don't make any appointments for me." He left the hotel without seeing Jasmine, figuring the roses were enough and the card said he'd call. That would have to suffice until he could give her his full attention.

Entering the parking garage, his Benz was waiting, cool, calm and collected. He, on the other hand, was sweaty, hot and stressed.

His anxiety had reached a teeth-grinding level, and Sumo was the reason. Just one peep out of his mouth, and the DEA would have enough to lock him away for life.

Taking a weary breath, he flipped open the glove compartment and reached for the Rolaids to calm his stomach and Quaalude to calm his nerves. Swallowing them down dry, he fired the engine and shifted into gear. The tires squealed as they hugged the curves of the garage and then out to the main strip.

Arriving at his estate, the dogs came out to greet him and instantly sensed his mood. Frank was focused on the meeting and charged to the house to prepare. Without a whimper, they followed close behind and stopped outside his office door. Frank unlocked the vault and entered. He grabbed the duffle of cocaine for the exchange, and within minutes he had everything back in order and locked up tight.

The dogs sat up as he came out and obediently followed him back to his car. Frank shot out of the estate and careened down the mountainside. When he pulled into the Zenith Cove parking lot, Chung Lee was there waiting for him.

The day was perfect for their meeting, cool and overcast. The beach was empty, and not a soul was in sight to witness the transaction. As he pulled up next to Chung Lee, they gave each other a quick nod. Then he latched onto the bag and got inside Chung Lee's silver Porsche 911.

"Nice day, huh?" Chung Lee said and handed Frank a briefcase of money.

"Perfect." Frank popped open the case and fanned a stack of bundled bills. "Two fifty?"

"Yeah," Chung lee replied, giving Frank a quizzical eye. "You never check the money. What's up?"

"Not a thing." Frank looked side to side, ready to leap out.

Chung Lee grabbed his arm. "One more thing."

Frank sat down and pulled his arm free. "If you don't mind, I'm not here to discuss the weather or anything else." He started to get out again.

"Sumo called me."

Frank quickly turned. "Where is he—what did he say?"

"Said for me to meet him. Didn't tell me why or where yet."

Frank started plotting. "Do me a favor. Call me when you find out the details. I think I'll make a surprise visit."

Chung Lee smiled and held out his hand. Frank opened the brief-case and handed him two grand. "More." He wagged his fingers.

"It isn't worth more."

"I think it is." Frank pulled out another three and shoved it at him. Chung Lee nodded and stashed it inside his coat pocket. "Always nice doin' business with you."

Frank groaned and got out of the car and into his own. That con-firmed it, Sumo was now his adversary. Who he was working for was the next thing to resolve. Shifting into reverse, he screamed out of the parking lot with all ten fingers strangling the steering wheel. "You're as good as dead, Sumo," he hissed through his teeth.

SEVEN

J asmine found Yarah on the Big-Six doing the proverbial *timeout*. "So I gave out a little money—who cares? This is a lot better than doing the fifty-two card magic show for those asshole bosses. Do you know how ridiculous you look goin' from shuffling to some juggling act?" Yarah squawked.

"Yeah, I do it every day," Jaz groaned.

"I'm surprised there isn't garlic hangin' around all their necks, they're so freakin' superstitious!" She grabbed a peg on the Big-Six and spun the wheel as hard as she could. "Watch this. I've been practicing it all morning." The wheel clicked like a frenzied tap dancer. "I can make it spin around thirty-two times."

Jaz giggled. "If it had wings it could probably fly."

"Not without me on it and right out of here!" They both laughed.

Jaz looked at her watch. "I'm going down to get a cup of coffee before break is over."

"Get me a cup. I should be tapped out any minute."

"We have the same break?"

"Yeah, somebody screwed up. But I won't tell if you don't."

Jaz chuckled. "See you down there."

Just as she sat down with their coffee, Yarah came walking up. "Did you remember how I like it?"

"Black with two sugar lumps."

"Yep, just like my men." Yarah grinned and took a sip. "So when are you going to see what's-his-butt again?"

"You mean Frank? I don't know. I hope soon. It's been a long time since Carl, and he doesn't even count. I'm ready to feel alive again . . . even if it hurts."

Yarah gave her a cockeyed look. "That doesn't sound like you. Are you feelin' all right?"

"I feel great. You just haven't heard me talk about a man before."

"You left out, in a good way."

"Okay, in a good way. But I'm not one of those man-haters. I just haven't been interested until now.

Yarah shook her head. "There's just something about him. He's too perfect in that too-good-to-be-true way. You know what I mean?"

Jaz closed her eyes and smiled. "Yes, I do."

Yarah handed her a napkin. "Here, wipe the drool off your chin."

When Jaz returned to her game she saw the roses and realized she'd forgotten to tell Yarah about them. She giggled to herself. "She'll be eating her words when she sees these."

The day had finally reached the end of the eighth hour. Jaz picked up the vase of roses and carried them into the lounge. Yarah saw her and rolled her eyes then walked over with her palm forward. "Don't tell me, let me guess. Mr. Wonderful?"

"See, you knew exactly who they were from," Jaz said and set them on the bench next to her.

"Did you thank him or are ya doin' that tonight?" Yarah asked.

"Actually, I went by the front desk to do that, but he'd left for the day. I'd sure like his hours, if you can call them that."

"Then, I guess you'll have to thank him tonight." Yarah smiled, arching a brow.

When Jasmine arrived home, she set the vase of roses on the table as Yarah's "words of wisdom" came to mind. *Was Frank too good to be true?* She knew that wasn't possible, although he had the sentiments, moves, and good looks that made her wonder if he was real.

After dinner and homework, Jaz put the kids to bed and snuggled on the couch. The card said he'd call, and the day was almost over. Her eyes struggled to stay open, but the warmth of the crackling fire and subtle scent of her violet throw lulled her to sleep. Falling deep into a dream, she heard someone knocking at the door. She tried to get up, but her legs were rooted like tree trunks. With each knock, she thrashed and struggled until finally whirling her body off the couch.

Sitting up disoriented, she heard it again. Then she realized it wasn't a dream. Someone was actually knocking at the door. Securing her robe, she went to the window and spied through the curtain. It was Frank, and he was walking back to his car. She knew if she opened the door it would be an invitation to her vulnerability—if she didn't, she would never know what she was missing. "Frank!"

He turned and saw her leaned against the doorway, hip cocked and hair mussed. "You are home." He started walking toward her.

"I was asleep. What brings you here?" she said smiling innocently.

"This chilly night." He folded his arms. "You in the mood for a little company?"

She bit her lip, thinking twice. "Maaaybe . . . for just a little while." Stepping aside, she let him in, and he purposely brushed against her. Something spirited was on his mind, and her fortress was starting to crumble. "Want a glass of wine?"

"Does a cat purr?" He grinned and came up behind her, nuzzling the fine hair on the back of her neck.

She squirmed as goose bumps rose with his breath. "That's a yes, I take it?"

"That's definitely a yes." His large, firm hands began massaging her neck and down her shoulders as she attempted to pour the wine.

Her head fell forward, and her body swayed with ecstasy. "Umm, that feels sooo good," she moaned.

"Like that?" He lifted her hair and kissed between her shoulder blades, inching down her back.

"Does a dog bark?" she murmured.

He chuckled. "Very clever."

She turned around and handed him his wine. "You better take this before I spill it."

"Yes, as I remember, you're good at that." A mischievous smile curled on his lips.

Clips of the sensually torrid scene became vivid, and her face flushed. "Oh, that's right. I spilled my wine, didn't I? I'm so clumsy when I'm distracted—or not." She giggled.

"Ah, but I wasn't even there. How were you distracted?" His eyes teased.

She turned back around and corked the wine. "It felt like you were."

He grinned. "I bet it did." He took her by the hand and led her to the living room. She floated across the floor, following effortlessly. Setting their glasses on the coffee table, he stretched out on the couch, leaned back, and then patted between his legs. Still rapt by his spell, she nestled down as his thighs embraced her fairy-light body. "Now, isn't this better?" he whispered and gently coaxed her head back against his chest.

Relaxed with eyes closed, Jasmine felt the rapid thumps of his heart on her back. It was magically surreal. Two people enjoying each other's company, snuggled quietly, sipping wine in front of a crackling fire. *Was she still dreaming?* He swept her hair with a finger. "You haven't said a word. Is this quiet-time?"

She took a sip of wine and rested her head back on his chest. "Well, it is pretty quiet." She kept her eyes on the dancing flames, feeling a fire building inside her.

"So you're all right with this: us together on the couch?" He gently rubbed her leg, releasing all the remaining tension.

"To be honest, it feels good but a little strange. It's been a long time . . ."

"Since you've been with a man?" he murmured and brought her face around to his. Their eyes closed and mouths parted. They pecked slowly and softly, tasting the subtle sweetness of each other's passion. The fervor rose and their bodies turned, melding, arching, and pressing deeper into a hot devouring kiss.

Frank slipped his hand through the front of her robe, exploring her silky nightgown for rigid points. He felt her limp, willowy body let go and lowered his head, kissing down her neck to the exposed supple crease between her breasts.

Jaz succumbed to his touch and was engulfed like a brittle limb in a blaze of flames as his lips sent chills to the tip of every hair follicle. The feeling was beyond her imagination and made her moan out loud, which Frank took as a green light. He rolled on top of her, driving his straining jeans into her hips while trying to raise her nightgown. His tongue lashed, his hands groped, and their bodies burned with passionate sweat. Breathless and spinning, she was slipping further away than she wanted. She tried to free herself from his grip, but he had her pinned. Tossing, she gasped, "Frank, I can't . . . we have to stop." He held her down and kept kissing her. "Frank, stop!"

Panting, he sat up and combed his fingers through his hair. "I'm sorry, I don't know what got into me," he uttered, grabbing his wine and dousing his flames. He knew if he didn't control himself, she may never want to be alone with him again.

"Thank you." Jaz pulled herself up and tied her robe closed. He was more than she could handle and difficult to resist. It was time to say good-night. Letting out a yawn, she hoped he would take the hint.

"I guess that's my cue." He slugged back his wine and stood.

Jaz stood up next to him. "Well, it is getting late and I have to work tomorrow."

Clutching her shoulders, he stared into her dazed, blue eyes. "All right, but we're not finished. What are you doing Friday night?"

She angled her head. "I know there's something going on . . . oh, I'm modeling lingerie."

"Oooo, can I come?" He rubbed his hands together.

"Sorry, women only."

He pulled her close, and his dark eyes penetrated. "Will you model for me sometime?"

She pointed at the clock. "I can't if you don't leave. I'll turn into a pumpkin at midnight."

Reluctantly, Frank headed out the door to his car. He turned before getting in and pressed his hand to his lips.

Jaz smiled, watching from the doorway. "Whew," she uttered and shut the door.

The next morning, Frank was just entering the elevator when the front desk manager called to him. "Excuse me, Mr. Pazzarelli!" He held the door open as she hurried over to him. "Sorry, but you had a phone call this morning from Dr. Carmen Lucio. He wanted you to call him as soon as you got here."

"Did he leave a message?"

"No, but he said it was urgent."

"Thanks, Jill." Frank let the door close, envisioning Sumo's surprised face. He chuckled to himself. *You picked the wrong person to fuck with . . . you're mine now.* Entering his office, he thumbed through his book of phone numbers and called Carmen's personal line.

"Dr. Lucio."

"Carmen, it's Frankie."

"Frankie! I tried you at home then the casino—"

"Just tell me, is it Sumo?"

"Yes, I have him in a private room in ICU. I told him I needed to run some more tests."

Frank squeezed the phone. "Just keep him there. I'll be right over."

"Oh, he won't be leaving. He's quite sedated."

"Perfect! See you soon." He went across the hall to inform Linda he would be gone.

She was busy typing with the phone perched on her shoulder and looked up to see him standing next to her. "I'll call you back. Yes, Mr. Pazzarelli, can I help you?"

"Linda, would you take my calls? I'm going to the hospital, and I won't be back for an hour or so. And inform the front desk, too."

She grimaced. "Are you all right?"

"I'm fine, but my friend . . ." he shook his head, "may be on his last breath."

"I'm sorry. I'll say a prayer for him."

"He'll probably need it."

Frank burned out of the parking garage and headed along the shoreline to the Tahoe Community Hospital. His mind was racing as fast as his anger. *He better have a damn good reason why he was at Jasmine's game and a damn good reason why he didn't call.*

Entering the sliding glass doors, he marched to the front desk and cut in front of a man. "Can you tell me where—"

The receptionist cut him off. "Sir, you're going to have to wait your turn. I was helping this man." Then she proceeded with her questions.

Frank leaned over the counter. "I don't think you understand. This is an emergency!"

The oversized, square-faced woman stood up, narrowing her eyes to sharp razor slits. "Everyone here has an emergency. Now, if you'd kindly."

"I don't kindly anything." He took a step closer and hunched down eye-to-eye with her. "I want Dr. Lucio, and I want him now!"

The woman flinched with every word then dropped to her chair. "J-just a minute, and I'll call him." She dialed the phone with a quivering finger. "Uh, Dr. Lucio there's a man here—"

"I'll be right there."

Frank was still glaring at her like a hungry lion.

"He'll be right down," she murmured.

He gave a quick nod and walked over to the water fountain to soothe the burn in his throat.

Dr. Lucio approached Gladys, who was still disturbed by the confrontation. "Where is he?"

She pointed. "Over there."

Carmen rushed up to Frank and held out a hand. "Frankie, how are ya, buddy?" They shook hands.

"I'll be better after I see Sumo. Where is he?"

"Like I said, I've kept him in ICU." He cupped his mouth. "Things can go wrong there . . . if you know what I'm saying."

"Yeah, like in about one minute." Frank followed Carmen down the long corridor, his hands clenching and extending as if preparing for the strangulation.

Carmen approached the last room in ICU. "He's in here."

Frank opened the door and looked around. "Where?"

Carmen stepped in. "What?" He looked at Frank. "Maybe one of the nurses took him to the bathroom."

Frank jerked the severed tubes hanging from the pedestal and stuck them in Carmen's face. "Does this look like he's taking a fucking piss?!"

"Frankie, I'm telling you. He was here." Then his eyes grew wide. "Wait a minute. There was a new nurse here last night, a student. It's possible she has something to do with this. I'll go see if anyone knows anything about her." Carmen dashed out of the room to the nurses' station while Frank paced the room, putting the pieces together.

Sumo had to be working for Marco. Otherwise, why would Marco accuse him of dealing with another supplier at the yacht club and be mad enough to kill. Frank assumed his lengthy explanation resolved the misunderstanding and regained Marco's trust . . . but if he didn't. His stomach twisted. *Marco will stop at nothing to get what he wants.* Frank wasn't going to take any chances. Sumo had to die.

Carmen quietly entered the room. Frank turned. "What'd you find out?"

"Sorry, Frankie, everyone thought she was an intern. There's no record of her." He shook his head. "I don't know what to say. What's going on, anyway?"

"Nothing you need to know. Just some unfinished business." Frank walked to the door. "If you hear anything, get a hold of me immediately." Carmen nodded.

In the morning Jasmine came waltzing into the women's lounge humming a tune. She waved to Yarah, opened her locker, and sat down on the bench to put on her vest.

Yarah studied her with a curious, narrow glare. *Hmm . . . too cheery . . . too somethin'.* Then it hit her. She slammed her locker and strutted over to confirm her suspicion. "You did it, didn't you? You thanked him for those roses?!" She folded her arms and jutted a foot. "Girl, look at me."

Jaz kept wrestling with her necktie, trying to achieve the perfect knot. "Did what?" she asked coyly.

"You know—the hoochi-coochi."

Jaz stood up and casually walked to the mirror for a final assessment. "What makes you think that?" she asked, grinning.

"For one reason that stupid smile on your face. And when did you ever hum? You never hum. In fact, I don't think I've ever heard you hum since I've known you."

Jaz looked at Yarah. "We didn't *actually* do it."

"Uh-huh, and I'm not *actually* standing here. I'm just a figment of your imagination."

"Oh good." Jaz exhaled. "I thought I was going crazy."

Yarah whined and stomped her feet. "Come on, tell me. Did you or didn't you?"

Jaz looked up and angled her head. "Is it possible to do it with your clothes on?"

Yarah burst out laughing. "Until you . . . I didn't think so." She held up a hand. "You know what, never mind? I don't want to know."

"Okay, but—"

"But what?"

Jaz started up the stairs and looked back. "It was good . . . really, really good."

EIGHT

I t was Friday night. Jasmine whirled into the parking lot of the Cove and found an empty spot next to Yarah's car. They agreed a cocktail would help set the mood to model lingerie for twenty romances-hungry women.

Wandering through the bar, peering back and forth, Jaz expected to spot Yarah's hair in a second. But it was so dark there was barely enough light to see in front of her face. As she walked past the last table, an unmistakable voice resonated. "They should call this the *cave* not cove."

Jaz wheeled around to see Yarah flash her teeth with a wide smile. "Oh, thank goodness." She sat down and leaned over the table. "I knew this was a meat market, but I didn't know it was a *mystery* meat market."

"Yeah, my luck, I'd roll over in the morning and see the most wanted layin' next to me." They both laughed.

"Did you order a drink?"

"No, I was waitin' for you."

Just then the bartender shuffled over. "Excuse me, ladies, but there's a gentleman on the other side of the bar that would like to buy you two a drink." They gazed over to where he was pointing but could only see a dark silhouette.

Jaz shook her head. "I don't know, Yarah. Next thing you know he'll want to join us."

Yarah hunched down with one hand to her mouth. "Jaz, it's a free drink—that's all!" She sat up and smiled back to the faceless stranger as the bartender impatiently waited. "We'll both take a Long Island ice tea, and make it top shelf," Yarah said.

Jaz shot her a look. "Please tell the man thank you for us," she added.

"I'll do that, but I think he'd rather hear it from you." The bartender left.

"Now look what you did. We have to go over and thank him." Jaz huffed.

Yarah flipped her wrist. "We'll thank him on our way out."

In a few minutes a waitress came over with their drinks. "This is from the man at the bar." She set the drinks down on the table and scurried away.

Holding their drinks high in the direction of the dark figure, they saluted to his kind gesture. "I don't think he's coming over," Jaz said, squinting.

"See, you worry too much, girl. Women like us can get whatever we want, so you better get used to it."

After finishing their drinks, they decided to head to Vonda's house. One was enough, and their curiosity had them antsy to find out what was in store. Jaz put on her coat and started for the bar as Yarah made a detour for the door. "I thought we were thanking that man?" Jaz said.

"You can. I'll wait outside. This place gives me the heebie-jeebies."

Jaz wandered up to the bar and looked around, but no one was there. "Excuse me. The man who bought us a drink, did he leave?" she asked the bartender.

He shrugged. "I don't know; maybe he's takin' a leak."

Hmm, perfect timing. She rushed up to Yarah. "I think he's in the bathroom. Let's get out of here." They hurried to their cars unaware the stranger was watching them.

Yarah rolled down her window. "Follow me. I know where Vonda lives." She took off with Jaz trailing and the stranger lurking behind. When they pulled in front of Vonda's house, Marvin Gaye could be heard from the street. Yarah got out of her car clicking her fingers. "Sounds like she's gettin' in the mood."

"I wish I was," Jaz muttered.

"Oh, come on. It'll be fun, ya big prude."

They rang the doorbell and waited, yet no one came. The music had drowned out any chance of hearing the tiny chime they were making. So they walked inside. "Yoo-hoo, Vonda!" Jaz called as they looked around.

Vonda came from the hallway. "Oh, hi! I thought I heard someone out here." She glanced at her watch. "You're early."

"Is that all right? We're curious to see what we'd be modeling," Jaz said.

"Sure, follow me to the bedroom. I'm not quite ready. I still have refreshments to set out, chairs to. . ." She began mumbling in German and raking her fingers through her hair.

"I can't understand her," Yarah whispered to Jaz.

"I think she's having a conniption. That's a German meltdown."

They held their mouths muffling their laughter.

Vonda stood in the doorway of the room. "This is your dressing room. Everything is hanging in the closet or folded in the dresser."

Yarah walked over to the closet, slid open the door and gulped. "Oh my God, it's like a bordello smorgasbord." She swept her fingers through the hangers. "Looks like you haven't sold a thing. There's a lot of stuff here."

"I haven't, you guys are my last hope. I thought women liked sexy underwear, but apparently they don't."

"You've been hangin' out with the wrong women," Yarah cackled. "Don't worry, you'll make money tonight—I guarantee it."

Jaz locked on a skimpy black baby-doll nighty and pulled it from the closet. "This looks like Fredrick's of Hollywood kind of stuff." *I bet Frank would love this one.*

"I know they're quite revealing, but when the women see how pretty they look maybe they'll sell. I'm in need of some money since tokes haven't been good this month."

"So you were serious about coming to my game drunk and rude," Jaz joked.

"No, but it is a thought." Vonda chuckled.

Twenty chatty women were gathered in the living room eating, drinking and waiting for the risqué show to begin. And each minute they waited the volume of their voices amplified.

"It's getting loud out there," Yarah said, standing in front of the mirror while admiring the nightgown she had chosen. It was shimmery gold with spaghetti straps and a slit up her thigh. "What do ya think? Sexy, huh."

"Wow—turn around."

Yarah spun, then posed with her leg angled through the slit. "If this doesn't sell, I'm keepin' it."

Both began fiddling with their hair when they heard: *"Bring on the show, bring on the show."* They looked at each other with wide, frightened eyes. "You better go before they stampede. I'm not ready yet," Jaz said.

Yarah licked her fingers and smoothed back a few loose hairs around her forehead. "All right, you want it, you got it." She opened the bedroom door, pulled back her shoulders and strutted out as if on a New York runway. Jaz was still deciding between something skimpy and something sheer when Yarah returned. "Oh my God, they're animals," she said, panting. "What's Vonda feedin' them?"

Jaz didn't respond. She was zoned out rummaging frantically through the closet until a pink teddy caught her eye. Putting it on, she arranged her hair to hang over the itsy-bitsy lace bodice. "How's that, can you see my nipples?"

"What!? Who cares? You have the body so flaunt it."

"I'm serious. Is it too see-through?" She turned side-to-side.

Yarah rolled her eyes. "Believe me, they'll never know you have nipples." They both laughed.

Holding her hair in place, Jaz trotted out to the crowd of howling, clapping women. They had her spinning one way then the other. When she finally came to a stop, nothing was covering her nipples or her breasts. The outfit had turned sideways.

"I'll take it!" a lady shouted. "Easy on, easy off. That's what I like!"

The night was a success, and together they made Vonda over four hundred dollars, more than she'd hoped for. Jaz and Yarah were changing into their clothes when Vonda entered. "So, did you each pick out an outfit?" she asked.

Yarah started raking through the closet and pulled out the gold satin nightgown.

"I thought you sold that," Jaz said.

"No, I told 'em it was clingy and hot."

"Uh-huh." Vonda raised an eyebrow. "I was surprised that didn't sell." She turned to Jaz. "What about you?"

"Well . . . it's not exactly for me, someone else." She held up a black lace baby-doll."

"Mmm, sounds interesting. Anyone I know?" Vonda asked.

"Maybe, Frank Pazzarelli, the hotel manager at the Palace."

Vonda fluttered her hand in front of her face. "Oh my, he's gorgeous. I'd be all over him like apples on strudel."

Yarah groaned, "She is. Now can we please change the subject?" She gazed around the room at the rejected negligees' strewn everywhere. "We probably should clean this mess up for you."

"That would be nice, and I'll start on the living room," Vonda said.

When all was clean and put away, Yarah and Jasmine left with their outfits, bantering about the rest of the evening. "Come on, just one cocktail," Yarah begged.

"I can't. I promised the kids I'd be right home after the pajama party." Jaz got inside her truck, determined to stay firm on her word.

Yarah pouted off to her car. She pulled away and looked at Jaz with an exaggerated frown and waved.

Jaz giggled, waving back and waited for her truck to warm. When the smoke cleared she adjusted the mirror from a light glaring in her eyes. Then she saw the outline of a person walking toward her. She watched for a moment, trying to make out a face, but her instincts told her to step on the gas.

Shifting the truck into gear, she took off before the person was visible. At the next street, she made a quick right and then another at the next corner. Now confused, with no idea where she was or how to get out, the eerie light caught up with her. Frantic and afraid, her eyes darted from the mirror to the street signs, looking for anything familiar. But her sense of direction was as scrambled as her thoughts.

Around she went with the car following every turn and every swerve, not letting her out of their sight. "Who is that!?" Jaz shouted as tears welled, turning everything into a dangerous blur. Wiping her eyes, she saw a yellow house and remembered Vonda lived just down the street. Spitting rocks and burning rubber, she raced down the road and up Vonda's driveway. Slamming on the brakes, she ran to Vonda's front door and pounded with both fists. "Vonda! Open the door! Let me in, let me in!" Her trembling legs buckled with each hysterical scream as the black car sat idling like a demon in white smoke.

The door flew open. "Jasmine! Oh my God! What's wrong?" Jaz pointed and collapsed to her knees as the car sped off in the night. Vonda looked out but didn't see anything. She only heard the screeching wheels. Bending down, she helped Jaz up and took her to the couch. "Who was that?"

Jaz buried her face in her hands, trying to shake her fright. "I don't know. They followed me from your house."

"Should I call the police—what should I do?" Vonda asked, wrapping her arm around Jasmine's shivering shoulders.

"I just want to go home," Jaz said, wiping her eyes on her sleeve.

Reaching to the table, Vonda snagged a box of tissues and handed her one. "Of course; I'll take you. Just tell me what happened first."

Jaz shook her head, trying to find a starting point. "I was followed—no chased! Someone was waiting for me outside your house." She wiped her eyes and blew her nose. "It was so terrifying. I didn't know what to do."

"Why didn't you come right back?"

"I got lost! How do you get out of this neighborhood, anyway?" she cried out.

Vonda gently squeezed her shoulder. "I'm so sorry, but I'm glad you made it back here. They might have followed you home."

Jaz looked at her. "I never thought of that."

"Did you get a good look at the person?"

"No, it was too dark."

Vonda got up and went to the window. "Well, they're gone. Maybe it was just some kids trying to scare you."

"Or maybe they had me mistaken for someone else. I don't know . . . it all seems like a nightmare," Jaz whimpered.

Vonda patted her leg. "Leave your truck here, and I'll take you home right now."

"You wouldn't mind?"

"Not at all, and you'll have it back tomorrow morning." She helped Jaz to her feet."

When they pulled into her driveway, the lights were on and the children's faces were in the window. "They're probably worried. I told them I'd be home an hour ago," Jaz said as they got out of the car.

"Well, at least you're all right." Vonda wrapped her arm around her back and led her up the walkway.

As they reached the door, the kids scurried out to meet them. "Mom, what's the matter? Have you been crying?" Justin asked.

"Just a little. I don't feel very well." Jaz didn't want to scare them, especially if it was only a prank.

Shauna hugged her. "You must feel really sick. You look like you've been crying all night."

"I'll be fine. I just need to lie down on the couch." She waved to Vonda, then went inside and locked the door. "Why don't you two go to bed, it's after ten."

Saddened, they kissed her good-night and went to their rooms. Jaz checked the door again then peered out the living room window for the black car. It felt like someone was out there, if only she knew why. Pacing with confusion, she decided to call Frank and let him know what happened.

He was lying in bed when the phone rang. "Hello?"

"Frank, hi, it's Jasmine."

He tucked his arm under the pillow. "I didn't think I'd hear from you tonight. I thought you'd be out late."

"Something horrible happened." She sat down at the kitchen table and wiped a trickling tear.

He pulled his arm from under the pillow and sat up in bed. "What do you mean something happened? Are you all right!?"

"I'm okay now, but when I left the lingerie party someone chased me around the neighborhood in their car. I've never been so scared in my life."

His jaw tightened as thoughts began to spark. "Someone chased you. I don't understand."

"Yes, I think they were waiting for me. I got lost and couldn't find my way out, and when I finally made it back to Vonda's house they drove away."

Frank was now standing with his hand clenched. *Sumo!* This time he had crossed the line and was tampering with something too valuable to be replaced. "Did you see the person?"

"No, it was too dark." She rested her forehead in her hand. "I thought it might be kids playing a joke, but I can't imagine why someone would do that."

Her theory bought Frank some time to confirm his suspicion. "Listen to me. I'm going to find this person. I don't want you to worry any longer." He was going to make certain Sumo never followed her again.

She raised her head. "You are—how?"

"I have my ways," he responded firmly. "Right now, you need to get some sleep. We'll talk in the morning. Trust me, everything will be just fine."

"All right . . . thank you." Jasmine was relieved she'd called Frank and went back to the couch to relax.

Hanging up with a burn to kill, Frank went to the study to pour a scotch. Staring at the ice cubes, strategizing his revenge, he first had to find out when and where Chung Lee was meeting Sumo. Then he would pay a visit and end it before his *dream girl* was merely a dream.

Glancing at his watch, he went to his office to make the call. Sipping, with the receiver to his ear, the phone rang continuously. He dialed the number again and still no answer. Slamming down the phone, his mind spiraled with wrath. If Chung Lee was involved then his multimillion dollar operation was being sabotaged.

Frank sank into his wing-back chair, drowning in emotions he'd never known. All his life he lived on the edge, and the risk was meaningless. Now the desire to love had manifested the desire to live. If his life was in danger, then anyone connected to him was also in danger. *Jasmine!* Infused with a thirst for love, he would do anything to protect her . . . even if it killed him.

CHAPTER

NINE

S itting at the head of a long glass table, Marco Gamboli dipped his narrow, pointed fingernail into a black satin pouch of refined white powder and lifted it to his nostril. In one hefty snort, it quickly disappeared. His hunched wiry frame and ghastly gaunt face rendered a man who was dying. Not until his voice was heard and strength felt, did it prove him otherwise. He leaned back, clasped his hands and drilled his sharp eyes into Sumo. "Now I'm ready. What did you find out?"

Sumo looked down, evading his constricting sneer. "I haven't had much luck, but I know where she lives." His rotund body jiggled as one leg nervously bounced.

"You know where she lives," Marco repeated, setting his hands on the table. "Well, I don't give a fuck where she lives. I want you to bring her here!"

Sumo nodded and wiped the sweat from his forehead. "I will, but Marco—"

"It's Boss!" Marco gripped the table and shot off his chair. "You are working for me now!"

"Yes, yes, Boss," Sumo stammered.

Still standing, he glared at Sumo. "Now finish . . . but what?"

"But I'm allergic to her perfume. I almost fuckin' died!" he said, opening his hands.

Marco dropped back into his chair and burst into guttural laughter. "Her perfume almost killed you," he laughed and wheezed, hovering over his desk. "Oh, I gotta tell the men this one." Then he wiped his eyes and became stiff as steel.

"Really Boss." Sumo wagged his head. "The paramedics had to take me to the hospital. I don't know if I can do this." He looked away and lowered his head.

Marco pushed from his chair and walked around the table. Lifting his skinny arm, he struck Sumo across the face with the force of a two-by-four, hurling him to the floor. "Frank is a traitor! He deceived me. He also needs to be reminded who is boss. Capiche!?" Sumo tried to scramble to his feet, but Marco had zero tolerance for weakness and came back with a blow to his groin. Sumo dropped over, clutching his stinging testicles as Marco stood over him. "Just thought I'd make myself perfectly clear."

Jaz awoke on the couch wet with sweat after replaying the chase over and over in her sleep. Remembering it was Saturday and the kids had their craft class, she got up to wake them and make a pot of coffee. Then it came to her; she didn't have her truck.

Just then, they came scurrying from their room and headed for the door. "Bye Mom, we're leaving," they said and waved.

"Wait a minute and I'll walk you." After the scare last night, she was leery of them being alone and hurried to her room to put on some clothes.

"Why—it's just down the road?" Justin whined.

"I don't care. I'll just be a minute." She gave him a look that thwarted an argument.

Justin went outside to wait and came running back inside. "Mom, your truck's here!"

Jaz looked out the window and there it was, just as Vonda said. "All right, then I'll drive you." In her robe and slippers, she loaded them and locked both their doors.

Shauna looked at her curiously. "Why are you doing that? We're not going very far."

"Just to be safe." Jaz put the truck in reverse just as Frank drove up the driveway. *Hmm, I wonder what he wants.* She waited for him to reach her truck then rolled down the window. "Good morning."

Startled, he turned and walked up to her window. Then he peered in and gave the kids a friendly wave. "Where are you headed?"

Justin cut in before she had a chance to speak. "Are you here to take my mom out again?"

"Not right now, but I hope later." He winked and smiled at her.

"I'm surprised to see you. What's going on?" she asked.

"I thought I'd come by and see how you're doing." His eyes swept over her attire. "You're still in your robe."

"I know, I just got up. I'm taking the kids to their craft class."

"Mom, we're gonna be late," Justin blurted.

"Okay, okay. I've got to go. I'm sorry."

Frank took a step back. "No problem. I'll call you later."

Jaz started to roll up the window then hesitated. "I'll be right back. If you want, there's a fresh pot of coffee inside."

His face beamed. "Sounds great. I haven't had my coffee yet."

"There's a key hidden under a loose board at the back door."

"I'll find it; you hurry up." Frank parked his car next to the curb and walked to the back of the house. He spotted a board missing nails and looked under it. Lying in the dirt was a key. To him, it was more than just a key. It was the key to a door that hadn't been opened in a very long time.

Unlocking it, he walked in and smelled the roasted aroma of freshly brewed coffee. It was a warm, cozy welcome to a cold, hungry man. Hanging his coat over a chair, he poured a cup and curiously looked around. Then something nudged him to find her room. Just a peek at her bed sounded as enticing as her in it. Opening doors, he quickly distinguished which room was hers and entered titillated with curiosity.

It was exactly how he pictured it, comfortable and unpretentious like her. He stroked the lace quilt which was meticulously folded to the foot of her four-poster bed. Then he pictured her body beneath it, hair sprawled and skin peeking through. Gingerly creeping over the hardwood floor, he picked up a small framed picture from her dresser. It looked like her parents by the resemblance. Then something in her closet caught his eye, and he carefully slid the door open a little wider. *Hmm . . . so she does own one.* Hanging on a satin hanger was the sexy black nighty she got at the party. Little did he know, she'd gotten it just for him.

Suddenly the back door opened and then shut. He darted from her bedroom into the bathroom. "Hello . . . Frank?" Jasmine looked around and saw him coming out of the bathroom.

He casually strolled up and greeted her with a kiss. "That was way too long." He pulled her close to his chest, feeling her ample unbound breasts under her robe. Sliding his hands from her back to her sides, he grazed over the soft roundness. "It's almost ten-thirty and the kids are gone. I could make a habit of this," he murmured.

She gave his tie a playful tug. "Habits are hard to break, you know."

"So I've heard." He started kissing her ear and felt her pull back from his grip.

"Hold on a minute," she said, thinking of a way to slow him down. "I never gave you the grand tour of the house." Giving him no choice in the matter, she led him to the living room. "You may remember this room," she said, holding out a hand.

He gazed down at the couch, envisioning their first passionate kiss. "It's a little fuzzy. Can you refresh my memory?" He yanked her into his arms. Then, one step at a time, he backed her to the couch and laid her down on the seat.

Lying defenseless to an overpowering longing, she let him untie her robe and linger over her breasts. Frank took his time around her nipples, down her stomach and along her legs. "You are amazing, Jasmine," he whispered and began unbuttoning his shirt.

Her eyes were closed until he placed her hand on his bare chest. She sprang forward and saw him half undressed. "I don't think—"

"Shhh . . . I want you."

"But . . ."

He placed a finger on her lips. "I think it's mutual."

His magnetism was stronger than any force she had encountered, and a deprived yearning begged her to indulge. "Not here. Come with me." She got up and led him down the hallway to her bedroom.

Sweeping her up in his arms, he kicked the door shut and carried her to the bed. Her strawberry hair spilled like wine, and her body surpassed all his lustful dreams. Letting his pants drop to the floor, a devilish smile curled as he climbed on the bed. Inching closer, ready to dive, she sprang off the bed. "Where are you going?" he said, turning on his knees.

"There's too much light." She went to the window and pulled the curtains, spotting the black car. Focusing, she gasped and turned to Frank. "It's the car. It's here! It's here!" she screamed.

He grabbed his pants and ran from the bedroom out to the front porch, catching only a glimpse of the back bumper. *Sumo obviously had a close eye on the house.* Grasping the railing, feeling his world being snatched from his fingertips, he had to act fast and find the people involved. Then, starting with Sumo, he'd take out one body at a time.

When he walked back into the bedroom, Jasmine was curled on the bed. He sat down next to her and stroked her hair. "I'll catch this person . . . I promise you," he whispered and kissed her tear-stained face.

"I think I should call the police. This has gone far enough."

"Not yet. Let me see what I can find out first." Frank couldn't take the chance of getting the police involved. That could easily put him at risk—never to see her again. As he gazed down at her limp body and into her misty eyes, he fought the urge to finish what they started. She looked so vulnerable and willing, but this time his rapacious libido would have to wait. "I need to know something," he murmured, wiping a tear from her cheek.

She looked up at him. "What is it?"

"Can I have a rain check for whatever was going to happen this morning?"

She lifted and pressed her lips to his. "Catch this guy, and I'm yours forever."

"Consider it done." He stood, brushing a hand over her body. "I'll call you later, and lock the door after I leave." When he left, an empty ache pierced his heart. This was a first which confirmed what had to be done. *No one was taking Jasmine from him—no one!*

Jaz listened for the door to close then wrapped in her robe and went to lock it. From a slit in the curtains, she watched until Frank was out of sight. Then she went to the couch to unravel her tangled thoughts. From the stalker to what almost happened in the bedroom, there was so much to think about her head was going to explode.

One thing she did know, which didn't need a second thought, this time it would be love, and only true love, that bound their hearts together.

TEN

F rank raced down Kingsburg Grade with regret fueling his desperate state of mind. If he hadn't invited Jasmine to the charity ball for everyone to see, she would be safe. Now she was the target, and he was the reason. His only salvation was to find the person who ordered the job, before Jasmine found out about him.

After scouring the streets and over the grade, with no trace of Sumo, Frank went home to make a call to the Martinez cartel. Anatoly, Carlos and Geno were brothers with connections that traveled throughout Mexico, Central and South America. If anything was going down, they would know about it.

When Frank arrived at his estate, he went directly to his office and saw the light on his answering machine flashing. Eager to hear if it was Chung Lee, he immediately sat down and pressed the button. *"Hi Frankie it's Mimma. Haven't heard from you in a long time . . . actually since the charity ball. You didn't stay long. Where'd you go? I miss you. Call me. Ciao baby."*

Mimma was the last person on his mind, even if she was stunning with a voracious need for sex. Knowing her, she'd demand to start up right where they left off, lips-to-lips, discussing what was on her mind. Normally he was up for it, but Jasmine was the only woman he wanted his lips touching. Then his eyes darted to the blinking light again. *Wait a minute!* She was Marco's sister.

He contemplated the idea of letting her get close to him—play her game but by his rules. After all, she did say he was the only man who understood her, and they belonged together. The pestering phone calls insinuated that was her mission. However, there were things to consider that made him hesitate. Mimma was possessive, manipulative and venomous. If she ever found out his heart belonged to Jasmine, they would both pay in blood. But with time ticking and lack of another plan, this was the easiest way to find his answer.

The phone felt like a gun to his head with his finger on the trigger. "Hello?"

"Mimma, it's Frankie."

"Ahh, hello darling. Guess you got my message." She leaned back on the black velvet chaise and crossed her legs.

He took an apprehensive breath. "I've been thinking about you, too. But you know how work is."

"No, thank God, I don't." She took a sip of her morning mimosa.

"So tell me, what have you been up to?" Frank asked insipidly, not like the man she knew, which sparked an inquisitive reaction.

Mimma sat up and set her glass on the table. "That's it! What have I been up to!? Darling, I believe you've lost your charm. Are you not feeling well?"

Frank realized if he was going to pull this off, he'd better be more like himself. "I guess all work and no play makes a very dull boy, as in I've lost my shine, if you know what I mean."

"Mmm . . . that's more like it. Just call me lemon pledge." Mimma stroked her cleavage as visions of debauchery stoked her fire. "So when and where, darling, and make it fast."

"Tonight, at my house. That is, if you're up to it. I know I am." He bit his lip with the poisonous, regretful words.

"Let's see, a polish and a lube. Will you need air in your tires, too?" She let out a playful giggle.

His mind wandered with perverted thoughts. At the liberated age of fifty-one, Mimma had the body of a thirty-year-old: firm, thin and toned. Her black, shiny hair was cut just above her shoulders in a sassy bob with straight bangs, highlighting her emerald green eyes. Her skin glowed and her teeth sparkled, but her experience with men drew all the attention.

"Why not? A little air in my tires would make for a better ride. Why don't you come over around seven?" Frank said.

"Seven is perfect. I think I can fit you in. No pun intended." She giggled again.

Frank fought to stay on track. "All right. Can't wait to see you. Ciao, baby." He hung up and walked over to the intercom button. "Clive, can you come to my office?" Within a couple minutes there was a knock at his door. "Come in."

Clive entered wearing a jogging suit. He was as fastidious about his health as he was with the estate. "Did you need something, sir?"

"Yes, I'll be entertaining tonight, and I want you to prepare something for dinner."

"Of course. Did you have something special in mind?" Clive stood with his hands resting on his hips.

"I'm thinking heavy and rich." Frank's intent was to entwine romance and dinner into an undetectable ploy. Knowing Mimma, she'd decline the indulgent food and want to go directly to the bedroom. They'd swap secrets and the night would end soon after.

Clive angled his head, confused. "Heavy and rich . . . ?" He held up a hand. "Never mind, I won't ask, but I do need to know how many guests."

"Just two, around seven-thirty."

"Very well." He nodded and left the room.

Mimma sipped her mimosa, beaming with sheer satisfaction. Her brother's ruse played out exactly the way he'd expected. She didn't like deceiving Frankie like that, but Marco was blood, her only blood. Setting the goblet down, she picked up the phone to enlighten him of her date. Her long red fingernails dialed then tapped on the phone as she waited for him to answer.

"Yeah?" A harsh, raspy voice answered.

"So, my sweet dear brother, how do you want to pay me, a deposit, or should I just come over and get it?" Mimma leaned back and smiled.

Marco let out a tar-riddled cackle. He knew his plan would work. Mimma loved money as much as herself. She would never turn down ten grand for doing something *else* she loved, something she couldn't buy: Frankie. "You don't think the son-of-a bitch suspects anything, do you?" Marco huffed.

"Not at all. He's just a man who can't resist a woman like me."

"Just get me the information, and I'll give you the money."

Her eyes snapped open, and she pointed at the phone. "That was not the deal! You said you'd pay me if he took the bait."

Marco grabbed the edge of his desk and stood. "I'll pay you when the job is done!"

"Oh really. Since your rules have changed so have mine. If you want the information it's another ten grand. I don't come cheap."

Marco's temples bulged with rage. "You are cheap! You just don't know it."

"Do I get my twenty grand or not?"

He flopped down in his chair. "All right, all right, you'll get your fuckin' money."

"I knew you'd see it my way," Mimma said with delight and hung up. *A long night of sex and pillow talk with Frankie. What better way to make twenty grand?* She raised her glass in a victorious salute.

ELEVEN

J asmine drove to work as if trying to outrun fear. Squealing into the parking lot, she circled around for a spot up close. But as usual, the one thousand employees who arrived by 8:00 a.m. got first choice of the good ones. After a futile search, she headed to the back of the lot, where she normally parked, and took a thorough look around before getting out. It appeared she made it there without being followed.

Grabbing her purse, she headed for the entrance in a quick stride. Weaving between the parked cars to avoid being seen, she was almost there when a car raced by and backfired. Leaping in the air, she screamed and noticed a crowd of people laughing at her.

"It was only a car," one lady said, chuckling.

"Sounded like a gun to me!" Jaz replied and scurried off to the women's lounge. Entering, the women were going through their pre-game primping rituals, misting perfume and hairspray, while exchanging their morning whines. And for the first time it brought a sense of comfort to her frayed nerves.

Yarah saw Jasmine sitting stoically in front of her locker and could tell something was wrong. She immediately suspected Frank. Shutting her locker, she strode up ready to say *"I told you so"* but chose a subtler approach. "I knew it was just a matter of time before that no-good-son-of-a-bitch hurt you."

Jaz gazed up at her. "It's not Frank. I think I'm going crazy with that black car."

"Black car?"

Her eyes sprang open. "I haven't told you, have I?"

Yarah's hands hit her hips. "Haven't told me what? *What* haven't you told me?"

Jasmine began rattling off how she got lost after the lingerie party, and someone in a black car chased her around the neighborhood. That if she hadn't made it back to Vonda's house who knows what would have happened to her.

Yarah's mouth dropped, and she sat down next to her. "Who would do something like that?"

Jaz wagged her head. "I don't know. I've racked my brain."

Yarah cackled, finding humor in the situation. "You can't rule out the slim-balls with gold chains and white loafers, or the dorks in plaid pants and toupees—all the guys we won't go out with. It could be one of them."

Jaz cracked a smile. "I'd laugh but I'm really scared. She walked to the mirror and finished buttoning her uniform vest. "I wish this was bulletproof."

Seeing her genuine fear, Yarah walked up and put her arm around her shoulder. "I have an idea. Let's sign the EO list, and we'll spend the day together. What do ya say?"

Jaz leaned her head on her shoulder. "Thanks, but you know we can't afford it, and truthfully I feel safer here."

"Well, if you change your mind I'm in. And I don't care what it costs."

Walking to the pit, Jasmine thought about Yarah's true friendship, and the sacrifice she would make—one she would do for her, as well. Then she saw her game and regretted saying 'no' to the EO. Every seat was occupied by an obnoxious young man. They were hollering and spilling their beers while doing a round of cheers. Jaz tapped the dealer on the shoulder, and he looked at her with *"just shoot me"* written across his face. Then he motioned with his eyes toward the empty toke box. Letting go a sigh, Jaz reached for the deck just as Tony came scrambling up to her.

He brushed his lips against her neck. "Get rid of them, and do it fast." Jaz nodded, comprehending fully, and then innocently smiled at her players.

"All right, we finally got something to look at," one of the studs bellowed to his buds. Then he leaned forward and peered at her name tag. "Hey Jasmine, are you lucky today?"

She looked up while preparing the cards for assassination. "I don't know. You're my first."

The man's mouth opened wide, and he leaped off his chair. "Whoo-hoo! Got that boys—she's a virgin!" Then he sat down and high-fived his grinning friends. Jasmine noticed heads turning from every angle of the casino to see the *virgin*. Tony even winked at her. Putting her mission into fast motion, she added the *slice and dice* to the shuffle, and then quickly tossed out the cards.

Right off the bat, three of the men shook their heads and stood. They could see where this was going: to the poor house. After four more rounds, the remaining three were ready to leave just as a western dressed man walked up to the game.

He looked at them and tugged on the brim of his gray cowboy hat. "How's she doin', fellas?"

"Sit down. Let's see what you're made of," one replied.

"Sounds like my kind of game." The cowboy sat firm and adjusted in his seat as if a brand new saddle. Reaching inside his tan brushed-leather jacket, he pulled out a brown paper bag and scattered ten sealed bundles of money across the green felt. Then he sat back and folded his arms. "There's two thousand in each of those." His bottom lip bulged with a stash of chew.

Jaz felt her heart race. This was sure to attract every boss like flies at a picnic. Glancing over at Tony, she called out, "Changing twenty thousand." Tony pushed off the podium and eyeballed the money, giving her a quick up and down with his head. Lining up the bundles, she counted each down then brought out twenty thousand in checks and slid them to the cowboy.

He grouped them by color then clapped his hands. "All right, let's get this show on the road!"

The three men hovered to watch, but the one-man posse made it clear he wanted lots of elbow room. After several intermittent huffs and glares, they finally left him alone.

Having lived in Montana, Jaz was accustomed to a wrangler's no-nonsense attitude and welcomed it with some down-home hospitality. "So, where are you from?" she asked, tossing him two cards.

"Casper, Wyoming." His voice rattled as if he'd been riding all day on a hot dusty trail.

"Are you staying with us?"

"No. Hit this." He motioned with his hand.

She gave him a ten. "Where are you staying?" She thought a pleasant conversation would bring some solace to an already stressful day.

"Shit! I meant to double down." He tilted his hat back and narrowed his eyes. "Darlin', as you can see, I ain't here to flap jaw. Now, is there anything else you need to know or can we play cards?"

Jaz buttoned her lip, ready to toss the cards, when a man resembling Albert Einstein walked up to her game. He placed a finger on his chin and peered over his wire-rim glasses at the empty chairs, as if contemplating sitting.

The cowboy turned to see what Jasmine was intrigued with, giving the odd man a thorough examination. Then he opened his arms to him. "Well, are you gonna just stand there or what?" The man mumbled a few words to him but didn't sit. The cowboy turned. "Just deal the cards," he ordered.

Jaz tossed the cards while the fuzzy headed man observed and muttered visibly under his breath. It looked like he was blatantly counting the cards and finally took a seat. "I think I'll play now." He reached in his vest pocket and took out a silver bell, red button and a shark tooth, placing them around his betting circle. Then he pulled out five one-hundred dollar bills and laid them on the table.

Jasmine had seen a lot of superstitious antics and started to say something when the cowboy beat her to it. "This is a blackjack table not a toy box!"

The man looked up at him then at Jaz. "These aren't toys. They bring me luck, and I can't play without them." His voice was panicked.

Jaz knew his lucky charms wouldn't fly with Tony. "I'm sorry, sir. You'll have to remove them. Nothing is allowed near your bet." The man tilted his head and gazed at her as if she was speaking another language.

This opened the gate for the gritty cowboy. With a sweep of his hand the charms hit the railing, and the old man went into a frantic fit. "Oh no!" He pulled at his hair. "You don't understand. I have to win. This is all the money I have."

The cowboy chuckled. "You think those toys are gonna change your luck? That's a bucket of hogwash."

"Hogwash! These precious things have made me a lot of money." He quickly gathered them up and arranged them around his circle again.

Jasmine could see he was in a desperate state of mind and motioned for Tony to come. He slithered up behind her. "You know the rules."

"I know, but just this once," she pleaded.

Tony studied the man, who was blinking like a dog begging for a bone. "These bring you luck?" he asked.

The man's droopy face came alive. "Yes, yes they do."

Tony pointed at Jaz, narrowing his eyes. "Just this once."

Jasmine quickly counted down his money. "Changing five hundred."

Tony cocked his head. "Five hundred . . . go ahead." Jaz slid out a stack of green checks and waited as the man recounted each one.

The cowboy set out three one-thousand dollar bets then looked over at the white-haired man. "Hey feller what's your name, anyway?" he said, holding out a broad hand.

"It's Irwin," he muttered and shook his hand.

"Irwin; my name is Dusty—Dusty Rogers. What do you say we kick some ass on this here blackjack table?" Irwin lowered his head, cowering to his comment, and placed a fifty-dollar bet in his circle.

Jaz flicked two cards to each bet and waited for Irwin to make his decision. Blinking repetitively, he peered at his cards hesitant to hit or tuck.

Jaz thought she'd lend some advice. "I have a ten showing. I can tell you what the book suggests."

"I know how to play. I've been playing this game longer than you've been alive."

The suspense was driving Dusty crazy. He stood and began prancing like a thoroughbred in a starting gate. He had three thousand dollars riding on this round. He leaned over toward Irwin. "Let me see what ya got, partner."

Irwin flashed his cards. "It's a sixteen."

Dusty winced. "Never mind, you're on your own. Bar none that's the toughest hand." Irwin reluctantly tucked his cards as Dusty swept for his first hit. Tossing the hand face up, he went to the second hand, looked and tucked. Scooping up the third hand, he started to tuck then scraped for a hit. "Goddamn it!" He slapped his cards on the table and sat down.

Jaz turned over her cards and took all the bets with a twenty. She reshuffled the cards, keeping her mouth shut as the men counted their checks and made their next bet. She had learned the hard way, it was better to remain quiet with a straight face than say something to defuse the tension. More times than not it didn't.

Dusty slid a stack of black checks that totaled two-thousand into his betting circle. Jaz called out to Tony, "Checks play to the limit."

The action grabbed his attention, and he stepped closer to observe. "Okay, plays to the limit," Tony repeated then called surveillance.

Jaz ran her hand across the felt, waiting for Irwin to make up his mind. "Are you betting this round?" she asked.

"Yes, just one minute." After seeing Dusty's bet, he decided to follow his lead and placed a four-hundred dollar bet in his circle. "I'm ready," he uttered and gripped the railing as Jasmine dealt the cards. "Hmm, a twelve, I hate twelve's." He hunched, perplexed, then swept for a card. Jaz hit him with a seven, and he happily tucked.

Dusty shoved his cards under his bet and watched as Jasmine hit her sixteen with an eight. "Yi-haw! That's what I like to see," he bellowed, hammering his fist on the table.

"We won! We won!" Irwin cheered.

Tony was now in the hot seat and standing right behind Jaz. "Get it back," he snarled in her ear. Big payouts attracted big suits: Roman Chandler, the shift manager; David Sly, the assistant shift manager; and Paul Cusimano, the casino manager. The way they paced, cracking their knuckles, it was like the money was coming out of their pockets.

Irwin stacked all his checks and stared passionately at them. Hesitating, he pushed them to the betting circle then positioned his *"good-luck"* charms around it just so.

"Are you sure?" Jaz asked, noticing sweat build on his forehead.

"Yes, yes, I'm sure." He had been keeping a running count of the cards, and they were in his favor to win.

Dusty set out two bets, one thousand each, then rubbed his hands together and hollered, "Deal the cards!"

Jasmine tossed the cards and waited for Irwin to hit or stay. "It's a thirteen . . . it should have been a twenty," he whimpered.

Dusty peered over at his cards, pondering his strategy. "Partner, you're neck deep in a barrel of rattlesnakes. You're likely to get bit whether you move or not."

"If I lose this hand I'll kill myself," Irwin uttered, shaking his head. Then he reluctantly shoved his cards under the last of his money.

Jaz had a two showing, the dealer's ace. She glanced over at Irwin. His face was tense with fear. Beating him would make her feel horrible, but if she didn't the bosses would make her feel worse. Either way she was doomed. Briskly turning over her hole card, a nine appeared and she hit it with a ten. It was a twenty-one, the hand the bosses wanted to see.

"Shit—damn—gopher guts!" Dusty shouted and stomped.

Irwin sank into his chair as deathly gray replaced the pink hue in his face. Jaz couldn't bear to make eye contact with him, feeling the tug of guilt. She looked down with her eyes steady on her hands and heard Dusty clicking his chips, but not a word from Irwin.

Then, like a crack of thunder, a gunshot echoed throughout the casino, piercing the silence with an ear-deafening magnitude. Jasmine gasped as warm liquid covered her body and face, then everything faded to dark. The cards dropped to the table, her knees folded and she collapsed to the floor.

Tony bolted from the podium and ran to her side. "Jasmine, Jasmine . . . can you hear me?" He lifted her head, staring in disbelief, and then dropped to the floor next to her. Paul Cusimano witnessed the entire unnerving incident and hobbled over to the game. Both stood paralyzed to the point of speechlessness, staring at the bloody scene.

"Excuse me, let me through!" a man said, wedging his way past the shrieking spectators. He approached Tony and Paul. "I'm Dr. Jerome Jensen, let me help." Tony pulled to his feet and nodded as the doctor went to the victim. He checked his pulse then approached the stunned cowboy, who had blood, hair, and brain fragments covering his left side. "Are you okay?"

"I . . . I ain't sure, but I'm not hurt," Dusty stammered with chewing tobacco drooling from his chin.

Dr. Jensen led him to another chair away from the scene. "Stay here and try to relax. You'll be all right." The shivering cowboy sat down and took a few staggered breaths. Jerome turned to Tony and Paul. "Have you called the police or paramedics?"

"I just did. They'll be here in a minute," Tony said.

Jasmine moaned and opened her eyes. Then she saw blood splattered on her clothing. "What happened? Is this my blood!?" she yelped.

Dr. Jensen knelt down next to her and placed his jacket under her head. "No, you're going to be okay."

She blinked, wrinkling her nose. "Then whose blood is it, and who are you?"

"I'm Dr. Jensen. There was an accident, but everything's under control." He didn't go into a lengthy explanation. She was already upset and confused.

"An accident?" Jasmine saw the crowd swarmed around her game but couldn't see anything else. "What's going on, and why are all these people here?" Her light head forced her back down. "I don't feel very well," she uttered and closed her eyes.

As the color drained from her face, Tony bent down next to the doctor. "Is she gonna be okay, Doc?" he asked concerned.

"She's in a state of shock and probably should go home. I'd be glad to take her."

Paul and Tony nodded in agreement then Paul asked, "Mind if I see some I.D. first." Dr. Jensen pulled out his wallet and handed him his identification. Paul examined it then leaned down next to Jasmine. "Dr. Jensen is going to drive you home. Is that okay?"

Her eyes fluttered open. "Sure, I guess so, but I still don't know what happened."

"You fainted, but the doctor said you'd be just fine."

"I wonder why?" she mumbled, remembering nothing of what happened.

Just then a paramedic walked up with a wheelchair. Tony took it and pushed it toward her. "Here doll, let me help you." He gave her his arm, positioned her in the seat, and then set each foot on its rest.

His concern was so out of character that Jasmine was more bewildered than when she awoke on the floor. She twisted around and gazed up at him. "I think I'll be all right but are you?"

His lips attempted a smile. "Just sit back and shut up."

TWELVE

Tony wheeled Jasmine through the hotel and out to valet like a load of gold going to an armored truck. She kept her mouth shut like he said. There was no sense in questioning his compassion and risk waking the sleeping tyrant.

Jerome followed close behind and withdrew his valet ticket. "I'll be just a minute." Then he hurried off to the booth to retrieve his car. Sliding his ticket under the window, he expected immediate service, but the two attendants were oblivious and carried on like two bickering crows. He rapped on the glass. "Excuse me. This is an emergency. I need my car."

They turned around. "Sorry man, we didn't hear you. Do you have your stub?"

"Yes, it's right there." He pointed. They both laughed and started arguing about who was going to get his car. "I'm not sure if you're aware, but there's been a tragedy in your casino. It's imperative I get someone home as quickly as possible."

Their eyes bugged. "Oh, sorry man," one said and raced from the booth to get his car.

Jerome walked over to where Tony and Jasmine were waiting. "It should be here soon." He patted Jasmine's hand, and she gazed up at him as if for the first time. The bright sunlight vividly accentuated his features. He reminded her of Nick Nolte but more refined. His face was ruggedly handsome yet baby smooth, and his thick blonde hair tossed in the breeze. She roved over his broad chest, noticing his white knit polo shirt hung loose around his waist. He wasn't anything like the doctors she was used to and looked way too young to be one.

The wheels of his car screeched to a stop in front of them, and the attendant jumped out. "I got it as fast as I could," he said panting.

"Thanks, I appreciate it," Jerome said, taking two dollars from his wallet and placing them in his hand. He turned to Jasmine. His ocean-blue eyes sparkled and dimples creased. "Okay, you ready?" She smiled and nodded at him.

Tony helped her out of the chair. "All right, get the fuck better and I'll see you in the morning."

Dr. Jensen jerked his head around, giving Tony a stern glare. "Excuse me."

"Oh, pardon moi." Tony held up his hands. "A doctor is present."

"And a lady," Jerome said firmly.

"Yeah, well, she's used to it."

Jaz could see where this was going. "We better go. I'll see you tomorrow, Tony."

Dr. Jensen placed a hand on her shoulder. "That may be too soon. I think you'll need at least a couple days of rest."

"But I can't afford it." She grimaced.

"Don't worry, I'll see that the dealers cut you in on the tokes," Tony said and smiled.

Jasmine gave him another once-over, still baffled with his unusual concern. "I'll call you in a couple days then." He nodded and walked back inside.

Winding down the window, Jasmine inhaled the crisp air in hopes of refreshing her foggy head. She couldn't imagine fainting from something she didn't remember and presumed it was stress induced by the person in the black car. *Frank had better stay true to his word and catch this person, whoever they were.*

Dr. Jensen climbed in and put both hands on the steering wheel. "So, where to?"

Jasmine pointed. "Make a left up here, and then at the first light turn right onto Kingsburg Grade."

"You live on the mountain?"

"About midway."

"That's nice. I love the mountains. They keep me in check— remind me how small I am in a humbling sort of way."

"That they do . . . don't they?" Jaz said, gazing out the window. Then she turned to him. "So where do you live, Dr. Jensen?"

His dimples dug deep. "First, please call me Jerome, and I live in Loveland, Colorado.

"Oh, I have a sister who lives there."

"Really? Does she look like you?"

"We have a likeness, but Suzy has that Heather Locklear city glamour, and I guess I'm more of an Ellie Mae Clampett."

He chuckled, glancing at her. "Nothing wrong with that."

The road climbed high over the valley, winding around steep ravines to a lookout point of the Sierras and sparkling lake below. Jerome looked out his window at the magnificent panoramic view. "It's really amazing up here."

Jaz marveled at the sight. "Isn't it funny how you drive by something every day and not *really* see it until someone points it out?"

"I think that's called too much on your mind." He grinned. "So how long have you lived here?"

"A little over three years. And why are you here, business or pleasure?"

"Mainly business, a convention for plastic surgeons. But I'm really not a meeting kind of guy, just couldn't pass up a free trip to Tahoe."

She winced. "I hope I didn't mess up your plans."

"To be honest, I wasn't expecting this. Although, one good thing came of it."

"Oh yeah?"

"I met you." They smiled at each other.

She noticed her street coming up ahead. "I'm the next street on the left, Benjamin Road." He made the turn, and she pointed to a secluded drive. "I'm the cedar and rock home on the right."

Pulling into the driveway, Jerome was taken by the secluded serenity of her property. It was far from the road, against the hillside and nestled in a grove of aspens and evergreens. A wrap-around deck encircled the house, and a porch swing gently swayed in the breeze. He noticed a pile of wood next to the garage that needed to be chopped and railroad ties alongside the driveway that needed to be realigned. Other than that, the only thing the home lacked was a strong pair of hands. "This is beautiful," he said, scanning the surroundings.

"Thank you. It's our summer home—actually my mother's. It was just collecting dust, so I thought it would be the perfect place to start over."

"Looks like the perfect place for anything."

"Yeah, there's a lot of good memories here." She reached for the door handle.

"Hold on, let me do that for you." He jumped out and hurried around to open the door. Latching onto his extended arm, he led her up the porch and waited as she unlocked the door.

Walking inside, Jaz held the door open for him. "Please come in."

Jerome stepped in, and his eyes immediately gravitated to a few scattered toys on the floor. "I see you have children?"

She saw Justin's ball and mitt lying in front of the TV. "Yeah, sorry it's a little messy."

He reached down and grabbed the mitt, sticking his fingers in it. A boyish grin grew as he examined it, turning and punching it with his fist.

"What about you, do you have children?"

He looked up. "No, I . . . I don't." He placed the mitt on the table as a wall of silence enveloped the room. "Well, I guess I'd better let you get comfortable."

Jaz sensed she'd hit a sensitive topic and complied. Sinking onto the couch, she kicked off her shoes and grabbed her throw. "So is there anything I should or shouldn't do?"

"The only requirement is rest, and at least one day from work." He smiled. "Most of my patients like that prescription."

"Sounds like my kind of medicine." She chuckled.

He walked to the door. "If you don't mind, I'll call you later and make sure you're doing all right."

"I'm sure I'll be fine. You've gone far beyond the call of duty."

"Well, you don't know me, that's pretty much how I do things." His eyes were resolute and reassuring.

"Then sure, thanks." She wrote her phone number on a scrap of paper and handed it to him.

"All right, now get some rest—doctor's orders." He started to leave. "Oh, I'm staying at the Paradise Palace. If you need anything call me."

"Okay," Jaz said and smiled.

THIRTEEN

J az slipped into a t-shirt and sweat pants then grabbed a book to read for the requisite R and R. She wasn't feeling as stunned from fainting rather dazed and confused as to the reason why. Whatever the cause, she prayed it would soon surface.

As she started into the book, her eyes became heavy, and she rested the book on her chest. Drifting to sleep, clips of a scene eased into focus. She saw Dusty and Irwin playing blackjack and then heard: *'If I lose this hand I'll kill myself.'* A loud blast rang out and warm liquid sprayed her face. After that everything went dark. Her eyes popped open, and she sat up straight. "I didn't think he meant it!" Feeling sick to her stomach, she got up to make a pot of tea and decided to call Frank. He'd probably want to know she went home and the reason why.

"Hello?"

"Frank, it's Jasmine."

He looked at his watch and felt his heart flinch. "What's going on? Aren't you supposed to be working?"

"Yes, but I went home early. Something horrible happened at my game."

He bounced off his chair. "Are you all right?"

"I'm okay now, but a doctor had to take me home after I fainted."

"What happened?"

"Until now I couldn't remember . . . but a man shot himself on my game. He said, 'If I lose this hand I'll kill myself.'" Feeling weak, she sat down at the kitchen table. "Do you know how many times I've heard that?"

Frank gripped his forehead. "I could imagine a lot." He sat back down with visions of the scene exploding in his head. "But you're sure you're all right?"

"I think so."

"Uh, you said a doctor brought you home?"

"Yes. His name is Dr. Jerome Jensen. He said he was here for a plastic surgeons' convention."

"That's right. We're hosting it at the Palace. I'll have to thank him for his help." Frank had no intention of thanking Dr. Jensen. He wanted to make sure he was in fact a doctor and not another threat to Jasmine.

"Well, he just left a few minutes ago—probably heading back to the hotel."

"Listen, the best thing for you right now is to get some rest. Take a sleeping pill if you have to, and we'll talk in the morning." Frank couldn't take any chances of Jaz interrupting his night with Mimma. She was his link to Marco, and it was vital he get to the source sabotaging his world.

Jaz let out a heavy sigh. "Believe me, I don't need a pill. I can barely keep my eyes open now. I'll just talk to you tomorrow."

"Sounds good . . . I'm glad you're okay. Sleep tight."

"Thanks, I will."

Frank hung up with a burning blend of panic and revenge searing inside him. The time bomb was ticking at a deathly pace, and tonight had to be absolutely perfect, right down to the satin sheets and silk pillowcases. Squeezing the tension in his neck, he poured a scotch while plotting his process of elimination, one person at a time. Dr. Jensen now, Mimma tonight.

Leaving his estate, he drove to the hotel and pulled up to valet. He figured it was quicker than the garage, and he wasn't going to be long.

"Good afternoon, Mr. Pazzarelli. What can I do for you?" the attendant said. Then he looked side-to-side and leaned down to his window. "Or should I say, what can you do for me?"

Frank cocked his head. His eyes darted to the attendant's nametag. "I have no idea what you're insinuating, Randy. Just park the fucking car."

Randy stepped back. "Hey, it's cool, it's cool. Forget I said anything."

Frank got out with angry eyes. "Keep it close."

"It'll be right here, Mr. Pazzarelli."

Frank walked inside replaying what Randy said. The comment sounded as if he knew something, and he had been meticulously careful to keep his operation covert. He was taught leaks create fractures, and fractures create floods, all of which create destruction. Getting off the elevator, he walked past Paul's office and then stopped. Something came to him. Lately, Paul had been inquisitive of his monthly trips. It was possible the storm was gaining a stronger force, using credulous people. *One more person to add to his list.*

Entering his office, he sat down at his desk and picked up the phone. Paul's reaction to Randy's comment may have a flushing effect.

"Yes," a charred, crackling voice answered.

"Paul, it's Frank."

"Where the hell have you been? You wouldn't fuckin' believe what's been going on here!" Paul panted after each emphasized word.

"I know, I know, I heard, but I've been tied up with other business." He swiveled his chair and faced the terrace. "It was suicide, right?"

"Yeah, it was a fuckin' mess. The dealer on the game fainted and had to go home," Paul wheezed.

"Are they all right?" Frank inquired to sound uninformed.

"Yeah, I think so." Paul shook his head and took a drag off his cigarette. "You should have seen it. This crazy fucker takes out a gun, points it at his head, and blows out his brains right on the fuckin' game. Tony and I stood there like two fuckin' girls. We didn't know what to do, but thank God a doctor was there to help. In fact, he took the dealer home." Paul stamped out his cigarette and lit another.

"Is the doctor staying with us?" It was crucial Frank appeared completely in the dark.

"Yes, his name is Dr. Jerome Jensen. He's staying in suite 1036."

Frank grabbed a pen and wrote down his name and room number. "All right, thanks." Paul was about to hang up when Frank caught him. "There's something I wanted to ask you."

Paul blew out a stream of smoke. "Yeah, what?"

"A kid in valet asked me something quite peculiar. I thought I'd run it past you—see if you've heard anything."

Paul flicked his cigarette. "Well what is it, or do I have to fuckin' guess?"

Frank set the pen down and leaned back in his chair. "He wanted to know if I could do something for him."

"Something as in . . ." Paul rolled his hand in the air.

"I don't know—didn't say." Frank kept it vague.

Paul was silent then blew out his answer. "I have no fuckin' idea, but I'll find out. What's his name?"

"Randy."

"All right. I'll let you know."

Frank hung up and left his office. He entered the elevator and pushed the tenth floor. Dr. Jensen was next on his list.

After three knocks a voice called out, "Who is it?"

"It's the hotel manager, Frank Pazzarelli."

The door opened to a dripping wet, solid body with only a towel wrapped around his waist. Frank was surprised to see such a young, fit man and thought he might have the wrong room. "I'm sorry to intrude, but were you the doctor who assisted with the fatal accident in the casino today?"

"Yes, I'm Dr. Jerome Jensen."

Frank studied his eyes. "I have a quick question for insurance purposes." He presumed by Jerome's educated assessment he could determine his credibility and possibly the answer he was looking for.

"Okay."

"Can you tell me the condition of each person when you arrived at the scene?"

Jerome tightened his towel. "Sure. From my brief examination, the dealer was in a state of shock with no apparent injuries. The cowboy was stable and coherent, vitals normal. The victim was dead due to a high-velocity projectile gunshot to the head. The powder burns indicated self-inflicted, which I stated in my report." There was no hesitation or faltering with his account.

"Thank you. I haven't read it yet but I will." Frank nodded. "That should be all for now. I'll call if I need anything else." He was convinced Dr. Jensen had no connection, and his intention with Jasmine was strictly professional.

"No problem, that's fine." Jerome started to shut the door then hesitated. "I'm not sure if you knew this, but I drove the dealer home. She wasn't capable at the time. I told her I would call and check on her later tonight. I can give you an update on her condition, if you'd like."

"Tonight?" Frank asked, sweating under his white starched shirt.

"Yes, if that's all right?"

"Actually, I have a pretty busy evening. I'll call you in the morning."

Jerome shrugged. "Fine."

"Great. I'll talk to you tomorrow." Frank smiled and left.

Jerome closed the door, but something about the visit didn't quite settle with him. He wasn't sure if it was Frank himself, his abrupt visit or the questions pertinent to the accident, which were detailed in the report. Walking back into the bathroom, he finished drying off as the suspicious feeling took root.

CHAPTER

FOURTEEN

J asmine's attempt to rest and relax wasn't going as easily as expected. The stalker was now more haunting than Irwin's suicide. She tossed on her side with her back to the window, then tossed again facing the window. Knowing she wouldn't sleep until her nerves were settled, she got up to look out the window.

The view of the street was blocked by the trees. A better vantage point was the deck. Taking hold of the door handle, she felt it twist in her hand. Terror rippled up her spine, feeling a presence on the other side. With fumbling, frantic hands, she tried to latch the lock but wasn't fast enough, and the door flew open.

"What's going on?" Justin squawked, walking inside.

Her body went limp. "Justin, you scared me."

"Mom, why are you home?" He stared at her curiously.

She searched for words, reluctant to divulge the grisly shooting. She didn't want them restless like her. "I didn't feel well, so I came home early."

"You've been sick a lot," he said, grabbing an apple from the fridge.

"Where's your sister?"

"She's comin'."

Jaz stepped outside on the deck and scanned the area. The breeze mischievously played with her hair, and the herbal aroma of the evergreens filled her lungs. On any given day it had healing powers, but today the air whispered an eerie message of caution. Then she heard a faint voice call from down the street. Jaz waved to Shauna and waited on the porch.

Strolling up, Shauna's eyes gradually narrowed. "Mom, what are you doing home?"

Taking a deep breath, she looked her in the eyes. "I fainted, but I'm all right. So don't worry."

"Something is wrong, isn't it? You're never sick, and now you're fainting."

Jaz could see she was upset and put her arm around her shoulder. "I fainted from something that happened at my game. It had nothing to do with me or my health. I'm just a little tired, and I haven't been sleeping well." She took a quick glance around the property before shutting the door and locking it.

Shauna set her books on the table and folded her arms. "You would tell me if you were sick, right?"

"You'd be the first to know. I'm sure a day of rest on the couch, and I'll be better in no time." She swept a stray curl from Shauna's tense face then walked in the living room to lie down.

"Well, if you need anything, I'll be in my room." She grabbed her books and left.

"Thank you." Jasmine stretched out on the couch, tucking her throw under her chin. Having the children home, she was able to let her mind drift to a peaceful place and was soon sound asleep.

After Frank finished his regimen of reports and phone calls, he walked to valet to get his car. An eager young man saw him, jerked his keys from the peg board and ran up to him. "Here you go, Mr. Pazzarelli."

Frank took the keys. "Thanks . . . where's Randy?"

Douglas shrugged. "I don't know. Would you like me to try and find him for you?"

"No." Frank slipped the man a five and got in his car. *Hmm . . . maybe Paul meant what he said and took care of it.* Returning to his estate, Frank turned off the engine and sat in his car for a moment. The pressure of the night with Mimma was sitting like an anchor on his chest. Without question, she'd demand the usual: seduction, sex and satisfaction. He'd have to play along if he expected to get what he wanted. Although, this time it wouldn't be as easy. Mimma wasn't the type to give up information like she did her body. The night would have to be unsuspecting. A romantic interrogation with a subtle approach was the plan.

Frank looked down to see Tank and Tasha with their tongues hanging out, sitting patiently next to his car. "If only women were like you," he uttered under his breath. Getting out, he patted each on the head, and they joyfully followed him to the house.

Clive saw him arrive and opened the door. "Good evening, sir."

Frank sighed, "I wish it was a good evening."

Clive angled his head and his eyes softened. "You look distraught. Is there anything I can do for you?"

"A scotch would be great. I'll be in my office." Trudging down the hallway to his office, Frank sat down at his desk and decided to call Geno Martinez since his last attempt was diverted by Mimma's message. Retrieving the key from the hollow book, he opened the top drawer of his desk and scanned down his list of phone numbers. After dialing, he sat back just as Clive knocked on the door. "Come in."

"Your drink, sir." He walked over and handed it to him then quietly left the room.

Sipping and staring at the intricate art on his Ming vase, he waited for Geno to pick up the phone.

"This is Geno."

Frank set his glass down. "Geno, it's Frankie."

"Ahh, Frankie my man. How the fuck are ya, Amigo?"

"Truthfully, I've been better."

Geno leaned back and lit a cigarette. "That doesn't sound good. What's goin' on?"

"I need your help."

"You sound pretty fuckin' desperate." He motioned for his wife to leave the room.

"Yeah, I've lost both my men, and one of them is tailing my woman. I think Marco's behind it, but I need to know for sure."

Geno nodded while taking a long drag. "Tell me their names, and I'll see what I can find out."

"Chung Lee Chen and Tommy Tanaka, goes by Sumo."

"Then what? What do you want me to do?" Geno reached for a bottle of tequila and poured a shot.

"Nothing. Just let me know if you hear anything."

"I can tell you this. I know Marco's been sniffin' around, but that's normal for him. He'll stick his nose in any crack if he thinks it stinks." He swallowed the shot. "But I didn't think it was yours."

"How did you hear this . . . did someone tell you?" Frank took a sip of his drink.

"It's my job to know about every fuckin' thing that moves around here. If I don't, then someone gets hurt. You know what I'm sayin'? So do me a favor. Keep your nose clean and lay low. I'll get back to ya."

"All right." Frank hung up agonizing over the throes of his situation as well as the repercussions. If it was Marco, he could end it right then and take him out himself. But then he would be on the lam for the rest of his life, and that wasn't in his plans with Jasmine.

Slugging down the last of his drink, a savory smell of garlic and butter tugged at his nose. He looked at his watch. He had one hour before Mimma arrived which gave him just enough time to shower, dress and prepare for the performance of a lifetime.

Leaving the office, he went to see what was cooking in the kitchen and found Clive hunched over the stove. He came up next to him and leaned over the simmering pot. "That smells great. What is it?"

Clive turned. "Oh, a creation I've been laboring over. Indulge your palate on this." He held out a bite on a long wooden spoon.

Frank sucked it down. "That's fabulous."

"It's my creamy garlic Alfredo with a touch of sherry. Something deliciously rich, as you requested."

Frank rubbed his hands together. "Sounds perfect." He dipped the spoon in for another sample. "Oh yeah, she'll hate this."

Clive glared at him disappointedly. "May I please be informed as to why I'm preparing such a delectable disaster?"

Frank chuckled. "Easy. I don't like Mimma, and I want her visit as short as possible—an in and out kind of thing, so to speak."

"Oh, I see . . ." Clive's eyebrows arched. Frank licked his fingers and smiled.

"I'll get it!" Jasmine called out, wandering from the couch to the kitchen to answer the phone. "Hello?"

"Girl, what is goin' on?! Now all of a sudden you're in the middle of gunfire! And from what I heard, you're damn lucky to be alive!"

"I can just imagine all the stories going around," Jaz said and sat down.

"Yeah, and you know how everything gets so freakin' twisted around. Someone told me you had a gun, and I knew that was bull. Then I heard someone shot you, and I thought that was possible. Then two players dueled it out. Girl, it's been a freakin' nightmare not knowing what really happened. Tell me, was the bullet meant for you or not?"

"No, but I thought it was, which is why I fainted and woke up on the floor." She sighed and shook her head.

"After what you've been through, who wouldn't? So how'd you get home?"

Jasmine's head shot up. "A cute doctor took me. Dr. Jerome Jensen."

Yarah slapped her side. "How do you do it? Even when it's bad it's good."

Jaz chuckled. "Bad or good, I've had enough excitement for a lifetime."

"For both of us! Listen, I'm getting ready to leave work. Do you want me to come over?"

"Actually, I'm supposed to be resting—doctor's orders. And you know Shauna, she loves to mother me."

"Girl, she's more like a nun than a mother." They both laughed.

"Well, just call me if you need anything. Oh, and by the way, everyone wants to thank you."

"For what?" Jaz asked.

"Tony took a week off!" Yarah burst out laughing. "We owe you big time, girl. Thanks for taking one for the team."

"He's not so bad."

"What!? Did I hear you right?" Yarah spouted.

Jaz grinned. "As a matter of fact you did."

"You must be sick. Do what the doctor said and get plenty of rest. I think you're still in a state of shock."

Jaz chuckled. "You're probably right, but I should be back tomorrow."

"Why?" Yarah rolled her eyes. "Milk this as long as you can."

"I can't. I need the money."

"Money—money—money. Why does it always come down to money?" Yarah huffed.

"Not everything does."

"Name one thing."

"Love . . . true love."

"Like I said, you're still in a state of shock. Good-bye and good-night."

Jaz chuckled and hung up. Returning to the couch, the phone rang again. She assumed it was Frank checking on her and answered in a delicate, weak voice. "Hello?"

"Jasmine?"

"Yes."

"This is Jerome Jensen. How are you feeling?"

"Oh, Dr. Jensen. I'm feeling a lot better, thanks."

"Good to hear. Is anyone there to help you?"

"My kids are, and Shauna takes better care of me than I do."

He smiled. "Sounds like you're in good hands, but I'd still like to see you before I sign the release to work. When would be a good time to come over?"

Jaz looked at the clock. "It's seven now. Around nine would work. The kids will be in bed then." She cupped her hand to the phone. "I didn't tell them what happened. I don't want them to worry."

Jerome nodded. "I understand. I'll see you then."

"Okay, good-bye."

"Good-bye."

FIFTEEN

F rank put the finishing touches on the table: long tapered candles in the center and a single rose across Mimma's plate. Then he went to the study, switched on the gas fireplace and selected a soft saxophone collection to set the mood. His plan was to convey the right message in the shortest amount of time. And if all went accordingly, he would know if Marco was the instigator by the end of the evening.

Stepping back to admire the romantic ambiance, everything was perfect except one thing, Jasmine wasn't there. Frank drifted to their last conversation and hoped she was sleeping. To ease his mind and eliminate the possibility of her calling, he decided to check on her.

Glancing at his watch, it was exactly seven, when Mimma was to arrive. *Just a quick call.* Picking up the phone, he dialed just as the doorbell rang. His back stiffened with the second chime. Hanging up, he could only hope Jasmine was fast asleep.

"I'm coming," Clive mumbled in a fast pace. He opened the door. "Good evening, Ms. Gamboli." He gave a cordial nod. "I'll take your wrap. Frank is in the study. I'll go get him."

"Thank you." Mimma turned and admired herself in a large oval mirror on the wall. She had selected a dress that was sure to lead him to her snare. It was slinky and shimmery-green that played cunningly with her alluring, emerald eyes. The neckline was cut low, exposing all but a sliver of her pearl white breasts, and a slit ran up to her hip for expedient pleasure.

Frank came walking toward her with his arms outstretched. His silky, dove-gray slacks rippled with his stride, and his black hair brushed against the collar of his pale blue shirt. "Don't you look like a million bucks," he said, grinning.

"More like twenty million to be exact," Mimma said, posed with one hand out and one leg through the slit of her dress.

He gently took her hand and kissed it. "Actually, beauty like yours is priceless." Then he lightly kissed her lips. Their eyes danced rhythmically to the devil's tune.

"And don't you forget it, darling."

He smiled and led her down the hallway to the study, where the fire burned. "Would you like a drink?" he asked, opening a glass cabinet stocked with the finest liquor. Next to it was an open cellar, boasting expensive, rare wines from around the world.

Mimma eyed his collection. "I've always said you were equipped."

"I would say prepared. So what would you like?"

"Whatever you're having."

"Scotch neat it is." He poured two drinks and handed her one. "To priceless beauty." They clinked glasses and took a sip. Stepping closer, he ran a finger from her neck down to her enticing cleavage. They both knew exactly how to play one another, yet neither fathomed they were on the same mission.

Mimma strolled gracefully toward the fireplace while gazing about the room. "You have exquisite taste."

"Thanks. Only the best . . . like you."

"Yes, and why not, if you can afford it. She picked up a figurine, examined it and then set it down. "But I'm surprised; the little business you do for Marco can't support a magnificent place like this. You must have some hidden treasure you haven't told me about." She wasted no time getting right down to business, just in case she was distracted later.

Frank wasn't suspicious. Mimma was notorious for her intrusiveness. "There's a lot I haven't told you, but isn't that the air of mystique—not knowing everything about someone?"

She nuzzled up to him and stared into his eyes. "Well, for your information, I happen to love a good mystery." Advancing her mission, she dipped a finger in her drink and traced his lips. His tongue caught the drips, and she pressed her mouth over his, lingering into a deep, ravenous kiss. She let his excitement rise then teasingly pulled away and strutted over to the bar.

Frank swallowed the bait and the hook. When it came to the rituals of seduction, Mimma was the master. He casually strolled up to her and pecked at her neck. "Let's talk about you . . . which is far more pleasurable," he uttered.

"You mean other than being a bad girl?" Mimma said, letting her head fall back.

His mouth reached for hers. "Uh-huh," he moaned, closing his eyes.

"I'll tell you my dirty little secrets if you tell me yours," she said, keeping it playful and unassuming.

He glided a finger up the slit of her dress while biting his tongue not to shout, *It's Marco, isn't it?! He put a contract on my woman and stole my men!* "Why don't you go first?"

"I think that's called pillow talk," she said and walked to the couch. Sitting down, she made sure her thigh was generously exposed.

Frank subtly pressed on and sat next to her. "So what's Marco been up to? I haven't heard from him in a while, and we usually have a sit down once a month to discuss business."

Mimma flipped her wrist. "You know men. They use you and then on to the next. It's what they do."

Frank's muscles tightened. "Does that mean he has someone else working for him?"

"Quite honestly, I don't know. But he has been curious about you. Why haven't you called? Do you not need my brother anymore?" she asked directly.

"I don't call Marco. He calls me!" Frank took a gulp of his drink.

"Then perhaps it's a little misunderstanding between you two." They avoided being straightforward with each other for their own selfish reasons. Jasmine could end up dead and Mimma without a dime.

Clive entered the room. "Pardon me for intruding, but dinner is being served in the dining room."

Frank stood up and held out a hand. "Shall we finish with our dirty little secrets later?"

"Why don't we leave out the secrets and get right down to dirty?" she said and took his hand.

"My intentions exactly," he muttered, leading her to the dining room.

Mimma stopped at the entrance. "Darling, this is exquisite. The candles . . . the rose . . ."

He waved a hand. "Just for you." Pulling out her chair, she gracefully sat. Then he took a seat as Clive presented a bottle of Sauvignon Blanc.

"Something smells wonderfully delicious. What are we having?" Mimma swirled her tongue around her red lips.

"I believe Clive prepared garlic Alfredo over linguini with garlic toast." Frank mused with his four-step plan. Dine, decadence, divulge, and dash.

Mimma bared her teeth. "Sounds . . . uh, nice."

Clive poured two glasses of wine and set a loaf of sliced garlic bread on the table. Frank passed the bread to Mimma. "You have to try this. It's delicious." He fanned the buttery aroma toward his nose.

"No-no." She waved both hands. "You don't want to ruin perfection, do you?"

He pulled off a hunk and held it to her mouth. "Indulge, please, Clive would be offended if you didn't."

"Maybe just a nibble." She opened her mouth and let Frank feed her, sucking the butter off his fingertips. "Mmm, that *was* delicious."

He grinned. "We might have to ask for another loaf."

"Darling, that's not what I'm talking about." She put his fingers in her mouth the exact moment Clive entered the room.

He gruffly cleared his throat and set a silver tray with two covered dishes on the table. Removing the lids, he stood with his hands clasped. "My specialty, bon appetite."

Mimma gazed at the mound of gooey linguini and then at Clive. "I know, I know, you'll be offended if I don't eat."

"Of course, what chef wouldn't?" He scooped a portion on her plate while exchanging glances with Frank.

Mimma attempted a smile then picked up her fork and spoon. Trying to find the right angle to dig in, she looked up to see Frank and Clive intensely watching her. "What!?" she spouted.

"Nothing, but you are Italian. It shouldn't be that difficult," Frank said and swirled a spoonful then stuck it in his mouth.

Huffing, Mimma stabbed a clump, swirled it, and put it in her mouth, but one stubborn noodle clung to her chin. Inch-by-inch, she sucked the noodle in until finally reaching the end. Setting her silverware down, she wiped her mouth and faced Frank. "I'm sorry, but there's one thing I don't suck and that's noodles!"

Clive coughed and scurried from the room with his hand over his mouth.

Frank laughed. "Nothing like speaking the truth."

"Really, I'm not hungry. I'll just watch you and sip my wine. Believe me that will be much more satisfying."

Frank set his fork on the plate. "Well, I'm not eating without you. So let's go to the study and talk about what you *do* like." His plan was working. Step one: check. On to step two.

"Now that sounds absolutely delicious." She batted her long, black lashes and stood from the table. Frank held out his arm and escorted her to the study while contemplating his next move. He poured her a snifter of cognac, hoping for the same effect as a truth serum.

She came up behind him and rubbed her breasts against his back. She knew all the angles and moves to get him just where she wanted him. Her long, red fingernail scaled up his back and over his shoulders. Then she began to massage him deep and slow. "How does that feel, darling?" she purred in his ear.

He turned and handed her the glass. "It would feel better upstairs."

"So what are we waiting for?"

Step two: check. "I'll lead the way." Walking upstairs to his master suite, he opened the door.

Mimma brushed past him, touching and sniffing like a dog leaving its scent. "Very nice, darling, and quite the view." Wandering out onto the terrace, the cool breeze whipped up her dress, revealing nothing but polished bare skin.

Frank came up behind her and lowered her dress straps off her shoulders. Like a delicate butterfly, it floated to her pointed high-heels. She turned around and extended her arms along the railing, letting him linger over her body.

The moon's iridescent glow outlined her sculpted figure, from the sweeping curve of her breasts and sharp pink nipples, down to her tapered ankle bone. As Frank sipped his cognac, taking in the view, he unconsciously strayed from his mission. However, her plan was working perfectly. *Now get him in bed and swap secrets.* Strutting back into the bedroom using body language dripping with perversion, Mimma turned and motioned with a finger to follow. Then she crawled up on the bed and posed invitingly.

Frank was powerless and surrendered to his manhood, climbing on top of her. Lying between her legs, he closed his eyes and began kissing her lips and down her neck, visualizing Jasmine. Mimma let out a heavy moan, bringing light to whom he was kissing. He stared down at her with the impulse to jump off, but that would undermine his ploy. He had to stay on track and finish the job he'd started.

Taking a hold of her wrists, he lunged, unleashing his revenge and retaliation like a savage animal. Mimma felt his fury and not his passion. She pushed back angrily, trying to get away, but her strength was not enough to tame his anger. Frank kept hammering harder and harder as she bucked and tossed until coming to a panting stop. Rolling off her, his chest rose and fell as he found his breath.

Mimma sat up, raised her hand, and slapped him across the face. "You hurt me, you son-of-a-bitch!"

The sting intensified his resentment. He leaped off the bed, snatching his pants from the floor and stormed out to the terrace. He looked up at the sky. The stars were out with a big lover's moon as streaks of silver rippled over the lake.

It was a night of brilliant beauty, but his eyes were blinded by a painful void. Frustrated, standing alone, he realized his plan was slipping away. More importantly, his priority was slipping away. This was not about him but the woman he loved. And if he wanted her safe and alive, his best odds were to go in and apologize. Turning around, he saw Mimma silently watching him. He had to make a move and slowly came up to her. Gently embracing her shoulders, he uttered, "I'm sorry. Let's go back to bed, okay?"

She pulled away from his hands. "Only if you play nice."

"I promise I'll be on my best behavior."

A smile curled, and her hips swayed. "Well . . . all right, but I'd love some champagne. Will you be a dear and get me a glass?"

Great idea. "I'll get a bottle."

"Even better."

Frank returned with a chilled bottle of Dom and a dish of fresh strawberries. He found Mimma lying across the bed on her side, smiling seductively. Pouring a flute, he bit off the stem of a strawberry and dropped it in her glass. "Here baby."

"That looks luscious." She took the glass and held it high. "To us."

He raised his glass, tipped his head back and guzzled it down. Then he leaned over, took her glass and set it on the table. Desperate for answers, he slid in next to her and slowly made his way on top again. His mouth lowered onto hers, and he began kissing her ever so lightly.

She stared up at him, batting her lashes. "I was starting to think you didn't like me."

"How could you think that?" He smiled and brushed a finger across her cheek. *I've got her just where I want her.*

She squirmed with delight, convinced beyond words that he was hers. Now all she had to do was weave him into her deviant web for Marco.

CHAPTER

SIXTEEN

J erome headed up Kingsburg Grade to Jasmine's house, remembering it was about three miles to the crest of the summit and then left on Benjamin. It was dark and signs barely visible, but he recognized the large rock formation at the corner of her street.

Making the turn into her driveway, his headlights flashed on someone under the deck. He slammed on the brakes and switched on the high beams, catching only a glimpse of a giant person running into the woods.

Jasmine saw the lights of a car shining through the living room curtain. She looked out and saw Jerome sitting in his car, as though he was at the wrong house. Then he got out and jogged to the back of her property. "What is he doing?" she uttered to herself.

Walking out onto the porch, she watched as he walked along the edge of the woods. Jerome noticed her and waved for her to get back inside. Then it hit her. The person in the black car was back! Dashing for the door, she scurried inside and locked it. Then she peered out the window to see Jerome walking toward the house. She met him at the door with eyes wide and wild. "You saw someone, didn't you?!" She gasped.

"Yes . . . who is it?" Jerome entered and locked the door.

She shook her head then wobbled to the couch and crumbled. "He's back."

"Who's back?" He sat down next to her.

Jasmine gazed at him with tears brimming. "Someone has been stalking me, and I don't know who it is, but they won't leave me alone." She wrapped her throw around her shoulders and clutched it tightly around her body.

Jerome stood and looked for the phone. "We need to call the police. I think they were trying to break in."

"Frank didn't want me to call the police, but I can't go through this anymore. I'm so scared."

"Who is Frank and why doesn't he want you to call the police?"

Jasmine wiped her face and rested her head back against the couch. "Frank Pazzarelli is my boyfriend. He wanted to investigate before I got the police involved and promised me he'd catch this person."

Jerome angled his head. "That name sounds familiar. In fact, I think I just met him. Is he the hotel manager at the Paradise Palace?"

"Yes, that's Frank."

"I wonder why he didn't mention you when we spoke today."

Jaz studied him. "You met him?"

"He came to my room this morning to ask me a few questions about the shooting. But that's beside the point. Why didn't he want you to call the police? Your safety should be his utmost concern."

Feeling weak and parched, Jaz went to the kitchen to get a glass of water. "Well, at first I thought it might be a prank. You know, some kids trying to scare me." She reached into the cupboard for a glass. "Would you like some water?"

"No thanks."

"But when I saw the same car from my bedroom window, I knew it wasn't. Frank told me he'd catch the guy and not to worry. So I've tried to but I can't," she said, sighing.

Jerome met her in the kitchen. "How many times have you seen this person?"

"Truthfully, I haven't actually seen them." She took a gulp of water then went back to the couch and sat down.

Jerome followed her. "The person I saw was a very large man, over three hundred pounds I'd say."

Jasmine's mouth dropped. "A really big man came to my game the other day. At first I thought he was drunk, but then he fell to the floor having a seizure. The paramedics came and had to take him to the hospital." She looked at Jerome. "You don't think it could be the same person do you?"

"I don't know, but I do know you've experienced more tragedy in one week than most people do in a lifetime." He shook his head. "A man has a seizure and a man kills himself, both at *your* game! On top of that, you're being stalked! I'm sorry, but as your doctor and friend I'm going to override Frank's decision. You need to get the police involved. It's too dangerous not to."

"I agree, but first let me call Frank and tell him what just happened." She went to the kitchen and called him while Jerome looked out the window.

Frank stared breathlessly at the phone while satisfying his sexual obligation. His gut told him it was Jasmine, and this *definitely* was not the time to talk. After six pestering rings, Mimma reached for it. "Don't answer it!" he bellowed, but it was too late.

Jasmine started to hang up when she heard a female voice answer.

"Hello?" Mimma said, panting out of breath. Jaz opened her mouth but couldn't speak. "Is someone there?" Mimma wheezed.

Frank rolled to his side, holding his hand over his eyes and clenching his jaw.

"Ah . . . is Frank there?" Jasmine asked hesitantly.

"It's for you, *lover-boy*." Mimma pressed the phone to his ear. Frank sat up and glared at her, wanting to bite off her head. Jasmine felt her throat swell and her hand lose all feeling as she listened to heavy breathing.

Frank had to say something. It would only cause more suspicion if he didn't. He closed his eyes and prayed it was anyone but the woman he loved. "Hello?" The noose tightened around Jasmine's neck, and the phone fell from her grip, crashing to the table. Frank heard the thud and slammed down the phone. "I told you not to answer it! Who was it?"

"I don't know—some twit." Mimma glared at him through narrow, blazing slits. "So who is the little slut, anyway?"

Frank's hand formed an angry fist, ready to defend his woman. Instead, he flew out of bed and raked his fingers through his hair while pacing the floor. "It's time for you to go, now!"

Jerome saw the whole thing. "Are you all right?"

"Uh . . . yeah." Jasmine robotically picked up the phone and replaced it in the cradle.

"Was he there?"

"No, he wasn't there. I'll call him later."

"I'm calling the police then."

Jaz walked to the couch and folded like a rag doll. Drawing her knees to her chest, she stared blankly at the TV, trying to hold her composure. As she listened to Jerome describe what he saw to the police, tears came flooding down her cheeks. Now *Lover Boy* could be added to her list of nightmares.

The couch sank next to her, then Jerome put his arm around her shoulder. "Listen, you really shouldn't stay here tonight. It's possible the person will return." She nodded and wiped her cheeks. He gently rubbed her shoulder. "I'm sorry this is happening to you. You've been through so much, and your health and safety is paramount." She nodded again as they gazed helplessly at each other. "The police said they would investigate and keep a close eye on your house. They should be here any minute." He consoled her oblivious of what was really going through her head. "Why don't you go pack a bag for you and the kids and come back to the hotel with me?"

"Okay." She stood, wobbling side-to-side, feeling like her head was hollow and body made of twigs.

Jerome held onto her arm. "Are you all right?"

"Yeah, just a little shaken. I'll be fine." When she left to get the kids up and pack a bag, the phone rang again.

"Do you want me to answer that?" Jerome called.

"No! I don't feel like talking to anyone."

"All right." He sat back and let it ring.

Fuming, Frank slammed down the phone. He was going to try and repair the *misunderstanding*. Mimma flew out of bed like a formidable tempest and stood with her arms folded and feet apart. Frank's demand not only stoked her coals but seared her flesh.

Ever since she laid eyes on him, he had been unattainable. She was not going to let a little mix-up like this ruin what she'd been wanting for a long time. Marco could keep his money. It wasn't worth losing Frank for it. A new plan was vital and fast.

She crept up to him cool and seductive. "Darling, you don't want to kick me out. The night is just beginning." Tracing a finger lightly over his chest and around his nipples, a mischievous grin replaced her hesitant lips. Frank swatted her hand away, but she knew she still had an ace in the hole. She would apprise him of Marco's suspicion. That would get his attention, and if he wanted to stay alive he'd better keep her *very, very* happy.

There was one thing Mimma didn't know, one important detail Marco deliberately kept from her: Frank had a woman. Knowing her desire for him, it was the only way to ensure the job was done and done right. Otherwise, no amount of money Marco offered her would have mattered.

Spiraling with anger and frustration, Frank sat down on the bed and lowered his head in his hands. More than anything he wanted to divulge his love for Jasmine—that the evening was a charade to confirm his suspicion of Marco. But then *both* women would be mad enough to kill him themselves. There was no way around it. He had to let Mimma have her way.

Taking a deep breath, Frank put his plan in forward motion. Walking over to the table, he picked up the bottle of champagne and poured each a glass. Then he crept up behind Mimma and leaned close, whispering in her ear, "So, where were we?"

She slowly turned around and took the glass from him. "As I said, the night is just beginning. You just need to relax, darling." She set her glass down and began massaging his back.

Frank let his head drop forward as she manipulated him into sub-mission. "Mmm . . . that feels nice," he said, tasting the poison of each paralyzing word.

"See darling, you want me." She pressed her breasts against his back, taunting him to take her in his arms and carry her back to bed. But Frank stood limp and numb, as if incapable of moving. Mimma kept massaging him, wondering if she had lost her touch or her age had weakened his interest. Shunning that thought, she led him to the bed and slithered on top of him. Slowly and passionately, she worked her tongue down his body.

Frank closed his eyes, imploring his body to react. Instead, he lay induced by a power beyond his control. "Sorry . . . I don't know what's wrong."

Mimma dropped down next to him and stared at the ceiling. She was convinced his inability to get aroused was because of her. Or this was all fun and games and he'd had enough. *Well, she hadn't!* One way or another he would be hers. A villainous smile curled. It was time to reveal her ace. She rolled over and stroked his chest. "I have some-thing of interest to you." She grasped his chin with her blood-red fin-gernails and turned his head toward her. "Do you know how much I want you, darling?" Her emerald eyes raced.

"You've made it pretty clear."

"Did you know more than money?" She swirled her fingertip around his lips.

He forced a chuckle. "Is that possible?"

"For you, yes." She sat up and looked intensely into his eyes. "Marco is paying me twenty grand to . . . let's just say, be with you tonight. But . . ." she hesitated, "I think I'd rather just have you."

Frank grabbed her arm. "I knew it! Marco is behind this, isn't he?"

"I'm not going to tell you anything until you let go of me!" He released her with a shove, then bolted off the bed. Confused, Mimma slowly made her way back to him and placed her arms around his waist. "Why are you so angry? What do you mean, behind this?"

"Why is he paying you?"

"It doesn't matter. I love you, and I want us to be together," she cooed, resting her head on his chest.

He held her back and looked into her pleading eyes. "It does mat-ter, more than you know. What does he want?"

"He wanted me to find out what you've been up to. He thinks you have deceived him. That you're dealing behind his back."

Frank shook his head. "What makes him think that?"

"He is not a stupid man—look around." She pointed at his luxurious surroundings. "You live like a goddamn king!"

Frank narrowed his eyes. "I invest and wisely, I might add."

"Frankie, the word is out. You make frequent trips to Guatemala, and you're working for someone else. Believe me when I say, Marco will not tolerate it. You will be killed."

He pulled her arms off him and walked to the window. "Where did you get this information?"

She crept up behind him. "I overheard Marco on the phone. He didn't know I was there." She touched his cheek. "Darling, listen to me. I'm telling you this for your own protection. I think there's a snitch . . . maybe in the hotel."

A line dug deep between Frank's eyes. "You know this?"

"Not exactly, but I heard my brother's rage and your name mentioned. After that, he was waving money at me with a proposition."

Frank paced the room, raking his fingers over his brain. His first thought was Paul, but why would he risk his hush-money of five G's a month when he had no proof? Then he stopped and looked at Mimma. "So what do you want? There has to be something."

Mimma smiled, walked over to the table and picked up her glass of champagne. Holding it toward him, she uttered, "Just you." Then she took a sip and sat down on the bed. "Honestly, I thought it would be easy money, but when you asked me to leave I couldn't risk losing you. It's not worth it to me."

"What will you tell Marco?"

"Nothing. Simple as that."

Frank came to her and gently ran a hand over her leg, executing a new approach. "You have to tell him something, or I'll no longer exist. You don't want that, do you?" His eyes turned soft and amorous.

"Of course I don't. I will do anything to protect you—to protect us. That is why I'm telling you this."

He sat down next to her and stroked her face. "Then, what will you say to Marco?"

She nuzzled against his hand. "I'll convince him there's nothing to worry about. You showed me your investment portfolio, which clearly is very lucrative." She looked at him straight dead in the eyes. "That is the truth, isn't it?"

"Yes. I have nothing to hide." He felt cornered with his *"do-or-die"* situation, but it was imperative she trusted him.

"Then we have nothing to worry about." Mimma rose to her knees and began lightly kissing his lips. "You still want to kick me out?"

He parted his mouth and let their tongues touch. "What do you think?"

"I think you would be a fool if you did."

SEVENTEEN

F rank glanced around the gray gloom of the Palace in search of a warm soft glow, but Jasmine was nowhere in sight. Oddly, he felt a sense of relief. Telling her he had to compromise with the devil to keep her from harm's way, wasn't far from the truth. Finding out the devil was a woman, she'd probably want him to burn in hell. Certain there was nothing he could say that she would possibly understand, he headed for his office.

The front lobby was crowded and noisy with check-ins and checkouts. Fortunately, he was able to shuffle past undetected and entered the elevator. At this point, stacking the customer's rants on top of his would have him leaping off the terrace.

Approaching his office, he noticed the door was left ajar. Peeking inside, he saw a man sitting in front of his desk obviously waiting for him. He walked in and shut the door loudly, alarming the stranger.

Dr. Jerome Jensen stood and turned around. "Good morning." He politely held out his hand. "Your secretary let me in. I hope you don't mind."

Frank shook it. "No, that's fine. Please sit." They both sat down.

"I know it's early, but I needed to talk to you right away." Jerome wasted no time. Frank's reaction was the reason for his visit. "I made an appointment to see Ms. Woods last night to make sure she was stable enough to return to work." Frank felt his tie constrict. "When I pulled up to her house, a man was under her deck. I believe he was trying to break in." Frank's eyes widened and mouth opened. "Jasmine said someone has been stalking her. She also said that it hadn't been reported to the police." Jerome leaned forward, emphasizing his concern. "This could be a dangerous man, and if you are her *boyfriend* like she said, then I suggest you take a more aggressive stance on the matter."

Frank stared blankly at him. Jasmine apparently disclosed their relationship. "I will, and I absolutely agree. I haven't talked to her yet. Is she all right?"

"She's a little shaken, so I brought her and the kids back to the hotel with me last night. They're in room 3030. I assume being the hotel manager you can help her out with that."

Frank jotted down the number. "Yes, thank you, I will." His mind raced. "Listen, for the record, can you describe the person you saw?"

"It was dark, so I didn't get a good look at him, but he was a very large man—three to four hundred pounds."

Frank nodded, trying to keep his wrath unnoticeable. "And what did the police say?"

"That's one of the reasons I came to speak to you. They will be here sometime this morning to take a statement from Jasmine and me. I thought I'd let you know, in case you had any questions or just wanted to be there."

"Yes, of course. Thank you." Frank stood up to imply *it was time to go!*

Jerome was perceptive and walked to the door. "I'll see you later then. And hey, nice office."

Frank forced a smile. "Thanks." As the door closed, he stepped from his desk and out onto the terrace, which invited him to take a closer look down below. The rocky shore could end it all quick and easy. Then he envisioned the soft, supple body of a woman that nourished his dreams. A face so naturally beautiful, the delicate curl of her lips, her freckled nose that wrinkled when she laughed, and the sweet smell of rosewater in her lush strawberry hair.

While thinking of her, unfamiliar emotions pooled inside him: fear, guilt and desperate love. Jasmine was everything he desired and now couldn't have. He must talk to her, but what would he say? No words other than I love you described what he was feeling. It was useless. She wouldn't believe him anyway, knowing he was with another woman.

He looked down at the rocky ground and contemplated the drop. Feeling uneasy with the temptation, he went back to his desk and stared at the piece of paper with 3030 written on it. And it stared back like a jury in a courtroom with a guilty verdict. Despite the futility, he had to see her.

Pacing his office, Frank rehearsed out loud what he would say. "Jasmine, I'm sorry, but there's—" He shook his head. "Jasmine, I know you're mad, and there's no excuse for what I did, but—" He squeezed his hand into a tight fist and slammed it on his desk, then he left to grovel at her feet.

The walk down the hallway was like trudging through a blazing hot desert without water. By the time he reached the door he was parched, wringing wet and out of breath. Taking his handkerchief from his pocket, he wiped his brow and timidly rapped on the door.

"I'll get it." The door opened to a breathtaking view of Jasmine in her robe peering out the patio window. "Hi Frank," Shauna chimed.

Frank didn't respond. He stood with his mouth parted, staring at the awesome sight.

Jasmine turned and met his gaze then boldly secured her robe. With her head high, she confidently strode over to him knowing exactly what to say. His face read like a worn book, one she knew well, having gone through it several times with Carl.

"I saw Jerome this morning," Frank muttered. "He told me what happened last night." His fingers reached for her. "Jasmine, I'm really—"

She cut him off. "I don't need an explanation or sobbing justification. It just didn't work, that's all!"

Frank closed his mouth, wanting desperately to tell her the truth. "Just tell me one thing. Are you all right?"

She jerked her head back. "I'm fine." The words stung with vengeance. Yet he could see through her bulletproof façade she felt the same way he did: hopelessly sick inside.

He nodded. "Well, I'm glad you're here at the hotel." His eyes darted and fluttered, tortured by her confused, despondent face.

"I need to go," Jasmine said and started to shut the door.

Frank stopped it with his hand. "Please let me know if there is anything I can do to help." His eyes pleaded for mercy.

She brushed away a straggling tear, then nodded and shut the door.

Justin ran up to her. "Mom, what's the matter?"

She held him tightly to her side. "Nothing. I have everything I need right here."

Frank stopped by the front desk, informing them the police would be arriving soon and to call him when they did. Then he went back to his office to make some calls. The first on his list was to Mimma. He wanted to know, verbatim, Marco's reaction to her explanation and make sure she'd absolved him of any suspicions.

After two rings Mimma answered. "Hello?"

"Mimma, it's Frankie."

"Mmm . . . you must have read my mind," she purred.

He was not in the mood for her sexual innuendos. "Did you talk to Marco?"

"I just got home, darling."

"You left my house three hours ago! What the hell have you been doing?" he snapped.

"I have my priorities, and Marco is not *first* on my list. I will see him at noon. That's soon enough." She listened to a long pause of silence. "Are you still there?"

"Yes." He was contemplating his only priority: Jasmine's safety.

"Darling, I will call you after I talk to him. What's the big hurry, anyway? It's not like your life is in danger . . . yet." She mocked.

"I know Marco, and you need to talk to him as soon as possible. It's imperative he trusts me completely."

"I've never heard you beg before. I find it quite unattractive." She sat down and crossed her legs. "So, what do I tell him about your escapades to Guatemala? You never explained that to me."

Frank was caught off guard. He hesitated, but a suitable answer came to mind. "I invest in antiquities, and one of my clients is a Cuban importer. His store is in Santa Lucia."

"Oh, how fascinating. You'll have to show me all your treasures someday."

"Next trip I'll buy you something special. How does that sound?" It was essential to keep Mimma convinced as well as her brother.

"That's sounds wonderful, darling. I *love* surprises."

"Then clear everything up with Marco, and I'll make that my priority."

"I will, don't worry. Ciao baby."

Frank hung up satisfied with their conversation, though wrestled with what could go wrong that hadn't already. If Mimma ever found out about Jasmine, it would take more than the ocean to douse her fire. Keeping her under lock and key was vital, at least until he no longer needed her. Massaging his head with that debilitating thought, the phone rang with a jolting disruption. "Yes?"

"Mr. Pazzarelli, there are two detectives here."

"Thank you, I'll be right down." He walked calmly to the lobby and greeted the two men with a hefty handshake. "I'm Frank Pazzarelli, the hotel manager."

"I'm Lieutenant Griffin, and this is Sergeant Mitchell."

"I was told the police were coming not detectives. Sounds pretty serious," Frank said, folding his arms.

Lieutenant Griffin spoke. "Well, that's what we're here to find out. We need to speak to an employee by the name of Jasmine Woods. Apparently, someone tried to break into her house last night. The report was called in by Dr. Jerome Jensen. We'll need a statement from him, as well."

"No problem. I'll have a clerk call their rooms right away." Frank left and approached the front desk. "Judy, would you please ring Jasmine Woods in room 3030? Let her know there are two detectives here to take a statement, and also Dr. Jerome Jensen in suite 1036." She nodded and immediately called their rooms, giving each the message.

Frank came back and clasped his hands. "They should be here any minute, so I'll just excuse myself. I have a busy day." He didn't want to stir up Jasmine's anger, turning a simple meeting into a hostile interrogation.

"Sir, if you don't mind, we also need a statement from you."

"Regarding what?" Frank asked sternly.

"A man was admitted into the hospital after having a seizure at Ms. Woods' blackjack table. Dr. Jensen stated there could be a connection, possibly the same man. So, we'll need information pertinent to that day."

Frank cocked a foot and shoved his hands in his pockets. "What do you want to know? I could probably answer it right now."

"For starters, a list of guests staying at the hotel that day, blackjack players as well as surveillance footage, anything that could establish a link."

"That's a lot to compile. It may take a day or two."

"You don't have a problem with that, do you?" The detective noticed Frank's uneasiness.

"No, not at all." He shook his head.

Lieutenant Griffin gazed over at the loud, bustling crowd. "When everyone gets here, is there a place we can all sit down without this disturbance?"

"Yes, we have a conference room down the hall." Frank peered down at his watch as anxiety started to build. He wished he'd been able to discuss a few things with Jasmine before the meeting. *What if she mentions they were seeing each other when everything started happening and that he didn't want to call the police? What if Dr. Jensen does!?* A wet film glazed his forehead, thinking of all the what-if's. "They should be here by now. I'll have Judy ring their rooms again."

Just then Frank saw Jasmine walking toward them, and his heart sank with pangs of guilt. He tried to draw their eyes together, but she defiantly resisted.

She held out her hand while approaching the officers. "Hi, I'm Jasmine Woods." They shook hands with her.

Jerome hurried up to them. "Sorry, I hope you haven't been waiting long. I'm Dr. Jerome Jensen." He held out a firm hand. The detectives acknowledged him then gestured for Frank to lead the way.

They entered a small board room with an oblong table and six black swivel chairs. There was also a long counter with a coffee pot, cups and assorted teas. "Would anyone care for something to drink," Frank asked nervously.

"I'm fine," Sergeant Mitchell replied, and the others nodded in agreement.

Lieutenant Griffin began, "We'd like to speak to each of you individually and ask that no one interrupts." He motioned with a hand. "So, if everyone would please take a seat we'll get started." Jerome sat down, and Jasmine sat next to him.

"Why don't you sit there," Sergeant Mitchell said to Frank, forcing him to sit opposite of Jasmine. They looked at each other like two boxers on their final round, both beat and bruised.

The deposition started with Frank, pertaining to the seizure incident. Sergeant Mitchell read, "The report states that Mr. Tommy Tanaka had an allergic reaction to perfume which caused a seizure at Ms. Woods' blackjack game. He was then taken by the paramedics to the Tahoe Community Hospital." He looked directly at Frank for confirmation.

"That's right," Frank answered, trying to keep cool and calm.

"According to the phone conversation with the police and Dr. Jensen, Mr. Tanaka fits the description of the perpetrator at Ms. Woods' house. Do you know this person, or have you ever seen him before?"

Jasmine studied Frank, noting every facial twitch and nervous blink. He probably looked scared to them. To her, he looked guilty. She wanted to shout and pound her fist. *"This is irrelevant! The only question that should be asked is how could you betray Jasmine!?"*

Frank repeated the question, "Do I know this person, or have I seen him before? I believe he has been a guest of ours prior to this incident, but I don't know him personally." Instantly, he felt the persecuting glares of Jasmine and Jerome. *Could they detect he was lying?*

"Thank you, Mr. Pazzarelli. That's all for now. However, we still need that information we requested as soon as possible."

"Yes, I'll have my secretary get right on it."

"Ms. Woods, you're next." Jaz sat up tall and looked straight at them with true Montana grit. Frank stayed to observe. He didn't want to be caught off-guard if bullets started flying. "Have you ever seen Mr. Tommy Tanaka before the seizure episode?" Lieutenant Griffin asked.

"No."

"Have you seen the person stalking you?"

"Actually, no. They were inside their car."

"Can you describe the car?"

"I don't know the model, but it was a mid-sized, black sedan."

"When did you first notice someone stalking you?"

"It was last Friday night after I left a party. They followed me . . . more like chased me around the neighborhood."

"If you wouldn't mind, can you be more specific?" The detectives made notes as she spoke.

"As I was warming my truck to leave I noticed headlights in my rearview mirror. At first I didn't think anything of it, but then I saw a dark figure walking toward me, so I took off."

"Then what?"

"I got lost and circled the neighborhood, looking for a way out, and the car stayed right behind me."

"Go on."

"Then I finally made it back to Vonda's house, where the party was, and the car sat idling in front of her house until Vonda let me inside."

"Did you call the police?"

"No. I thought it might be a prank—maybe some kids trying to scare me."

"Have you seen the car again?"

"Yes, one more time at my house."

"Do you know anyone that may have a vendetta with you, perhaps a player here?"

"No." She shrugged.

"Thank you Ms. Woods. We'll be in contact. You're excused." Frank swallowed a sigh of relief. He was sure a finger was going to point directly at him.

"Would you mind if I stayed?" She wanted to make sure something wasn't said she needed to hear. *Who knows what other little secrets are going on in Frank's life?*

"Fine with us," Lieutenant Griffin said and turned to Jerome. "Mister. . . I mean Dr. Jensen, you're next." Jerome was sitting like the Lincoln monument, personifying a statue of unwavering justice. His shoulders were square, knees slightly apart, feet firmly on the floor, staring into the face of righteous truth. "Okay, tell us from the beginning what you saw the night you reported the intruder."

Jerome first disclosed his encounter with Jasmine at the scene of the shooting to establish the relationship and timeline.

"And why were you at Ms. Woods' house last night?"

"I wanted to make sure she was able to return to work, which requires a physical assessment before I sign a release."

"Did you release her?"

"I didn't. After the incident with the prowler, I brought her here to the hotel where she would be safe. I'm recommending at least a couple more days of rest."

"How long are you staying in Tahoe?"

"The conference ends tomorrow, but I can stay another day or two until Jasmine returns to work. After that, I'll find a referred doctor to take over."

Frank interjected. "I have a personal friend at the Community Hospital, Dr. Carmen Lucio. I can give him a call if you'd like." He was eager to get Jerome out of the hotel and out of the scene. One less person to deal with.

"Is that all right with you?" the detective asked Jerome.

"That would be fine. I trust Frank's judgment since he *is* Jasmine's boyfriend." Suddenly there was a different picture as all heads turned to Frank and looking quite confused. "I'm sorry, I assumed they knew," Jerome said calmly.

This was exactly what Frank was afraid of. One incriminating slip could end any chance of him getting back with Jasmine and open an entirely new investigation. "I didn't mention it because no one asked," Frank defended.

The interrogation took on a new angle. It was now a group session. The detectives turned to Jasmine. "Is that correct, are you and Frank dating?"

Jasmine hesitated. "Well, yes." She chose the easiest way out to void more confusion or questions. And she really had nothing to hide except the knife in her back.

Frank's jaw relaxed with a drop. He wasn't prepared to delve into the reason why they just broke up.

"So Frank was aware that someone has been stalking you."

Jasmine looked at Frank in despair. "Yes."

"What action was taken?" Both detectives, Jerome, and Frank, sat motionless waiting for her response.

"Frank said he wanted to investigate before getting the police involved."

Lieutenant Griffin tapped on his chin, eyes blindly wandering. He turned to Frank. "I can't quite understand why you wouldn't call the police when your *girlfriend's* life was at stake."

Frank clasped his sweaty hands. "Like she said, we first wanted to rule out if it was just kids trying to scare her. I never thought for a minute it would get to this point."

Sergeant Mitchell looked at Jasmine. "So when Dr. Jensen called the police this was the first time it was reported?"

She nodded and uttered, "That's correct." She knew the questions would lead to the inevitable.

"Did you inform Frank the police had been contacted?"

Jasmine looked at Jerome, knowing he was right there to confirm the call. "Yes, but when I called he wasn't there."

Frank could have jumped up and kissed her. *But why was she protecting him?*

Jerome kept a close eye on Frank. There was something about his naivety that was unsettling. He seemed like the type that would trust no one, especially if Jasmine was in danger.

"Where were you last night when this happened?" Sergeant Mitchell asked Frank.

Frank chuckled nervously. "This sounds like I'm under investigation. I was out." He kept his eyes locked on the detectives, avoiding Jasmine's knife-throwing glare.

"Where and what were you doing?" Sergeant Mitchell asked again.

Frank straightened. "Now wait a minute. What I do in my personal time is my business."

"It's just a simple question, Mr. Pazzarelli. We're not implying anything. But if you're uncomfortable answering, you don't have to."

Frank didn't want to look like he was hiding anything. That would only raise more suspicion. "It's no big deal. A friend came over to my house to discuss some business, that's all."

The detective cocked his head. "But you said you were out, and Ms. Woods said when she called you weren't home. So, were you there or not?"

"I was *outside*. I never heard the phone. We were sitting on the deck most the night."

Jerome remembered Jasmine dropping the phone and her immediate depressed state of mind after the call. Something was up that neither one wanted to confess. Jerome decided he would ask a few questions when he had some time alone with her.

The detectives conversed quietly then stood. "Looks like we have enough for now, but we'll be in touch with all of you if we need anything more." Lieutenant Griffin turned to Dr. Jensen. "If you could please give us a forwarding phone number and address we would appreciate it."

"No problem, and I'll be here another couple of days if you need to get ahold of me."

"Thanks." They both gave a nod and left the room.

"I'm sure we'll be talking later," Jerome said to Jasmine and stood up to leave.

"Yes." When he left, she got up and headed for the door as Frank pulled her back by the arm. Embraced to his chest, she struggled furiously to be freed, but his hungry kiss weakened the fight. Her defiant mouth opened, becoming soft and yearning.

The door closed with their wavering bodies while they feverishly fulfilled a requited need. Clinging and drowning in his love potion, two words brought the excitement to an immediate halt: *Lover Boy!*

Jaz shoved Frank back and raked her fingers through her hair. "Just leave me alone, please."

Frank held out his arms. "But Jasmine—"

"But what, Frank, what?"

He stood lifeless, eyes wide and mouth gaping as if hanging from a noose.

"That's what I thought!" She spun out the door, leaving him squirming and dangling.

EIGHTEEN

M arco peered out from a turret of his stone and stucco castle, built on a sprawling mountainside of yellow pines and blue spruce. It resembled the home he and Mimma grew up in with their parents. For over a century, the Gamboli winery in Vomero, Italy was revered for its Pinot noirs and Sangiovese varietals. Marco helped run the fifty-acre vineyard when he was just a boy. When he reached the age of eighteen, he had mastered the art of wine making.

Mimma grew up resenting the winery. She believed her parents loved Marco and the winery more than her. And when she reached the age of eighteen, she had mastered the art of love making.

Unexpectedly, the hundred and twenty years of cultivated perfection came to a tragic end when Marco and Mimma's parents were killed in a train crash. The estate and legacy were theirs to carry on, yet without the Gamboli spirit they both fell into a deep pit of darkness.

What did survive the devastation was their passion for money. As need fueled Marco's want, he found a new resource. It was cocaine. Not only did it suppress the painful memories, but it became a main-stream of infinite income. Marco quickly organized a small cartel in London, England which presented the potential of becoming more powerful than he imagined. The demand forced him to expand his operation into the United States, where the largest hotspot was located, California.

Lake Tahoe's remote environment had the familiar comforts of Italy and bordered the lush money-pit. It was the perfect place to transplant his roots and start over. Mimma followed Marco, being her only blood and to escape the haunting memories in Vomero.

Parking her silver Jaguar under the large portico, Mimma got out as Sylvester Michael Ferretta ran out of his station to greet her. He was the son of Michael Ferretta, Marco's trusted friend and international liaison. He was a stout, muscular, virile young man in the peak of his prime. "Good afternoon, Mimma. You're looking fine today."

She pulled her sunglasses down and winked. "Thanks Sly. Would you let Marco know I'm here?"

"My pleasure." He pushed the intercom button inside the guard sta-tion and watched her hips strut toward the front door. She turned and smiled, feeling his eyes grope her buttocks then entered the front door.

"Marco, where are you?" She tossed her purse on top of a round marble table, illuminated like a kaleidoscope by the surrounding stained glass windows.

"You're late!" he shouted, standing at the top of the stairs and look-ing down at her. His sharp, thin body shifted down the stairs. "Come to the study."

"It's nice to see you, too." She followed him to a room of polished rich cherry wood and soft tanned leather.

Marco shut the door behind them, sat down at his desk and opened a family crested humidor. Pulling out a cigar, he shoved it in his mouth and leaned back. "Now, tell me everything. Who is Frankie working for?"

Mimma suddenly felt parched and casually strode to the wine cabinet. Pouring a glass of pinot, she swirled it and then meandered back to the wing-back chair. Sitting, she took a sip and crossed her legs. "He's not working for anyone . . . only you."

"Bullshit!" Marco hammered his fist on the desk.

"It's the truth! He has another business and investments."

"How do you know this?" Marco squinted through baggy slits.

"I saw his files, books, the records, everything!" She wanted Frank and was willing to lie for him.

Marco shook his head. "I don't believe you. Why would he show you this?"

She relaxed back. "We talked about his beautiful possessions and how he acquired them. Then he told me of his business in antiquities." She took a sip of wine. "You know, Marco, I am a woman and he is a man. Do you doubt my capabilities?" She smiled and raised an eyebrow.

"I know Frankie, and he wouldn't show you or anyone else his records."

She flipped her wrist. "Then you don't know the power I possess. Besides, I wanted some investment tips since he's done so well." She took another sip of wine. "Not to mention, I made him an offer he couldn't refuse." She licked her lips, grinning smugly.

"This isn't worth twenty grand. You're nothing but a . . ."

"Ah, ah." She wagged her finger. "Let's not get nasty. I don't want your money, anyway."

Marco pulled the cigar from his mouth and studied Mimma long and hard. "You are turning down my money? This isn't like you." He rose from his chair like a corpse rising from the grave and leaned over the desk. "Why don't you want my money like you goddamn demanded!?"

"That's not important." Mimma looked down at her glass and swirled it.

"It is important! Have you made a deal with Frankie?"

Mimma sat idle and cool. "I can assure you, I did not make a deal with Frankie. What I tell you is the truth." This time Marco would not drag her dignity through the mire for his pleasure.

Marco collapsed in his chair, shaking his head. "I should have known. What a fool I am."

Mimma stood defiantly and set her glass on the desk. "Whatever you're thinking, you're wrong! You know nothing!"

He let out a raspy chuckle. "I know plenty." He pointed at her with his cigar. "Before you get yourself in too deep, you should know this." His lips curled into a tight sneer. "He's fucking someone else."

Mimma lunged at him with dagger eyes. "Frankie is only fucking me. This discussion is over!" With her chin up and shoulders back, she marched out of the study, snagged her purse and bolted out the front door.

Sylvester was at his post and saw Mimma storm out of the house. He quickly ran up to her car and opened the door. "Have a good day, Ms. G."

"Ha!" Mimma slid in and sped out in a screeching fury with Marco's words pricking her skin like razor-sharp thorns. *Could it be possible that Marco speaks the truth? But why would Frankie invite me over for dinner and make love to me?* His breathless words saying he wanted her echoed in her head. Driving and thinking, it suddenly became clear, and she began laughing aloud. "You bastard, Marco! You can't fool me. I know your evil ways," she bellowed. He was trying to turn her against Frankie, testing her breaking point. Everyone knew Frankie loved women but had never fallen in love . . . until now. Mimma smiled with sweet satisfaction of her brother's failed attempt of deception.

The gate to her villa opened, and she pulled into the circular driveway. Immediately, she went inside to call Frankie, as he'd adamantly insisted. With a quick kick of each foot, the Italian red leather released its pointed pinch. Then she stretched out on the black velvet chaise lounge and dialed the hotel.

"Paradise Palace, may I help you?"

"Frank Pazzarelli," Mimma said, twisting her raven hair between two fingers.

"Just one moment and I'll ring him."

"Hello, this is Frank."

"Hello, darling."

"Mimma—good. Did you talk to Marco?"

"Yes, we had our little chat. I can't stand him. He can be so mean and manipulating sometimes."

"Why, what did he say?" Frank said, leaning closer to his desk.

"Well, I explained to him you were only working for him—that you had an antiquity business."

"And?"

She rested her head back. "And he didn't believe me, but I lied for you, darling. I told him I saw your books and records of your investments."

"So . . ." Frank waved his hand, "how did he manipulate you?"

"First, he accused me of making a deal with you, because I refused his money. I told him I didn't—"

"What!? You refused his money! Why?!" Frank spewed.

"I told you last night that I was not going to accept Marco's money. Besides, I have plenty."

Frank stood, jutting a hand in the air. "Don't you see, it looks like you *are* making a deal with me! God damn it, Mimma!" He clutched his forehead.

"Darling, I did what you wanted me to do."

Frank dropped to his chair. "So tell me, does Marco believe I'm working for him and only him?"

"I'm sure he does. He tried to turn me against you and told me you were fucking someone else, but I didn't buy it. That's Marco's way of getting you to break. I know my brother. He tests you with his wicked games, to see if you are telling the truth or not." She stared at her fingernails. "Darling, don't worry. It didn't work. I thought to myself, why would Frankie invite me over for dinner, have a rose on my plate and make love to me all night long, if there was another woman?" Her lips curled and her tongue swirled. "You want me, don't you darling?"

There was nowhere to run. Frank was caught between the teeth of both Gamboli's. Three words dribbled from his frozen jaw. "You did good."

Mimma giggled with delight, "I hope you can relax now. You are far too uptight, my love." She sat up. "Listen, I have plans for the day, but I want to get together later tonight. We can celebrate. See you around eight. Ciao."

Frank hung up with a groan. He would have to comply with Mimma's wishes but only until Jasmine was safe.

Jerome saw Jasmine walking down the hallway and called to her. She turned and waited for him to catch up to her. "Pretty intense meeting, huh?" she said as he approached her.

"Yeah, it turned out that way, which is why I wanted to talk to you. Do you have a minute?"

"Sure. What is it?"

"You think we could go somewhere to talk, maybe the coffee shop?"

"Okay . . . you look worried."

He shrugged it off. "I just have a couple questions that didn't get answered, that's all."

The hostess sat them at a table that overlooked the Water's Edge Golf Course. Jaz gazed out the window at the bright green fairways glistening with dew. "Do you golf?" she asked Jerome.

"No, my friends discouraged me from trying. It sounded like three hours of frustration rather than fun." He chuckled. "How about you?"

She nodded. "I used to play in a women's league in Montana, but I haven't since I moved here."

He angled his head. "I'm surprised they even have golf courses in Montana. Isn't it around thirty-below most of the year?" He chuckled.

"Yeah, we used snowballs instead of golf balls," she said.

He chuckled again and kept a relaxed grin as his eyes lingered over her hair, down to her nose and around her lips.

Just then the waitress rushed up holding out a pot of coffee. "Would you like some?"

They each turned over their cups and nodded. After filling them, Jerome clasped his hands and placed them on the table. "So, you were saying?"

"Oh, it was nothing." She took a sip of coffee. "You said you had a couple questions for me."

"Yes, and they may sound a little intrusive, but I feel it's important to know everything."

"Well, you *are* my doctor."

"And friend," he added and smiled. "It's about last night. After you made the call to Frank you seemed very upset. I assumed it was because of the prowler, but something's telling me there's more to it. He lowered his head and touched her hand. "Jasmine, you can tell me the truth. Did you talk to him?"

She nervously looked out the window. "No, not exactly." Her teeth clenched, remembering those two heart-stomping words.

"I'm a good listener. Is there anything you need to talk about?"

"It was just a little misunderstanding." She pulled her hand from under his and held onto her cup.

"Normally I don't pry into people's affairs, but any information will help this case." He sat back and rested his hands in his lap. "And to be honest, it looked more like contention between you two than anything else."

Jasmine couldn't hold her anger in any longer. Her glassy eyes revealed her pain. "A woman answered the phone."

"Oh . . . and I'm guessing she wasn't there on business."

"No. She called him *Lover-Boy!*"

"Well, maybe it was a misunderstanding like you said. Did you talk to him about it?"

"Yes," her voice faded. She took a sip of coffee. "And it's not a misunderstanding . . . it's over."

Hearing that, Jerome felt it was timely to express his feelings about Frank. "How well do you know him, if you don't mind me asking?"

"Well enough," she stated firmly, trying to salvage her self-respect.

"I'm sorry, I shouldn't even be saying this, but there's something about him that doesn't sit right with me, and I don't know what it is."

"I'm not sure what you're insinuating. I think he's a man with a lot on his mind and a hotel to run. In truth, I'm just not his type. So life goes on." She swept her hair over her shoulder and stared out the window.

Jerome could see he'd crossed the line. It was obvious she still had feelings for Frank. He started to apologize just when the waitress appeared, this time with a pad and pen.

Her bright red curls matched her bright red lipstick. "Okay, what would you two like to eat?" She stared blankly, chomping on a piece of gum.

"Oh, nothing for me." Jaz waved. Her appetite left after thinking about the phone call.

"I'm fine too," Jerome said with a nod.

"Okay, I'll be back with the bill." She swiftly turned.

Jerome reached over the table and gently held Jasmine's hand. "I'm sorry. I care about you, and I don't want anything to happen to you. Right now you are in danger until they catch this person. I thought I'd stay a day or two longer to make sure you'd be okay."

Jasmine could see he was deeply concerned for her welfare, which was more than Frank had on his mind. He was more concerned with his quota of women and who was next on his list. "I think I'll be fine but thanks."

"Are you sure? It's no problem."

Jasmine nodded with a brief smile.

Jerome pulled a pen from his shirt pocket and grabbed a napkin. "I don't have a card on me, but this is my number in Loveland. If you need to talk about *anything*, please call me."

Jasmine took the napkin and folded each edge, pressing a crease, then stuck it in her pants pocket. "I probably should take advantage of the kids being gone and take a nap. I'm feeling a little drained after that meeting."

"I think you should."

Parting their ways, Jaz turned and called to Jerome. "Can I work tomorrow?"

He looked back. "Get a good night's rest, and I'll release you in the morning." He pointed a finger. "That's doctor's orders."

"Okay, Doc." She waved and headed to her room. Jerome watched her walk away, feeling something awaken inside. Something he expected never to feel again.

CHAPTER

NINETEEN

Yarah found room 3030 and knocked on the door. She waited a minute and then knocked again, this time hard enough for the entire floor to hear. Jasmine sat up, disoriented. "Who is it?"

"I thought your best friend," Yarah answered sarcastically.

"Yarah! I'll be right there." Jaz whirled off the bed and hurried to the door. She was expecting a big hug, but Yarah was waiting in a perturbed stance, hip cocked, arms folded, and eyes set on incinerate.

"So when were you going to tell me?" she said and waltzed in.

"Right after my nap. How did you know I was here?"

"I tried calling your house this morning, and when no one answered I got scared. So I called Frank here at the hotel."

"You called Frank!?" Jaz screeched.

"Why not? You two are connected at the hip, aren't ya?"

"Connected as in . . . you mean . . ."

"Yeah, makin' waves, mattress dancin'—havin' sex!" Yarah threw her hands in the air.

Jasmine looked away. "Well, we were getting there, but I guess he was tired of waiting. He's now some other woman's *lover-boy*."

"Whoa, back up." Yarah sat down on the bed. "Start from the beginning, like why you're here in the first place."

Jaz sat down next to her and gave her a detailed account of everything that had happened.

"I don't understand. Who would want to stalk you?" Jasmine raised an eyebrow. "I didn't mean it that way, but only wacko's do that kind of stuff."

"I know . . . I knew what you meant, and there's probably hundreds of players I've upset. But I can't think of anyone that sticks out like a crazy maniac. If I don't count Tony."

"Yeah, he's the only one I know." Yarah giggled, then her eyes lit up. "Hey, going back to lover-boy, tell me all the juicy stuff."

Jaz huffed and walked to the patio door. "You were right. I called him last night to tell him what happened, and a woman answered the phone."

"Yeah, then what?" She rubbed her hands together, totally absorbed.

Jasmine glared at her. "This is heartbreaking not exciting."

Yarah let her face droop. "Is that better?"

"Yes." Jasmine went on. "Anyway, she said, 'it's for you, lover-boy,' and then there was a long pause and a lot of breathing. I mean a lot of breathing and then he said hello."

"So maybe he just ran in from outside."

"Nice try. He confirmed it this morning—it's over."

"I'm sorry. What did he say?" Yarah walked over and put her arm around Jaz.

"Nothing worth remembering."

"Well, it could've been worse."

Jaz looked at her with glassy eyes. "How's that?"

"If Jerome hadn't come to check on you, who knows what would've happened."

"I know. I feel sick when I think about it. Yarah, I'm really scared, but I'm just as depressed."

Yarah's somber eyes gradually widened with thrill. "I've got just the cure!"

"If you do then we'd be bazillionaires," Jaz said in an apathetic tone.

"Listen, remember that cop from California that always plays at your game? You know the one. He keeps buggin' you to go out with him?" Her eyes sparkled with her ingenious plan.

"You mean Stan?"

"Yeah! There's no better cure than the hair of the dog that bit you."

"Hair of the dog? This isn't a hangover!"

"I know, I know, but it's the same rule. If a man hurts you, it takes another man to get over him. It's female law 101."

Jaz wagged her head. "I don't think so. I've had enough of those three-legged monsters. They're just a heartache waiting to happen, and my heart can't handle one more."

Yarah laughed. "Come on . . . besides he's a cop! He could protect you from that lunatic, and who knows, maybe catch him!"

Jasmine knew Yarah wouldn't let up until she changed her mind. "Okay, next time he comes in I'll take him up on it, but only on one condition."

"What's that?"

"I'll have him bring a friend and we'll double date. If I'm doing it so are you."

"No! You need the cure—not me."

Jaz raised her chin and folded her arms. "Then forget it."

"All right, all right." They chuckled and slapped palms. "Well, I guess I better go and let you get some rest."

"Probably should, doctor's orders."

Walking to the door, Yarah turned and pointed. "Stay out of trouble."

"I'm trying," Jaz sighed as she left. Then she climbed into bed and stared out the patio door. Her eyes wouldn't shut as the blue sky beckoned her for a breath of fresh air. It had been awhile since she'd sat outside to relax, and the tug was overwhelming.

Throwing the blanket off, she walked out onto the balcony and gazed at the sparkling lake below. The water looked so cool and tranquil, yet her thoughts were hot and fractious, taking her against her will to Frank. She envisioned the way he looked at her, kissed her and touched her after the meeting, as if he still had feelings for her. Just not enough to keep him faithful. *He's probably seeing his lover tonight!* Her nails gripped the railing as she shook her head, trying to shun the visual of them in bed. Yarah's idea of going out with Stan might be just what she needed to block out his betraying face.

Now completely awake and unable to sleep, she came back inside and looked at the clock. The kids weren't expected back until five. With that, she threw on a sweater and left to take a stroll through the casino. As she entered the pit—the pit of death. She noticed her blackjack table had been removed, and a patch of new carpeting was in its place. An eerie voice whispered: *"If I lose this hand I'll kill myself."*

Feeling sweat bead on her forehead and stomach sour, she turned to leave when Tony came strolling up to her. She took a breath, preparing for his cynical lambasting. "Hi Tony."

"What do ya know; the casino queen is up and about."

She smiled, angling her head. "I thought you were off for a week."

"No, just a day. Can you imagine all the happy bubbly people around this fuckin' joint if that happened?" He gave her a perplexed once-over. "You don't look so good. Did the doc release you?"

"He said he would in the morning." Then she put a hand on her hip. "So what's wrong with the way I look?"

"I don't know—somethin's missin'. He shrugged. "But hey, who am I to say, I'm missin' about twelve inches." He laughed.

Jaz was taken aback by his jovial mood and cracking a joke, especially about himself. Then it came to her. "You seem happy, maybe a lady in your life?" She smiled teasingly.

He shuffled up to her nose-to-nose. "Let me tell you about me and the dames. The only time they make me happy is when I *pay* them to make me happy! And this ain't the time or place. Ya got it?" Jasmine nodded, taking a step back from his hot breath. "Then I'll see you in the morning." He turned.

"Wait a minute." His head pivoted around. "Can you stick me somewhere easy? I'm not up for the frontline yet."

He folded his arms, and rocked back on his heels. "You want somethin' easy? Hmm . . . okay. You and the Big Six, all week, easy enough?"

She shrugged and gave a cockeyed smile. "I guess I asked for it."

"It ain't too late to change your mind."

"No, I'll take it."

He shook his head and left.

Frank returned to his office after the grueling, heart-ripping meeting to tackle the next thing on his agenda. He sat down and rang Paul's office.

"This is Paul."

"Paul, it's Frank. I need to talk to you. Are you busy?"

"If it's about that kid, Randy, I had a talk with him. He's no longer here."

"Did he explain what he meant?"

"Yeah, and he said he was sorry. He was just hustlin' a toke."

Frank thought about it. Maybe he did overreact. All the chaos going on had driven him to the brink of paranoia. "I appreciate you speaking to him, but you didn't have to fire him."

Paul stamped out his cigarette. "Those guys are a dime a dozen. Who gives a fuck?" He pulled out another and lit it. "Hey, what's the status on that dealer we sent home? You have an update?"

"As a matter of fact I do. Dr. Jensen brought her here last night. Apparently when he went to check on her, he saw a prowler snooping around her house."

"A prowler? Did he call the police?" Paul asked anxiously.

"Yeah, two detectives were just here to take a statement from him and Ms. Woods." Frank was careful to keep all names formal. The less information, the less conspicuous.

Paul blew out a stream of smoke. "Talk about a black cloud. A shooting—a prowler. Next thing you know, she'll be in the obituaries."

Frank felt his knees buckle. "Let's hope not."

"All right, so is that it, because I have a shit-load of work to do before the daily count." Paul wheezed out of breath.

"Yeah, that's it. I'll let you go." They hung up.

Paul sat back, stamped out his cigarette and picked up the phone.

He had to make an urgent call.

"Yeah?"

"Sumo, it's Paul. We need to talk. Meet me at the Ridgeway Diner. It's on Highway 80 heading west about half an hour out of town. I'm on a tight schedule, so don't be fuckin' late!" He slammed down the phone, grabbed a full pack of cigarettes out of the top drawer of his desk and slid them inside his suit jacket.

Reaching for his cane, he stood with a grunt and lumbered to the elevator. He glanced back over his shoulder, hoping to slip out of the hotel without anyone noticing, specifically Frank. It was crucial he meet with Sumo and warn him to back off. Knowing the police were involved changed everything. The chances of Sumo getting caught and implicating him was a risk he wasn't taking.

Paul pulled into the gravel parking lot of the Ridgeway Diner. To his surprise, Sumo was there waiting for him. "What do ya know, he's early," he murmured and parked next to him. They exchanged nods then sauntered inside the restaurant like two butcher-ready hogs.

The diner was quaint with family photos hanging along the walls of hunting and fishing trips. Their prized trophies were mounted with the name and picture of the proud sportsman next to it. Paul remembered it fondly when he stopped in for lunch one day on his way to San Francisco. The pictures reminded him of the hunting trips he had with his father before his crippling accident.

Sumo pushed his chair aside, grabbed a wooden bench from the entrance and sat down. Paul took the petite vase of daisies off the table and placed it on the table next to them. He picked up the menu. "The chili is good. Real spicy if you like it that way."

"I don't want the fuckin' chili. I want this job done and get out!" Sumo ranted.

Paul grabbed his wrist. "That's why I called this little meeting. You almost got caught!" He leaned over the table, his saggy jowls jiggling. "I just found out the police are involved. You need to disappear and somewhere far."

Sumo jerked his wrist free. "I get paid first."

"For what? You don't have the girl. You're goddamn lucky to be alive, let alone get paid. If it wasn't for my daughter posing as a nurse, Marco would have checked you out his way. I saved your big fat ass!"

Sumo shook his head. "But you don't know Marco. When he wants a job done, he expects it done."

"What's the big deal about this woman, anyway?" Paul said, shaking out a cigarette.

"You don't know who Jasmine Woods is?" Sumo asked quizzically.

"Yeah, she's a dealer at the Palace. Other than that, Marco told me nothin'." Paul lit his cigarette and pointed it at Sumo. "Personally, I don't give a fuck who she is. I just want the money."

Sumo kept his eyes steady and his mouth shut. If Marco didn't tell him anything, then that's the way he wanted it. "Well, her perfume almost killed me. And I don't want to end up in the hospital again."

Paul leaned over the table. "Then back off! The heat's on, and I'm not goin' down with you."

"So what are you gonna do?"

"I'll come up with something. Now let's eat." He flagged down the waitress. "We'll take the chili with lots of onions and cheese." He sat back and rubbed his hands together.

The young girl batted her big brown eyes. "I'm sorry, sir, but we're fresh out."

TWENTY

When Frank arrived home, Clive and the dogs met him at the door. "Good evening, sir. They couldn't wait to greet you." He stepped back and gasped. "Good grief, you look dreadful."

Frank looked in the foyer mirror and pinched his pasty, pale cheeks. His eyes were bloodshot and his face lined with anxiety. "Truthfully, I feel worse than I look," he uttered.

"If you don't mind me saying so, you need some rest."

"I need a drink."

Clive looked up and huffed. "I'll get you one, but please go relax for goodness sakes."

Frank lumbered to his office with the dogs following close behind. They stayed outside the door as he went in and sank into his chair.

Resting his head back against the cushioned leather, Clive returned with his drink. "Sir, your scotch neat." He walked over and handed it to him. "However, a bed would do much better," he murmured then turned and left.

Frank swirled the amber liquor, lost in thought, noticing the light on the message machine was blinking. He pushed the button, taking a swallow. *"Frankie—Geno. I made a few calls. Yeah, your man Tommy Tanaka is working for Marco, but no word yet if there's a contract's out on your senorita. I'll call when I know more. Later."* Frank squeezed his glass until it shattered, cutting his hand. He watched a trickle of blood slowly drip to his desk and hissed, "Your blood is next, Sumo."

Leaving his office, he took Clive's advice and went to his bedroom. Collapsing on top of the satin spread, his eyes grew heavy and gradually closed. Deep into sublime darkness he drifted, and then a goddess appeared. She gracefully walked up to him dressed in a flowing white gown. Her hair swirled over her shoulder like rich, dark honey. He stroked her creamy skin, letting his fingers linger over her delicate face.

As he slowly lowered his lips onto hers she suddenly turned into a black-haired witch. His eyes snapped open. *Mimma! Eight o' clock!* Feeling the effect of his scrambled brain, booze and sleep deprivation, he was in no condition to see her tonight. He pushed the intercom button.

"Yes," Clive answered.

"If a woman calls for me, I'm not in." Frank knew positively that Jasmine wouldn't be calling.

"Very well, sir. Would you like supper tonight?"

"No, I'm not hungry."

"Should you need anything else, I'll be in my room reading. I'm right in the middle of a superb mystery novel."

"All right." Frank went back to bed, eager to see Jasmine again. For now, it was the only place he could touch and hold her the way he longed to.

Paul shuffled to his office, relieved to have returned without anyone knowing he'd left. Hanging his cane on the arm of his chair, he sat with a heavy sigh. It was now up to him to figure out how to finish the job on his own. He knew by Marco's reputation, Sumo's warning wasn't to be taken lightly. Though his offer was enough money to retire comfortably, it was contingent when the job was done. Then his squinty eyes grew round. *How convenient that she is staying at the hotel.* He picked up a pack of cigarettes, lit one and called Marco to apprise him of the fortuitous development.

"Yeah?"

"Marco, it's Paul. I have some very interesting news."

"It better be. I'm eating my dinner."

Paul hunched over his desk, resting on his elbows. "The woman you want is staying here at the hotel. This could work to our advantage. The closer the better, you know?"

Marco set his fork down, wiped his mouth and rose to his feet. His eyes grew red and his finger jabbed. "I'm tired of waiting! I came to you because I thought this would be a simple task—you being the casino manager and her being your dealer. But apparently she keeps outsmarting you idiots." He pounded his fist on the table. "I don't care *how* you do it or *where* you do it; just bring her to me!" Marco slammed down the phone.

Paul glared at the phone then hung up. With a fast swipe, he latched onto his cane and hobbled out of his office to the elevator. He got off at the front lobby then waddled over to the registration desk. "Hey, Anna."

"Yes, Mr. Cusimano?" she replied politely.

"Can you look up a guest for me? Her name is Jasmine Woods. What room is she in?"

The young attendant quickly scanned through the hotel registry. "Here she is, room 3030."

Paul jotted down the number. "3030," he mumbled to himself. He gave the girl a nod and limped away to the parking garage.

Jasmine and the kids had just finished dinner in the coffee shop and were leaving when they ran into Jerome. "Well hello," he said, acknowledging all their faces with a wide smile. "I was just heading up to my room to give you a call, but this is better. How are you feeling?" he said to Jasmine.

"I feel great." She smiled, shooting him a look and then at the kids. Jerome immediately caught on that she hadn't disclosed the details with them. "Yeah, we just had dinner, and now we're heading up to the room to watch TV."

Justin interrupted. "Mom, who is this man?"

"Don't you remember Dr. Jensen? He brought us here last night."

Justin shook his head. "Not really. I think I was still asleep."

"Then let me introduce you again." Jaz waved her hand. "Dr. Jensen, this is Justin and Shauna."

Jerome shook Justin's hand. "Hi, you can call me Jerome." Then he shook Shauna's hand.

"I remember you," she said.

"That's good, and I remember you." He smiled.

"Mom said bugs were trying to get in our house, so we're having it extra-mated," Justin said.

"You mean exterminated?" Jerome chuckled.

"Yeah, that, but I think we're going home tomorrow."

Shauna gave Justin a nudge. "You don't have to tell everyone about our bugs."

Jasmine quickly took over. "Well, we'd better be going. Say good-night to Dr. Jensen, kids."

"It was nice to see you again," Shauna said.

Jasmine looked down at Justin. "I don't remember seeing you before, but it was nice to meet you."

"Nice to meet you, too." He patted his shoulder. "You're very lucky," he said to Jasmine.

"Yeah, I think I'll keep 'em."

"Well, have a nice night. Oh, and I'll have that release ready for you in the morning."

Jaz angled her head. "Is it possible to get it tonight? I'm taking the kids to school in the morning, and I'd hate to miss you."

"Sure. What time?"

She looked at her watch. "Say about . . . eight-thirty."

"No problem; I'll bring it to your room." He started walking then turned. "Hey, would you like to meet me at the Kazbah for a glass of wine instead?"

"Sure, that sounds great. I'll see you there, same time."

As they walked away, Shauna looked back at Jerome and tugged on her mother's sleeve. "Mom, he's cute, and a doctor!"

Jaz glanced back at him. He was all that. Yet to her, he looked like another man and another heartache.

Paul went home to conjure up a foolproof plan. After three cigarettes and three vodka gimlets, he came up with something that would play on her compassion. First, he would turn off the surveillance cameras on her floor. Then he would go to her room and inform her that a detective contacted him and needed to investigate her home. When she arrived, he would be there to assist in the investigation. *She shouldn't be suspicious of that.* Then he would trip, claiming he injured his bad leg and needed immediate medical attention. Feeling compassionate, she would drive him. Then he would pull out a gun and personally deliver her to Marco himself. He let out a raspy chuckle. "Malibu, here I come."

CHAPTER

TWENTY-ONE

Shauna and Justin were settled in for the night, along with strict instructions not to open the door for anyone, no matter what. Jasmine showed them how to dial the hotel operator, if they needed her, and more importantly to chain the door after she left. After a quick glance in the mirror and a puff of perfume, she went to the door. "Okay, I won't be long and remember—"

"We know, Mom. Don't open the door for anyone," Shauna said.

"And lock the chain." Jaz waved a kiss good-bye and left after hearing the chain slide through the latch.

Standing at the doorway of the Kazbah, she looked around for Jerome and decided to peek inside. It was decorated in Arabic décor with large, colorful rugs, beaded curtains, and the tables sat low with tasseled pillows for seating. She walked back out just as Jerome had arrived. "Hi, I was looking for you."

He smiled. "I thought *I* was early."

"You are—we both are. I was just a little anxious to get out after napping most of the day."

"How do you feel?" He touched her shoulder while his eyes caressed every feature of her face, lingering long over the golden high-lights of her fresh ripened strawberry hair.

"Actually, I feel great." She was looking forward to relaxing with a glass of wine, but mainly to set her eyes and mind on someone other than Frank. He had a way of completely consuming her thoughts, and she needed a break.

"Wonderful. Shall we go in?" Jerome opened the door as Jasmine walked through. "This looks interesting," he said, looking around.

"You may want to pick somewhere else, unless you don't mind sitting on the floor," Jaz said.

"I don't know. It looks kind of fun. How about you—do you mind sitting on the floor?"

"No, but I'm glad I didn't wear a skirt."

"You and me both." He chuckled.

The waitress approached them dressed in a jeweled bikini top and bottoms with a sheer flowing skirt. A chain of coins looped around her waist jangled melodically as she moved. "Come right this way," she said and escorted them to a corner table then gestured with her hand to sit on the pillows.

Kneeling down next to them, she lit the candle on the table as her bronzed breasts heaved amply over the gold beaded bra. "Take a moment to look over the menu, and I will be right back." Her allur-ing lips and dark painted eyes momentarily averted their attention from her exposed, glistening skin. Then she glided away.

"Quite authentic," Jerome said, looking around again. The room flickered with musk scented candles, casting an exotic sultry ambiance of glimmer and smells. Then his eyes gradually set on Jas-mine's face, illuminated softly by the candle's glow. "This might sound forward, but you look beautiful tonight."

She smiled, appreciative of his candor. "Thank you." He looked handsome, too. His blonde hair was loose and natural, and his deep blue eyes sparkled against his black dress shirt. Then, like that, her mind wandered off to Lover-Boy and what he was doing or rather *who* he was doing. Unconsciously, she shook her head to rid the thought.

Jerome noticed. "Are you all right?"

"Oh, um, my hair was tickling my face."

Just then the waitress jangled back to take their order. "Have you decided?" She batted her long thick lashes and parted her shimmery, tinted lips.

Jerome looked at Jasmine. "What would you like to drink?"

"Just a glass of merlot, please."

"Make it two," Jerome said.

The waitress nodded. "I'll be right back." As she floated off like a gypsy in the night, Jerome began recounting the events of his stay, some of which were perilous while others memorable and poignant.

While he spoke, Jasmine saw beyond his strong, forthright exterior to a man of gentle and genuine kindness. He seemed unreal, or maybe she had been hurt so many times she didn't know a man possessed those attributes. But there was something else—something that reminded her of her father. He exuded with such ease, a sense of security and true honesty that she unexpectedly sighed out loud. Jerome smiled and his dimples creased deep.

"Did you hear that?" she whispered.

"It's all right. I liked it."

"I think I needed this."

"I think we both did." Their eyes danced together by candlelight, each entranced in their own thoughts. "I almost forgot." He reached into his upper jacket pocket and pulled out a piece of paper. "Here's your release, signed and ready to go."

"Thanks." She took it and put it inside her purse.

Just then, the waitress was back with their wine. Bowing down, she set the glasses on the table and smiled seductively at them. "What can I get you to eat?"

"Are you hungry?" Jerome asked Jasmine.

"No, I'm still full from dinner."

"I guess we're fine." After the waitress left, Jerome held his glass up to Jasmine. "I know this may sound trite, but here's to your health."

They clinked to his toast and took a hearty sip. Setting his glass down, he clasped his hands. "It was nice seeing Shauna and Justin again. I really didn't get a chance to talk to them before. They seem like great kids."

"Thanks, they are." Jasmine wasn't sure what more to say, remembering the topic of children struck a nerve with him.

"I guess they're comfortable with you being out tonight?"

She nodded. "They're pretty easy going. I think the divorce instilled a resiliency. Nothing really upsets them." She took a sip of wine. "No such luck with me. It did the opposite. I have a tendency to be overly cautious."

"As you should be," Jerome said as his eyes held firm with hers. "Is their father involved in their lives?"

"No, but I try to reassure them he still cares and loves them, which is difficult to believe when he never calls." Her eyes descended.

He squeezed her hand, seeing her obvious frustration. "I'm sure having a mom like you, they'll be just fine."

She smiled. "I try, but there is one thing a mom can't do."

"What's that?"

"Replace a dad."

His glassy eyes expressed his sympathy. Then someone came to mind as well as his character. "What about Frank? Is he good with your children?"

Jasmine was caught off guard. She shook her head. "He really didn't have a chance to get involved with them." Then she quickly changed the direction to avoid Frank's tenacious spell. "What about you? I'm surprised you're not married with kids," she inquired, trying to reopen that door.

His eyes drifted away, and the silence translated his visible pain. "That's a long story . . . one for another day." It was obvious he was not ready to let her near his personal life. "Tell me about Montana. It must've been a beautiful place to live." Both avoided the topics that changed their mood.

She welcomed the new subject, exhaling internally. "Let's see . . . I lived on a ranch near the city of Missoula. We raised Arabian horses, and at one point we had eleven, including the foals." Jerome sipped his wine and listened as if she were reading him a bedtime story. "Just down the road from us, Crown stables held show clinics every Saturday. It had always been a dream of mine to have a show horse. So, I thought, why not. And guess what?" Her sapphire eyes raced. "One of my fillies took a blue ribbon in every show, even won the West Coast Regional."

He set his wine down. "Wow, that's great."

She looked down. "It was . . . and then life goes on."

He saw her slipping away with the fond memory. "That must have been quite a sacrifice, leaving all that behind."

Her eyes met his. "Probably the hardest thing I've ever done. But through it all, I found out sacrificing makes you appreciate what you're striving for."

"Tell me, what are you striving for?" he asked, captivated.

A playful smile curled. "I guess everyone is allowed to dream, right?"

"I try to at least once a day." Little did Jasmine know she was casting a spell of her own, and he was being swept away like a bird in a storm.

She closed her eyes and smiled. "I dream of a life surrounded by peaceful beauty and every day you wake up happy." She looked over at him. "It's out there . . . somewhere."

Just then flute music wafted through the subdued crowd, and a belly dancer appeared. Her tambourine jingled as she weaved through the tables, slinging her hips at the low-seated crowd. The night was exactly what Jasmine needed, and as they relaxed in each other's company, sipping their wine and watching the dancer, a voice came over the paging system.

"Jasmine Woods. Paging Jasmine Woods. Please call the operator."

Her eyes darted to Jerome. "That must be my kids!" She jumped off the pillow and frantically hurried to the hostess. "I'm Jasmine, where's the phone!?"

"It's on the pillar over there." She pointed.

Jaz ran to the phone and dialed the operator. "I'm Jasmine Woods!"

"Let me connect you to security."

A man's voice answered. "This is security."

"Yes, this is Jasmine Woods. What's wrong?" Her voice trembled.

"Apparently someone tried to break into your room. Luckily, the kids called the operator, and she immediately informed us. The person was gone by the time we arrived."

"I'll be right there!" Jasmine hung up and saw Jerome standing next to her anxiously waiting to hear what happened. "Someone tried to break into our room. I've got to hurry!"

They rushed through the casino, bustling past the meandering crowd. When they arrived at the room, the door was open a crack. Jaz pushed through and saw two security guards sitting at the table with the children.

"Mom!" The kids ran up to her. "It was so scary," Shauna cried. "There was a knock at the door, and we thought it was you, but when I asked who was there, they didn't answer. Then they tried to unlock the door." The kids clung to her side, whimpering in fear.

"It was a good thing they locked the chain," one of the security guards said. "I guess when the person realized they couldn't get in they took off."

"The stalker knows I'm staying here!" Jasmine cried out. Then she looked at the security guards. "The cameras in the hallway. They'll have a picture of who this is."

"We already checked and for some reason they weren't working." He shrugged.

"What's a stalker, Mom?" Justin asked timidly.

Jaz realized she'd announced the reality of her nightmare. She wrapped her arms around both children. "There's a man that's been following me. I thought it would be safer if we stayed at the hotel."

Jerome added, "But the police are going to find him and make sure this doesn't happen again."

"So we don't have bugs?" Shauna asked.

Jaz stroked her hair. "I'm sorry. I just didn't want you and Justin to be frightened."

A security officer interjected. "So the police know about this person?"

"Yes, they know," Jasmine said.

"Well, to be safe, I'd check out of this room," the officer said.

"Mom, you're Wonder Woman, remember? Nobody's gonna hurt you," Justin said.

"You're absolutely right. This guy doesn't know who he's dealing with, does he?" She tried to subdue their fear as well as her own.

"Listen, I have a suite with two rooms. Why don't you stay with me?" Jerome said.

"That's probably a good idea, ma'am," the security officer said.

"Please Mom, please," both children begged.

"All right but just tonight."

After Jaz and the kids gathered up their things, they went with Jerome to his suite. He led them to their room to get situated then left and went out to the balcony. Shauna and Justin cuddled together in one bed as Jaz sat down next to them. She kissed their cheeks and tucked the blanket around them. "Everything will be okay. You get some sleep, and I'll be back in a few minutes." They nodded and closed their eyes. Taking the blanket off her bed, she wrapped it over her shoulders and went to the terrace to find Jerome.

He was looking out over the dark, glittering sky and turned when he felt her presence. "Are they all right?"

"I think so." She came up next to him.

He shook his head. "I don't know what to do. I feel so helpless."

"So do I." Tears began welling. "I'm about ready to pack up and grovel my way back to Montana. I don't know if I can take this any longer."

He rubbed her quivering shoulder. "I've made up my mind; I'm not leaving until I know you're safe."

"You don't need to do that," she whimpered.

"Yes, I do."

Lying with his eyes open, listening to the phone ring, Frank's head pounded and body stiffened knowing Mimma would be furious if he wasn't home. To compromise his plan now would be foolish. He had no choice but to complete his mission. Lifting the phone, he heard Clive rambling through his rehearsed answer. "Thanks Clive, I've got it."

"Oh, I thought . . ."

"I'm back."

"Very well." He hung up, looked up and went back to his book.

"What was *that* all about?" Mimma asked.

"Just a misunderstanding. So how are you?"

She was in her room primping with the finishing touches. "I'm almost ready. I miss you, and I can't wait to see you." She blotted her lips on a tissue then pursed them in the mirror.

"I know, I miss you too, but I'm really tired. Can we make it another night?"

Her eyes narrowed. "No! I want to see you tonight. And I was just about to leave." Then her red lips curled. "But I have an idea that might change your mind." She smiled devilishly at herself in the mirror. "How does a nice hot bubble bath and massage sound . . . hmm, darling?"

Frank closed his eyes and let out a futile sigh. "I have to say that does sound nice, but I've had a long day and will probably just fall asleep on you." He gave it one last try to beg out without her recognizing his desperate plea.

Mimma stomped. "I'm not taking no for an answer." Then she hung up and left the house.

Frank pushed the intercom button.

"Yes?"

"Mimma will be here soon, and I'll get the door."

"Is there anything else you'll be needing from me?"

"No, I can handle it . . . at least I think I can."

"Good night, then."

"Good night." Frank sat up and ran his fingers over his five o'clock shadow. He grinned. *She's gonna hate this.* Reaching down, he peeled off his thin gray socks, unbuttoned his white dress shirt and let it hang open. Heading down to the study, he turned on the surveillance monitor then went to pour a drink. It had come to the point where nothing was working to alleviate his stress, not even his scotch.

After downing one, he poured another just as the doorbell chimed. Grumbling under his breath while taking a long swallow, he strode to the foyer to get the door and glanced up at the monitor to see Mimma fussing with her hair while applying lipstick. Giving her a moment, he opened the door. "Hi baby."

"Hello darling." Her eyes wandered from his sexy smile to the black hair that trailed over his dark, olive chest and down his trousers. "Don't you look delicious," she said, sweeping a finger across his chest and entered.

"So do you." He sauntered down the long marble hallway with the tails of his shirt flying to each side. Mimma's high heels clicked right behind him.

"Where are we going, darling?" she asked excitedly.

"Upstairs to the bedroom," he said without stopping. He was going to do what had to be done and as fast as possible.

"You don't waste any time. You bad boy."

Frank had only one thing on his mind: comply and say goodbye. It wasn't just sex anymore. It was a game with only one winner. He entered his bedroom and headed straight for the bathroom to draw a bath.

Mimma kicked off her heels and followed him inside. "You feeling dirty?" she whispered in his ear.

"This is for you." He leaned over, twisted the gold knob and hot water rushed from an arched faucet into a marble oval tub.

"I thought you liked dirty girls," she purred, stroking his cheek with her red fingernail.

"I like them wet, too." He swirled vanilla bath milk into the steaming water and swished it around. Then he dimmed the lights and lit four large candles at each corner of the tub. Standing back, he crossed his arms, casually posed and said, "Take off your dress."

"Oooh . . . Mimma likes." She squirmed. "Now say it like you mean it."

Frank was amused by her attitude. "I said take off your dress, and do it now!"

Fixated on his penetrating glare, Mimma wrapped her arms around her back and unzipped her dress. Sliding it off her shoulders, she let it fall to the floor. Frank became aroused and went to her. Hooking a finger through her bra strap, he pulled her body close to his. Mimma resisted teasingly, but he scooped her up and set her in the sudsy water.

"Darling, my bra and panties!"

Frank didn't care if she had on her shoes. It was all just a role in the script, one scene at a time. "I'll be right back." He left the room to get a bottle of chilled chardonnay and heard the phone ring.

The intercom speaker buzzed. "I'm sorry to disturb you, sir, but this man insists on talking to you. He said his name is Mr. Tommy Tanaka. Shall I tell him you're unavailable?"

Sumo! "No, I'll take it."

"Darling, where are you? The fun is just beginning," Mimma squealed from the bathroom.

"Just a minute, I have an important call to take. I'll be right back." Frank left the bedroom and went across the hall to a guest room for privacy while Mimma pouted and sank down into the bubbles to wait.

"Hello."

"Frankie, it's Sumo." Frank held his tongue, giving no indication he knew anything.

"Sumo, I've tried to get a hold of you. You're a hard man to reach."

"I've been busy . . . business, you know."

"So, why the unexpected call? What's going on?" Frank fought to remain calm as his fist clenched at his side.

"I have some information. Something you need to know."

"Let me have it," Frank responded cool and fast.

Sumo had his own plan brewing. One way or another he was getting paid. Then he would disappear. "I know some stuff—a lot of stuff! About someone you might say . . . is very close to you."

"How close?"

"Fifty G's."

"That's pretty close."

"Meet me at ten o'clock just past the Y. I'll be parked behind an abandoned gas station. You'll see it."

"Ten at night?"

"Yeah!"

"This better be worth it."

"It is. Just bring the money."

Frank hung up, feeling one step closer to having his arms around Jasmine. Then he heard Mimma call out to him, bringing him back to his servitude. He walked downstairs, opened a bottle of chardonnay, snatched two glasses, and strolled back into the bathroom.

Mimma sat back and smiled, resting a foot on the outer edge of the tub. "I thought you forgot about me, darling." Her knee waved back and forth, enticing his eyes.

"That's impossible."

She splashed water at him, released her bra and slipped off her panties. "Here, this is for you." She tossed the wet bra at his face and he caught it with his teeth.

Like before, his torment began to surface, compelling him to unbuckle his belt and take off his shirt. Naked and rigid, he stepped into the tub with two glasses of wine and nestled between her legs. They each took a sip and fused their lips in a slippery, wet kiss as their bodies rushed and collided beneath the water. The night was an academy award winning performance with nothing but a riveting climax and all for a woman not even there.

TWENTY-TWO

T he smell of fresh brewed coffee stirred deliciously in the air, rousing Jasmine from a restful sleep. She peeked over at the kids and then quietly tiptoed from the room to get a cup.

Jerome was sitting on the terrace reading the paper and sipping his coffee. Jasmine wandered out to greet him. "Good morning," she said, cuddling a cup with both hands.

He turned and saw her standing in the doorway wearing the roomy, white t-shirt she'd borrowed from him last night. Her long bare legs and mussed hair captivated his attention. He set the paper and coffee down on the table and folded his arms, grinning. "I see the t-shirt worked for pajamas."

She held it out. "Yeah, thanks. I'll go back later and look for my nightgown and whatever else we left behind." She sat down, drawing her knees up under the t-shirt and sipped her coffee while entranced by the view. The sun was just beginning to peek over the summit, frosting the lake in shimmery gold. "It's beautiful, isn't it?" she murmured.

"I don't think it's ever looked prettier," he said, gazing at her. "And speaking of pretty, how do *you* feel?"

She turned, feeling his eyes. "I feel wonderful. I haven't slept that good in weeks."

"I'm glad. You'll probably need every ounce of strength just to walk in the casino today."

"I know. I tried yesterday and regretted it." She shuddered. "I don't think I'll ever get those words out of my head." Jerome angled his head. "You know, what the man said before he . . ." She looked down at her coffee.

"Oh, yes." He leaned toward her concerned. "Do you think you can do it? Because if you can't, I'll recommend another day of rest."

"I think I'll be okay. Tony assigned me the Big Six all week, and that's as easy as it gets."

Jerome sat back. "Good. Easy is what you need." As they sipped their coffee in the cool breeze and breathed in the fragrant scent of pine, Jerome noticed her deep in thought. "Something has you thinking," he muttered.

She looked at him, resting her cheek on her knee. "I wish I could go home and get back to my normal routines."

"And what's that?" He was curious about this woman who stirred his dormant body awake.

She closed her eyes, daydreaming of the perfect morning. "I wrap in my robe and take a cup of coffee out to the porch swing. I breathe in the fresh air, listen to the birds . . . pray, think." She chuckled. "Probably too much of that, but it all seems to put me in the right frame of mind."

He knew exactly how she felt. His home and routines were what kept him going every day. "Well, now that the stalker knows you're here, I don't know which place is safer. What do you want to do, stay or go home?"

Her eyes were a persuasive misty-blue. "I want to go home, and I'm sure the kids do, too." She had another reason jabbing at her: to get as far away from Frank as possible.

Jerome sat back. "I have a feeling I couldn't stop you if I wanted to, and I'd probably do the same thing." He set his coffee cup on the table. "Why don't we do this? I'll follow you home and make sure everything is okay, and if all appears safe and undisturbed, then—" Jaz jumped up and put her arms around his neck. "I guess that was the right decision." He chuckled.

Wiggling his big t-shirt down, she pulled away. "I'm glad you understand."

"Understanding is not the problem—worrying about you is."

Her eyes grew big. "Hey, I bet I could get Yarah to stay with me."

"Who's Yarah?"

"My closest and dearest friend. She's always in for a little adventure."

"This is more than a little adventure. Does she know everything that has happened?"

"Yes, and the police said they would patrol my house." She touched his shoulder. "Please don't worry . . . you can go home. I'll be fine."

He placed his hand over hers. "That's a big request, but if you're sure your friend will stay with you, then I will."

"I know she will."

Jerome looked at this watch. "All right, I'll call and catch the next flight out. You better wake the kids."

"It shouldn't take us long. I'll get 'em up and ready right now." She took off to the bedroom.

Jerome nodded, absorbed in the comment he just made. *You better wake the kids.* There was something odd about it, as if he'd said it before. Taking a deep breath and one last gaze at the beautiful setting, he went inside to pack.

Shauna and Justin were following Jasmine around like two zombies, yawning and mumbling in rebellious protest as she busily gathered their things. "I know, I know, I hear you, but we need to have everything packed when Jerome is ready to leave. He's following us to our house before he flies home." She hollered to Jerome to tell him they were checking the other room for anything they missed.

163

"Okay, I'll meet you there in fifteen minutes." When Jasmine and the children left, Jerome experienced a peculiar paternal emptiness. Uncertain of the reason, he tried to shrug it off, but the feeling gripped his heart as he continued to pack.

Jasmine slipped the key in the lock and slowly twisted the silver round door handle. Poking her head in, she took a long look around then entered the room.

"Is everything all right, Mom?" Shauna asked.

"Everything's fine. Just start looking around for anything we missed, and stick it in this bag." She placed a small black suitcase on top of the bed.

Justin started swinging his fists in the air. "It's time for Wonder Woman," he sang out, "pow-pow-pow!" He jumped on the bed and then brought it to a dead stop. Turning to his mother, he asked, "Mom, why does Jerome have to leave? He could stay and protect us."

She gave him a quick smile then opened the dresser drawers. "Because he lives and works in Colorado."

"Maybe he could stay a little longer. Did you ask him?" Shauna pleaded.

"Listen, we'll be just fine, and I'm going to have Yarah stay with us, anyway." She tried to convey a sense of security while desperately trying to believe it herself.

Jerome rapped on the door three times. "Hello?" He pushed the door open wide enough to stick his head inside. "You guys ready?"

Jasmine walked over and pulled it open. "Just about."

Jerome stood with his hands in his pockets, watching them shuffle around the room. "I just don't feel right about this. I don't know what it is, but it's the same feeling I had packing."

Justin figured that was his cue. He walked up to Jerome, wrinkling his freckled nose. "Do you want to stay with us? You can have my room."

Jerome clutched his shoulder. "That's quite an offer, but I can't take your room. People would be coming over at all hours of the night needing me to help them. I don't think you want that, do you?"

Justin shook his head. "No, I guess not." Then his eyes sprang open. "I know—I know! You can have Shauna's room!"

"No way, Justin! I don't want strangers coming in my room, either."

Jasmine stepped in. "No one is giving up their room." She stood between the kids and put her arms around their shoulders as if posing for a photo. "I guess we're ready."

The snapshot prodded Jerome mysteriously. "Then we'd better go," he uttered, latching onto their bags and followed them out the door.

After a very anxious ride up Kingsburg Grade, Jerome pulled into their driveway and scanned the area. From the outside, everything appeared to be in place and undisturbed. He patted Jasmine's hand. "Stay here. I'm going to take a quick look around." He walked the property, over the deck and along the edge of the woods. When he returned, Jaz and the kids were waiting next to the car with their luggage in a pile. "Coast is clear out here, but I want to look inside." After searching every room, he came back and helped them into the house.

Jasmine drew in a breath and smiled as she entered. "Umm, it feels so good to be home again." The kids took off for their rooms while they sat down on the couch. "Thank you so much, Jerome. I really appreciate everything you've done, especially being there for the kids and me."

"I'm glad I was here to help. I care about you." He smiled and his blue eye glistened. "Oh, don't forget to call your girlfriend."

"I won't."

As he stood to leave, a sudden pounding came from the front door. The kids came out of their rooms and ran to Jasmine's side. Jerome held out a hand. "Wait here! I'll get it." He peeked from the living room curtain then hurried to the front door.

"Sir, we have orders to investigate if anyone comes near this house. Do you live here?" Standing before him were two police officers holding a baton in one hand and the other hovering over their gun.

Jasmine overheard the conversation and quickly went to the door. "He's my doctor, Dr. Jerome Jensen. I'm so glad to see you. Are you patrolling my house?"

"Yes, ma'am. We've been instructed to keep your house under constant surveillance. I'm sorry for the inconvenience."

"No, I'm relieved you are. Thank you."

They tipped their heads. "Please don't hesitate to call 911 if you need assistance at any time." They turned and walked away.

"Well, that makes me feel a lot better," Jerome said with a heavy sigh.

Jaz folded her arms. "See, we'll be fine."

Jerome looked at his watch. His awaiting departure didn't allow much time to dally. Standing with a loss for words, an inexplicable pang wrenched his gut. It felt odd leaving them behind, as if they had bonded like a family. He dug in his wallet for a business card to write on but only found an old grocery list. Jotting down his phone number, he handed it to Jasmine. "Just in case you threw away the napkin."

She took the tattered piece of paper and watched a sturdy man become a shy, tenuous boy. "Well, good-bye." He reached out and took her hand, giving it an affectionate squeeze.

She slid it from his grip and wrapped her arms around his neck, giving him a hug instead. "Good-bye," she murmured, slowly pulling away from him.

Jerome walked to the car and turned before getting inside. "If you ask me, Frank is a fool. You're too beautiful of a woman, inside and out, to be treated like that."

Jaz leaned against the door and smiled, watching the little boy change back into a pillar of strength. His words resonated with the same power. He was absolutely right. Frank was a fool.

TWENTY-THREE

Frank burst through the entrance of the Paradise Palace in a combative, unstoppable mindset. His longing for Jasmine gnawed painfully, which intensified his resentment toward Mimma. He had gone above and beyond, obliging her spontaneous demands. Enough is enough! It was time to cut the dangling leash. Tonight, Sumo would be gone, and the clock would stop ticking. Next was Mimma.

Pushing the elevator button, Frank watched it descend to the lobby. When it opened, he hesitated getting in and looked toward the casino. He had to get a quick fix and took off to find Jasmine. Just seeing her was a shot in the arm, bringing him back to life and diligent to his mission.

Strolling from pit to pit, through all the blackjack tables, he finally spotted her dealing the Big Six. Standing in awe, he watched her body move like a willow, swaying back and forth, as an insatiable desire to make love to her overcame him. He wanted to march over and take her right on the table in front of everyone.

Feeling a tenacious draw, Jasmine averted her attention from the game in search of what it was. And there, behind a row of slot machines, was *Lover Boy* in all his pretentious glory. She tried to resist his grip, his stare, but he held her hostage and defenseless as if both hands were tied behind her back.

"Earth to Jasmine," a lady said, tapping a silver dollar on the glass table top.

"Oh, sorry." Jasmine came back to the game and spun the wheel. But that brief moment while held by his grip, she saw flashes of their sweltering passion. They were lying on the couch with a roaring fire dancing off their bodies, embraced in a long, passionate kiss, savoring an irresistible yearning. His hand touched her skin, brushing over her breasts and down . . . *Wait a minute! What was she doing?! He was not going to get away with this—leaving her in a state of limbo—loving him and hating him.* There was only one way to put an end to this: have the last word.

Frank noticed a visible change in her expression. It was not one of love but of contempt. Immediately, he turned and walked to the lobby. All he wanted was a look. He got what he came for and that was enough.

Entering his office, he noticed a handwritten note on his desk. *See me when you get in. Paul.* It wasn't unusual they met to discuss morning issues. Often Paul wanted his opinion with occasional rants or problems in the casino. Frank did the same with hotel issues. They weren't friends but shared a business camaraderie which was mutually appreciated. Frank rapped twice and opened the door.

Paul looked up as his eyes sank into baggy, wrinkled slits. "Frank, come in," he grunted with a cigarette bobbing from the corner of his mouth. "Shut the door and sit." He coughed while waving to enter.

Frank shoved the door with his fingertips. "I'll stand, if that's all right."

"Fine. Just thought you should know the police contacted me. They have a possible suspect with who's been hasslin' our dealer."

Frank now felt like sitting. "Do they know his name?" he asked, maintaining his innocence.

"Not yet." Paul crunched his cigarette and lit another. "But they're on to him. Said they'd call me when they have more information."

"Let me know when they do."

"Should be today or tomorrow."

Frank left Paul's office spinning with perplexity . . . something wasn't right. *Had the police caught up with Sumo, or was Paul in on it too? Maybe this was just a diversion.*

Trying to piece it all together, he sat down at his desk with the intention of refocusing on work, but all he could think about was plotting Sumo's demise. It was time to take him out. With his military background and mercenary assignments, it would be as simple as pulling the trigger. He just needed the right course of action for the execution, which had to be fast, unexpected and not too messy.

Leaving his desk with unfinished work, Frank drove home to prepare for his meeting with Sumo. Careful planning eradicated failure. A lesson to be learned only once. As he whirled into his driveway, Tank and Tasha hurried over to meet him, and together they marched, heel to toe, like three soldiers ready for combat.

Entering the house, Frank went directly to his gun cabinet and unlocked the glass and metal door. Then he pulled a chain attached to a hidden latch which released the backboard. Inside was a priceless collection of rifles, automatic pistols, revolvers, and his faithful partner, Walther PPK. He affectionately gripped the piece and attached the silencer, uttering, "We have work to do." Jabbing the cold, steel barrel down the back of his trousers, he shut the cabinet door and locked it.

A tempest gathered strength as Frank paced his office, rehearsing every last detail of his stratagem. *Can't forget the fifty G's. It's gotta look right. Let him see the money then blow off his fuckin' head.* Punching his fist into his palm, his mind spun with preconceived images of what would happen next. Each step, movement and thought was propelled by his bloodthirsty retaliation.

The money was next. Lifting the Ming vase from the table, Frank pushed the button, and the wall slid open. After unlocking the vault door, he withdrew ten bundles of cash from a wine crate and placed them in a silver briefcase. Then, returning everything precisely back in place, he had to figure out one last step: where to hide four hundred pounds.

The bottom of Lake Tahoe was his best option. But getting Sumo on the boat, without a witness, seemed impossible. Torching the car with Sumo inside was another. Although, the fire and smoke would draw immediate attention. Somehow, he had to contrive his demise without a trace of evidence leading back to him. His eyes opened wide. *I'll bury him on my property. No one will ever find him there.*

With a plan in motion, Frank went to the liquor cabinet and poured a scotch. Downing it in one gulp, he welcomed the burn as it rippled down his throat. Now he was amped and ready for action. Just then a loud crack of thunder struck with surprise. Hurrying to the window, Frank saw dark clouds moving in and circling the valley. A flash of light grazed the sky, and another sharp crack pierced the silence. Within seconds, sheets of rain hit the ground, turning the driveway into a rushing river.

This was not part of the plan, but nothing was going to stop him now. He was getting Jasmine back, and then he was done—ready to start a new life.

Glancing down at his watch, it was 9:15. Time to go. He checked the magazine and silencer on the gun, opened the briefcase and placed it on top. There was no room for one slip-up. Sumo was just as deadly when it came to eliminating the enemy. With briefcase in hand, Frank started out the door just as the phone rang. Clive buzzed him on the intercom.

"Yes," Frank answered quickly.

"Ms. Gamboli is on the phone. Would you like to take the call?"

"No! Tell her I'm not home."

Clive looked up and shook his head. "As you wish."

Frank clutched the case to his chest and ran to his car, bracing against the whipping rain. Setting the briefcase on the seat, he darted to the garage to get one more crucial item. He needed a large sheet of plastic to wrap around Sumo's body. Stains in his trunk would be incriminating evidence.

Casing every corner, he found a large white canvas tarp and quickly unfolded it. He had to make sure it was big enough to do the job. Satisfied, he dashed back to his car and stuffed it in the trunk.

"Okay, that's everything," he murmured to himself and took off into the stormy night.

The road coiled down the mountainside like a black, slippery snake, and pockets of water had created an obstacle course, compromising his time of arrival. Frank dodged the holes and took every curve cautiously. He knew Sumo, and he wasn't leaving until he got paid.

When arriving at the bottom of the grade, Frank depressed a button next to the rearview mirror, and a trickle of light illuminated his watch. It was 9:45. He had fifteen minutes to get there. His nerves turned hard as stone, and his conscience went blank. This was an ingrained process before taking out the enemy. Then he envisioned each step of his diabolical plan. First he would get inside Sumo's car and place the briefcase on his lap. Next, he would wait for the exact time to open the case. Then, without faltering, pull out the gun and put a bullet right between his eyes.

Shifting the mirror, Frank checked to see if anyone had followed him. So far, he was still alone. Up ahead, he spied a gas station with weathered boards nailed over the windows and tumbleweeds rooted between the gas pumps. He slowed down and turned into the muddy driveway, noticing tire tracks leading behind the building. Creeping to the back, he spotted Sumo's car parked inside an open shed.

Sumo saw him and started to open his door, but Frank motioned for him to stay. Not one step could be deviated. Parking close to the building and out of sight from traffic, he pulled on his gloves and latched onto the handle of the briefcase. He could see Sumo watching him like a hawk tracking its prey. Calmly, with the case in hand, he got out and looked side-to-side. Then he crept to Sumo's car and swiftly got inside. Drawing in a breath, he choked on the suffocating stench. "You smell like shit."

"I feel like shit." Beads of sweat were clinging to Sumo's greasy forehead. His clothes were stained and wrinkled. The same attire Jasmine described a week ago. "You have the money?"

Frank's heart raced like a runaway semi. "I have it, but first tell me what you know."

"Show it to me!" Sumo demanded.

Frank couldn't open the briefcase—not yet. "Not until I know it's worth it to me."

Sumo smirked. "Have you been fuckin' some broad named . . . Jasmine?"

Frank wanted to blast him right then for just saying her name. "Who the fuck wants to know?"

"It's Marco, man. He's gonna take whatever he wants and right now it's her."

Frank grabbed Sumo by the collar and shook him. "Why! Why does he want her?"

Sumo pried Frank's hands off him. "Because he knows you fly to Guatemala and wants you to talk."

"What else does he know?"

"Not a lot, suspects you're runnin' guns."

"Nothing solid?" Frank asked, staring into his beady eyes.

"No, and believe me he's tried."

"What about you?"

Sumo grinned. "He doesn't think I know a fuckin' thing. If he did, I wouldn't be sittin' here."

Frank sneered. "So why are you working for him?"

"Money. What else?"

"I didn't think you'd fuck me for him." Frank glared. "And what about Chung Lee—where's he?"

Sumo chuckled. "Probably the easiest ten grand I ever made." Then his eyes went stone cold. "Hear me out. If you don't pay tribute to the boss, that juicy Jasmine won't be fuckin' you no more. Catch my drift?"

Frank's blood boiled. "That's not worth fifty fuckin' G's!"

"No, it's worth a hundred fuckin' G's, but I'm running a special tonight." He burst out laughing.

Frank grasped the briefcase with both hands and flipped open the latches. Sumo had his eyes closed and head tipped back, still humored by his remark. "Here's your fuckin' money." Frank slid his finger around the trigger and pointed the PPK right between his eyes.

Sumo reared back, choking on his last gasp of air. "No Frankie— no!"

Frank gritted his teeth and fired. The magnitude of the shot whiplashed his head, coating the rear window with brains and blood. A gurgle gushed from Sumo's mouth, then his forehead hit the steering wheel. Frank wiped the tiny, red specs off his gun and put it back inside the briefcase.

Scoping the area again, it appeared the rainy night played perfectly to his advantage. The next step was getting Sumo's body from point A to point B. After retrieving the canvas from the trunk, he placed it next to Sumo's door. Then he grabbed hold of his arms and began tugging, but it was like pulling a cement truck out of a mud hole. This required more than sheer strength. It called for absolute and resolute mind over matter.

Stabilizing his stance and digging his heels, Frank willed the dead weight from the seat to the canvas, and Sumo landed in a heap. Stretching him out and then rolling him in the tarp, Frank dragged him to his open trunk. He wasn't stopping with the arduous feat until the final step of the assassination was accomplished.

Slamming the trunk, drenched in sweat, he leaned against his car and uttered, "You're right, Sumo, that *was* worth a hundred fuckin' G's."

TWENTY-FOUR

The dogs ran and barked behind Frank's car as he drove through the entrance gate and circled to the back of the house. He rolled down his window to hush them, though no one lived nearby, and immediately they contained their excitement to a high-pitched whimper, following until he parked.

Exhausted, sitting with his hands glued to the steering wheel, Frank let out a heavy sigh as the dogs anxiously waited for him to open the door.

He forced himself out, patted their heads and opened the trunk. Instantly, they sniffed the scent of fresh blood and began pacing the perimeter of the car as he stared down at the wrapped mound. "To the house," he commanded and pointed. They looked at him determined to stay. "Sorry, not this time." He grabbed their collars and marched them inside the house. He was not taking any chances of them wanting a piece of Sumo.

As he walked back to the car, depleted of energy, he realized the giant dilemma before him. Unless he had a crane, it would be impossible to remove Sumo by himself. He had no choice but to ask Clive for his help. His *mind-over-matter* method was depleted as well. Glancing back toward the house, he saw his bedroom light was still on and went to ask him.

He rapped on his door. "Yes, come in," Clive said, peering above his glasses as Frank entered. "Good grief! What happened to you?!"

Frank was wild-eyed and winded. "Clive, you gotta help me. I didn't want to bring you into this, but I have no choice." He took a deep breath and held onto the door.

"But, I—I."

"Please, I need your help."

Clive sat up and set his book down on the nightstand. He had never seen Frank in such a state of mind. "By the looks of it, you need more than *my* help. You need a hospital!"

"I'm sure I do," he huffed, "but right now, you'll do."

Clive stood. "May I ask what it's for?"

"There's something in my car that I can't get out alone."

"Stop." He held up a hand. "I can assure you, I don't want to know any more. Just give me a moment to change."

Frank waved. "Come like you are. It'll just take a minute."

Clive glared at him, grumbled under his breath, threw on a robe, and followed him outside. When he saw the bulging canvas in his trunk he froze in stride. "Sir, I don't think I can do this." He gulped hard.

"Well, I'm sure as hell not leaving it in my trunk."

Clive didn't say another word and slowly inched forward. He stood and stared quizzically at the canvas. "Not knowing the contents of this massive lump, one could only hope it is nothing more than a snoozing hippopotamus," he muttered.

Frank chuckled. "Good guess." He walked inside the garage and found the wheelbarrow then positioned it next to the back bumper.

Together, they struggled and tugged on the tarp until the body was resting on the edge of the trunk. Then with a guttural heave, Frank pushed while Clive yanked and Sumo dropped with a thud.

Bent over, holding his knees, Clive gasped for air. "Is that it . . . can I go in now?"

"Yes, go back to bed, and keep the dogs inside." Frank wheezed.

Clive wandered back inside the house, shaking his head and mumbling about his job requirements.

Frank slid a shovel next to Sumo's wrapped body, lifted the handles and then proceeded with the final step. Straining with every step, he trudged into the darkness of his five-acre wooded estate. Glimpses of rodents darted from his feet and pine trees clawed at his hair. An owl screeched and swooped overhead, protesting his intrusion. But nothing was stopping Frank until Sumo was six feet under.

Reaching a clearing, he dropped the handles and caught his breath. It was perfect: surrounded by large rocks and far from any civilization. Planting his shovel, he began digging a hole large enough to engulf his nightmare. Then he pushed the wheelbarrow to the opening, raised the handles and watched as Sumo flopped into his coffin of dirt. When the last shovel of soil was tossed, Frank gazed down at the freshly turned grave and muttered, "Sorry Sumo, but you didn't have a fuckin' prayer."

Yarah agreed to stay with Jasmine until the stalker was caught. It was now day five and Jasmine woke feeling a sense of normalcy. Her visit yesterday to the Douglas County police department helped ease her mind. Sergeant Mitchell informed her there had been no report of a person fitting the perpetrator's description anywhere, but they would still keep an APB on him. He also assured her they had a drive-by surveillance status on her house for another couple weeks.

"We'll be right back," Jasmine called to Yarah as she was heading out the door to take the kids to the bus stop.

"Take your time," Yarah hollered back. She was still in bed relishing a moment of peace and quiet. She had never been the kid type and justified her lack of interest with one profound statement: *"Can't have them, so why want what you can't have?"* It was never discussed why she couldn't, and Yarah respected Jasmine for that. Her private life was just that—private.

When Jasmine returned, they took a cup of coffee out to the porch swing and talked about the positive things in their lives which soon digressed to a less popular topic: work. Relenting to its necessity, they pushed off the swing and went in to get ready for eight hours of it.

"It's time to go!" Yarah bellowed at the door. Jaz came from her room, slung her purse over her shoulder and grabbed the keys. "Wait a minute. I'm going to work. Where are you goin'?"

"What do you mean?" Jaz said, shrugging her shoulders.

"By the looks of it, you're tryin' to impress somebody . . . maybe *lover-boy?*" Yarah smiled, gloating with her astuteness.

"Have you lost your mind? I could care less about Frank! He's nothing but an egotistical, male chauvinist, lying, cheating, don't even get me started!" She took a breath, calming her instant flare-up.

"Geez, I think I saw your lungs."

"Sorry. It's just that he won't let me go. I caught him staring at me the other day, and it brought up all these memories that I wish I didn't have."

"Maybe *you* won't let *him* go. Ever think of that?"

"Believe me, I'm trying but he's sooo . . ." She stomped her feet and slapped her sides. "See!?"

"Girl, you got it bad. My mama use ta say: 'A man that good-lookin' is just one lie away from the truth.'"

"Well, your mama's right. He had me believing that Prince Charming was actually real, but now I know he's still just a fairytale." The cuckoo clock began chirping, and Jaz looked up. "It's almost nine. We better go."

Yarah glared at the bird as it reeled back inside. "You better hide, if you know what's best."

Frank arrived at the Paradise Palace early and invigorated. He had regained new life from one momentous death. In the drug world, it was survival of the fittest. People could disappear at any time of any day. The way he saw it: it was Sumo's day.

Mimma, on the other hand, wouldn't be as easy to eliminate. This required the tools and skills of a specialized surgeon. When all was finished, not a hint of scarring left in sight.

He reached for the phone to call Paul and find out the latest report on Sumo. His answer would confirm if he was involved or not.

"This is Paul."

"Paul, it's Frank. I was wondering if you've heard back from the police."

Paul sat up, hacked and then stamped out his cigarette. "You seem pretty curious. Is there a reason?"

"Not really; just following up on my report for the detectives."

The last time Paul spoke to Sumo he had ordered him to disappear. He searched for an answer. "Yeah, they called me yesterday. "I guess they spotted him in Arizona somewhere. Wanted for burglary, rape— a list of shit." He paused to light a cigarette. "Damn, I can't remember his name, but he's our man. Big guy: three to four hundred pounds. Probably in fuckin' Mexico by now." Paul let out a raspy cackle.

"Good to hear. Thanks for the update."

"No problem." Paul hung up and blew out a stream of smoke with his eyes fixated on the wall. *Marco promised him he'd be leaving all this bullshit behind. But it was getting too difficult, possibly deadly, if he didn't get the girl.* A trickle of sweat pierced the corner of his eye, and then a hot poker stabbed at his chest. Dropping his cigarette, he jerked at his tie as his lungs labored for air. He called out for help, coughing with every attempt. His eyes bulged, his hands reached, kicking and thrashing he fell to the floor. With one last struggle and one last breath, his dream, his fear, his body let go.

Frank sat back in his chair, consumed in thought. Paul was lying but why? He wasn't the type to get involved in something risky or dangerous. Bitter and impatient he was, but he wasn't deviant. Then he remembered what Mimma said. Jackpot! He's the rat. *So my five grand a month wasn't enough to keep him quiet. That could only mean one thing: Marco's money was. I'll take care of him later. Right now, on to Mimma.*

Frank decided to take a jaunt through the casino. It usually cleared his mind, and Jasmine's face fueled his fire. Slipping on his suit jacket, he left his office just when a bloodcurdling scream echoed through the hall.

"Oh my God! Oh my God! Somebody help!" Carla cried hysterically, running from Paul's office.

Frank ran up to the doorway and saw Paul lying next to his desk. One hand was resting on his chest, fingers around his tie, and eyes bulging with fright. He walked up and knelt down next to his head. Reaching with his fingertips, he gently closed his eyes.

"Is he dead?" a voice asked from a crowd at the doorway.

Frank glanced back. "Yeah, he's dead. Looks like a heart attack. Has anyone called an ambulance?"

"I did," Carla whimpered. "Here's a blanket. You might want to cover him up." She handed Frank a thin thermal blanket while holding her hand over her mouth. "I told him he smokes too much . . . I told him," she muttered, shaking her head.

The ambulance came and took Paul away, leaving most in a somber mood. Frank, on the other hand, was thinking two down one to go. After everyone went back to their duties, he strolled through the casino as previously planned.

People were cheering and galloping from one slot machine to the next. Others were laughing and clapping while playing at the tables. There was an illusion of glamour in the casino—a facade in which the people knew nothing but what they saw. Otherwise it would be a crime, and no one wanted to see that.

Scanning the pit for Jasmine, all he wanted was a glimpse, yet she was nowhere in sight. Just then a fragrant breeze came up behind him and then quietly brushed past. His eyes drilled into her back, imploring her to turn around. But she stubbornly kept steady with arms swinging, hips slinging and feet proudly marching. Frank smiled. Even mad she was everything he wanted.

CHAPTER

TWENTY-FIVE

The news about Paul's death saturated the *Tahoe Times*. He had been a resident of Lake Tahoe for forty years. Thirty-five of them he worked at the Paradise Palace and fifteen of those as casino manager. Frank laid the paper down on the kitchen counter and took a sip of coffee, inspired by an idea. Having a wake would present the perfect opportunity to personally meet with Marco.

According to Sumo's last words, Marco had nothing to prove which meant *he* had nothing to hide. A sardonic smile twisted upward as his mind began to scheme. *What better way to rid the attention of a woman than with the attention of another woman? Better yet, with many women.* He would invite a gathering of people from famous to faceless. Mainly the beauties he'd promised to call or sleep with and of course Mimma. It would be a competition, to say the least, and he would be first prize.

He envisioned the fantastically ingenious scene like a boy hitting a homerun. Mimma's jealously would ignite as he embraced, kissed and mourned with all the other beautiful ladies. Her intolerance would torch their so-called love affair. He would, understandingly, let her go and then resume where he left off: in love with the woman of his dreams.

Frank got up to pour another cup of coffee and looked out the window to see Clive chasing after the dogs. Curiously watching him, he thought it was strange behavior for Clive, more so that the dogs wouldn't respond to his command. He set his coffee down and walked out to help with the situation.

Clive stopped to catch his breath and staggered over to him. "Good morning, sir."

Frank angled his head. "Why are you running after the dogs?"

"Oh . . . well, if you must know. The dogs have found something unusual." He took a winded breath. "I haven't gotten close enough to clearly make it out. They've been tossing it back and forth like a bloody badminton birdie. I beg of you, can you lend me a hand?" He panted.

Frank walked toward the squabbling dogs. "Tank—Tasha! Come here!" The dogs aborted their play and stood at attention. Without another word, they obediently marched over to him.

Clive crept up to what had kept them amused for hours and shuddered, cupping his mouth. Frank pointed at the dogs to stay and went to see what was so revolting. Clive stepped back, curling his lips. "Where do you think it came from?"

Frank bent down to examine the object. It was the remains of a finger gnawed to the bone. Without question, it had to be Sumo's. His mind exploded with what other body parts were scavenged from his grave. He had to revisit the site. "Clive, take the dogs inside." He quickly held each dog by the collar and walked them to the house. Frank took out a handkerchief from his pocket and picked up the finger. Chunks of flesh dangled from the bone, and the fingernail was completely chewed off.

With a shovel, he followed the trench the wheelbarrow made on that rainy, ominous night. Today the sky was clear, but the forest was dark and eerie, as if something beyond his imagination was waiting for him. Every step into the wilderness he felt a step closer to danger. Looking up, he saw buzzards circling overhead and knew he was near. Then suddenly an icy shiver raced up his body, and goose bumps rose on his arms.

Next to the gravesite was a mound of dirt no dog could have possibly dug. Only one creature could've done this. The hairy beast that haunted him as a child.

Creeping up to the ravaged hole, deep imprints of long sharp claws were territorially stamped around the outer edge. He peered in and saw the white canvas shredded and blood-soaked. Only bone and clothes were left to identify Sumo's remains. Just then, twigs snapped and muffled angry snorts came from behind him. His body froze with an emotion never allowed—a rule instilled by his father, and a covenant driven into his core by the navy. But this was not just any fear; it was a childhood nightmare that suddenly became real.

He bolted down the path, leaving the shovel behind, running like the little boy in his dreams with flashbacks of those sleepless, tearful nights chasing after him. Terrified, heart pounding against his chest, he weaved through the trees, swatting limbs from his face, leaping over boulders, running for his life until he came upon his finely manicured lawn. Stumbling to the ground, he lay heaving and looked back over his shoulder. The forest was calm. His nightmare was nowhere in sight, and Mother Nature would finish the rest.

TWENTY-SIX

I t was the type of day at the Palace that Jasmine prayed it would be. No jackpots were ringing, no people were screaming, just the hum of the vacuum as a porter swept over the nape of the multicolored carpet.

Feeling a tap on her shoulder, she turned to see Connie's grinning face. "Welcome back to blackjack," she said, crossing her eyes.

Jaz laughed. "I have to say, the Big Six was a nice break. I think I'll request it more often."

"Ha, you're dreamin'. It's only for rehab or punishment, and I'm next." She pointed at her watch. "Go take your break, precious minutes are ticking away."

Jaz headed for the women's lounge to take a quick power-nap. Her quiet time last night was so enjoyable she stayed up until the TV quit airing. When she entered the lounge it was resonating with the usual opinionated chatter. This time it was about Paul Cusimano's death, which she had heard nothing of. Spying Vonda in a huddle of women, she went to find out what happened.

"You didn't hear!?" Vonda gasped, clutching Jasmine's shoulders. "They found him in his office hanging from his tie!"

Jasmine gulped. "Another death?! I think I need to go lie down."

"I'm sorry," Vonda winced, "but you asked."

Jaz walked away thinking: Jerome was right about the hotel. Finding two unoccupied chairs, she sat down on one and stretched her legs over the seat of the other, then rested her head back. As she listened to the drone of rants, it wasn't as annoying this time. In fact, it was just the opposite. The familiar tone lulled her to sleep and into a dream.

It was dark and cold. Her arms were tucked against her body, and her legs were curled close to her chest. There was movement beneath her, bumpy and smelled of gas. She tried to sit up, but the surroundings were too confined. Then she realized she was in the trunk of a car. Hearing Frank's voice, she called out to him. "Frank-Frank, help me! I'm in here."

Feeling a nudge, her eyes snapped open to a cascade of curly black hair and greasy red lips. "Sorry to wake you, dear, but I think you were having a nightmare. Are you okay?"

Jaz sat up and looked around. "Yeah, I'm fine."

The lady was still hunched over her. "You were calling out a name. I think you said Frank, Frank. That's when I woke you."

"Thanks." Jasmine gave her a faint smile. *Great! Now I'm saying his name in my sleep!* After putting the chairs away, Jasmine peered in the mirror at her hair. She wore it up and fastened with a clip. Loose curls fell along her cheeks, framing her face. It was a different look, more chic than usual, and definitely wasn't for Frank as Yarah had claimed.

With a fresh coat of lip gloss, she went upstairs silently praying that her game was the way she'd left it: dead. To Jasmine, a dead game was a moment of rare tranquility, held at a distance from all the greedy chaos.

Entering the pit, she spied Connie standing alone, hands idle, with a complacent look on her face. Jaz joyfully tapped her on the shoulder, grinning ear-to-ear. "Thanks, nice job."

Connie angled her head. "But I didn't do anything."

"My point exactly." Stepping onto the game, Jaz saw Tony leaned against the podium enjoying the tranquility as well. They exchanged a friendly nod, then she felt his presence sneaking up behind her. Before she could turn around, he leaped in front of her and wiggled all ten fingers in her face.

"No more boogie-man?" he said in a low, spooky voice.

She reared back. "So far so good." *If I don't count you!*

"Good to hear." He smiled and turned to leave.

"Hey, real quick, is it true about Paul?" she asked.

He shuffled back. "Quick! What do I look like a fuckin' auctioneer?" His mouth fired off like a welder's torch.

"No, but was he strangled by his tie?"

His eyes narrowed. "Who told you that?"

"You know, the women." She shrugged.

"Heart attack. That quick enough?" His toothpick twirled and teetered.

"Oh . . . that's terrible." Her voice drifted and she looked down.

"Yeah, well, I'm fuckin' next." He stepped closer, pointing his toothpick at her. "So do us both a favor, stay out of trouble. I need my beauty rest and not in the grave!" She nodded, trying to keep a straight face. *Yarah would have argued with that one.*

It was the end of an unusually calm day. No one died. No hurtful insults and no sight of Frank. Jasmine walked into the women's lounge to retire her vest and tie. It was 6:05 p.m. The time of day had miraculous powers in the casino. Just that morning no one was giving thanks to the Almighty and now they were. Then she noticed Yarah wasn't there yet, which was odd since she competed for title of "first out the door."

Throwing on her coat, Jaz was just about to ask if anyone had seen her when a hurricane blew open the door, and she came bursting through with arms and mouth flying in every direction. "Tell me! When did they start putting seat belts on the chairs!?"

Jaz stood back and giggled. "What happened?"

"You wouldn't believe it!" She stomped to her locker. "All I had is one guy—just one guy to get rid of, and then I could close my game!

But noooo he wasn't leaving, even after I beat him seven hands in a row! He just sat there like he was super-glued to the seat!" She jerked her tie from her neck. "Finally, I told him I was gonna throw up if he didn't leave." She grabbed her coat and slammed her locker door.

"Feel better?" Jaz said, grinning.

"Ahh . . . much. Now, let's get out of here!"

Pulling into the driveway, Jasmine saw Shauna and Justin watching out the window for her. She waved to them, and they met her on the porch, giving her a hug and kiss. Whether it was morning, noon or night her kids always made her happy and reminded her to give thanks.

"Hey Mom, were you Wonder Woman today?" Justin asked.

"No, thank goodness. Today was exactly the way I wanted it: easy, quiet and uneventful."

After dinner and TV with the kids, Jaz tucked them into bed, poured a glass of wine and settled on the couch to end the night in the same placid manner.

Taking a sip, she rested her head back in peaceful contentment. And as good as it was, she still felt a void—the void of loving a man.

Giving Frank another chance wasn't a problem with her heart, but there was with her head. A war was going on between them as each defended their territory. Consequently, there was no room for negotiating. It was time to listen to what her head was saying and learn from what her heart was feeling.

TWENTY-SEVEN

amantha was just seven years old and the only survivor of the
family vacation when their station wagon slammed into a jack-
knifed semi-truck on a narrow road in Estes Park, Colorado.

Fortunately, she won't remember the fatal crash or being flown by
helicopter to the Loveland General Hospital, where she was on a sev-
enty-two hour watch after fifty percent of her body was skin grafted
with the sparse remains of her family.

Dr. Jensen specialized in skin grafting and deemed one of the best
in the state. This achievement was vowed at the early age of ten when

his older brother, Johnny, a fireman, fell eight stories through a burning apartment building. His face was charred to the point of being unrecognizable which imprisoned him in booze, pain and depression. Everyone was grateful he was alive . . . everyone but Johnny.

One final, cold night, Johnny surrendered his soul with a note that stated he had to die to escape. That day, Jerome dedicated himself to saving others so they wouldn't feel the same sense of internal doom.

Nurse Powell quietly closed the door. "Yes, doctor, she's stabilized and sleeping. Now go home and get some rest."

Jerome massaged his forehead. "All right, but call me the second she wakes."

"I will, I promise."

Lumbering to his office, he grabbed his coat and keys, spotting a note reminding him to call Jasmine Woods. He picked it up, shoved it in his pocket and left the hospital.

As always, it was dark outside when Jerome headed home. Being one of two plastic surgeons at Loveland General, he hadn't seen a sliver of daylight since his return from Tahoe.

His truck sputtered in protest, having sat idle for endless hours. But Jerome knew its habits and gave the gas pedal two pumps then tried again. It rumbled awake with a favorite song playing on the radio. He turned up the volume, shifted into gear and started down a rural country road for home.

Making the final turn, he pulled up to his mailbox and crammed days of mail and newspapers between his legs. Then he proceeded up a winding driveway to the top of the hill. Reaching his rustic timber home, he parked and got out with the song still playing in his head. *"Brandy . . . you're a fine girl. What a goood wife you would be—"* Entering, he took off his coat and hung it on a wooden peg on the back of the front door. Keys and mail were tossed in a large green ceramic bowl on the kitchen counter. Then he peered inside the refrigerator.

His routine never varied, which enabled him to do it practically in his sleep. Grabbing a Coke, he went to the living room and collapsed in his sunken, leather recliner. With the Coke in one hand and the remote in the other, he took a sip and turned on the TV. His eyes fluttered, imploring to sleep, and as dark pervaded his world of light a jolting ring had him leaping from his chair. Jogging to the kitchen, he grabbed the phone. "Yes?"

"Dr. Jensen, she's moaning," Nurse Powell whispered.

"I'll be right there." He snatched his keys, threw on his coat and ran out the door. Whirling into the emergency parking lot, Jerome hurried through the sliding doors and entered the elevator.

The door opened at ICU. Nurse Powell was just coming around the corner, and they met face-to-face. He latched onto her arms out of breath. "Is she still awake?"

"She should be. I just left her."

After scrubbing, Jerome entered Samantha's sterile room. He stood next to her bed and watched as her eyes flickered open and mouth parted. "Shhh . . . everything's going to be all right."

She stared at him with cold, blank eyes—eyes that had a million questions then drifted back to sleep. Jerome left the room, drawing in a heavy breath. He knew if she survived, this was only a fragment of her suffering.

Nurse Powell came up to him. "She's a fighter. I think she'll make it."

He gazed at her with glassy eyes. "I've never wished this on anyone, but in her case, having amnesia would be a true blessing. Say a prayer for her."

"You're both in my prayers," she said, studying his face. "Tell me, when was the last time you slept? You look exhausted."

He shook his head. "I don't know. I can't remember."

"Why don't you go try? No one's in the darkroom, and I'll keep an eye on Samantha."

"But—"

"But nothing. You'll be no good to anyone if you don't get some rest. I'll come and wake you if there's an emergency." She pointed a finger at him. "You may be a doctor, but sometimes a mother knows best." Her large chest puffed out as she placed her hands on her hips.

"I guess I can't argue with that." He took off down the corridor and entered a storage room converted into a nap room. It was cramped and dark with just enough space for a gurney, which made do for a bed.

Wincing with the pain in his head, Jerome knew closing his eyes would help, but it also opened the door to that regretful day.

Dribbling down the basketball court . . . running, dodging and turning with swift control of the ball. Going up, leaping, fingertips letting go, then a sharp elbow to the eye and crashing to the floor in blinding pain.

It had been a year of lost time and a blur of surgeries to reattach his retina. Finally, through patience and perseverance, the last attempt was a success. Jerome expected all would be well and his career back on track, but he was wrong. Due to the extreme stress he endured that withered, insufferable year, he contracted brain cancer. Unfortunately, his was incurable and inoperable. The only glimmer of hope were the miracles he'd witnessed and all the experimental drugs readily at his disposal.

Lying awake, unable to repress the perpetual nightmare, Jerome remembered a close friend had just given birth to her first child. He decided to make better use of his time and got up to go see her.

Entering her room, he quietly approached her bed and gazed down at her angelic face while she soundly slept. Rachel was the *"girl next door"* and they had a special bond. Their families lived across the street from each other as they were growing up, and they vowed to be husband and wife someday.

The accident on the basketball court changed all that. Rachel deserved a man who could give her a family, like she wanted, and he couldn't. The numerous medications he took had serious side effects. The worst being sterility. Through it all, they'd remained close friends with a deep appreciation for each other's honesty.

While gazing down as she slumbered, her face mysteriously changed into someone else, someone he'd just met. He shook his head and blinked his eyes, knowing the effects of sleep deprivation. Quietly he left her room and headed back to his office with something on his mind. Sitting at his desk, he reached in his pocket and pulled out the note to call Jasmine. A smile rose as he dialed her number.

The hot cup of coffee warmed Jasmine's nose, and the dawn's early light soothed her goose-bumps as the gentle sway of the porch swing kept time with her thoughts.

Gripping the collar of her robe, she held it tightly against the morning chill and swallowed the last sip. Then she pushed off to go inside and get ready for work. Heading to the bathroom to start the shower, she heard the phone ring and expected Yarah's alarming voice. "Hello?"

"Jasmine?"

"Yes."

"Hi, it's Jerome."

"Oh, hi Jerome, good to hear from you."

"I was just calling to see how you were doing."

"I'm doing a lot better."

"Wonderful. Then I'm assuming the police caught the stalker, and everything is back to normal."

"Well, everything is back to normal, but they never caught the guy. Actually, I spoke to the police a few days ago. They said there's been no report of him anywhere. I'm praying he left Tahoe."

Jerome rested back in his chair, feeling relieved. "Are they still watching your house?"

"Yes, so that's reassuring." Jaz sat down at the kitchen table. "And how about you—how are you doing?"

"Uh . . . everything is back to normal here, as well." He wasn't going to add to her stress and divulge he also had a stalker, but unlike hers it wouldn't vanish. He continued with pleasantries. "And how's work, anything happening there?"

"Same as usual, someone else just died."

He sat up. "At your game!?"

"No, thank goodness, not this time. Our casino manager had a heart attack, probably from someone winning too much."

Jerome sat back and exhaled. "I'm telling you, there's something about that place."

Jaz glanced up at the clock, realizing she had to be showered and out the door in half an hour. "Jerome, I'd love to talk, but I need to get ready for work or I'll be late."

"Sure, no problem. Well, if you need anything, anything at all, just call me."

"Thanks, but all is well and I should be fine."

"Hopefully you will . . . call that is." *Hmm, did I just say that?*

"Sure, okay, well good-bye. And thanks again for checking on me."

"You're welcome. Take care."

Jasmine hung up the phone. *Did he say, hopefully you will?*

TWENTY-EIGHT

Strolling into work, Jasmine felt revived, energized and prepared to tackle whatever came her way. At least that's what she thought until she saw Frank standing directly in her pathway like a barricade blocking the road.

She wanted to turn around, but that would show weakness. *And she was . . . oh, yeah, Wonder Woman!* Inhaling, she walked toward him with every step sloshing between pain and passion. She tried not to notice how impeccably dressed he was, standing with one foot out, arms crossed, with a sly grin on his face. Then their eyes locked and he repositioned his stance. Face on, feet parallel, and he slipped his hands in his pockets.

She felt the heat of his eyes strip away her clothes and sear her flesh. He smiled but she couldn't, even if she wanted to, and boldly walked past him and into the lounge.

When the door shut, a puff of air hit Frank in the face. It was only a puff, but it felt like a two-by-four with a pain deeper and more intense than anything he'd ever experienced. Women had come and gone in his thirty-six years. Never had one made him fragile and powerless or incapable of speaking. There had to be something—a potion—hypnosis—a gun! To stop his misery. He had reached the breaking point in which life without Jasmine was killing him. One way or another he was going to get her back.

Meandering back to his office, fondly entranced, he contrived a new plan. He contemplated all of Jasmine's characteristics and qualities. Her true nature was kind and not spiteful, so his approach would have to prey on that—something she would never suspect and easily fall for. He had an idea: get her advice for Paul's wake. She would never suspect a mournful man in suffering.

Facing the mirror, he pinched the tender, thin skin under his eyes until they turned red and watered. *To be more convincing, he had better look the part.* Then he raked his fingers through his hair and loosened his tie. "If this doesn't get her, I don't know what will," he uttered. Looking at his watch, he calculated her break was over and she would be back at her table. With game plan rehearsed, he left his office to find his one and only.

Gazing around for his bright sunshine, he spotted Jasmine standing alone. This was exactly what he'd hoped for: her undivided attention for his spectacular show. He felt certain the persona of a pathetic man would soften her heart. For full effect, he pinched under his eyes again and timidly walked toward her.

Jasmine noticed him and could tell by his skittish gate and drawn face something was wrong. Frank grabbed the front edge of his suit coat and nervously tugged at it, emphasizing his despair. Then he approached her game with tears dripping down his face.

"What's the matter—are you all right?" Jasmine asked concerned.

He looked down then back at her. "That's why I was waiting for you this morning. . . I really needed to talk to you." He moved in closer. "I'm sure you heard about Paul."

"Yes, I did, yesterday." She studied him, wondering if this was one of his mastermind ploys, but he seemed too upset.

"He was a good friend of mine. We went way back. God! I still can't believe he's gone." He closed his eyes and shook his head.

"I'm really sorry. I didn't know him very well." She nipped at her bottom lip, not sure what to say.

Frank gazed at her with red, glassy, imploring eyes. "If it's not too much to ask, I was wondering if you could help me."

"Uh . . . what is it?" She felt her muscles stiffen.

"It's nothing really, just a little advice."

"Advice about what?"

He cleared his throat. "As a close friend, I feel I need to do something for him. You know, a memorial to pay tribute. Maybe a gathering of friends and family." He looked away, trying to prompt more tears. "But I'm not sure what to do, and I'm too distressed to think about it." He held onto the edge of her table. "Can you help me . . . please?"

Jasmine looked side-to-side for any eavesdroppers then leaned toward him. "Considering what I went through with you, you don't deserve my advice. You really hurt me!" Her nostrils flared with each retaliatory word. "But, I am human."

"I know, I'm sorry, and I wish for just this moment you could forgive me." As he desperately gazed at her, he could see she was beginning to fold.

Her face softened. "Well, I've never been to a memorial, but I think your idea of having a gathering of friends and family would be enough."

"Could you help me?"

"Don't you have a personal secretary to assist with your social affairs?"

"I do, but Linda doesn't have time for this. Everyone's bogged down with extra duties now that Paul's gone." He squeezed out one more tear.

Jasmine opened her mouth to respond just as two men approached her game.

Frank nodded at the men. "I'll call you later." He turned and slowly walked away. *Yes! The perfect out.* Jaz watched him until he was out of sight, praying her date with Stan tonight would cure her like Yarah promised.

Brushing her hair while grumbling about the *"hair of the dog"* remedy, Jasmine was having second thoughts. At first it sounded therapeutic, and now it sounded crazy. The only reason she didn't cancel the date was Stan Niyol had the manners of a saint and one of the few men she could trust. His language was well-behaved and respectful of her. She knew every story commemorating his valor as a sheriff, as well as his Navajo history. Though she could tell by his military haircut and stout muscular physique, he was no man to mess around with.

Marty Bidziil was Stan's best friend and a detective. He stood six feet tall, wore a long braided ponytail and had eyes that could melt metal. He and Stan grew up together on the reservation, and their families had formed a strong solidarity. They believed their spiritual mission was to teach the Navajo philosophies, offering a better way of life. Both men held true to their duty until it was time to let their hair down. Then Stan turned to gambling, and Marty turned to women.

Yarah stretched out her long, tan legs as she unrolled the sheer black stocking from the tips of her toes. She stepped into a hot pink skirt and buttoned a tight white blouse, then she gazed in the mirror. She was ready to go on the outside but not the inside. Going on a date wasn't something she liked to do or wanted to do. But, for the sake of helping her best friend forget about Frank, she was willing to make the sacrifice. Picking up the phone, she called Jasmine.

Jaz was pacing the front room, peering out the living room window when she heard the phone ring. "Hello?"

"Are they there yet?"

Jaz rolled her eyes. "Please remind me why we are doing this."

"Because you need to get over that no-good, lyin', cheatin', and all those other things you said."

"I am, so can we call it off?"

"No. Are you ready?"

"About fifteen minutes ago." Then Jaz heard a car door shut. "Wait a minute, I think they're here. Gotta go!" She ran to the bathroom for a quick all-over check and a splash of perfume. Then she calmly walked to the front door to greet them.

Yarah hung up the phone and ran to the bathroom for a quick armpit check. She raised her arms. "Oh shit, I'm a big sweaty-mess!" In one quick motion, the top went flying and she threw on option two. A half an hour later and another shirt change, she heard a knock at the door. Pasting on a happy smile, she opened the door. "I was just about to call search and rescue," she said.

Marty grinned. "Are you lost?"

"Are you looking?"

"All my life." They laughed, and then he grabbed her hand and walked her to the car.

The couples arrived at the Lakeview Hotel for dinner at the Emerald Restaurant. It was known for its fine dining and breathtaking view but mainly for their live entertainment.

"Good evening. Are you here for dinner or just cocktails," the hostess asked as they approached her.

"Dinner. Reservation for four under the name Niyol," Stan said.

The hostess ran a finger down the list then smiled. "Right this way." She escorted them through a white linen dining room and waved her hand toward a semi-circular booth. Yarah and Jasmine slid in first, next to each other, and then Stan and Marty each took an end.

Yarah gazed over at the ancient duet performing on stage. They both looked to be in their eighties, bald and wrinkled, wearing white three-piece suits with pastel blue ruffled shirts. One was pointing at the audience while singing: "Can't take my eyes off of you," as the other pranced his fingertips across the piano keys.

Leaning over the table, Yarah cupped her mouth. "Are you kidding me? This is *live* entertainment! They look dead to me." Everyone chuckled quietly.

Marty gazed around at the engrossed audience. "I think we came on the senior citizen night."

"Ding-ding! You win the prize," Yarah chimed.

"Is that you?" Marty asked, grinning.

"Ding-ding! You win again."

Marty and Yarah hit it off and playfully teased while Jasmine and Stan quietly watched. Their relationship had been built on boundaries and rules, creating an obvious nervousness sitting side-by-side. It wasn't until the wine and the four-course meal was consumed that each felt a little more relaxed.

Stan turned to Jaz. "You want to go dancing? I heard they have a good band at the Palace tonight."

Jaz started to answer as Yarah cut in. "That sounds fun! You up for some twist and shout?" she said to Marty.

Marty's other side was eager to come out and play. He ran a hand along the edge of Yarah's skirt and stroked her inner thigh with a finger. "You're lookin' at the man who invented the twist and shout." He let out a howl. Yarah grabbed his chin and planted a big kiss for all the gawking onlookers.

Jasmine gave Stan a forced smile. "Actually, dealers are not supposed to fraternize with customers at the hotel."

"Jaz!" Yarah spouted. "No one will catch us. Come on. For once break the rules."

Stan scooted closer to test the water. He snuck a hand on her leg and moved it up to her thigh. "I think we'd have fun. What do ya say?"

She tensed with his thigh massage. The "hair of the dog" wasn't doing anything but making her hair bristle. "Thanks, but I better not. If someone sees us we could get suspended." She gently placed his hand on the seat.

Stan could see NO, in capital letters, written across her face. And if she wasn't dancing, she definitely wasn't doing anything else. He raised his arms above his head and yawned. "On second thought, I am a little tired."

Jaz sighed, "Boy, you read my mind. The wine and dessert made me really sleepy. Would you mind if I called it a night?"

"Jaaazzz," Yarah whined again, "it'll be fun."

"You guys go ahead." She placed her hand over her mouth and coaxed out a yawn.

Marty gave Yarah a swat on her thigh. "Just you and me, baby."

"Okay mister twist and shout, let's see what you got."

Scooting out of the booth, Jaz glanced over at Stan. No doubt he was agitated. He had a perturbed look on his face with both hands in his pockets, fidgeting for his keys. Regardless, she was glad to end the date early. For starters, she wasn't in the right frame of mind. Secondly, their player-dealer relationship wouldn't be compromised, and lastly being seen at the Palace with a customer violated hotel policy. She touched his arm. "Thank you for dinner. I had a really nice time."

"Yeah, so did I. You ready?"

She nodded and he escorted her out while the love-birds followed behind, swaying arm-in-arm.

The drive home seemed longer than if Jaz had walked. Although, she made use of the time and apprised Stan of everything she'd gone through with the stalker.

Fortunately, that brought him back to the person she knew and liked, insisting on investigating the case himself. Walking her to the porch, he kissed her cheek and held her hand. "I'll see you tomorrow."

She smiled. "Yes you will . . . and thanks again."

"My pleasure." He squeezed her hand and let it slip away as he left.

After several cocktails, Marty spun Yarah from one end of the dance floor to the other. Their bodies teased and spirits begged for unbridled passion. Hooting and hollering, they kicked up a storm, parting the crowd to the outer edge of the floor.

Marty performed his version of Elvis, thrusting his hips, while Yarah shimmied around him like a burlesque stripper. Neither one was bashful of displaying what they wanted.

"Why don't we take this up to my room?" Marty said.

"I have a better idea. Let's take this up to your room." They both laughed and headed to the elevator feverishly entwined. Kissing and touching, the door closed and ascended to his floor. It opened and they stumbled out and weaved to his room.

Marty slipped the key in the door and whirled Yarah in by the arm. She landed on the bed, squirming and giggling, with her skirt hiked up to her hips. After attaching the 'Do Not Disturb' sign, he walked to the table and swallowed a shot of tequila.

"Come join me," Yarah said, patting the bed.

Marty set his glass down, dropped his pants, unbuttoned his shirt, and climbed on the bed. Diving between her legs, he grabbed the bottom edge of her skirt and yanked it over her waist, exposing her pink panties and black thigh-high hose. In a flash, she flipped him over and stood up with each foot straddling his body.

A smile curled at the corners of his lips. "Yeah baby, show me what you got."

Teetering side-to-side, trying to keep her balance, she unzipped her skirt and unbuttoned her blouse.

"Did you ever consider becoming a stripper?" He laughed.

"Hey, you try this," she squawked.

He latched onto her leg and pulled her down on top of him. Eyeing the pink lace bra covering her two cupcake breasts, he unhooked it and tasted her dark chocolate nipples. Yarah arched and moaned while his hand slithered off into private territory. Then his head went down to orally explore and immediately shot back up. "What the fuck!" he yelled at her in repulsion, scrambling to his feet.

Yarah lifted her head and gazed at him. "What?" she uttered.

"When were you going to tell me!?" he shouted viciously.

Rising to her knees with arms outstretched, she begged, "Don't I look like a woman?"

Marty looked down and shook his head. "Get dressed."

"Fuck you!" Yarah screamed and began gathering her clothes.

"Fuck you, too!" Marty snarled and sat down at the table, slugging another shot of tequila and swearing under his breath.

Before walking out, Yarah looked back at him with black streaks streaming from her eyes. "It didn't have to end this way, you know." Marty started to say something then waved for her to go. Crippled with guilt, regret and deep-seeded despair, Yarah staggered out the door.

TWENTY-NINE

Jasmine arrived at work extra early to hear every teeny-weeny detail of what transpired between Yarah and Marty after they left the restaurant. From what she vividly remembered, they hit it off quite well, and that was a first for Yarah. She normally kept men at an arm's length, proclaiming they were like owning a puppy. You love it, you feed it, it chews everything up, then it leaves you with a pile of crap. Jasmine hoped this one would be different and possibly everlasting.

As the lounge started to clear, Jaz looked up at the clock and decided to leave with the rest of the women. She assumed Yarah was running late due to a hangover but eventually would arrive.

Today she was scheduled in the dollar blackjack pit, which was odd yet a relief. The suspense of Yarah's absence had completely consumed her concentration, and that wasn't conducive for the frontline.

After pushing out the graveyard dealer, Jaz exchanged morning pleasantries with her players and shuffled the cards. Positioned, hands out, on the verge of dealing, she felt a tap on her shoulder. She turned expecting to see Yarah's annoyed face, but it was Henry's.

"This is my game," he groaned in her ear. He was a feeble geriatric with a permanent frown and sullen eyes. Jasmine always felt sorry for him, thinking he should be retired and enjoying the final phase of his life. But he was there every day with a limp in his walk and a scowl on his face—hating his life.

She clung to the deck. "I'm sure this is my game. I saw pit four, game five, next to my name."

"I know. It was a mistake . . . sorry." He reached out with a quivering hand and took the freshly shuffled deck.

Reluctantly, she smiled and apologized to her customers for the misunderstanding then turned to Henry. "Do you know where I'm supposed to be?"

"Where else, the frontline."

Sighing under her breath, Jaz trudged over to the purgatory pit—the bottomless pit—the fit pitchin' pit! And with every defiant step her brain wouldn't stop thinking about Yarah.

This wasn't like her. Money was always an issue. She even worked with a hellacious hangover. There had to be an unavoidable reason why she wasn't at work . . . maybe an emergency.

Turning the corner onto the promenade, Jaz heard her name being called as Stan walked up to her. "Thank God you're all right. I didn't see you in the pit, and after everything you told me last night, I thought something might have happened to you."

"No, I'm fine, but Yarah hasn't come in yet."

Stan set his hands on her shoulders. "That's another thing. Marty needs to talk to you. I think it's important."

"About Yarah?"

"Yeah, but you'll have to talk to him. I've got fifty-two cards calling my name." He made a U-turn and headed toward the pit.

Now she felt even worse, wondering what Marty was going to say and if Tony was in the pit . . . she groaned in utter misery.

It was an hour of what Jasmine anticipated, including Tony, but she finally made it to her break. Wandering through the casino, trying to find Marty, she spotted both Stan and Marty playing blackjack together. She came up behind Marty and leaned toward him. "So where's Yarah?" she uttered and they both turned around.

"Hey, I'm winning for a change," Stan said, rubbing his hands together.

Jaz smiled. "I was wondering where you went."

"I thought I'd try a different dealer. Don't get me wrong, you're still my favorite just expensive."

Marty was glaring at her and growled, "Let's talk." Stacking his chips, he got up from the table and motioned for her to follow. They walked far from the crowd and out of earshot. Then he threw his hands on his hips. "Was that supposed to be a joke—line me up with, with . . . her!?" His statement was paralyzing and commanded a reply.

Jasmine's mouth dropped to her stomach. "I don't know what you're talking about. What's wrong?"

He cocked a foot and folded his arms. "How well do you know *your friend*?"

She stiffened. "Pretty well. In fact, we're best friends."

"Did you know Yarah is—or was a man?"

Jasmine couldn't speak. Her confusion turned into a cyclone that was thrashing inside her head. "No, that can't be true. I've known her for three years. We've gone to the beach together. She's taken vacations with us. We just modeled for a lingerie party!" she rebelled.

Marty gazed into her swelling pools of blue. "I'm gonna tell ya, sweetie. She had me fooled, too."

Jasmine clutched her temples. "No, it can't be true. I've seen her and there wasn't . . ."

He touched her shoulder. "I know. She's had an operation. Listen, in my line of business you see it all, and to put it bluntly, there's a big difference."

A knot the size of a golf ball forced its way down Jasmine's throat. She gulped hard, trying to swallow. "I don't know what to say . . . except I'm sorry. I really didn't know."

Marty could see she was sincere and squeezed her shoulder. "Now that I know you didn't do it on purpose, apology accepted. So . . ." he looked toward the pit, "if you don't mind, I'm going to join Stan and see if his luck rubs off on me."

Jasmine entered the women's lounge as if on death row, head down, slow staggered steps and gazed at the telephone booth. One was available, and she wondered what she would even say. Words couldn't describe what their friendship meant to her. A tear dropped, and that's what Yarah needed to hear.

Sitting down in the booth, she closed the door and put a dime in the slot. The phone rang continuously until Connie knocked on the door and pointed at the clock. Jaz nodded and hung up. Taking a breath, she pulled herself together and trudged back to the pit.

Tony saw her and motioned her over with a finger. She cautiously walked up to him and stoically stood. "Heard about your partner in crime. Didn't know you girls were so friendly." He winked, twirling his toothpick. Jaz could feel her face turning red hot and turned to walk away before saying something she regretted. *But Tony knew everything.* Stopping, she pivoted back around. "Ooo, did I strike a nerve?" he cackled.

Her eyes narrowed. "What did you hear?"

He wagged his finger in her face. "Oh no, you can't fool me. I know your type." He stepped closer. "So, Mizzz *goody-two-shoes,* what's your story?"

"My story? I don't have a story."

"Well, your girlfriend does. We have it all on tape and it's pretty juicy, I might add."

"You have *what* on tape?"

"Ms. Lolita and some guy. They were doing everything but the hokey-pokey in the elevator."

"So where is she, what's happened to her?"

"Calm down—calm down. Nobody did anything to her. She did it to herself. She's been fired, gone, finito!" He rocked on his heels with a smirk on his face. "It's too bad . . . I kinda liked her. Easy on the eyes, if ya know what I mean." Then he pointed at her. "Let it be a lesson. You don't shit where you eat!"

Jaz swallowed. *Fired . . . gone . . . finito.*

After countless calls, Jaz sat down at the kitchen table to try Yarah one more time before she went to bed. Nine rings going on ten, she started to hang up when Yarah finally answered.

"Hello?"

"Yarah! I'm so glad you answered. I've been so worried."

"I'm sorry." Her voice was weak.

"Tony told me you got fired."

"Yeah, the bastards! I can't stand that place."

"He also said the elevator camera taped you with Marty."

"Pretty stupid of me, huh?" She burst out crying. "I should have listened to you, and now I have to move."

"Move! Why?"

"Are you kidding? I can't stay here. Once you're fired you're black-balled from all the casinos. You know I can't afford to be out of work. Not even a day!"

Jasmine paced the kitchen. "Let me get the kids to bed, and I'll come over."

"No, I'm not in the mood, thanks anyway. I'll figure something out. Don't worry."

"But I am worried."

"Listen, I'll just call you in the morning."

"You promise?"

"Yeah."

Jasmine hung up with a sick feeling she was going to lose her best friend—her confidant—her soul sister.

Early, before the sun rose over the mountain peaks, Yarah packed her car with necessities and anything else of value that would fit. She decided to leave without saying goodbye, knowing how Jaz felt about that word. Although, she did regret leaving her alone to the wolves of the trade, but she had no choice. Eventually, everyone would know the truth, and that was a whipping she couldn't endure again.

The cool breeze nipped at Jasmine through her terry cotton robe as she rocked on the porch swing and looked out over the valley. The leaves were donning their fall attire, and a cool restlessness carved the air. She never heard from Yarah, like she promised, and Yarah never broke a promise.

After the kids left for school, Jaz drove to the other side of the valley, where rent was cheap and close to the casinos. As she turned down Yarah's street, her heart shuddered at seeing her empty carport. She pulled into her driveway, walked to the porch and banged on the door. Waiting intensely for a reply, there was nothing. No movement, no calling, nothing.

She went to the window and peered through a crack in the curtains. Her lungs heaved and knees gave at the sight. Scattered scraps of newspaper foretold what she suspected, and tears of their beloved friendship let go. She sat down on the front stoop until her eyes finally dried. Man or woman, Yarah would always be remembered as her best friend.

After a mournful drive home, Jasmine solemnly walked inside the house and heard the phone ringing. Her eyes widened as she dashed to the kitchen and eagerly answered. "Yarah?!"

"No, guess again."

"Jerome?"

"That hurt."

"I'm sorry, is this Stan?"

"No—it's Frank! How many boyfriends do you have?"

"Ha! You should talk. What do you want?"

"I told you I'd call. Remember, you said you'd help me with Paul's wake?"

She angled her head. "Are you sure it was me?"

"Come on, let's not start off this way," he pleaded.

She lowered her head. "I'm sorry; I've had a really bad morning."

"Is there anything I can do to help?" He grinned with something brewing on his mind.

Her head shot up, remembering who she was talking to. "I think you've done enough, don't you?"

Feeling a sense of urgency, he had to confess his feelings before she hung up on him. "Jasmine, I have to be honest with you. I can't stop thinking about you. Your smile, your laugh, your touch. I could go on and on . . . I love you."

She coughed. "What did you say?"

"Do you want me to repeat everything or just . . . I love you?"

"That's what I thought you said." She clenched her jaw, trying to keep her words from firing out like bullets, yet it was too late. "Frank! You have no idea how much you hurt me! Just when I thought I'd take a chance again, I got my heart broke! Not only that, tossed out like three-day leftovers!"

"But I."

"Let me finish!" She picked up a spatula next to the stove and began waving it in the air. "I don't trust you. How could I ever trust you again? And what's a relationship without trust, huh!?"

He stood with his mouth open and hand extended. "Jasmine, what happened between us was for your own protection, because I love you."

The blood rose to her face, burning like a raging fire as she repeated his explanation. "What you did was because you *love me*!? I think I remember Carl saying something like that. I'm hanging up now."

"No, wait, please! I know it sounds absolutely crazy, and right now is not the time to explain, but when I can you'll understand. I really do love you."

"You're right, it does sound absolutely crazy," she spouted. "So, let's get back to why you're calling."

Frank exhaled, feeling weary. "It's for Paul's memorial. Can you help me?"

Rolling her eyes, she sat down. "What exactly do you want me to do?"

"I just need a little womanly advice; one that has credence and class like yours." He scraped for a morsel of her attention.

She conceded even though she couldn't organize a picnic in her frame of mind. Resting her forehead in her hand, she closed her eyes and took a deep breath. "Frank, I don't know, just do what you told me: invite friends and family, serve some food, and you might want to say something nice about him."

Frank was in the refrigerator rummaging for something to eat. His uncontested silence tested her patience even more. "Are you there? Did you hear anything I said?"

He straightened up. "Yes, I'm here. And I think that's exactly what I'm going to do."

"Then, if we're done, I'd like to get back to what *I* want to do."

"What do you want to do?" he asked curiously.

"I want to sit outside on the porch swing and have my coffee."

"Isn't it a little cold for that?"

"No, it's what I do. It gives me peace, and I need some right now." She hung up without a goodbye or second thought.

Frank walked outside, eating his ham sandwich with the dogs sniffing close behind for crumbs. He gazed up at crisp, clear sky as a chill rose up his spine. *Hmm . . . this is what she does? Must be that Montana blood in her.*

THIRTY

T he hospital was quiet, no moans, no outbursts, only the chime of the elevator as the nurses changed floors. Taking advantage of the opportunity, Jerome took off for the darkroom to catch a quick nap. His nightmare no longer loomed, and a fantasy had taken its place. To him, it was literally a sight for sore eyes.

Lying on the gurney with a blanket rolled under his head, he welcomed the dark in anxious anticipation. As his eyes closed and mouth curled into a smile, he let out a restful sigh just as the corridor reverberated with loud, panicked voices. Jumping up, he bolted out the door and followed the commotion to the emergency lobby.

Huddled together were four men dressed in plaid flannel shirts and grease stained jeans. "Hey, there's the doc!" one said, pointing. "You gotta help Chuck!" he bellowed as the injured man waved his bloody, rag-wrapped hand.

Jerome normally didn't work emergency, but graveyard ran a thin staff, so he volunteered when they needed help. "What happened?" he asked, peeling back the makeshift bandage.

"Got my hand caught between a cable and a tree," Chuck said and belched. "Sorry, I slugged down a few beers on the way over. I thought it would help with the pain."

Jerome examined the wound. "It's not too bad, but you'll need some stitches. Let's take you back." He wrapped his arm around Chuck and led him through the double doors into a curtained cubicle. "Take a seat. I'll be right back."

Chuck sat down on the blue-sheeted bed then laid back and rested his head. Jerome returned with a tray of suture material and instruments. He pulled a chair up next to the bed and carefully cut away the remaining blood-soaked rag.

Chuck looked down and winced at the torn flesh. "I've been a logger for twenty-two years. Never once got hurt and never once missed a day, but it all happened so fast, ya know?"

Jerome smiled. "Sounds like you're overdue for some time off. This is going to need at least two weeks to heal." He turned to prepare the anesthetic.

"Is it gonna hurt?"

"Not after I numb you."

Chuck saw the needle and struggled to get up. "I hate shots!"

"You'll be fine." Jerome gently lowered him, and after thirty sutures, and a pat on the back, he walked him out to his crew.

"Hey guys, wake up!" Chuck said, kicking the sole of his buddy's boot. "Doc finished stitchin' me up."

A giant bearded man stood up unsteadily. "You okay to drive?" Jerome asked him.

"Yeah, I'm fine. I don't drink. They just rub off on me." The burly brute latched onto Chuck's good arm with his massive hand. "Come on ya stupid dummy." He kicked the feet of the other two men who were still sleeping. "Get up; we're goin' home." They grumbled to a stance, and all staggered out the door.

Jerome hurried back to the darkroom to resume where he'd left off. And as every muscle sank and bone settled, he fell into a deep, deep slumber and then into his awaiting dream.

Through the mist of a mountain meadow, he sees a woman walking toward him. She's wearing a yellow blouse tied in front with blue jeans and cowboy boots. Her hair looks like autumn leaves falling over her shoulders. She smiles and takes his hand. They cling in a passionate kiss and crumble down to the lush dewy grass, laughing and staring endlessly into each other's eyes.

Jerome sat up and his eyes snapped open. This was not just a woman in his fantasy, this was Jasmine. And she had graced him with new light and hope.

Suddenly the door opened, and Nurse Powell stuck her head inside. "Dr. Jensen, I hate to wake you, but Samantha is asking for you."

Jerome threw his legs over the bed. "Tell her I'll be right there." Looking down at his sweat-stained scrubs, he grinned with the reality of their torrid intimacy. He couldn't ignore this or brush it off as insignificant. He had to see Jasmine and apprise her of his feelings.

Samantha had survived the critical stage and was now eating and wanting to know about her family. Jerome agonized putting her through more suffering after defeating the physical challenge. Yet, the consolation was a new family waiting for her with open arms. Standing before her door, he took a breath and calmly went inside.

The sixteen-hour day had its rewarding moments as well as arduous, but it was over and tomorrow was Jerome's day-off. He got inside his truck and gave it a couple rousing pumps. It shook awake then took off down the road for home.

Like his truck, his home held the same beloved reverence. It was a place that knew his pain and loneliness with a story similar to his own.

In the early spring of 82', Jake Thompson began construction on the timber frame home. It was his wife's dying wish to leave the world from a place of beauty and serenity. They searched until they found the perfect spot, nestled in the middle of God's country amid the forest and a meadow of wildflowers. Diligent, through all the elements, Jake worked hard to make her wish come true. But as time passed so did his true love. It was then the home was left unfinished and abandoned.

For a year, Jerome drove past the vacant structure, feeling an empathetic draw. It stood tall and majestic yet empty and alone, like him. All it needed was someone to give it life, and after several phone calls he located the owner. At first Mr. Thompson was reluctant to sell, proclaiming it was his wife's "little slice of heaven." Although, after Jerome disclosed his own tragic story, the man agreed they belonged together.

Throwing his coat over the peg and mail and keys in the bowl, Jerome made his pit-stop at the fridge. He peered in and saw yesterday's meatloaf from the cafeteria, which looked as delicious as a steak he was so hungry. Setting it on the kitchen counter, he opened a bottle of wine and poured a glass.

He had three things to celebrate: Samantha's recovery, a well-deserved day off and no more nightmares. Taking his wine and meatloaf to the living room, he flopped into his chair and turned on the TV. With every sip and every bite, his body slithered into peaceful darkness and back into Jasmine's open arms. They held, they touched, they yearned for each other in a love so intense, so awaited, they never wanted to part.

Stirring awake from the throb in his head, Jerome listened to the news on the TV, but nothing seemed more important than talking to Jasmine. She had staked a claim on his brain and not just when his eyes were shut.

He was convinced meeting her was linked to his existence somehow. It was time to stop dreaming and do something about it. Getting up from his chair, he went to the kitchen and dialed her number.

Jasmine lifted her head from the pillow and listened to the phone ring. It was early, but she thought it might be Yarah. Slipping on her robe, she hurried to the kitchen to answer. "Hello?"

"Hi Jasmine, it's Jerome. How are you?"

She rubbed her eyes and gazed at the clock. "I'm fine," she said, yawning. "How are you?"

"I'm great. I just finished my shift and actually have a day off."

She leaned against the wall. "That's wonderful—you deserve it."

He smiled, listening to her sleepy voice. "I was thinking . . . about Tahoe." *About you!*

"Oh yeah, you miss the drama?" she said jokingly.

"Something like that." He didn't want to start off too fast. "I'll probably be coming back soon."

"Really, when?"

"Next weekend." *Too soon?* He felt his heart gain speed.

"Well, if you'd like to get together, call me when you get in."

"I'd like that. I was hoping we could get together for lunch or dinner, if that's all right." *Too forward?*

Her eyes opened a tad wider. "Sure, okay." *Anything to forget about Frank.*

"Great. I'll call you when I get there."

"Sounds good. Talk to you then."

Jerome hung up feeling he'd missed an opportune moment to tell her the truth—that because of her he hungered to live and to love. That no other woman gave him such strength, greater yet, hope. That he sees them as a family, even if *how long* couldn't be answered.

The advice his family and friends gave him finally anchored: to be honest with the woman he falls for. And above all, don't stop living or denying himself happiness.

Until now, he believed his honesty would destroy any possibility of a relationship. Telling a woman he was impotent and dying of brain cancer sounded pathetically painful. But for some reason, the risk was worth taking with Jasmine.

It wasn't long after Jerome called that cupboards slammed, the TV blared and the relentless *"It's my turn,"* was protested every other minute. Morning was declared whether Jasmine knew it or not. Wrapping in her robe, she scooted into her knitted slippers and moseyed out to the family room.

"Hi Mom, I made you coffee!" Shauna blared over the cartoons.

Jaz walked over and kissed the top of her head. "Thanks. You know you're my favorite daughter."

"I know, and you're my favorite mother."

"And what am I!?" Justin squawked, jumping up and down.

"You're my favorite monkey." Chuckling to herself, she went to the kitchen and poured a cup of coffee then curled on the couch to join the kids.

Sipping and staring blankly at the TV, her mind drifted to Jerome and his early, unexpected call. She remembered their conversation, noting he didn't say *why* he was coming. Whatever the reason, it made her feel happy and excited to see him again, which was more than she could say for Frank.

Spiraling into his sticky web, she thought about the current crisis he created. If he hadn't been so deceitful, Yarah would still be there with a job and she with a friend. *So much for the hair of the dog remedy!*

Getting up from the couch and stomping off to refresh her coffee, she went out to the porch to soothe her raw emotions. Looking out over the patchwork of orange and yellow, she rocked and huffed while trying to fight off *Mystery Man*. But he had a sneaky way of weaseling his way into her thoughts.

There *was* something about Frank, as Jerome had said. For her, there was never a question of what it was. She knew exactly, as did every woman he encountered. Frank had the charisma that could charm a snake, the looks that could melt icicles, and the words to seduce a woman who swore men were only good for breaking hearts. Why, of all people, would she fall for someone like him?

Monday morning, the lounge was a war zone with every woman firing off their mouths. It seemed Yarah's dismissal perpetuated a revolt against men and their flagrant discrimination toward women. The consensual rant: they were never penalized for their misconduct and women were. Jasmine agreed with them. However, it reopened the wound she had tenderly sewn shut.

Marching upstairs to the casino floor and into the pit, Jasmine pushed onto her game which ironically faced a man fondling a woman half his age. Insidious things went on in the casino. She witnessed them every day. From PTA mothers to Cub Scout fathers, it bred a hunger to behave perversely and without a care who observed.

The couple facing her was the most typical. The older, polished man with the young, scantily dressed woman. After several cocktails anything could happen. Whether they were stopped or not depended on his financial credentials. Lots of money bought lots of action. No one sees anything—no one knows anything. Simple as that.

As the lovers stood to leave, Jasmine realized she still harbored the need for love as well as passion. Astonishingly, Frank hadn't extinguished that. The only problem was it required trusting a man. At this point, nothing sounded more challenging after Carl and Frank. Her eyes suddenly froze. *Speaking of the devil.* Watching him walk toward her, she took a firm stance and braced herself for his mind-altering, body-levitating song 'n dance.

Breathless, Frank reached out and grabbed the padded ledge of her table. His forehead glistened with sweat, his black hair was ruffled and his red silk necktie was set askew. "Hello beautiful." His words came out choppy and winded.

"What happened to you? Did you run to work?" She said, grinning.

"In a manner of speaking, I did, just for you." He let out a breath and ran his fingers through his hair.

"You better fix your tie, too." She pointed.

He adjusted it. "Is that better?"

"Not if you're trying to impress me." But she couldn't help see his sexy, vulnerable side. The side he never exposed. "What do you want, Frank?" she sighed.

He looked at the empty seats around her game. "I can see you're a very busy woman, so I'll make this fast."

"Please do."

"I'm going to start fresh with you—"

"Wait a minute!" She sharpened her glare. "Fresh with me!"

"You didn't let me finish." His eyes softened along with the tone of his voice. "I couldn't wait to see you, and actually I did run over before a customer sat down. Jasmine, I know you're hurt and confused, and there's a lot I need to explain. If you'd just give me one more chance you'll know I really do love you."

Stay strong! Stay strong! Her eyes searched, her body became tenuous, and her heart went soft and compassionate. Swallowing her regret, her mouth opened. "Maybe . . . but that's all I can give you right now."

He stepped back. "I'll take a maybe. And when you're ready, we'll put everything behind us and start over." His basset hound eyes beseeched forgiveness.

She cocked her head. "How many times have we done that?"

"Look at it this way. Love is limitless, if it's meant to be." He walked away then turned and blew her a kiss.

Jaz could hear Yarah screaming: *"Are you crazy, girl?!"*

Frank returned to his office and went over the list of guests for Paul's memorial. He had reserved the yacht club for tomorrow night, and if everything went as planned then goodbye Mimma and hello Jasmine. He picked up the phone and called Mimma to make sure she would be there.

"Hello?"

"Mimma, it's Frankie."

"Darling, where have you been? You haven't returned any of my calls. You had me so worried."

"Sorry baby, I've been out of town. Like I promised, I have a surprise for you." *Not the surprise she expected.*

"Oh goody. When can I see you?"

"That's the reason I'm calling. Tomorrow night I'm having a party at the yacht club to pay tribute to Paul Cusimano. I want you to be there." He leaned back in his chair.

Mimma sat up. "Of course, darling. What time?"

"My driver will pick you up at six-thirty."

"Not you?" She pouted.

"No, I have to be there early and get things ready." He was preparing for his great escape, without her.

"But I want to see you tonight . . . have a little party of our own." Her tongue circled her crimson lips.

"I can't; I'm working late."

She stomped her foot. "It's been too long."

"Listen, after the party—you and me. I gotta go. See you tomorrow." He hung up and gloated with ecstasy.

Mimma looked at the phone and hammered it on the table. "Bastard!"

CHAPTER

THIRTY-ONE

"What's cookin', good-lookin'?"

Jasmine turned to see Tony walking up to her. "Hi Tony, not much."

He pulled out a chair and sat down at her table. "So, what's the Brazilian babe up to these days?" His question touched a tender spot.

"I'm not sure. I haven't heard from her."

His cocky grin went flat. "You two haven't spoken?"

"No." Now her tender spot was throbbing.

"It ain't none of my business but don't you think that's a little strange, being bosom-buddies and all?"

Jaz whipped her hair over her shoulder. "I'm sure she's busy trying to find a job and a place to live. That takes time, you know."

He pointed his toothpick at her. "She wouldn't be in this mess if she'd kept her legs crossed. Hear what I'm sayin'?" He nodded and stood.

That one hit below the belt. Jasmine glared at him with fire blazing from her eyes and smoke blowing from her flared, freckled nostrils. "You have no . . ." She paused, shut her mouth and stared directly forward. Defending, retaliating, or proving a point with him would've set her back to square one, where everyone else was. She had been through too much to do that. Instead, she stood silently still.

"So, you do hear what I'm sayin'," he said and strutted back to his podium. Her lungs evacuated like a popped balloon. *You're right. It's none of your business!*

The first two guests arrived at the yacht club. Clive greeted the young ladies, took their coats and led them down the hallway to meet the host. Frank was sitting at a table in the lounge dressed to the nines. He was wearing a charcoal pinstripe suit, white French-cuffed shirt and black silk tie.

He stood barely remembering the voluptuous, blonde twins and graciously kissed their hands. "Thank you for coming and showing your respect," he uttered in a solemn voice.

They were clueless who Paul Cusimano was and had only met Frank once at a penthouse party. "No problem. We couldn't resist a party at the yacht club," one said.

The other nudged her arm. "Speak for yourself, Candy. I just think it's so sad, and I'm really sorry for your loss." She wrapped her arms around Frank's neck and kissed his cheek.

"Carla, you made it sound like I'm not sorry and I am!" She moved in getting a big hug and kiss, too." It was perfect. Not only did Frank get their names and sympathy, but Mimma glided in to see him smothered in lips and breasts.

He quickly lowered his head and moaned mournfully for a better show. "Oh Frankie, is there anything we can do for you?" Candy said as they both laid their head on his chest.

Frank stroked their hair. "No, but thank you. I'm usually not this emotional, but he was such a close friend." He peered from slits to see Mimma swaggering up to him.

She cocked a hip and folded her arms as sparks flew from her dark, green eyes. "I see you *do* have feelings. Very good, darling, very good. I was starting to think you were just another man."

Frank raised his head while clinging to the twins. "Mimma, I want you to meet two friends of mine. This is Carla and Candy."

"Hmm, Carla and Candy. Isn't that sweet?" She jerked her head and charged off to the bar.

"I don't think she likes us," Candy said, glancing over at her. The plan was working as expected. Frank could feel the sting of Mimma's venomous glare as she sat seething and sipping her wine.

"Oh, she's fine, don't worry about her," he said, giggling inside.

More guests began to arrive, and the room filled with a hum of sorrow and business but mainly pleasure. Single women were everywhere and floated over to express their condolences with an emotional kiss and generous hug. When the line of embracing reached the end, Frank looked over to the bar for Mimma, but she was gone.

Like a hound, he searched every room then went outside and gazed around the harbor. There was no trace of her anywhere. Thrilled his plan was a success, he continued with his performance, huddled with the women. Swirling his wine, deep in sorrow, he felt a stern tap on his shoulder and turned.

"Boss wants to see you—now!" Keys said, displaying a row of long pearly-whites.

Frank glanced around the room. *It just keeps getting better and better.* "I didn't know he was here. Where is he?"

"Probably too busy with the dames. He's over there." He pointed to a corner table as Marco's eyes latched onto him like blood-sucking leeches. Frank adjusted his tie and left the beautiful dames to chat among themselves.

Marco held out an arm, motioning him to sit. Frank pulled out a chair, rested back, and then casually took over the conversation. "I appreciate you coming tonight and paying your respect. Paul was a good man." He shook his head. "Tragic, wasn't it? So unexpected, but of course it always is."

Marco lunged at Frank. "I couldn't give a flying fuck about Paul. It's you I'm here to see." He held a fist steady at his face. "Listen, you no good son-of-a-bitch, stay the fuck away from Mimma. Or this pretty face of yours won't be pretty no more. You got it?!" He unclenched his hand and briskly tapped him on the cheek.

Frank held up his hands. "No problem. You have my word."

"That's good." Marco stood and gathered his men. "Let's get the fuck out of here." Single file, his entourage followed him out the door and into an awaiting limo.

Frank watched and grinned. It was the crescendo to a well-deserved celebration. He was *ordered* to keep his distance by someone you can't say no to.

Clive was shuffling about the room preparing to leave. "Sir, I do believe the staff would like to retire for the night. I've noticed them getting quite anxious."

"I'm ready. Just give me one minute with the ladies." Each had slipped him their personal request which he had willfully declined. Returning to the twins, he wedged between them and wrapped his arms around their waists. "Ladies, it was a pleasure seeing you tonight, but they're ready to close and we have to leave." He gave them a subtle pat on their backs.

They clutched onto his arms and brushed their lips against his cheeks. "We decided we're not leaving without you."

He held them away. "I'm afraid you are." Then he gestured a hand toward the door. "Thanks again for coming."

"You don't know what you're miiiissing," they cooed harmoniously.

He grinned. "I have a pretty good idea I do, but I'm taken."

"I told you, Candy!"

"It was your idea to come, *Carla*." Flipping their purses over their shoulders, they strutted out while Frank watched and cursed himself. Then he redirected his thoughts to the success of the memorial.

Clive was waiting in the limousine when Frank came outside. He noticed him glowing with sheer delight and couldn't remember the last time he looked so happy. After he got in, Clive turned around. "I have to say, that smile is quite becoming. You should do it more often." Frank didn't say a word, just sat like a cat that had eaten a rat. "What, may I ask, has you so giddy?"

"Clive, it was a fabulous night—absolutely *fabulous*," Frank said, shaking his head and smiling.

"Yes, there was quite a turnout, if that's what you mean," he replied, looking at him curiously.

"That, my dear old chap, has nothing to do with it."

Clive rolled his eyes. "I see, just another one of your bewildering escapades."

Frank leaned back. "To say the least."

When they pulled into the estate, Tank and Tasha ran up to meet them. Frank got out and patted each on the head. "Tonight we celebrate," he said to them. They howled, following him inside the house and down the hall to the kitchen. He peered in the fridge while they sat licking their jowls.

Finding two T-bones, he dangled the meat above their heads as they pranced in place. "Take it!" he commanded. They leaped in synchrony, snatching the steaks from his hands.

While they were busy with their treats, Frank went to the study to pour a long celebratory drink for himself. Sinking into the soft, leather couch, he slowly sipped his scotch while mulling his next assignment.

He had to create a story so compelling, so believable, that Jasmine would take him back. Needing the right place and mood for such a task, he took his drink and climbed the stairs to his retreat.

Lying in bed with one arm under his pillow, Frank stared out the window into the midnight sky. He saw Marco's fist an inch from his chin and chuckled with his threat. His words were so poetic and couldn't have sounded any sweeter. Then he thought about Jasmine and how he longed to be with her. Having millions stashed in the vault, he could shut down his operation and offer her a life of infinite luxury. His eyes grew wide and wild. *That's it! No woman would refuse that.*

Looking over the horizon of people, Jasmine spotted her game and sighed. Smoke was rising from it like a sewer hole missing its lid. Every player had a cigarette in their mouth, a scowl on their face, transfixed on their cards. They were the deadheads—dead set on getting their money back no matter how many cigarettes, drinks or hours it took.

Stepping up to the game, she tapped the dealer on the shoulder. He instantly came alive as if she were the cavalry to save the day. Handing her the deck, he smiled at the docile players. "Thank you, everyone. I'm out of here." With one lively clap and a flash of his palms, he pivoted and shot out like a cannon ball.

Jasmine acknowledged her players with a friendly smile and warm welcome. Her innocent face and pink dewy lips had a way of inspiring hope with a chance to win. The five flat bodies inflated and began to move and speak.

"All right, things are looking up!" a man said and placed a fifty dollar bet down which triggered another, and the momentum rounded the table. "The pressure's on. Can you handle it?" the man said to her.

Bring it on! was what Jasmine wanted to say. "I'll try my best," she chimed, which sounded much sweeter. As she was shuffling the cards, her eyes gravitated to a monstrosity of red roses being delivered to the pit. It was the biggest bouquet she had ever seen in her life.

Fred, the pit boss, moseyed over to the fragrant garden and snatched the card from the holder. "So who's the lucky lady?" he said, grinning at the captive female dealers. Taking a peek, he replaced the card then casually went back to the podium and resumed his position

"Who are they for?" a player called out to him.

Fred placed a finger to his lips. "That's a surprise."

Now all the women were in a tizzy wondering who was the most loved, appreciated and deserving of the extravagant bouquet. Jasmine hoped it was Sylvia, a mother of six. Then there was Carol. She worked two jobs after her husband was permanently injured. Or maybe Trudy, as an apology from her abusive boyfriend. Twenty long minutes went by with four women in the pit.

Carol was the first to be tapped off her game. The pit grew silent. Even the customers stopped playing to listen. Eagerly, she plucked the card and read the envelope. "To the owner of my heart . . . Jasmine," her voice trailed off in despair.

Jaz winced, feeling the penetration of each woman's disappointment.

"I knew they were for you," one of her players commented.

"Really? Why?"

"I don't know—you have that unattainable air about you."

Hmm . . . why can't Frank see that! Just then she felt a tap on her shoulder. Her relief was there to push her out for a break. "Good luck, everyone. See you all in twenty minutes." Clearing her hands, Jaz handed the deck to the incoming dealer and started down the walkway.

"Hey, don't forget your roses!" the woman hollered.

"Oh yeah, thanks." Jaz grabbed hold of the gaudy monstrosity and held it out as if a rotten sack of potatoes.

"Need some help?"

Jasmine turned to see Frank grinning like a bouncing baby. She handed him the vase. "*Help* wasn't exactly what I was thinking, but yes, thank you."

"Did you read the card?" he said, walking next to her. "No, not yet. I'm afraid to."

"Just read it." He hugged the vase and brushed his hand over her cheek. "I mean it. I love you and I miss you. Please forgive me." His brown eyes batted passionately.

"Frank . . ."

He held up a hand. "Don't say anything right now. I'm taking these to the bell desk, and when your shift is over you can tell me then. He plucked the card and placed it in her hand. "Now, go take your break."

Jaz didn't respond, just sighed, and marched off to the lounge. It wasn't Frank she was mad at—it was her, for being such easy prey. Somehow, someway, he had the power to walk right through her brick wall like it wasn't even there.

When she reached the lounge, it was nearly vibrating with feverish banter. So she decided to open the card before going inside.

Please forgive me. I want you in my life and no one else.

I love you,

Frank

The words tugged at her heart. He obviously was very sorry. *Wait a minute!* Something was missing, something very important. No one else sounded like *only her* and not her children. Finding the flaw in his gallant ploy, she pushed through the door and went inside.

Connie saw her come in and galloped over. "We want details!"

"And lessons," another said. It appeared all the women had heard about the spectacle and crowded to hear her response.

Jasmine wasn't prepared to be cornered nor questioned. "I don't know what to say . . . it's really nothing."

Connie's mouth unhinged. "What!? Are you kidding me? I heard it was three dozen."

"It probably was." Jaz sat down and exhaled. "But this person wants to be in my life and I don't."

Connie's hands flew out from her sides. "Isn't it that good-lookin' dude that runs the hotel? Who could resist that hunk?!"

Jasmine saw all the incomprehensible eye-rolling as the women shook their heads and walked away. She began to question herself. *Maybe Frank did have a forgivable excuse . . . maybe she owed him that much.*

"Are you sick? You must be," Connie said, placing the back of her hand on Jasmine's forehead.

"I'm fine. We just got off to a rocky start, and I don't want to get hurt again, that's all."

Connie slapped her butt. "Hurt me, baby, hurt me."

Jaz couldn't help but laugh, but she was serious in every sense of the word. She latched onto Connie's shoulder and looked her square in the eye. "Be careful what you wish for. It really does hurt."

It wasn't long before the disgruntled chatter headed up the stairs to the casino. Jaz glanced in the mirror before going up, and a confused, lost soul stared back. It looked as if her entire being was in search of an answer. One she didn't have.

When Jasmine returned to her game, Tony walked up to her holding a clipboard. This meant one thing: early out. The little voice inside her head screamed with both hands waving, *"Yes, yes! I will, I will!"* Her responsible voice put a sock in it. *"You can't, you can't. You have bills to pay."* He looked at her. "Yea or nay?"

Jasmine opened her mouth, but only a groan trickled from her lips.

"I don't have all fuckin' day. What's it gonna be?" He looked at the customers and shrugged. "Whoops, I slipped."

"No, no thanks," she stammered.

"Now, was that so hard?" He took a pencil and crossed off her name then went to the next dealer on the list. Little did he know how hard that was? It was as hard as saying *NO* to Frank.

Making it through the eight grinding hours, Jasmine said her final "good luck" then went to the lounge to change out of her uniform. After that, she headed directly to the employee exit, climbed in her truck, rolled down the window, and took off with the cold air whipping through her hair.

It felt absolutely wonderful but not as wonderful as having the willpower to refuse Frank and his three dozen, long stemmed, red roses.

Slipping into a t-shirt and sweat pants, Jaz poured a glass of wine and snuggled on the couch with the kids. Taking a sip, she relaxed back just as the phone rang.

Shauna jumped up. "I'll get it."

"If it's Frank I'm not home."

"Hello?"

"Hi, is Jasmine there?"

"Who is this?"

"It's Jerome. Is this Shauna?"

Shauna put her hand over the receiver. "Mom, it's Jerome!" She came back. "Yes, this is Shauna. How are you, Dr. Jensen—I mean Jerome?"

"I'm great. How are you?"

Shauna rocked side-to-side, rattling on enamored. "I'm doing fine and no one's tried to break in our house. Mom said the prowler is gone, thank goodness."

Jerome kicked off his shoes and leaned over the kitchen counter. "I'm glad to hear that. Hey, I thought I might come to Tahoe and visit for a couple days. I was hoping we could all get together."

"That sounds fun." Jaz was standing next to Shauna. "Well, here's Mom. See you soon."

"Okay, see you soon."

"This is a nice surprise. Are you at work?"

Jerome smiled, hearing her voice. "Actually, I'm home. I decided to join the regular crowd and sleep at night."

Jaz sat down at the table. "What made you switch?"

"I guess it was time for a change."

"I hear you there. I'm ready for a change, too. I just don't know what it is yet."

Jerome knew exactly what it would be, if he had it his way. "I'm calling to tell you I'll be in Tahoe tomorrow. I get in around two o'clock."

"Oh, that's great!"

"I know. I'm really looking forward to seeing you and the kids again."

Jasmine's eyes darted at the door as someone rapped melodically on it. "Excuse me for a second." She called to the kids, "Can you see who's at the door?"

Justin got up and spied through the curtain. Frank was standing with the rejected bouquet of roses. He hollered back, "Mom, it's Frank! And he has a giant bouquet of roses!"

Her eyes bugged, knowing Jerome heard every blasted word. She timidly got back on. "Ahh . . . sorry about that." She winced.

"Sounds like you have company," he muttered, deflated.

"I don't know why he's here. Believe me, I haven't been seeing him."

"Well, you better go see what he wants, or at least rescue the roses." Jerome tried to sound unruffled.

"Mom! Frank is still at the door. Do you want me to let him in or what?" Justin shouted.

Jaz covered the phone with her hand. "Just tell him to come in. I'll be just a minute." As Frank entered, she decided to end the conversation with an embellished finale. "I'm so excited you called, Jerome. I can't wait to see you tomorrow! Call me when you get in."

He perked up and smiled. "I can't wait to see you, too. I will—I'll call as soon as I get off the plane."

"Sounds great!" Jaz hung up, grinning from ear-to-ear. She walked into the living room and there, standing in the corner next to the door, was a different Frank. His clothes didn't have the usual *never been worn* look. His slick, ever-ready hair was disheveled. But what really got her was the look on his face. It reflected an absence of worth. She felt like reaching out to comfort him, but she also knew he was a man of many disguises.

"You forgot these," he said and held out the roses.

Shauna and Justin were more entertained with them than what was on TV. With eyes glued, they watched and listened while eating their popcorn.

"Why don't we go out on the deck for some privacy," Jasmine said, giving them a stern glare.

Frank set the bouquet on the kitchen table and followed her outside. She walked to the swing while he walked to the railing and looked out over the wooded ravine. "I heard you talking to Jerome. He's coming to Tahoe?"

Jasmine sat down on the swing but kept it steady. "Yeah, he'll be here tomorrow." She leaned back and gaze up at the speckled sky just as a star fell. Closing her eyes, she made a wish. The same wish as always. "Frank, the roses are very beautiful . . . but you don't know me. I'm not easily bribed."

He turned around to see her head tilted back with the moonlight dancing off her face. "You're beautiful, you know that?" Walking over, he eased down next to her and put his arm around her shoulders. "If I wanted to bribe you, I would give you this night. This starry, magnificent night," he turned her face with a finger, "every night."

Leaning down, he tenderly kissed her lips and her wall, brick-by-brick, crumbled to dust and her armor of iron melted like butter. "Jasmine, I want you in my life forever," he whispered softly between kisses. "We belong together. I will take you away from all of this, and you will never have to want again." Taking her face in his hands, he pressed his mouth over hers while his fingers slid down her cheek and over her sweatshirt.

She arched as his fingers brushed over her yearning body, and his magical power kept her longing for more.

"Mom, are you going to be long?!" Justin bellowed from the door, breaking Jasmine from his spell.

Her head shot forward, and her eyes popped open. "No, I'll be right in." She stood up and glared at Frank. "How do you do that?"

He looked up and smiled. His wavy, black hair dangled over his dark, devilish eyes. "You haven't seen anything yet."

"Probably not, but don't forget what I said," she huffed.

He tilted his head. "I think I already have."

"I can't be bribed!"

He chuckled. "We'll see about that."

Jasmine went inside and shut the door—mad, confused, and falling head-over-heels again.

THIRTY-TWO

I t was Saturday early afternoon. Shauna and Justin were with their
friends, and Jerome was expected to arrive in Tahoe around two
o'clock, which gave Jasmine time to catch up on neglected chores.

Switching on the stereo, she tuned into a country channel and
"Take Me Home Country Roads" was playing. It was a sentimental
favorite, so she cranked up the volume and began singing along.
Around the kitchen she twirled with the broomstick. The next song
she two-stepped through the living room with the vacuum. In record
time, the house was clean and laundry done. Now it was her turn.

Drawing a bath, Jasmine slithered into the fragrant lavender bubbles and closed her eyes. While drifting into a steamy euphoric trance time drifted too, and before she knew it the cuckoo clock chirped twice. *Jerome!*

Springing from the tub, she grabbed a towel and raced to her room. Sorting through her closet for something to wear, she heard the phone ring and presumed Jerome was right on time . . . or so she thought. "Hello?" she answered excitedly.

"Is this a day off, or are you avoiding me?"

"Oh . . . hi Frank," she said, disappointed.

"Well, at least you got my name right this time."

His cynicism hit a nerve, and she went from bubbly to boiling. "For your information, this is my day off. Unlike you, I don't have the luxury of leaving work whenever I want."

He sat back and smirked. "You could, just name the day." He looked out the window, envisioning her in a long flowing white gown. "I'll never forget the first time you were here at my office. Man, you turned me on. You still do . . ."

"Frank—stop!" She pulled at her hair. "Jerome will be here any minute and I'm not ready."

His muscles tightened. "What do you see in him, anyway? Besides, he lives two states away."

She grinned. "Is that jealousy I hear?"

"Him!? No." Frank wasn't going to admit it had been gnawing at him like a dog on a bone. "Did he say *why* he was coming?"

"I'm assuming business." She looked at the clock. "Listen, I've got to go." She also knew in a matter of seconds she'd need a quick exorcism if she talked to him any longer.

"All right. I'll talk to you later. Hey, don't have too much fun." He listened for her response, but the line was dead.

Jaz went to her room, babbling to herself, and resumed pawing through her closet when the phone rang again. Her eyes narrowed and teeth clenched. With long, brisk strides she marched to the phone, this time prepared. "Now what?!"

"Uh . . . sorry, I think I have the wrong number." The phone clicked.

Jasmine recognized the voice. It was Jerome! Then the phone rang again. She let it ring twice, then answered in a sweet, cheery tone. *"Hello!"*

"Jasmine?"

"Hi Jerome! Are you here?"

"Yeah, whew, I'm glad it's you. I called the wrong number and got someone having a really bad day."

"Hmm, well, now you have me!"

He liked the sound of that and stretched out on the freshly made bed. "So how are you?" He rested his head back and pictured her face.

"I'm great. How are you—how was your flight?" She regained her excitement.

"My flight was smooth, and honestly I've never felt better."

"Well, I'm sure changing shifts made a big difference. I don't know how people can work those late hours. I'd be a walking zombie."

"I *was* a walking zombie." He was anxious to see her and felt they were wasting precious time. "I'm really looking forward to seeing you and the kids. When can we all get together?"

His request sounded almost odd, having the kids included in his plans. "They're at their friends right now, but I expect them home in an hour. We can get together then, if you'd like."

"Sounds perfect." Jerome looked at his watch. "Let's see, it's 2:15 now. Say, 4:00 I'll pick you up. I thought we could have a picnic by the lake. How does that sound?"

He couldn't have painted a more perfect picture. "I would love that, and I'm sure Justin and Shauna would too."

"All right. I'll grab a bucket of chicken and see you then."

"We'll be ready. Oh, is there anything I can bring?"

He grinned. "Can't think of anything else I need."

Jasmine jogged to her room and stormed through her closet. She found a comfortable yellow cotton blouse and put it on with a pair of jeans and boots. She let her hair hang loose, added a touch of lip gloss, a light spray of perfume, and she was ready.

Looking for her purse, she heard the phone ring again. "I may as well be the operator," she uttered to herself. Not sure who to expect, she answered in a soft voice. "Hello?"

"Jaz, it's Frank."

She took a deep breath. "Yes?"

"For your information, there are no conventions scheduled for physicians at any of the hotels."

"Thank you for your thorough investigation."

"Just thought you should know."

"Thanks, I've gotta go. Bye." She hung up thinking about Jerome's visit. *Was it just for her?*

At 3:30 the door flew open, and the kids came barreling in the house. "Hi Mom, we're home!"

"Hi! Guess what we're doing today?" Jaz said, standing with her hands on her hips and a wide smile. They both stared at her curiously. "Jerome is in town and wants to take us to the lake for a picnic."

"Whoo-hoo!" Justin hollered and leaped in the air. "Can we go to Camp Garrison, where you can rent bicycles and watch the fish in the trout pond?" he asked almost out of breath.

"I think that's a great idea." Jaz put her hand on Shauna's shoulder. "What about you, does that sound fun?"

"Sure, I kind of like Jerome." Her view of boys had changed. They were now past irritating to intriguing. "Do you like him?" she asked with a timid smile.

"If you mean as a friend, yes. I think he's a very nice man."

Justin opened the refrigerator. "I'm hungry."

"You'll have to wait. Jerome is bringing fried chicken, and he'll be here in fifteen minutes."

Justin shut the refrigerator door. "But I'm hungry now!"

"And you'll be hungry later. That's what happens to boys your age. You eat and eat until you're a big hairy man."

Justin gulped and his face blushed. "Oh, I know what this is all about. It's about the birds and bees stuff, isn't it?"

Jaz put her arm around his shoulder. "Well, you're close, but we'll talk about that another day."

"Good, 'cause I don't want to know what they do." Then he scurried off to his room.

As the cuckoo clock struck four times, the kids heard a knock at the door. Shauna looked out the window to see Jerome standing on the porch. "Mom, Jerome is here!"

Jasmine called from her room. "Let him in, please. I'll be right there." Feeling a little nervous, she glanced in the mirror, smoothed down her hair and took a deep breath. Then she casually walked out to meet him wearing the same attire he'd envisioned in his dream.

He swallowed hard when she came into view. The woman who kissed him every night in his sleep just became real and was walking right toward him. Her lush autumn hair, innocent smile and tranquilizing sapphire eyes were more beautiful than he remembered. "Wow, you look amazing."

Jasmine almost stumbled when she saw him. The sophisticated doctor in his business suit and tie was left home, and his windswept rugged twin had taken his place. She lingered over his denim shirt, working down every pearl snap until resting on his western, silver belt buckle. From his faded, frayed blue jeans to his cowboy boots, he wasn't anything like she remembered.

"I like your cowboy boots," he said to her.

"I like yours too," she uttered, and ascended back to his ocean blue eyes. "You look—different."

He smiled and his dimples creased. "I don't always wear suits."

Then he turned to the children. "Hey guys, want to go on a picnic?"

Justin shoved his hands in his pockets. "I'm not that hungry. I'm gonna try to stop eating."

Shauna burst out laughing. "What? You stop eating. I'd like to see that."

Jasmine stepped in. "I'll explain later." She winked at Jerome.

Jerome put a hand on Justin's shoulder. "I don't know about you, but I love fried chicken."

Justin shrugged. "I do too, but I don't want to turn into a big hairy man."

Jerome chuckled. "I think you've got awhile before that happens, and a lot more eating to do."

Justin let out a sigh. "I am pretty hungry."

"So am I." Jerome said, rubbing his hands together. "So let's go to the lake and have a picnic." He opened the front door and waited as Jasmine and the kids shuffled outside.

"Oh boy, a jeep! This'll be fun." Justin yelped as everyone climbed into a seat.

"It might be a little cool and windy so button up," Jerome said and took off down the road.

From the summit of Heavenly Valley, along the peaks of the Sierras, and across to the North rim, they could see for hundreds of miles.

Jaz pulled her hair from her face and looked over at Jerome. His hair lashed in the wind, and the sun gleamed over a growth of whiskers, giving him an edgy, rough appeal. His entire presence exuded such masculinity that just being with him made her feel safe and secure.

Jerome felt her scrutiny and glanced over at her. "Anywhere in particular you want to go?"

His words roused her from her trance. "Oh, ah, yeah, there's a great picnic area on the California side called Camp Garrison. It's really beautiful."

"Sounds perfect, just point me in the right direction."

Justin leaned between them. "Do you like to ride bicycles, Jerome?"

"I do, but I haven't been on one for quite a while. Why?"

"Because you can rent 'em there, and it has a trout pond, too."

Justin's excitement was contagious. Shauna and Jasmine recounted a memorable day they spent fishing and riding bikes around the wooded pathway. It was something they planned to do again someday.

"Then I think it's unanimous. We'll ride bikes and see trout." He glanced at Jasmine the same time she looked at him, and each felt strangely connected.

Reaching Camp Garrison, Jerome found a secluded spot with a picnic table and a trail leading down to the lake. Jasmine laid a checkered tablecloth on top of the table while Jerome passed out paper plates, and the bucket of chicken.

The kids finished in a flash then ran off to have a rock skipping contest, opening an opportunity for Jerome to disclose his desires.

Staring across the table at Jasmine and her inviting eyes, he eased in slowly. "So, you've been well and back to your regular routines?"

She relaxed, and crossed her arms on the table. "I've been okay. My friend, Yarah just got fired. She was the one who stayed with me after you left."

"I'm sorry to hear that. What happened?"

"Oh, it's a long story." She waved. That night had been permanently locked away, never to be reopened again. "But what really hurt is she just took off! And I know she would have found a job if she'd tried." She locked eyes with him. "I've always been a firm believer that if there's a will there's a way."

That was music to Jerome's ears. "I like the way you think," he said and smiled.

She shrugged. "It's gotten me this far." Feeling comfortable, she broached a question that had been nudging her after Frank's call. A slow smile curled. "Why did you come to Tahoe? Was it for business or—"

"Hey, Mom and Jerome! Come and see the tiny fish swimming around. There's a ton of 'em," Justin called.

Jasmine chuckled. "We'll probably have to continue this later."

"I'd love to. Maybe we could get together for a glass of wine or something."

"Okay. Tonight would work."

"Great. Tonight it is."

They left the picnic site and walked to where the kids were playing. The blue sky was fading into soft pastel pink over the undulating swells of the lake. "It's really beautiful here. I can see why you chose this place," Jerome said.

"It is," Jaz uttered, enveloped in the bliss.

Justin piped in. "Jerome, do you want to see the trout pond or ride a bike?"

Jaz laughed nervously. "We're not going to get an ounce of peace with him."

"That's okay." Jerome ruffled up Justin's hair. "Boys will be boys."

"That's right! Come on and I'll show you." Justin took off running down the path with Shauna behind him. Jerome felt an urge to hold Jasmine's hand as their fingertips collided. Then he remembered she'd just received roses from Frank and thought it might be too soon. There was a perfect time for everything and tonight would be his.

THIRTY-THREE

When Jasmine arrived at the Pier Pub she spotted Jerome's jeep right next to the door, which meant he'd arrived before the dinner crowd or miraculously was at the right spot at the right time.

It was a local favorite, including hers and Yarah's, and was always packed from morning to midnight. Circling around, she left the lot and wedged in next to the curb down the street.

When she walked in Jerome was sitting at a corner table next to the fireplace. That, too, was a coveted spot. He waved to her and smiled.

She waved back and strolled up to him. "Well hello stranger, mind if I join you?" she said playfully and took off her coat. He stood up glazed with perspiration and welcomed her with a firm hug, exposing his rapidly beating heart. "You're shivering," she said.

"I was a little cold, hence the fireplace." He motioned with a hand. In truth, his nerves were dangling like live wires, worrying about the outcome of his confession. He hung her coat over her chair and waited as she sat. Then he sat and looked into her eyes, down her hair and over her black scoop-neck sweater.

What he saw was more than a beautiful woman sitting across from him. He saw his single life changing into something he never imagined: a family. It was almost as if he was looking into the future. "I think you get prettier every time I see you."

She smiled humbly and clasped her hands. "Thank you, and so do you . . . I mean, look very handsome." His dark brown sweater emphasized his blonde hair and muscular chest.

Leaning back, he caught his breath. "I hope you don't mind; I ordered us a bottle of wine."

"Sounds great."

Just then the waitress shuffled over. "Here you go." Her round eyes fluttered as she uncorked the bottle. Then she poured a glass for Jerome to sample. He gave a nod and she filled their glasses, leaving the bottle on the table.

Jerome held up his glass. "Here's to a wonderful day." They clinked and took a sip. Then he set his down and gazed at her like a love-sick boy. "I feel sorry for any man who lost you. They were clearly out of their mind."

She chuckled. "And all this time I thought I was out of *my* mind." He cocked his head, puzzled by her comment. "Well, I'm stretching it a bit. But I do believe there's a true love for everyone. That is, until lately, and now," she smiled briefly, "I don't know what to believe."

Jerome leaned toward her. "Jasmine, you're every man's dream and should be treated like a queen. Don't ever stop believing that, and whatever you do, don't settle for less."

Jasmine felt his words stitched into her heart. "No man has ever said anything like that to me before."

He rested back. "Like I said, they were clearly out of their mind."

The moment prompted Jasmine to seek the answer she never received. She took a sip of wine and casually asked, "You never got a chance to tell me why you're here."

Jerome looked at her, then down at his wine and swirled it. "Well, there's a lot to it." He drew in a breath, suddenly feeling like a cornered rabbit. "I guess I'll just say it the way it is. I like you a lot. You've been on my mind . . . a lot."

She listened patiently as he searched for the right words to piece together. "And, if you're not in a hurry, I'll give you the long version to make this a little more understandable." She nodded, intensely locked on his face. "I play basketball, and during a game I was elbowed in the eye. It detached my retina." His eyes became turbulent waves of blue. "I've had several operations, nine to be precise, to reattach the retina. And due to the extreme trauma, I contracted a disease." He saw the muscles in her face stiffen. "It's brain cancer. I don't know how long I have . . . they told me—"

Her emotions exploded. "I'm so sorry, Jerome." Her eyes filled with round tears. "Is there anything the doctors can do?"

"There's something *I* can do and that's join the living. Ever since I was diagnosed, I've denied myself of feeling. Feeling good—feeling bad. I've basically been living a numb life. It seemed a waste of time to feel anything, knowing I wouldn't be around much longer. So I devoted myself to making others feel good."

He shook his head with his hands out. "I don't know what you've done to me, but I want to be among the living again." He took her trembling hand in his. "This is the first date I've been on since . . . I can't remember." Jasmine just stared at him. She couldn't move, couldn't speak, couldn't breathe. "I never felt right denying a woman the hope of having a family or a husband she deserved. It would hurt me as much as them." His face grew animated. "Do you want to know what opened my eyes?" She nodded. "All the comments I hear from my patients."

"Like what?" she murmured, trying to keep her composure.

"How long do I have to live? And, will I be okay?" Jerome raised his hands. "Who knows? That's a question I can't answer. No one really knows. So why should I deny myself the chance to *really* live when this seems to be the universal question?"

Jasmine clutched the stem of her glass with both hands. It felt like the power of his voice would surely knock it over. She gazed at him and moved her lips, but the words came out in slow motion and garbled. "I-I don't . . . I-I think . . ."

Jerome lifted her chin with a finger. "They gave me six months. It's been a year."

"So, there *is* hope," she said, feeling her blood begin to pump.

"Well, I do have access to any drug that comes along. So why not try everything?"

"Something's working then—keeping you alive," she said, revived.

"I think more than anything, I refuse to give up." He leaned forward. "And now my will to live is stronger than ever. Jasmine, you're the one who's making it stronger." He brushed a tear from her cheek. "Listen, I know we live far from each other, but things change and anything can happen. All I know is my nightmares are gone and replaced with your face. I can't ignore that." The momentum of his energy surged like a river as he passionately declared his desire for her.

"And that's why you're here," she uttered.

"Yes." He gripped her hand, transferring all his energy with the need for understanding.

Remembering how evasive he was on the topic of children, Jasmine asked, "Are you not able to, you know, have children?"

"Unfortunately, the medications have negated that entirely."

Hearing his story, and seeing the renewed spirit it in his eyes, she *now* felt like the cornered rabbit. He didn't know she was experiencing her own crippling battle. Like him, it was the reason she was alone. All her life she had dreamt of the perfect love—one that was constant, unconditional and made her feel alive.

Knowing his life could expire any day, it shed a dreary, flickering light. She wanted to feel love long and deep, without the imminent fear of having it ripped from her heart again. They both sat back, pondering in silence all that was expressed, acknowledged and felt. Yet, he waited breathlessly for her to speak.

The room was hammering as if with her own heartbeat. She gave him a sympathetic smile. "Jerome, I'm thankful I've replaced your nightmares, but I-I just don't know what to say." Her face revealed the words she couldn't express.

"I know, and you don't have to say anymore. Just understand I had to take the chance and find out your feelings." He looked down at his wine and took a sip. "It was pretty farfetched to even think you'd consider me and my deep-dark secret." Steadying the glass, he looked into her eyes. "You just seem so perfect for me. You're strong, honest and intelligent, not to mention beautiful. And you've already experienced motherhood and have two wonderful children. I could never find another woman like you if I searched the world over." His earnest eyes exposed emotions raw and forthright.

This time, Jaz reached out and put her hand on his. "I'm not saying I don't want to see you again. It's just that . . . this has been a lot to take in. I need some time to process it. I like you, too." What she saw in Jerome was a man who defied death. A man of strength and tenacity. A man who had more compassion for others than any person she'd ever known. The words unexpectedly fell from her lips. "I guess it's worth a try."

Jerome grinned, regaining vision of his foolish dream becoming real. "That's all I ask, and if it doesn't work, then at least we can say we tried. What do we have to lose?"

Jaz smiled, although his comment left a resounding clang in her head. *What do we have to lose?*

The waitress rushed in to give them their check. "I didn't want to interrupt you, but my shift is over and I'm closing out. Can you settle this now, please?" She set the receipt on the table.

"Sure." Jerome pulled out his wallet and handed her enough money to include a tip. "Keep the change."

"Thanks. You two love birds have a great night." She swished away.

"I should be going too. I'm exhausted," Jasmine murmured as every muscle in her body quivered with intense overload.

"I'm sure our conversation is the reason. I feel like I've been riding a roller coaster all night." He chuckled. His sense of humor soothed the bitter truth of what actually took place.

Leaving the Pier Pub, he slid his fingers through hers, and his warmth and strength as before enveloped her with security. "Where are you parked?" he asked.

She pointed down the street. And as they walked hand-in-hand, she couldn't comprehend how someone like him could be so deathly ill. It just didn't seem possible or humanly fair.

Reaching her truck, she hunted for her keys while he hunted for a way to see her again, just one more time. "Listen, you can say no and I'll understand, but I'd love to take you to dinner tomorrow—any restaurant, you pick."

His request would give her time to get to know him better and make a more conscientious decision. "Well, I've heard of a steakhouse on the other side of the lake that's supposed to be fantastic."

His eyes sparkled. "What's the name and I'll make reservations."

"North Point Grille. It's a bit of a drive."

"Sounds perfect. I'll pick you up around six." He lightly kissed her cheek then opened her door.

Jasmine climbed in, stuck her key in the ignition and touched his arm. "Thank you for being so honest. It means more to me than you know." *One particular face came to mind.* "So, until tomorrow."

He nodded and shut her door then opened it again. "I forgot to ask. What's your favorite flower?"

"Hmm . . . I'd have to say wildflowers." She looked at him curiously.

He shut her door smiling and walked back to his car.

As she pulled away from the curb, a tide grew strong, and the repercussion of his devastating news hit her like the crushing waves of the sea. Her lungs heaved for air as tears welled and poured. It was more than she wanted to know, or prepared to know, the reason for his visit. And now she'd given *two* men a morsel of hope, telling them: *"It's worth a try"* and *"Maybe."* What was she going to do?

THIRTY-FOUR

To accommodate the load and optimum profitability, Frank custom fit his Cessna by removing all the seats, except the pilot's, then added extra fuel bladders for a non-stop flight. On a normal run, he carried one-hundred to one-hundred and fifty guns, but this wasn't a normal run. This would be his last with a tight fit of two hundred. After that, he was done. Frank paced as the phone rang several times.

"Yeah!"

"Mac, it's Frank."

"Lucky for you I forgot my keys. I was just headin' out the door."

"I'm making a run on Monday. I need two hundred this time."

"Of what, and hurry up? I got a sweet young Chiquita in the car waitin' for me."

"I want one-hundred M-16's and one-hundred Mac-10's. Frank had his list honed down to the most demanded.

"I'll have 'em ready. Fuck no, I'll be out of town."

Frank massaged his forehead. "Just stash them in the barn, usual place, and I'll get them before I leave."

"Pay me first. It'll be forty G's this time."

"I'm not making two trips. You'll have to meet me."

"When?"

"Tomorrow night, 6:00 on the last level of the parking garage at the Palace."

"Forget it . . . too risky."

"We'll be alone. I'll make sure of it."

"If you don't, I guarantee you'll regret it." Mac slammed down the phone.

The morning sun blazed through the window, nudging Jerome awake. He turned on the TV and listened to the news as his eyes adjusted and headache faded. Then he anxiously got up to start the day.

Today he was on a mission, which had nothing to do with Jasmine, but rather the man who deceived her. His distrust with Frank never subsided and had pestered him since he left Tahoe. To put it to rest, he decided to do a little investigating and see what secrets the casino held hostage.

Not having a course of action, Jerome knew elevators were a good source of information. All he needed was a crumb, or tidbit of gossip, to substantiate his suspicion. Leaving the room, he took the elevator to the 6th floor. This was the administrative level. When it opened, he stayed and waited as a woman entered.

They rode quietly together while he thought of something to say. Luckily his stomach growled which instigated a conversation. "The food looks good," he said, gesturing to a poster displaying the buffet menu.

The woman grinned. "I take it you don't work here?"

"No, just visiting."

"Then I recommend the coffee shop. At this time of day you'll be waiting in line forever. That is, unless you get a line pass from one of the pit bosses."

Jerome angled his head. "How do I do that?"

"Just sit down at any game and play for a while. It doesn't have to be long. Then ask the dealer to get you a line pass for the buffet. My friends do it all the time. It's the best way to avoid an hour wait."

"Great. I'll do that." Jerome thought he'd dig a little deeper. "So, I'm guessing you *do* work here?"

The mid-aged woman pushed her glasses back to the bridge of her nose and looked up. "For seventeen years."

Jerome nodded. "You know, I wanted to personally thank the hotel manager for my room. Can you tell me who that is and where to find them?" he asked to open an informative conversation.

"Oh, that's Mr. Pazzarelli, but he's a hard man to track down." The elevator door opened, and she hurried out as more people bustled inside. "Have fun and good luck," she said and waved.

"But-but . . ." The door closed. Next stop, the casino. A stroll around the main floor could be a fortuitous detour to the buffet.

Spotting a dealer standing alone at a game, Jerome surmised by his good looks and cocky grin, he was probably in the loop with the latest scoop. "Hi, mind if I try my luck?" he glanced at his nametag, "Brad."

The dealer motioned with his hand. "Pick a seat." Then he began shuffling the cards. Jerome took the first chair and tossed a twenty dollar bill on the table. "You feelin' lucky?" Brad asked, grinning.

"Not sure what I'm feeling—hope it's luck," Jerome said and smiled.

"Where you from?" Brad asked as he slid a stack of silver dollars to Jerome.

"I was just going to ask you the same question. Your badge doesn't say."

"You know the casino; they have a reason for everything. If my name tag doesn't say where I'm from, then you'll probably ask, like you did, and a conversation starts . . . like it did."

"Boy, they nailed that one, didn't they?" Jerome chuckled.

"Yeah, they don't miss a beat. Anyway, I'm from Nebraska." He held the deck ready to toss the cards.

Jerome set three dollars in his circle. "Nebraska, I remember it being a big sea of green."

"You mean all the cornfields?"

"Yeah, for hundreds of miles it seemed."

"That's why I left. My dad was a farmer, his dad was a farmer, and I was supposed to be one." He shook his head. "I'm not a farmer and never will be." He scraped away Jerome's losing bet then waited for his next.

"So what brought you to Tahoe?"

"My sister vacationed here and told me about it. Nebraska doesn't have mountains, and I've always wanted to learn how to ski. And, it just seemed like a really cool place to live."

"How about this hotel; do you like it here?" Jerome set another bet in the circle.

Brad stopped dealing and stared at Jerome. "Oh, I know who you are. You're one of those shoppers. I say something wrong, and the next thing you know I'm written up." He smiled big and wide. "Everything is just peachy-creamy here."

Jerome angled his head. "We're just having a friendly conversation, nothing else."

Brad looked side-to-side. "You're not here to score me on my customer service bullshit—I mean bullcrap?"

"Nope, just thought I'd try my luck before breakfast."

Brad shot him two cards. "I like it here okay. The casino manager just died, which, don't get me wrong, turned out good for us dealers. He was a real asshole, and the biggest sweater in the joint."

"Sweater?"

"You know, sweatin' over every nickel paid out."

"Oh, I see. So who's in charge now?" Jerome carried on nonchalantly.

"Who knows, why do you ask?"

"I have a friend here, Frank Pazzarelli. Do you know him?"

"I think he's the hotel manager."

"Yeah, that's him."

"I see him around now and then, but he doesn't talk to me. No offense, but he struts around like he owns the joint."

Jerome chuckled. "That sounds like Frank. I guess nothing's changed. Hey look, he doesn't know I'm here and I wanted to surprise him. I thought I'd leave a college photo in his car. You wouldn't happen to know where he parks, would you." Jerome turned over his cards and watched his last three dollars get scraped into the rack.

"He probably parks on level two with the rest of the suits." He pointed to the promenade. "If you follow that walkway to the lobby, you'll see the elevator to the garage on the right."

"Thanks. Uh . . . you wouldn't happen to know what he's driving, do you?"

Brad grinned. "You can't miss it. It's the nicest car in the garage. A big black Benz."

"He always had a thing for nice cars," Jerome said and casually stood. "Well thanks for all your help, Brad. And remember, this is a surprise."

He shrugged. "Like I said, we don't talk."

Before breakfast, Jerome decided to take a quick side-trip to the parking garage and locate Frank's car. Getting off on the second floor, he walked the length of the garage and down every row but didn't see a black Benz. His stomach growled again, giving the two-minute warning. He left for breakfast and to plot his next move.

Walking through the casino, toward the buffet, Jerome ran into a long chain of people and realized he'd forgotten to get a line pass. Since the last attempt cost him twenty dollars, he made a U-turn, taking the woman's advice, and went to the coffee shop instead.

Sipping a cup of coffee while digesting a stack of blueberry hot cakes and bacon, he remembered something else the woman said: *"He's a hard man to track down."* Jerome was prepared to do whatever it took to ensure Jasmine's safety.

With a full belly and renewed energy, he went back to the garage to find Frank's car. Knowing he didn't associate with others, it was probably his best resource for loose ends or hidden secrets. Roaming every level with no luck, Jerome disappointedly headed back to the elevator just as a car went screeching past him. He quickly turned and watched a black Mercedes Benz careen around the bend and drive to the upper level. *Now we're getting somewhere.*

Hurrying into the elevator, he got off on the casino level and waited for Frank to enter. Hunched and hidden from view, he began to grow impatient. Something was holding him up—something he needed to know. As he stood, ready to investigate, the elevator opened and out bolted Frank.

Jerome ducked down and watched him march by in a focused, determined stride. He followed at a distance, keeping an eye on him, weaving through the people until he entered the main elevator. Now, while the coast was clear, Jerome went back to the garage and proceeded with his undercover digging.

The elevator opened on the last level, level five. He immediately spotted Frank's car. It was the only car there, which he thought was strange. But it wasn't as strange as where he'd parked. His car was tucked in a corner, next to the stairwell, and far from the elevator. *Hmm . . . obviously intentional.*

Scoping the area to make sure he was alone, he dashed to the car and crouched down between it and the wall. He tested the passenger door handle. It was locked. Then he scooted around to the other doors, they too were locked. Searching every inch and crevice for a way in, he noticed the passenger window was open a crack. Recalling a similar situation in his younger days, he opened the door with the dipstick.

Slinking to the front of the car, Jerome wedged between the bumper and the wall and released the hood. Taking another quick look around, he pulled out the dipstick and quietly lowered the hood.

Scurrying back to the passenger window, he bent the tip of the dipstick and inserted the loop through the crack of the window. Holding onto the bent tip, he slid the loop down the window to the door handle, slipped it over, gave it a swift tug, and the door opened. Returning the dipstick to the oil port, he secured the hood and climbed inside the car.

Like a snake, Jerome slithered over the seat to the glove compartment and sifted through the contents. Other than a multitude of pain relievers and antacids, there was nothing out of the ordinary. He pulled up the floor mats and checked under the front seat. Still not a crumb of incriminating evidence to go with.

Creeping over to the back seat, he spied a folded blanket on the floor behind the driver's seat. He carefully lifted it, and his eyes snapped open. *Jackpot!* A metal briefcase was tucked halfway under the front seat. He raised his head and peered out, feeling a presence lurking. Fortunately, it was only his rattling nerves.

He quickly brought the case to his lap as a splat of sweat hit the shiny surface then another. Wiping his head and case dry, he held his breath and depressed the two side locks. Surprisingly, they snapped open. *Frank, you're slipping up.* With brow creased and his teeth clenched, Jerome slowly lifted the lid. "Whoa, what do we have here?" he muttered, thumbing through a stack of bundled bills.

Just then, a ding echoed through the garage like a Sunday morning church bell. Jerome looked up and his heart stopped, seeing Frank standing outside the elevator with a maintenance man. He couldn't hear what they were saying, but it sounded like they were in an argument. Regardless, he had to get out and fast.

Shutting the case, he pushed it back under the seat and set the blanket on top. Extending his finger up like a telescope, he locked the door he'd entered and unlocked the back door then quietly slipped out.

Staying crouched to the ground, he listened to them argue as Frank demanded to have the level closed until the next day. Then he heard shoes clicking against the pavement and coming closer to the car. Posed like a sprinter with every muscle quivering, Jerome waited for the precise moment to escape. The stairwell was his only option.

He heard keys jangle, and then the car door opened. As the door shut with a loud bang, he dove around the corner and down the concrete stairwell.

Sprawled and breathless, not moving a muscle, the car engine started, and then tires screeched out of the garage. Jerome let out a heavy winded sigh, climbed to his knees and staggered inside.

Frank raced home after realizing he'd left without his partner. If something went wrong he wanted the odds even, and Walther was the only one that could do that.

Storming through the door to his office, he unlocked the gun cabinet and released the latch. And there, posed like a high-class hooker, dressed to kill and ready for action, was his beauty. Frank shoved the gun down his pants as Clive poked his head around the door. "I thought you were gone," Frank said, surprised.

"No, actually, I'm waist-deep in laundry," Clive replied. "And pardon me for saying, but you've certainly gone through a bushel of briefs lately." He huffed.

Frank groaned, "It's been one of those weeks."

"I see." Clive started to leave then turned. "As for dinner, I thought—"

"Don't bother; I'll be home late."

Clive smirked. "Well, I suppose that's a fair consolation for washing your skivvies." He shot him a look and then off he toddled.

After locking up the office, Frank headed back to the Palace now prepared for the unexpected. It was essential to predict the unpredictable.

Though his relationship with Mac was going on four years, by no means were they friends. Mac was as mean as he was dangerous and wouldn't hesitate to kill him if things went awry. Frank greased the maintenance man to make sure the garage level was closed. That, at least, would reduce the risk of a witness.

Linda knocked on Frank's office door. "Yes?"

She peered in then entered. "Excuse me, Mr. Pazzarelli, I don't mean to interrupt, but while you were gone a woman named . . ." she looked at her note again, "Mimma Gamboli called."

Frank sat up. "What did she say?"

"Here's the message." She walked over and handed it to him then stood with her hands clasped.

Frank gave her a brief smile. "Thanks. You can leave now, and close the door."

"Of course, but I thought you should know the message is verbatim. She even made me use two exclamation marks and then read it back to her. I have to say, she was pretty upset you weren't here when she called."

"Really? How's that?"

"She was yelling about where you were and who you were with. I told her you were gathering the daily reports, but I don't think she believed me." Linda shrugged. "Sorry."

Frank nodded. "Thanks."

"Sure," she sighed and left his office.

Frank read the note.

Meet me at the Pine View bar tonight at 6:00 and don't be late!! Mimma.

"Fuck!" Frank slammed his fist on the desk then stormed out onto the terrace. Grasping the railing, he squeezed the cold steel as if trying to wring the life out of it. *I have to be here for Mac. I'll deal with Mimma later.* Making his decision, he went back inside and over to the bar to pour a drink. Slugging it down, he bellowed, "Fuck her!" He poured another. "And fuck Jerome, too!"

THIRTY-FIVE

I t was a bittersweet struggle for Jasmine. She wanted to see Jerome again and get to know him on a deeper level. He had all the qualities she wanted in a man and the mindset of how she should be treated, which was rare in her eyes. Yet the reality of his health siphoned the thrill and depleted her desire. It just didn't seem right her faith in true love was constantly tested every time she met a man.

Nudging the porch swing with her heels, she thought about all the people she had loved and lost. Her father, Hyrum, came to mind first, posed in his three-piece suit.

He was a man of moral and financial dedication, yet seldom allowed time to embrace love. She drifted to Carl, the father of her two most precious treasures. His actions were dictated by a bottle and insisted his money could buy what she wanted. What she wanted didn't cost a dime.

A smile surfaced as she pictured Yarah and her flaming orange hair. She was the catalyst in her emotional recovery—insisted on having fun, expected nothing but the best and always there for her no matter what. She let out a sad sigh. Then there was Frank or was it Frankie—who knows? He was seductively enticing, charismatic, gorgeous, but a man who betrays. Not only that, wanted a second chance!

Tilting her head back, she looked up at the sky and saw a man she would love to love. The only problem was he was clinging to life for his *dear life!* She closed her eyes and called out to the heavens, "Tell me what I should do."

The Lady Luck bar was right in the middle of the casino and off the main promenade. It gave Jerome a bird's eye view of people coming and going. He figured Frank had to pass through sometime and when he did he would be hot on his trail.

The bartender walked over to him. "Sir, can I get you something to drink?"

Jerome twisted around. "No, I'm fine."

Nodding, he examined his face. "Were you in a fight or something?"

Jerome angled his head then realized he'd scraped his face in the fall. He touched his cheek. "Oh, yeah, I tripped on the stairs in the garage. Probably looks worse than it feels."

"I was gonna ask who won. It didn't look like you did." He chuckled.

"That bad, huh?"

"Nothin' a little Tequila wouldn't help."

"Spoken like a true salesman but I'll pass. I have a little business to take care of."

"Okay, just holler if you need anything." He smiled and walked away.

Jerome twisted his stool back around and glanced at his watch. His date with Jasmine was nearing. If Frank was up to something, he'd better do it quick. It was one thing to prove his distrust, but to jeopardize a wonderful evening with Jasmine wasn't worth it.

Combing the area, his eyes narrowed on someone walking his way. It was the man he was looking for. He quickly turned to keep his cover and waited a few minutes, then he slowly pivoted back around. Frank was nowhere in sight. "Now where'd he go?" Jerome muttered, looking back and forth. Digging in his pocket, he pulled out a dollar bill for taking a seat and left to expand his search.

Staying off the main walkway, Jerome took a jaunt through the slot machines, surmising it was the safest route for staying covert. Unbeknownst to him, Frank was thinking the same thing. As they both whipped around the corner their heads nearly bumped, meeting eye-to-eye in total surprise. "Whoa, that was close. How are you doing, Frank?" Jerome said and held out his hand, playing the credulous guest.

"It's Jerome—right?" Frank chose to appear complacent.

"Yes, it is." *That's odd. He knows who I am.*

"Sorry, I'm bad with names."

Jerome smiled and shrugged. "We all have our faults."

Frank studied his face. "You look a little rough around the edges. What happened?"

"Oh, that." He shook his head. "I'm a klutz sometimes. I tripped on the stairs."

Frank nodded. "Hmm, well . . . we all have our faults. It was nice seeing you again, but I'm late for a meeting."

"Yeah, I was just heading to my room. Have a good night." Frank refrained from saying, *"you too"* and left.

Jerome darted back behind a row of slot machines and released a stifled gasp. He watched as Frank charged on, entering the parking garage elevator. Panicked, he knew if anything was going to happen he had to be there.

Just then a group of people in uniforms walked up to the elevator. Jerome joined them as they all got inside. "Long day?" he asked, presuming they were employees.

A young girl sighed, "Yes, thank God it's over."

"I know, my tush is killing me," a slim, petite man said then looked at the man next to him. "How about yours, Richard?"

"I think I have bruises."

"Wanna compare!" Everyone burst out laughing.

They arrived at the second level, and everyone except Jerome exited. He climbed three more levels. As the door opened, his breath became shallow and body began to tremble. He felt like a rat caught in a trap, but he couldn't back out now. It was imperative to know Frank's intent.

The light switch was next to the exit door. He turned it off to avoid any chance of getting caught. Quietly and slowly, he pulled the door open a crack.

Peeking through the slit, he saw Frank sitting in his car. Something told him the silver case was the reason. Needing a better vantage point for viewing and listening, Jerome scanned the area. It appeared the only place was the stairwell, where he got hurt. More challenging, it was behind Frank's car.

Sweat trickled and his heart thumped, calculating how to get there without being seen. With a steady eye on Frank, ready to dash, he stiffened as a silver truck crept up the driveway.

Closing the door to a slit, Jerome sat low and watched as the truck parked next to Frank's car. Then the driver got out. It was too dark to make out any identifying features, but the man was big and brawny, wearing fatigues and army boots. He cautiously walked around to Frank's door, and the silver case exchanged hands.

Jerome had his ear pressed to the crack, straining to hear the conversation, when his sweaty palm slipped off the handle and he fell to the floor.

Lying paralyzed with fear, Jerome peered out the crack of the door. The big man was already in his truck, and Frank was running toward him with a gun.

Thinking fast, Jerome had two options. He could hide behind the door and escape after Frank entered. Or he could act like he was lost and trying to find his car. Instinctively, one or the other was going to happen. He prayed for the escape.

Scrambling to his feet, he hid behind the door just as the elevator dinged and door slid open. It was perfect timing. He started to lunge, but the door blocked him as Frank burst in waving his gun.

In a flash, Jerome snuck out behind him and sprinted for the infamous stairwell. He ran down the stairs, opened the door and charged inside the hotel. Gasping for air, he leaned against the wall until fully composed then hurried back to the casino.

Frank saw the elevator door close without seeing who got inside. With Walther still in the air, he watched as it stopped on the casino level. "You're dead . . . whoever you are." He wasn't concerned about the forty grand he'd sacrificed or that his supply of guns was gone. It was Mac and his zero tolerance for the slightest deviation, and this looked like a setup.

Mac raced home ready for action. He was well rehearsed for this type of scenario and routinely performed drills to perfect the unexpected ambush. The most important and vital rule was leaving no trail. This meant no evidence of any kind, nothing and no one. Next, a new identity and life in Mexico City.

"More olives!" Mimma screamed at the bartender. With legs crossed and fingers strumming, she sat at the Pine View bar and stared out the window.

"I'm coming, I'm coming; hold your whores," he groaned under his breath. Holding up a skewer of olives, he pointed it at her. "That enough?"

"Just put them in my martini," she snarled.

He dropped the skewer with a splash and walked away, shaking his head.

One-by-one, Mimma plucked each olive off with her teeth. "You son-of-a-bitch!" she screeched.

"What?" The bartender said, glaring back at her.

"I'm not talking to you."

"Good, then I'm not talking to you," he uttered.

"I mean, I didn't call you the son-of-a-bitch. I was calling someone else the son-of-a-bitch," she slurred.

"Oh, I see. Well, I hate to break this to you lady, but you're sitting alone."

Mimma waved him off like a pesky fly. Then she stood dazed and wobbly, clutching her chair. "You've disrespected me for the last time, my darling." Tossing back the last drop of her martini, she snagged her purse and weaved toward the door.

"Hey lady, your bill!" the bartender called.

"Mimma stopped, pulled out a hundred-dollar bill from her black satin purse and let it fall to the floor. "That should be sufficient." In her five-inch heels, she staggered out the door to where Sly was waiting.

He noticed her and hurried from the limo to help. "You all right, Ms. G?" he said, opening the car door.

She put her hand on his cheek and looked straight into his dark, hungry eyes. "I will be after you take me home and fuck me."

A surge of heat rose from his groin to his face. "I'd love to . . . you're beautiful and all, but . . ."

"But what? I'm too old!"

"No! Marco would kill me if he found out."

"Who's going to tell him, huh?" She put one foot in the car as her limp, inebriated body folded to the seat. Sly set her other foot in then pulled her dress down, covering her polished, porcelain buttocks.

"I'm a stupid, stupid man," he sighed and shut the door.

Mimma pulled herself to a respectable position when she heard the engine start. She leaned forward and whispered in Sly's ear, "There's plenty of room back here my sweet, young stallion."

Gazing in the mirror at her, it took him to a scene from one of his dreams.

It was late and Mimma had been drinking. She ordered him to drive her to a remote place. He did. Then she made him pull over and get in the back with her. They kissed, running their hands all over each other. She laid back, raising her red dress up to her hips and motioned with a finger. He climbed between her legs and gave it to her, like she demanded.

"Mimma, I'm taking you home. God knows I'd love to fuck you but I can't." Hearing no response, he glanced in the mirror. Her head was back, mouth open, passed out cold.

THIRTY-SIX

W ithout a minute to spare, Jerome hurried down the promenade to the main elevator. His date with Jasmine was less
than an hour away, and he still had to pick up flowers.

Approaching the lobby, he saw Frank positioned like an armed
guard, robotically looking back and forth. He hesitated, tempted to
turn around and take the stairs, but this was his golden opportunity
to clear his name. Plastering on a crooked grin, he casually strode up
to him. "We gotta stop meeting like this," he said, chuckling.

Frank was in no mood to speak, especially to him, and just nodded.

"Oh, guess what?" Jerome lightly punched his arm. "I just won my money back. It took a while, but as they say: 'perseverance is a virtue.'"

"That's great." Frank kept his eyes steady on the crowd, weeding out his suspect.

Jerome shoved his hands in his pockets. "Well, I can see you're busy. Have a good night." He nodded and walked inside the elevator. When the door closed, his chest deflated and jaw unclenched. It felt like he'd just stepped out of a mobster movie, minus the killing.

As he quietly ascended to his floor, his mind sifted through the scenes, scrutinizing what to tell Jasmine and what to leave out. Either way, it would seem just as unbelievable as it was to him.

Entering his room, he glanced at the clock on the nightstand. He had a half an hour to shower, pick up flowers and get to Jasmine's house. Taking no chances, he decided to call and let her know he'd be a little late.

"Hello?"

"Hi Shauna, this is Jerome. Is your mother there?"

"Hi Jerome! Yes, she's getting ready. I'll get her. Have fuuun tonight."

"Thank you; we will."

"Hello?"

"Jasmine, how are you?" he asked politely.

"I'm fine . . . unless you're calling to cancel."

"No, I'm just going to be a few minutes late, that's all." He sat down on the bed.

"Wonderful! I'm not ready, still trying to figure out what to wear."

He loved her candor. "That shouldn't be too hard. You'd look great in anything."

"Oh, I was hoping you'd say that. Then don't be surprised if I'm wearing jeans and a t-shirt," she chuckled, "just kidding."

He chuckled, too. "Wear whatever makes you comfortable. All I want is to see you." He felt the minutes ticking away, minutes with her. "Listen, if I hurry, I should be there around seven. Is that all right?"

"That's perfect."

"Great. I'll call the restaurant and let them know the change."

"Okay, see you soon." She hung up.

The jeep hugged the winding curves up Kingsburg Grade while Jerome's angst over Jasmine's reaction increased. There was a fine line between what he'd witnessed and not being accused of invading Frank's privacy.

It was possible she might even misconstrue it as an attempt to defame his character to better *his* odds. Nevertheless, the subject was very delicate and each defining word should be thought out carefully.

Pulling up to her house, Jerome noticed the curtains quickly close. It looked like someone was in charge of arrival duty. Taking a deep breath, he ran his fingers through his hair, grabbed the bouquet, and just as he reached the front door it sprang open.

"Hi Jerome! Come in, she'll be right out," Shauna said, eyeing the flowers. "Those are beautiful. Good choice." Then she scurried down the hall to get her mother.

Jerome stood, feeling like he was in high school going to the prom. Nervousness raced through his body. Although, it was better than the fear he'd just experienced.

Justin walked up to him with a bowl of popcorn. "Want some?" he said, stuffing in a mouthful.

"Sure. I love popcorn." Jerome took a handful. "My parents made me popcorn before they went out, too."

"Yep, and when Mom forgets I remind her." They conversed comfortably. And just as Jerome's heart found a normal rhythm, it began beating like thunder again.

Jasmine appeared wearing a sky-blue sweater and skirt with a belt cinched around her waist. Her vibrant hair of sun-kissed red swirled loosely over the blue and took his breath. "You look like a sunset . . . the most beautiful sunset," he uttered and swallowed.

"How sweet. You always say the nicest things." She crept closer, wincing at his face. "What happened?"

He wasn't about to go into details right then. "Stairs." He shrugged.

She touched the petals of a flower in the bouquet. "These are beautiful."

"Oh." He held them out to her. "I couldn't find wildflowers. Hopefully, these will do."

"I love daisies." *He remembered.* She took them to the kitchen. "Give me just a minute while I put them in water."

Jerome followed her in, and as she reached for a vase his eyes gravitated to her round buttocks. It wasn't like him to gawk, but it was more sensual than if she'd been standing completely naked. "Would you like me to get that for you?" he asked before his face framed his guilt.

"Nope, I got it." She pulled it down and filled it with water then arranged the flowers on the kitchen table. Standing back, she gazed at them. "They sure brighten the room, don't they?"

"Yes, just like you." He wanted to take her in his arms and kiss her.

She smiled at him. "Thanks. Well, I guess I'm ready."

After giving last-minute instructions, they clasped hands and walked out to the jeep as Shauna and Justin watched from the window.

"I like him."

"So do I."

Driving along the lakeside, Jasmine gazed out the window at the diamond-dappled sky and then looked at Jerome. "It's strange, but when I see a starry night it reminds me of Montana."

Jerome glanced over, soaking in every word—every unforgettable minute. "And why's that?"

"I don't know. I guess I did a lot of staring out . . . hoping, longing, praying . . . and waiting."

"Waiting for what?"

"Hmm, good question. A miracle moreless."

"I hear you there." He had prayed many nights for a miracle himself.

It was an intimate hour of laughing and telling stories when they arrived at the North Point Grille.

The restaurant resembled a rustic hunting lodge with a big front porch and firewood stacked next to the door. Inside, the floors were of hardwood with a large Navajo rug at the entrance. And in the corner of the room, a massive stone fireplace blazed with a crackling fire.

Jerome gazed around, intrigued. "This is my kind of place."

"It's amazing," Jaz said, still clutching his hand.

Just then the hostess approached them. "Do you have a reservation?"

"Yes, they were changed to eight o'clock under Jensen," Jerome said.

The hostess verified the reservation then took them to their table. "A lake view, as you requested." She extended an arm.

Jerome helped Jasmine off with her coat, and as she turned around they exchanged a brief kiss. They, too, had a crackling fire blazing in the corner. He pulled out her chair, and after taking their seats, a pudgy waiter with a pencil-thin mustache shuffled over to them.

He bowed quickly. "Good evening. May I get you something to drink, perhaps from the bar?"

Jerome looked at Jasmine. "Would you like some wine?" She nodded and smiled. "A bottle of your finest Cabernet Sauvignon, please."

"Right away." The waiter left and silence dominated the air as each wrestled the quandary which plagued their minds. Jasmine was reluctant to start a relationship, and Jerome was reluctant to divulge the scene.

Sensing his accusation could do more harm than good, his stomach churned and his throat constricted. Yet, for the sake of her safety, he had to tell her. "There's something I need to discuss with you . . . something I saw tonight."

She watched his face turn from tender to tense. Clasping her hands on her lap, she gave him her full attention.

"Your wine, sir," the waiter said, approaching their table and presenting the bottle to Jerome. Then he uncorked it, poured a sip and handed it to him. Politely swirling, sniffing and sipping, Jerome nodded, chomping to finish what he'd started.

The waiter smiled while lingering with his refined routine, pouring each a glass and then meticulously wrapping a white linen cloth around the neck of the bottle. "Have you had a chance to look over our menu?" he asked as his mustache twitched.

"Not yet," Jerome answered anxiously as Jasmine sat riveted in suspense.

"Fine. Let me tell you about our specials tonight." He proceeded to recite each one in delectable detail, unaware they were both sitting on pins and needles. "Now, enjoy your wine and I'll be back in a moment."

Jerome took a breath and began again. "Tonight, in the parking garage, I witnessed something that may confirm my feelings about Frank." He could see her face twist with confusion. Without delaying, he gave a dramatic account of what happened with the exception of breaking into Frank's car. He worried that would undermine his case instead of substantiate it.

Jasmine sat speechless, staring at him. "I can't believe it," she finally said, "running in with a gun? Are you sure he didn't see you?"

"I'm positive. I saw him in the lobby as I was going to my room. Believe me, he doesn't know it was me." Jaz looked down, feeling numb and strangely empty. Jerome touched her hand. "I vacillated with saying anything, but I care about you."

Drawing her hand back, she clasped them in her lap. "But nothing was really proven. Maybe—"

"You have to trust me . . . please." He gazed into her glassy eyes.

She nodded with a quick smile. "I'll keep my distance, but would you mind if we changed the subject?"

"Not at all. I was hoping you'd say that." He exhaled, and they both picked up their menu.

They drank their wine and finished their dinner as the night slowly lost its glimmer, allure and intimacy. Although Jerome's eyes still yearned, he saw a listless vacancy in hers. Looking out the window, he murmured, "It's beautiful out there with the moon reflecting off the water."

Jasmine gazed out. "Yes it is."

"Would you like to take a stroll on the patio?" he asked, desperately trying to regain the romantic mood.

She smiled. "Sure, that sounds nice."

They walked out to the railing and gazed at the luminous water in chilled silence. Jerome looked over at her, and the vibrancy she'd possessed earlier had faded. He didn't expect his vigilance would have such a negative effect. More regrettable, he didn't expect the intimacy to turn off so quickly.

"I probably should be getting back home," Jasmine said, clutching her wrap around her shoulders. Jerome's despondency translated his disappointment. She felt bad, but she could also relate.

Her life had been seasoned with disappointing events, and not one made any sense—even her date tonight. Falling in love with Jerome would be easy, but her heart was already in need of repair. How could she withstand another break, even worse, from him dying?

It was as clear as the crisp cold night, the evening was over. Jerome noticed her shivering and put his arm around her shoulder. "I guess I should take you home. It's getting pretty chilly out here."

"It is . . . thank you."

While the engine warmed, Jerome envisioned them dancing, laughing and snuggling, ending the evening with an unforgettable memory not one of regret. Praying for a change of mind, he asked, "The night is still young. Would you like to go somewhere else?"

She felt her heart throb, gazing into his blue, blue eyes. Yet, severing it then would be easier than prolonging it into a tear-jerking, heart-wrenching goodbye, and she despised goodbyes. "I'm sorry, I think I'd rather just go home."

"Okay." Jerome felt his chest deflate as if his heart had been removed. The words he wanted to say no longer mattered. It was too late. She'd made that perfectly clear.

When they arrived at her house, Jerome got out and came around to her door. "If you don't mind, I'd like to walk you to the door." The real reason was he couldn't just sit there and watch her walk away. He had to feel her fingers clasped with his and gaze into her sapphire eyes one more time.

"I'd like that." She smiled, taking his hand. And as they reached the porch an emotional awkwardness enveloped them. She looked up at the moon while he looked away nervously.

Like before, he turned into that fragile little boy. She touched his shoulder. "Thank you for everything, and I love the flowers." Facing her, he smiled with tears swelling. She rose to her toes and tenderly kissed his lips.

"Thank you, I needed that," he said, sliding his hand from hers and wiping his face. "I'd better go before I make a fool of myself." She nodded as her eyes filled. He walked away then hesitated before getting in the jeep. "If it's okay, I'd like to check in with you now and then to see how you're doing?"

"I'd like that." She smiled and brushed a tear, knowing it was the last time she would see him.

"Take care."

"You too," she whispered.

CHAPTER

THIRTY-SEVEN

Mimma woke that morning with fury plunged deep in her heart and headache so scull-crushing it was on the verge of nauseating.

Lugging herself from the bed, she teetered to the bathroom with her eyes closed and fingertips pressed to her temples. Fumbling for the light, she flipped the switch and slowly opened her eyes. "Oh my God! I look like Medusa!" she screamed, looking in the mirror.

Her hair was coiled into black little snakes that spiraled from her head with last night's hairspray. She pointed. "You will pay for this. I'll make sure of it!"

Wandering back to the bedroom, she noticed her black stockings were laying at the foot of the bed and shaped in a heart. A smile curled. "Mmm . . . you are sly, aren't you?" However, he wasn't the man she wanted to get her hands on. "Sonia!" she screeched, holding her temples.

The door opened. "Yes, Madame." Her eyes snapped open in fright. "What happened to you?!"

Mimma placed her hands on her hips. "I fell in love! Now, go get me some coffee and hurry!"

"Whew, I'm glad I haven't," she murmured and scurried out of the room.

Mimma paced, thinking of everything she had done for Frank, even defended him. Her anger boiled. "I should have let Marco kill you! You *are* just like the others. I was a fool to believe you are something that you are not!"

The door opened, and Sonia held out a cup of coffee. "Madame."

Mimma clutched the cup in her palms. "Now, draw me a bath. I have business to take care of."

After last night's scare, Frank was convinced he was being set up, or there was a hit out on him. He went to his office and made a call to Geno.

"Yeah?"

"Geno, it's Frankie."

"Hey man, how's it goin'?"

Frank sat down. "I'm still alive, if that's any indication. I think Marco wants me whacked. Have you heard anything?"

"No man, haven't heard a thing, but I'll ask my bros and make a few calls. In the meantime lay low."

"All right. See what you can find out and call me."

"I will." Geno hung up and immediately contacted Carlos and Anatoly.

Frank's narrow escape had him rethinking his priorities. It was time to begin his life with Jasmine. He knew a flame still smoldered inside her—the one he started, the one he kept hot. To wait any longer would give someone else the chance to take his place . . . possibly Jerome. Staring at the phone, he decided to call her and cash in his *"maybe."*

"I'll get it," Jasmine called to the kids. "Hello?"

"Good morning, beautiful."

The words felt prickly after hearing Jerome's shocking story. "Hi, Frank," she uttered.

"How are you?" He envisioned her stubborn but adorable face. "If you really want to know, I'm running late for work."

He grinned. "Pretty soon you won't have to worry about that any longer."

Her eyes widened, knowing how impetuous the casino was with firing people. "Why, what do you mean? Have you heard something?!"

"No, no. Think of the best thing not the worst."

"Well, if it has anything to do with you, I can't imagine." She huffed.

Her fiery temper teased him and he chuckled. "I'll tell you in person when I get to work."

"Fine." She hung up. However, deep down beyond the rules of right and wrong, mystery man had a way of keeping her wanting.

Frank arrived at the Palace and pulled into valet. He had unfinished business there, hearing nothing of what actually happened to Randy. It was possible *he* could be the rat, ruling out his first intuition as Paul. Every angle and every person had to be vetted. Otherwise, his *maybe* may as well be *never*.

Approaching the valet booth, Frank glanced at the attendant's name tag. "David, I'm Frank Pazzarelli, the hotel manager."

"Yes, I know who you are," he nodded. "Can I help you?"

"Yeah, a kid named Randy worked here. Have you seen him?"

He cocked his head. "Didn't he get fired?"

"That was my understanding. But I'm curious if you've seen him hanging around."

"Well, I know he has friends here, so now and then he comes by."

"Is he a friend of yours, and don't worry it won't affect your job."

David was shaking his head before he blurted out his answer. "No-no, he's not my friend. I don't know him at all."

Frank studied him. His quick, defensive comeback was a little too quick. "Can you find out who his friends are?"

"Uh . . . yeah, I think so."

"Do that, and I'll be back in a minute." Frank turned and marched inside the hotel.

David watched until he was out of sight then ran over to the store-room. "Hey man, Frank's onto you." Randy darted out from behind a wall. He was taking inventory of their cocaine stash.

"What!? How do you know?"

"'Cause he was just here askin' about you. You gotta get out of here. I don't want to lose my job, too."

"No way! I'm not fuckin' goin' down for everyone. If I get busted, we all get busted."

David raised his hands. "Do you have any idea what will happen to us?"

"Yeah, we'll all go to fuckin' prison—that's what!"

"If we're lucky! These guys don't mess around. We'll all be taken out to the desert and buried alive!"

Randy closed his eyes and began banging his forehead against the wall. "So what do we do?" he muttered.

David grabbed his shoulders and turned him around. "I say we leave town. Get our shit and split."

"Are we gonna warn the others?"

"No man, they're fuckin' on their own."

Frank took a detour before he went to his office, looking for his soon-to-be significant other. She didn't see him watching her laugh and socialize with her players or know that he was picturing them sharing a bed every night and making love every morning. She also didn't see him wipe the tears that had never dripped before her.

As a card flew from the table and onto the floor, Jasmine spotted his smiling face. "I see you," she muttered under her breath.

Two women noticed her round eyes turn into narrow slits as she stared off in the distance. They both turned to see what had changed her expression.

"Oh my, he could stop a train dead in its tracks," one said, fanning her face to the other.

"I'd say."

Jaz overheard them. "You got that right. He derailed me."

Now discovered, Frank strolled up to the game and nodded at the ladies then at Jasmine. "Before you leave tonight, I need to speak to you. It's important."

She glanced around her table. "Do it now. We're all friends here." She flashed him a daring grin as the five unknowns stared passionately at him with bated breath. "Go on." Jaz egged him on.

His eyes danced wild and hungry. "Let's run away—from all of this. I have enough money to live in luxury for the rest of our lives. It will be wonderful, just you and me. What do ya say?"

Jaz chuckled, "Uh . . . I don't think I can say it out loud."

"I'm serious. Please think about it." He backed away from her game and blew her a kiss.

Jasmine rolled her eyes and huffed, refocusing on her players. They were sitting star-struck with their mouths hanging open.

"How can you pass that up!?" a lady bellowed.

Jaz looked back at Frank and watched every step his long legs made in his wavy, black trousers until he faded out of sight. "I don't know . . ."

Frank hadn't had breakfast yet, and his unrequited request left him feeling exceptionally hungry. Across the street, Bill's served a $1.99 special that ran twenty-four hours and hard to beat.

He pulled a quarter from his pocket and bought a newspaper from the stand. As he waited for the light to change, a cold gust of wind whipped through his jacket, sending a chill down his back. He looked up to see an overcast of threatening clouds and raised his collar around his neck.

It was strange, he thought, how the day had turned from beautiful to gloomy in less than an hour. Shrugging it off, he read the headline on the front page of the newspaper. **New Study Reveals Coffee Can Kill You.** "Now that's a fuckin' scare." He chuckled then realized the light had changed and stepped off the curb.

With his nose deep in the paper, he started across the street when suddenly, out of nowhere, a car careened around the corner like a speeding bullet. His eyes darted up as a shot rang out. Then his body was rammed and dragged down the street until his jacket ripped free.

Lying face down in a pool of blood, Frank gurgled out a name—a name that nobody heard.

The casino doors flew open, and a woman came running in, screaming hysterically, "Oh my God! Oh my God! Someone's been killed! Call the police!" Then she collapsed on the floor.

Instantly, the docile crowd turned into hurdling pandemonium. Chairs flew, and people were trampled to get a glimpse of the bone-chilling horror.

Tony raced through the pit, informing the dealers to close their games and take a break. Jasmine was one of them. As she began counting down the deck of cards, one of her players apprehensively crept up to her.

"Um . . . that man . . . the one that blew you a kiss . . ." She shook her head and began sobbing.

Jasmine felt her head swim as the blood swooshed down to her toes. "No . . ."

"Yes," the woman looked up with tears trickling down her cheeks. "He's dead. I'm so sorry, dear."

"No! It can't be!" Clinging to the table, heaving for air and wailing in disbelief, her trembling knees gave way, and she sank to the floor.

The woman darted off in search of help and frantically snatched the sleeve of an elderly man playing a slot machine. "Come, a dealer has fainted! She's lying under her blackjack table. Please help me!"

The man grabbed his cane and followed her. When they arrived, Jasmine was already sitting up. "Dear, are you all right?" the mournful woman asked with the man standing next to her.

Tony leaped in front of them and held up a hand. "We got it under control. Move on, this ain't a freak show."

"I was just trying to help!" the woman spouted.

"You want to help—leave," he fired back.

The woman's mouth hit her chest. She marched off, and the old man went back to where he was playing.

Tony knelt down next to Jasmine. "Who's next, huh? It better not be me. If you remember, I want to go out with a smile on my face."

Jasmine couldn't speak. She just stared off in catatonic misery. He waved a hand in front of her face. "Hey! You there?"

She wiped her eyes. "Please tell me I'm not."

"I'm tellin' ya this. No sugar coatin' nothin'. Frank got whacked. This ain't no accident. Someone wanted him killed."

Her swollen eyes opened and she swallowed. "As in ma-ma-murdered?"

"No, as in Mickey Mouse—yes murdered! What's more, there was a bullet hole the size of a baseball in his fuckin' chest."

"I don't what to hear anymore!" She clenched her eyes and held her hands over her ears.

"Listen to me," he gave her a quick shake, "you and Frank were tight. Maybe he mentioned somethin' to ya. Do you recall any names, anything at all?" His beady eyes dug into hers for a clue.

Jaz mechanically shook her head back and forth while thinking Jerome was *right!* She wanted to tell Tony what he saw, but that could backfire and claim her the next victim. It was safer to let things lay as they were. "I don't know anyone or anything . . . nothing."

"Good. That's what I wanted to hear." He helped her to her feet. "Now go home, and I'll close your game."

The next morning Frank was on the front page of the *Tahoe Times*. The article disclosed the time, date, where it happened, and cause of his death. As for *who* and *why*, it was still under investigation.

Jasmine read his name aloud and ran a finger over his picture. It was hard to believe he was the person she knew and *wanted* to love. "How could I be so blind . . . is love that hard to see?" she murmured to herself as a river of tears rushed over her cheeks and down to her broken heart—a heart that couldn't take anymore.

It was time to get her life back on track and forget about love, especially true love, which included Jerome or anyone else. Shauna and Justin completed her, and that was all she needed.

CHAPTER

THIRTY-EIGHT

D r. J.T. Barton, Chief of Staff at Loveland General Hospital, glanced up over his wire-rimmed glasses to see Jerome coming out of OR. "Dr. Jensen, you're just the person I wanted to see. Do you have a minute?"

Jerome walked over, smiling. "Sure. Is everything all right?"

Dr. Barton set a hand on his shoulder. "As a matter of fact, that was my question to you. I heard you were chosen as one of the volunteers for the Philippine Outreach indenture."

"Yes, I was." Jerome relaxed and folded his arms.

"Well, I wanted to commend you on your generous obligation, but may I ask *why* you dedicated yourself to an endeavor of such magnitude? You've been a great asset to the hospital and community. I really hate to lose you." He studied Jerome beneath a cloud of fluffy, white hair.

"Thank you, Dr. Barton. Simply put, I felt I was the perfect candidate. I have no real obligations, unlike other physicians with families. And it would be an opportunity of a lifetime, so to speak."

He nodded throughout Jerome's explanation. "You are, correct me if I'm wrong, one of three plastic surgeons."

"Yes, that's right, as well as five GP's and two biochemists—ten total."

Dr. Barton squeezed his shoulder. "It sounds immensely rewarding to say the least, however, a greater challenge indeed."

Jerome humbly nodded. "Well, I can't think of a better way to utilize my skills, more importantly my time."

"I agree, son . . . I agree. But if you change your mind, you can always back out. There's still time."

"Not at this point. I signed the agreement. I'm now mentally and contractually committed for six months."

Dr. Barton smiled. "Given that, you have my full support." He patted Jerome on the back then proceeded down the hall.

After speaking to Dr. Barton, Jerome felt the full impact of what he was about to undertake, as if for the first time. The chosen ten would fly to Manila, Philippines and then board a truck to the Subic Bay Naval base where the supplies, including food and medicine, would be ready for them to take. Then they would journey deep into the jungle of Olongapo in the Zambales province of the Philippines and set up a triage tent as well as residence tents.

The mission was to treat the villagers who suffered from minor illnesses and diseases to burns and broken bones. It would be a monumental challenge, Jerome was aware of that, although minuscule to his own.

As his last patient was treated, Jerome called it a day. His limited concentration, and the intensity of his headaches were a significant sign his brain cancer was progressing. It was only a matter of time before his impairment would put his patients at risk. This, above all, confirmed a primitive atmosphere was where he belonged. Where his skills were deemed beneficial and his precision less scrutinized.

The next morning, Jerome woke to the day he had been purposely procrastinating—not that he was incapable but merely couldn't face the sorrow.

Today his home would be packed and cleaned. Selling it wasn't an option. In his mind, they each served their purpose well. It was only right to preserve what dignity was left and wither like him in the same meaningful way.

While sifting through files, discarding and organizing, he spied a receipt from Tahoe. It was of the trip when he first met Jasmine. Though the circumstance was horrific, the outcome changed his perspective on living and loving.

It had been nine days going on ten since he'd last seen her, but knowing he'd never see her again felt like eternity. *That evening*, before the mention of Frank's name, when they radiated with romance, the chemistry surged between them.

He saw it in her eyes and felt it in her touch. Why she turned off that light was understandable. No one wanted to fall in love when there was no future, only the reality of what to expect. Despite the ending, if he hadn't pursued his desire for her, the regret would have been more agonizing.

Jerome placed the receipt in a box and sat down in his recliner to take a breather. His heart ached with a pain so deep it was almost debilitating. He needed to see her one more time—one *last* time. Just to look into her deep blue eyes, touch her face, and hear her gentle voice would make his final passage easier.

Checking his watch and calendar, her shift was over in two hours, and he had four days before his departure to Manila. Maybe, just maybe, she would let him see her for a quick visit.

The gossip was like an unruly poltergeist, following Jasmine around the casino and whispering behind her back. She even felt Frank's presence, the same as when he would hide somewhere and watch from a distance. Yet the last time they spoke, the last time she watched him swagger off so confidently, before his last plea and blowing her a kiss, haunted her internally.

As the long sorrowful day came to a close, the women sent her home with their sympathy and hugs. But something else followed her home: monotony.

Walking inside the house, an ingrained routine began. She went to her bedroom to change, to the kitchen to cook, to the couch to relax and then to bed. It was the same thing every day and every night. Something had to change— somehow, someway.

Lying on her bed, staring at the ceiling, Jaz heard the phone ring. "Can you get that?" she hollered to the kids.

Shauna got up. "Hello?"

"Hi Shauna, it's Jerome."

"Oh, hi Jerome." She threw her hand on her hip and tapped her toe. "You know, I didn't get a chance to say goodbye before you left."

He smiled. "Well, that's one of the reasons I'm calling. I didn't get a chance to say goodbye to you either."

She giggled. "Isn't it a little late, you're already gone?"

"Nah, it's never too late."

"So, I guess you want to talk to Mom."

"Yes, is she home?"

"Yep, I'll get her. *Goodbye* Jerome."

"*Goodbye* Shauna."

Jerome sat down at the kitchen counter. His conversation with Shauna buckled his knees and brought him to tears. Now he had to find the strength for Jasmine. Waiting for her, he dried his eyes and calmed his nerves.

Shauna knocked on her bedroom door. "Mom, Jerome is on the phone."

"It's Jerome?" she uttered to herself. *He probably heard about Frank's death.* "Okay, I'll be right there." She pushed off the bed and went to the kitchen. "Hello?" Her voice was hesitant, remembering their last conversation and how it ended.

"Hi Jasmine, how are you?"

"Hi Jerome, I'm okay. How are you?"

He wasn't sure what to say, feeling jumbled with desperation. "Truthfully, not as good as I'd like to be."

"Oh no!" She placed her hand over her heart and sat down.

"Not that . . . I'm hanging in there. But there's something I'd like to talk to you about, and I'd like to do it in person, that is, if it's okay."

She lowered her hand. "Sure."

He smiled. "If I can get a flight out, I'll be there in two days."

"Sounds serious. Is everything all right?"

"Yeah, but I'd rather talk face-to-face. And, I miss you." He didn't expect that to come out but was glad it did.

Jasmine smiled. "I miss you, too." The words flowed so effortlessly, so naturally.

"That's good to hear. I'll call you tomorrow and let you know when I'll be there."

"Okay, have a good night."

"You too." Jerome hung up wishing they could have talked for more than a minute—more like a lifetime.

It was 5:05 p.m. and Jerome had just touched down at the Reno airport. Pangs of excitement raced through him like a child mystified with wonder on Christmas morning. In one hour he would see Jasmine and the kids. It was a day he never expected, and a day he'd never forget.

Carrying a small bag, he walked outside and saw a man dressed in a gold and navy suit. He was holding a sign with his name on it and eagerly approached him. "Hi, I'm Jerome."

The man turned his sign around and looked at it again. "Dr. Jensen?"

He smiled. "In the flesh. I used my title making the reservation."

"You earned it." He latched onto a baggage dolly and looked around. "Where's your luggage?"

Jerome held up his bag. "This is it. I'm not staying long."

The driver chuckled. "Either that or you're a nudist." He opened the door as Jerome got it. "So, where to?"

"Tahoe. I'm staying at the Swiss Inn. It's up Kingsburg Grade about midway." Jerome intentionally found a place near Jasmine and far from Frank. To see him again and risk a happy ending, was the last thing he wanted to do.

"I'll find it," the driver said and shut his door.

Jerome took a mental snapshot of the scenery as they drove up the canyon. It was hard to imagine he would never see it again, which made him wonder what he would say to Jasmine. Not mentioning the progression of his cancer was probably best, and focus on his mission in the Philippines. Although, the real reason was simple. He couldn't leave this world without seeing her one more time.

His eyes closed and dimples creased, picturing her in his big, white t-shirt with her knees folded underneath it. She looked so adorable he wanted to pick her up and hold her in his arms. "I would've loved to have loved you," he whispered as a tear escaped.

The hour seemed only a few minutes when the driver turned up Kingsburg Grade and pulled up to a quaint motel with a Swiss flag at the entrance. He looked back at Jerome. "Normally I'd get out and help, but I think you've got it under control."

"Hope so." Jerome paid him and then walked inside the motel lobby. He rang the bell twice while his eyes roamed the authentic surroundings.

Thumbing through postcards, coupons and flyers, he glanced at a newspaper at the end of the counter. Then he stepped closer and raised it to his face. **Hotel Manager Murdered.** A picture of Frank was next to it. His mouth dropped, and his eyes couldn't have opened any wider.

The clerk came out. "Yeah, can you believe that?" she said, shaking her head.

Jerome wanted to say: *Yes, yes I can!* "No, I can't. Do you mind if I take it. I'd like to read the article."

She waved her hand. "Yeah, take it. It's old news anyway. So, I'm guessin' you want a room?"

"Yes, one night." He glanced down at the date. *Why didn't Jasmine say anything?*

"Shocking if you ask me. You never know these days who's the good guy and who's the bad." She handed him the key then walked out the door and pointed. "It's around back. You'll see it—number seven."

Jerome jangled the key. "Lucky seven . . . I need it."

"You and me both." She flashed him a smile.

Tucking the newspaper under his arm, he walked around back and opened the door to his room. He looked around at the shabby, bare-bones interior and then thought about where he'd be living for the next six months. *I guess I better get used to it.*

Sitting down on the bed, he glanced at his watch. He had fifteen minutes before Jasmine got off work. It was just enough time to devour, digest and process every word of what happened to Frank. Lying back, he began reading:

Frank Pazzarelli, the hotel manager of the Paradise Palace casino, was killed in a hit-and-run shooting at the intersection of Main Street and 10th, Monday at approximately 11:00 am.

According to the forensic officer, after being struck he was dragged twenty-three feet until breaking free. The identity of those connected with this crime is still under investigation. The Douglas County Police Department urges anyone with information to immediately contact them.

Jerome set the paper down with his mouth gaping in astonishment. "Someone wanted him killed," he uttered. The last sentence of the article blared like a siren. *"Anyone with information . . ."*

He did. A vivid description of that formidable night was seared in his brain like a brand. The question was: should he say anything, should Jasmine, and why didn't she mention it?

After a moment to let Frank's death sink in, he looked at his watch and realized Jasmine should be home. Taking a deep breath, he called her.

"Hello?"

"Guess who?" he said, grinning.

"Jerome!" It was amazing. Just saying his name, the stress from the casino miraculously vanished.

"Yep, it's me and closer than you think."

Her eyes widened. "Where are you?"

"About five minutes away." He caught a glimpse of his face beaming in the mirror. He looked so different, so extraordinarily happy.

"Great. Tell me the name, and I'll pick you up . . . say in twenty minutes?"

"Perfect. I didn't rent a car." He opened the curtains and gazed out the window. "When you think you've reached Switzerland, that's where I'll be."

She laughed. "I hope you mean the Swiss Chalet?"

"That's the one."

"Then I'll see you soon." Jasmine quickly threw on a pair of jeans and boots, touched up her hair, and dabbed her lips with gloss.

It was like night had turned into day, bad into good, and she was alive instead of dead. A change was happening, the change she needed, yet nothing had changed with Jerome. The only explanation which made any sense was love had planted a seed, and she was feeling it bloom.

Remembering back to the first day she'd met Jerome, he'd made her feel worthy of concern and respect. To her, those were key elements of true love. So why refute the chance to experience this rare splendor, even if it was for an unknown time? Tonight she would tell him.

Breezing down the two-lane road, Jasmine arrived at the Swiss Chalet and spotted Jerome standing out front. He looked so thrilled to see her with his arms out and big smile. Pulling up next to him, she rolled down her window. "Hey, going my way?"

He leaned in. "Yes, I am."

"Jump in!"

He rounded the truck, leaped in, and their eyes met in blissful reunion. "It's great seeing you again. I've really missed you," he said, gently caressing her face with his eyes.

Jaz felt an apology was necessary before another word was said. "Jerome, I'm so sorry for the way I treated you that night. I was confused. So much had happened that—"

"Jasmine, you don't have to say another word. I'm just glad you agreed to see me again."

She nodded and smiled. "So am I, and . . ." She was on the verge of telling him her *good news* when he pressed a finger to her lips.

"I'll finish that for you. And I think we should go to the lake and catch the rest of the sunset."

She exhaled. "You read my mind." Looking behind the seat, she found a blanket and set it between them. "I have this if we get cold."

"It is getting pretty chilly." He grinned.

They pulled into Camp Garrison and parked in the same spot they had the picnic. Jerome snagged the blanket and Jasmine's hand. And as they took off down the path, she felt his energy transferring into her. It was so powerful, so overwhelming she couldn't wait to tell him of her bursting revelation.

Sitting on top of the picnic table, Jerome snuggled Jasmine close to his side and wrapped the blanket around their shoulders. They gazed out at the lake and watched a flock of geese ease across the pink and silver ripples. "It's just as beautiful as I remember," he murmured.

"More beautiful than I remember," she said, looking up at him. "There's something I need to tell you, and I can't hold it in any longer."

Jerome noticed her glassy eyes and assumed it pertained to Frank's demise. "Okay."

"I've been thinking about what you said. I know you live far away, but I can't see why we shouldn't follow our hearts, no matter how long we have. At least we won't regret what could have been, maybe even true love."

Jerome felt his heart plummet to the bottom of his saddened soul. Her words should have had him dancing. Instead, they hit him like a wrecking ball. Taking her hand, he pressed it tenderly to his lips as a tear hit her skin.

"What, Jerome? What is it?" Her eyes were wide with confusion.

He gazed into her turbulent pools of blue. "I'm going to tell you this the best way I can." He brushed a tear from her cheek. "My life has been rewarding, even more since I met you. Just to look at you takes my breath away—you're everything I've ever wanted and literally dreamed of. But I can't." He shook his head and looked away.

"I don't understand. I thought you wanted to make a try of it."

"It's too late. That's what I came to talk to you about. I signed a contract that I'm now committed to. I never thought I would have another chance with you."

"A contract?"

"I volunteered for a mission in the Philippines. Knowing my time is near, I couldn't think of a better way to use it before. . ." He swallowed and squeezed her hand.

She slumped to his side, spinning, empty and numb. "How long will you be gone?"

"Six months . . . but who knows?"

"Is there any way you can get out of it?"

"No, we leave in two days." He watched the geese float by, enrapt with their mate.

She looked down. "I don't know if I can say goodbye." Then she burst into tears.

He took her face in his hands. "Let's not." Kissing her hungrily, he felt her body shivering under his touch and swaddled her close to his chest. "Jasmine, will you let me hold you in my room?" he whispered.

She felt his heart beating against her cheek, and his request was exactly what she needed: to be comforted by the *one man* who made her feel loved. She nodded, wiping her tears away.

They drove to the motel, and Jerome pointed to his room. "I'm in number seven. And if you're wondering, yes, I am feeling lucky . . . lucky to have met you."

She chuckled, feeling something too—something deeper and stronger than the tempestuous ocean. "Come on." He took her by the hand and walked to the door. Unlocking it, he held it open for her. "Welcome to my humble abode, and I mean humble."

Jaz glanced around with her hands on her hips. "Not overbearing, well appointed, good layout, functional, could use a little—"

"Could use a lot!" he blared then flopped down on the bed. "But I bet the Ritz doesn't have a bed that can do this." He bounced up and down while the springs sang out a squeaky tune. She giggled at him, lost in his youthful spirit.

Then he brought the bed to a stop, and his face turned soft and amorous. Taking her by the arm, he pulled her on top of him. They stared breathlessly into each other's eyes, feeling something beyond words. With bodies pressed and heat rising, Jasmine lowered her lips onto his. They kissed as light as a butterfly and meandering as a meadow path, gently taking their time.

An impulse surged through Jerome's body, yet he knew he was powerless. "I can't . . ."

"Shhh . . . it's okay. Just being together in each other's arms feels wonderful," she whispered.

Without saying another word, he got up and gazed passionately down at her. Then he began removing his shirt, one button at a time, and let it fall to the floor.

Captivated, Jasmine watched with only a glint of moonlight to illuminate his body. A breath fluttered in her throat, roaming over his glistening muscles that rippled from the top of his shoulders to the bottom of his stomach. He smiled with her fascination and unfastened his belt. Sliding his jeans down to the floor, he stepped out of them and stood, personifying nothing less than hammered steel.

Climbing on top of her, their skin bonded in a sensation beyond any human sense, an infusion so hot their blood boiled, and their kisses suspended them high above the clouds. "I will miss you," he whispered, kissing her lips. "This night will keep me sane every day I'm alive." Then he sank down next to her, bringing her head to his chest.

Jasmine closed her eyes as tears pattered like rain on his skin. "I don't want to let go . . . if I do, then you'll be gone."

Jerome gently stroked her hair. "I won't be gone. I'll always be with you. But you have to promise me something."

"Anything," she whispered.

"Don't settle for a man who doesn't treat you like a queen."

She nodded. "I promise."

As the hours passed, the reality of their *last night* roused Jasmine awake. She looked over at Jerome's peaceful face and gently nudged him. "I need to go home now," she whispered.

He hugged her to his chest and kissed her head. "I know."

Gathering her clothes, she saw the newspaper on the floor. "You were right, you know. I wanted to tell you, but there was never a right time," she said, looking at the article.

"Honestly, I'm glad you didn't." He came up to her and wrapped his arms around her shoulders. Their weary eyes met. "I'm really sorry for what happened to him, but I'm thankful I don't have to worry about you while I'm gone."

She nodded as he kissed her long and deep one more time. They broke away, each sighing. It was the time they both had been avoiding. The time to say good-bye.

Staggering out to her truck, fighting to remain strong, they felt as if the world had come to an end. Jerome held her quivering body next to his and whispered in her ear, "I don't want to let you go."

She looked up into his eyes, and they both began crying, knowing it was for the last time. Desperately clinging, drenched in tears, Jaz slowly pulled away for both of them.

Jerome opened her door, and she feebly climbed inside. Starting the engine, she gazed at him through the window, remembering a man who loved her.

"You'll be in my dreams," he mouthed. Her quivering lips smiled and she headed home.

THIRTY-NINE

When the ten physicians arrived in Manila, two naval cadets were there to pick them up in a large military truck. They boarded the back, which was open on both sides, and sat side-by-side on two long metal benches.

The itinerary gave detailed instructions, stopping first at the Subic Bay naval base to pick up all the initial supplies then on to the compound.

As everyone got settled, they left the airport and took off down a muddy pitted road through a dense forest of bamboo, broad leafed plants and exotic flowers.

Jerome observed the foliage, fascinated by how different it was from Colorado's, while trying to absorb the brain-busting potholes gouged in the road. However, this time he wasn't alone in his pain. Groans of agony echoed from all the men every time they hit one.

Dr. Sean Whitmore bellowed, "It sounds like a maternity ward in here!" He was one of the general practitioners and had kept quiet until reaching his limit of whines.

"One more bump and my *ass* will need a sling," Dr. Ronald Westin, a plastic surgeon, groaned and everyone laughed.

"I'm sure I could make you a new one," Jerome said, chuckling.

Dr. Westin wagged a finger. "Ah, but the question is, whose ass would you use to augment mine? It sounds like we are all down to the bone."

"Are you kidding me? I have more than enough for *you* and every native in this God-forsaken country," Dr. Donald Hornsby blared, pointing at himself.

As the moans turned into giddy laughter, the doctors began to bond in a humble camaraderie. However, they didn't know humility was the key factor in selecting the pantheon. There was simply no room for a big head in their tight rudimentary quarters.

The physicians were from different states and ranged in age from thirty-six to sixty-two. Jerome was the youngest and Sean the oldest. Each gave a brief introduction, disclosing their poignant story of which precipitated their decision to volunteer.

Jerome deliberately left out one important detail. Getting *"special treatment"* for his disease was the last thing he wanted from anyone. In his eyes, they were there to treat *only* those who could not treat themselves, not him.

It had been nearly two hours of trudging deep into the jungle when the laughter stopped, and their groans equaled the rumble of the truck. Fortunately, they had reached their destination. Tired, sore, and staving off monstrous hunger pangs, they unfolded their knees, held onto their backs, and one-by-one set foot at their new home.

It was a welcoming surprise. The compound was completely set up and ready for operation, contrary to the agenda as step one of the mission.

Gazing at the premade structures, Sean held out his hands, tilted his head back and shouted, "Halleluiah! There is a God!" A spontaneous *"Amen"* followed.

There were eight tents made of white canvas and wood frames, and each was constructed for a designated purpose. The main tent was the largest. It was the kitchen, equipped with propane, battery and solar energy. Inside was a dining area, a cooking station and storage compartment. Down from that, approximately one hundred feet, were five resident tents set up with cots and lockers. On the opposite side of the camp was a medical supply tent, and next to that was the triage tent for their patients.

Jerome followed a savory smell wafting from the mess tent and spied a pot of stew simmering on the stove. "Hey, anyone hungry? There's something cooking over here calling our names."

One of the cadets smiled and rocked on his heels. "We knew you'd be hungry, so I whipped up my kitchen sink special."

"I hope you included all the fixtures. I could eat a bathtub right now," Donald spewed.

The cadet clicked his fingers. "Darn, I knew I forgot something."

Like a herd of cattle, the men stampeded over and took a seat around a long folding table, humming with every bite that it was the best stew they'd ever tasted.

While eagerly consuming, they soon realized they weren't alone. Onlookers from a nearby village were crouched in the trees observing their new neighbors. This was exactly what they were hoping for, deducing their means of advertisement was solely by word of mouth. And if all went as perceived, they expected the hospital to be up and running by morning.

In less than a week, Jerome's normal day was several hours of routine examinations and surgeries. Not until long into the night did he have a moment to relax and reflect.

Lying awake, he would gently turn the pages of his memories. Some were fading, others vivid and brought a smile. Some even made him laugh. Yet those of Jasmine, without fail, always brought a tear.

It had been four months and ten days. The mission, as everyone expected, challenged each doctor to strive beyond their limitations, adapt to the deficiency and constantly revitalize their ingenuity. Through it all, with everyone's diligence, it was a successful operation.

One night—one well deserved night, the ten men gathered around the fire-pit to relax and rejoice.

John Stanton, one of the biochemist, had invented cocktails from indigenous flowers, herbs and roots, and was eager for each to be tested and rated. He hurried back to his lab and returned with a tray of motley concoctions. "George, this one's for you. It's not Jose Cuervo but it's close," he said, handing him a specimen cup.

George was Hispanic and had spoken fondly of his rare collection tequila. He took the cup of cloudy mixture, swirled it, sniffed it and then swallowed it. He shuddered and smiled as it burned down his throat then held his cup out for more. "I think we have a new job for you, my friend."

There was a harmonious cheer as they passed around the surgical tray of John's specialties.

Sean stood and held up a finger. "I'll be right back." He darted off to his tent and returned with a wooden box. "I was saving these for a special occasion and this, I'm afraid, is as close as it's going to get." Opening the box, he handed each a hand-rolled Padron cigar. The men drank, laughed, told stories, and puffed away until utterly and joyfully inebriated.

John was aware of Jerome's pain, witnessing his anguish and hearing his sighs when he thought he was alone. Pulling his stool next to him, he handed him a cup. "I want you to drink this."

Jerome waved his hand. "No, believe me, I've had enough. I won't be able to work tomorrow if I have anymore."

"It's anesthetic—it should help the pain."

Jerome shook his head and looked down. "You noticed. I was trying to keep it a secret."

John set his hand on Jerome's leg. "Listen, I know pain when I see it. That's one . . . actually, that's the main reason I'm here."

Jerome studied him. "You didn't mention it when we were having story-time."

"And I don't recall you saying anything, either."

Sitting together, they peeled back the layers of their personal lives until reaching the core.

John was a widower. Twenty years ago his wife died of leukemia just as they were to start a family. Not only did he lose her but all the scrapbook memories they were planning to have. It perpetuated a turning point in his career. For ten years he had been an anesthesiologist. Now he was a biochemist with a new purpose of discovering cures.

Raising his cocktail high in the air, John uttered, "My darling, this is to you." Then he downed his drink and wiped his eyes.

Jerome drank the potion respectfully with him, wincing with the bitterness. "Hope it works."

"Don't worry, it will." John grinned. "Hey, I spilled my guts. Now it's your turn."

Jerome grinned, shaking his head. "That could take all night."

"So what?" John's arms flew from his sides. "Just lay it on me, bro." Then he hunched toward Jerome and spoke from the corner of his mouth. "Between you and me, I like girl talk." They both exploded into laughter, swaying back and forth in drunken amusement.

Listening to them cackle, Sean stood up and stumbled over to them. "For the sake of our sanity would you two hyenas please enlighten us with what's so funny?" John started to reply then began laughing again.

Jerome was holding his sides and caught his breath. "Oh, just a little girl talk, that's all." He and John doubled over in a gut-busting fit, and everyone began laughing clueless as to why.

When the gasps and panting came to a stop, the men called it a night and stumbled off to bed—everyone but John and Jerome. They set their cups down and envisioned their lost loves as the fire danced between them.

"Now that we're alone, tell me your story," John muttered, entranced by the flames.

Staring off into red hot coals, Jerome said, "Her name is Jasmine."

"Pretty name."

"Yeah, pretty inside and out . . . she's everything and more than I've ever wanted." His voice faded.

John turned to him, eyes wide. "This is only for six months. What's the problem?"

Jerome kept his eyes steady on the fire. "I'm dying."

John flinched, hearing the *same* words from his wife. "I'm so sorry. What's the diagnosis?"

"It's brain cancer."

"How long do you have?"

"The way I feel, not long. The initial prognosis was six months . . . . I'm going on a year and a half." Jerome saw the hopelessness in John's face. "I'm sorry. I didn't mean to ruin the party but you asked."

John sat stoically, eyes straight forward, gazing at the fire. Then his body began pumping with life, and he bolted off his chair. "It's all making perfect sense. This is why I'm here!" He stared fiercely into Jerome's eyes as if looking at his wife. "That cocktail you drank, the cocktails we all drank, they're products of this horticultural extravaganza!" He stood and waved his hand around the property. "We are standing in the midst of miraculous cures here."

Jerome smiled, trying to partake in his enthusiasm, but he had tried everything he could get his hands on and nothing had worked.

"Come on, bro, get excited with me," John chanted.

"Honestly John, I don't know if I'll even be alive tomorrow. The pain is consuming everything, my appetite, concentration—I've been feeling weak and unstable. I'm afraid it's just a matter of time."

John recognized that *"letting go"* stage all too well. It was where the battle ends and hopelessness defeats. He patted Jerome on the knee. "Why don't we call it a night? We both have a lot of work tomorrow."

The next morning came like a jackhammer on a metal roof. As eyes cracked open, the men lined up outside John's tent for his hangover remedy, except Jerome. He had slept in. He meandered over to the mess tent for coffee and breakfast as John was leaving.

"Hey, thought I'd see you up bright and early this morning like everyone else," John said.

Jerome scratched his head. "Whatever you gave me, knocked me out."

John patted his shoulder. "Good to hear. I made plenty, so help yourself."

"Thanks, I'll probably take you up on it." Jerome poured a cup of coffee and sat down at the table.

"Mind if I sit with you a minute?" John asked.

"Not at all." Jerome pulled out a chair for him.

"I wanted to thank you for listening to me last night. I know I was pretty drunk and probably made a blabbering buffoon of myself."

Jerome grinned and looked side-to-side. "Actually, I enjoyed our little girl talk."

John cackled, "So did I, but don't tell the other guys." He stood up. "Well, I must be off. There are places to go and people to see."

Jerome stopped him. "John, if you wouldn't mind, I'd like to keep my illness . . ."

He held up a hand. "Understood."

As the last patient was treated, it occurred to Jerome he hadn't seen John since their morning chat. He inquired with the others of his whereabouts. They, too, were just as curious.

Soon after, Robert, the accompanying biochemist, found Jerome. "I heard you were looking for John."

"Yes, have you seen him?"

"He left this morning to see the Shaman in Olongapo."

"Shaman?"

"You know, the village witch doctor. John said he gives him inspiration and clarity."

Sean overheard them talking. "Listen, whatever he's learning from that *witch doctor,* he has my blessing. I thought I was going to need a lobotomy this morning."

"Yeah, you and me both," Robert said, chuckling.

Jerome left the camp and took off down the dirt road to the bustling town of Olongapo. Arriving, he walked up to two young boys and introduced himself.

It was known for miles and throughout the villagers that the Americans were there to care for them. Respectfully, it cultivated a genuine indebtedness, and the boys were eager to help. They escorted him to the outskirts of the village and pointed at a primitive hut made of stone and clay.

Jerome entered through a cloth doorway and saw John sitting next to an archaic man wrapped in multi-colored material.

John turned. "Jerome! Come in, come in. We were just talking about you."

"My ears are burning," Jerome said in a quizzical tone.

"They should be. I want you to meet the village doctor." Jerome walked over to the woven rug, where they were sitting cross-legged. "He's pretty hard of hearing, so you need to come close." John placed a hand on the old man's shoulder and pointed to Jerome. "This is Jerome, the man I was telling you about." He pronounced each word loud and clear.

The tan wrinkled man grinned at Jerome with lips of puckered leather.

John looked at Jerome. "He's made some pretty profound discoveries, to say the least." Then he motioned to the shaman. "Show Jerome your potions," he said loudly.

The old man unfolded his legs and stood with ease. He walked over to a table of rusted canisters, glass bottles and wooden carved bowls. Then he pointed at something revolting and pungent, stewing over a small flame. "How would you like to be our guinea pig?" John said with wide, animated eyes.

Jerome peered into the pot and backed away. "It looks like something a cow regurgitated."

"Listen," John moved close and talked softly, "I know this sounds crazy, but I've been testing some of the Shaman's *"magical potions,"* he quoted with his fingers, "and with my biomedical research it's possible we could find a cure for you." John's eyes were wide, emphasizing his great news. Jerome had been a guinea pig for a year, and his lack of zeal was not what John was expecting. "Did you hear what I said, bro?"

"Loud and clear, John. You have no idea how many drugs, potions and super-pills I've taken, hoping one, just one, was worthy of its hype."

"So you're going to stop trying?" He pointed. "See that!" Jerome peered down at the green, slimy mixture again. "That, according to this shaman, has been curing cancer."

"What is it?"

The ancient man picked up a wooden spoon and began stirring the simmering goo. "Sang-hwang mushroom!" he spouted.

"What?" Jerome said, looking at John.

John was now hopping up and down, exhilarated. "That, my friend, is Sang-hwang mushroom extract or phellinus linteus, as I would refer to it. It's an ancient healing remedy that, for some *unconscionable* reason, has not hit our part of the world yet."

Jerome bent down and sniffed it. "If this cures cancer why wouldn't it be in the United States?"

John's eyes snapped open. "Can you spell *BUREAUCRACY?* I'm serious, Jerome. If this works, I'm going to find a way to cut through the red tape and get it approved. Then I'm going to start saving the lives that have lost all hope." He took Jerome by the shoulders. "Now, are you going to be my guinea pig or not?"

"What do I have to lose?" Jerome said, closing his eyes and opening his mouth.

The shaman scooped out a small portion and held it at Jerome's mouth. "Eat," he grunted.

Jerome cracked an eye and pinched his nose as the shaman shoved in the slippery green mixture. Jerome gagged it down as both men watched. "Umm, good," he said, rubbing his belly. "How many times a day do I have to eat this—?"

"Shit!" John spouted. "Normally, the texture of the mushroom is hard and tough. However, diluting it and cooking it actuates the chemical properties more quickly. Otherwise, it wouldn't be so disgusting. Now, back to your question. The dosage is three to six grams, three times a day." He waved his hand. "It's horrible, I know. Just think of it as grandma's goulash."

"What? My grandmother was an excellent cook."

"Okay, then my grandma's goulash. She was horrible. So how 'bout it—shall we give it a try?"

"All right, all right. I'll give it a try."

John administered the exact dosage three times a day at approximately the same time for the optimal efficacy. He kept a daily journal, noting Jerome's mood and side effects, ultimately signs of remission.

It had been a month from the first day of treatment that Jerome woke up feeling a significant difference. The sharp edge which usually prodded him wasn't there, and he had regained his equilibrium. He couldn't wait to tell John and reclaim a *Good Morning!*

Marching over, every step strong and steady, Jerome went straight to John's lab and found him hunched over his workstation, peering into a microscope. "Good morning, John."

John straightened and turned around. "Good morning to you, too. Why are you up so early?"

Jerome shrugged with his face beaming like the sun. "Did you hear what I said, *gooood morning?*"

John looked at him confused, his mind still occupied with his newest study. "Spell it out, bro."

"All right. G-O-O-D morning!"

John studied his face and replied, "Yes, it is."

Jerome raised his hands from his sides. "John, this is the first *good morning* I have had in over a year. I have no pain—I can't even describe how good I feel."

Comprehension hit John like an arrow between the eyes. Gasping, he dropped to his knees and looked up at the sky. "Thank you, Lord. I knew there was a reason you sent me. With every death there is life. And now, my darling, you did not die in vain."

One week to go and Jerome's six-month agreement with the Philippine Outreach indenture was over. Some of the physicians committed to another contract. Jerome was going home.

His cancer was gone and he literally felt reborn. All he wanted was to start a new life with Jasmine and the children. Although, now he had a new fear. It was possible she had found another man, believing he had passed.

He never called her after that teary night. The pain of going through another good-bye seemed unbearable. All he could do was pray she hadn't.

286

CHAPTER

FORTY

Thrashing and wringing wet, Jasmine woke from a frightening, recurring nightmare. Jerome was sleeping next to her in bed. His face was soft and lips curled in a content smile. She would lean down to kiss him and discover his body was stiff and skin icy-cold.

Every night, since their last night together, the nightmare found her. Darkness had become the hunter and she the prey.

Kicking off the damp blanket, she got up and went to the kitchen to heat up a cup of milk and vanilla. It was the remedy her mother would make her when she couldn't sleep. And she wished she was there to do it for her now.

It had been six months and ten days without a word from Jerome. With nothing to go on, Jasmine could only hope he'd fulfilled his mission and passed on peacefully. The true purpose of why he went made it easier to accept. Though within her heart an ache had come to rest. Finishing the milk, she snuggled on the couch with her violet scented throw and slithered off to sleep.

It wasn't long before the sun blazed through the living room window that Jasmine felt a touch on her shoulder. She lifted her head to see Shauna standing over her. "Mom, we're turning on the TV."

"What time is it?" Jaz said, rubbing her eyes.

"Eight o'clock."

"Eight o'clock!? Why didn't you wake me sooner? And why aren't you ready for school?"

"Duh, because it's Saturday."

"Oh." Jaz raked her fingers through her hair and moseyed into the kitchen to make a pot of coffee. Suddenly it dawned on her she had told Connie she'd work for her today. Mumbling and scolding herself for making that commitment, she ran to the bedroom and threw on her clothes.

It was the usual banter, same worries, same everything in the women's lounge. The only thing missing was Yarah's dry humor to cheer away the gloom.

Jaz put on her gold vest, cinched a knot in her tie and walked past the mirror. She knew exactly how she looked—exactly how she felt.

Entering the casino pit, she was immediately lambasted with Tony's apathetic sarcasm. "You look like shit! What's wrong with you?"

"Thanks, I needed that," she responded dazed and groggy.

He stepped closer, his toothpick bouncing at a threatening level as he studied her eyes. "You tie one on last night?"

Jaz coughed out a weak laugh. "No, I can't sleep."

"Well, wake up and stick a smile on your face. This is fuckin' *paradise* if you've forgotten!"

Although his words were harsh, they sent a message of truth. Until she found something better, the job paid her bills and put food on the table. It was her livelihood, if she could call it that, and she couldn't risk losing it.

Sticking *that* smile on her face, Jasmine approached her game with the determination of finding a new spirit.

After forty minutes of long-winded, insipid conversation, she realized her players weren't listening to her at all. They were looking around her at something more interesting.

Tony swaggered up to her with a cocky grin. "I don't know what you did from the time you got here until now, but it must've been good." Jasmine angled her head and shrugged. She had done the *guessing game* for six months and wasn't in the mood for one more day. He shook his head. "Aren't ya gonna ask why?"

"No," she answered.

"I think you should."

"Okay, why?"

"Look." He pointed across the pit.

Jasmine turned and felt the air in her lungs rush to her throat. It was as if God had sent her a rainbow. Sitting on top of the podium was a giant bouquet of wildflowers, and no one but Jerome knew they were her favorite flower. She stammered, "Wh-where did they come from?"

"Why don't you go see?" Tony waved for a dealer to take her place.

Jasmine moved toward the bouquet without touching the ground. Her body was weightless—her mind a blur of ecstasy as if it was all a nonsensical dream.

Trembling, she touched a flower, making sure it was real, and then saw a card perched in the center. Through a river of tears, she took the card and read it aloud. "I picked them myself."

Spinning around, eyes darting, she searched every visible inch for a man she thought was gone. The miracle she prayed for and wished upon every falling star was standing in the distance. Then a voice whispered to run and never look back.

With hair flying like the mane of a wild mustang, Jaz raced to Jerome and leaped into his open arms. He caught her and held her against his chest like their last night together. She clung and they cried, looking into each other's eyes.

Amid the noise and sea of people, they heard nothing and saw nothing, as if the only two people alive. It was a moment of rare tranquility, held at a distance from all the greedy chaos.

T h e   E n d

GLOSSARY OF TERMS

Action: A player's betting standards, including the amount of their bet.

Basic Strategy: A set of rules that optimizes the odds of winning.

Big Six: A large wheel that rotates with various betting denominations separated by pins.

Bill: Referred to as a hundred dollar bill.

Blackjack: An ace with a ten or face card.

Book: Referred to for rules of playing blackjack.

Call a hand: The length of time a player wins on a craps table.

Check or Chip: A token used for gambling in lieu of money.

Circle: An assigned spot on a table game to place a bet.

Cold: When a deck of cards is losing the majority of the hands.

Counting down the rack: To calculate the total value of checks in the rack.

Dead Game: An inactive table game.

EO: An early leave from work.

Eighty-Six: To be banned from a casino or property.

First Base: The first seat on a table game, to the dealer's left.

Frontline: Designated table games for high limit players.

George: A big tipper.

Hand: The cards in play.

Hawk: When a table game is closely watched.

Helps Hall: Where the employees eat.

High-roller: A player who has the resource to bet the table maximum.

Hit: A card given to a player to advance their hand.

Hole card: The hidden card under the dealer's exposed top card.

Hot: When a deck of cards is winning the majority of the hands.

House: The casino.

Negative Progression: Betting a large amount of money to win back a loss.

Rack: The metal tray that holds the checks on a game.

Relief: The dealer who gives the breaks.

Size: Cutting down a stack of checks using the index finger.

Snapper: A blackjack.

Split: When a player separates two cards for more betting options.

Stick: The long stick a craps croupier holds to maneuver the dice.

Stiff: A player who doesn't tip.

Sweat: A term used in reference to a casino or boss who reacts negatively to losing.

Tapped out: To release a dealer for a break.

Toke: A tip.

Twenty-one: When the cards add up to twenty-one (not the same as a blackjack).

Working the deck: To shuffle the cards until they run in the casino's favor.

Printed in the United States
by Baker & Taylor Publisher Services